FOR BEN OLSEN

Who keeps putting up with a bunch of crazy writers as friends,

And finds time to make our books better all the while.

BRANDON SANDERSON

GOLLANCZ
LONDON

Interior illustrations by Isaac Stewart and Ben McSweeney

First published in Great Britain in 2016 by Gollancz
An imprint of the Orion Publishing Group
Carmelite House, 50 Victoria Embankment, London EC4Y 0DZ
An Hachette UK Company

A CIP catalogue record for this book is available
from the British Library

ISBN 978 1 473 20825 4 (Cased)
ISBN 978 1 473 20826 1 (Export Trade Paperback)

1 3 5 7 9 10 8 6 4 2

Printed in Great Britain by
Clays Ltd, St Ives plc

The Orion Publishing Group's policy is to use papers that are natural, renewable and recyclable products and made from wood grown in sustainable forests. The logging and manufacturing processes are expected to conform to the environmental regulations of the country of origin.

www.brandonsanderson.com
www.orionbooks.co.uk
www.gollancz.co.uk

CONTENTS

ACKNOWLEDGMENTS

This book comes out in the year that will mark the tenth anniversary of the Mistborn series. Considering all the other things I've been doing, it seems like six books in ten years is a grand accomplishment! I can still remember the early months, writing the trilogy furiously, trying to craft something that would really show off what I can do as a writer. Mistborn has become one of my hallmark series, and I hope that you find this volume a worthy entry in the canon.

As always, this book involved the efforts of a great number of people. There's the excellent art by Ben McSweeney and Isaac Stewart—maps and icons by Isaac, with all the broadsheet art done by Ben. Both also helped a great deal on the text of the broadsheet, and Isaac himself wrote the Nicki Savage piece for it—since the idea was to have Jak hiring out his work now, we wanted to give that a different voice. I think it turned out great!

The cover art was done by Chris McGrath in the US, and by Sam Green for the UK edition. Both are longtime artists on this series, and their art keeps getting better. Editorial was done by Moshe Feder at Tor, with Simon Spanton shepherding the project over at Gollancz in the UK. Agents on the project included Eddie Schneider, Sam Morgan, Krystyna Lopez, Christa Atkinson, and Tae Keller at Jabberwocky in the US, all overseen by the amazing Joshua Bilmes. In the UK you can thank John Berlyne of the Zeno Agency, an all-around awesome guy who worked hard for many years to finally break my books into the UK.

At Tor Books, I'd also like to thank Tom Doherty, Linda Quinton, Marco Palmieri, Karl Gold, Diana Pho, Nathan Weaver, and Rafal Gibek. Copyediting was done by Terry McGarry. The audiobook narrator is Michael Kramer, my personal favorite narrator—and one I know I'm probably making blush right now, as he has to read this line to you all who are listening. At Macmillan Audio, I'd like to thank Robert Allen, Samantha Edelson, and Mitali Dave.

Continuity, all-around editing feedback, and countless other jobs were done by the Immaculate Peter Ahlstrom. Also working here on my team are Kara Stewart, Karen Ahlstrom, and Adam Horne. And, of course, my lovely wife, Emily.

We leaned extra hard on my beta readers for this one, as the book didn't have the chance to go through writing group. That team is: Peter Ahlstrom, Alice Arneson, Gary Singer, Eric James Stone, Brian T. Hill, Kristina Kugler, Kim Garrett, Bob Kluttz, Jakob Remick, Karen Ahlstrom, Kalyani Poluri, Ben "wooo this book is dedicated to me, look how important I am" Olsen, Lyndsey Luther, Samuel Lund, Bao Pham, Aubree Pham, Megan Kanne, Jory Phillips, Trae Cooper, Christi Jacobsen, Eric Lake, and Isaac Stewart. (For those wondering, Ben was a founding member of my original writing group with Dan Wells and Peter Ahlstrom. A computer person by trade, and the only one of us in that original group who had no aspirations toward working in publishing, he's been a valued reader and friend for many years. He also introduced me to the Fallout series, so there's that as well.) Community proofreaders included most of the above plus: Kerry Wilcox, David Behrens, Ian McNatt, Sarah Fletcher, Matt Wiens, and Joe Dowswell.

Well, that was a mouthful! These folks are wonderful, and if you compare my early books to my later ones, I think you'll find that the assistance of these people has been invaluable in not only slaying typos but also helping me tighten narratives. Finally, though, I'd like to thank you readers for sticking with me these ten years, and being willing to accept the strange ideas I throw at you. Mistborn is not quite halfway through the evolution I have planned for it. I can't wait for you to see what is coming your way, and this book is where some of that finally starts to be revealed.

Enjoy!

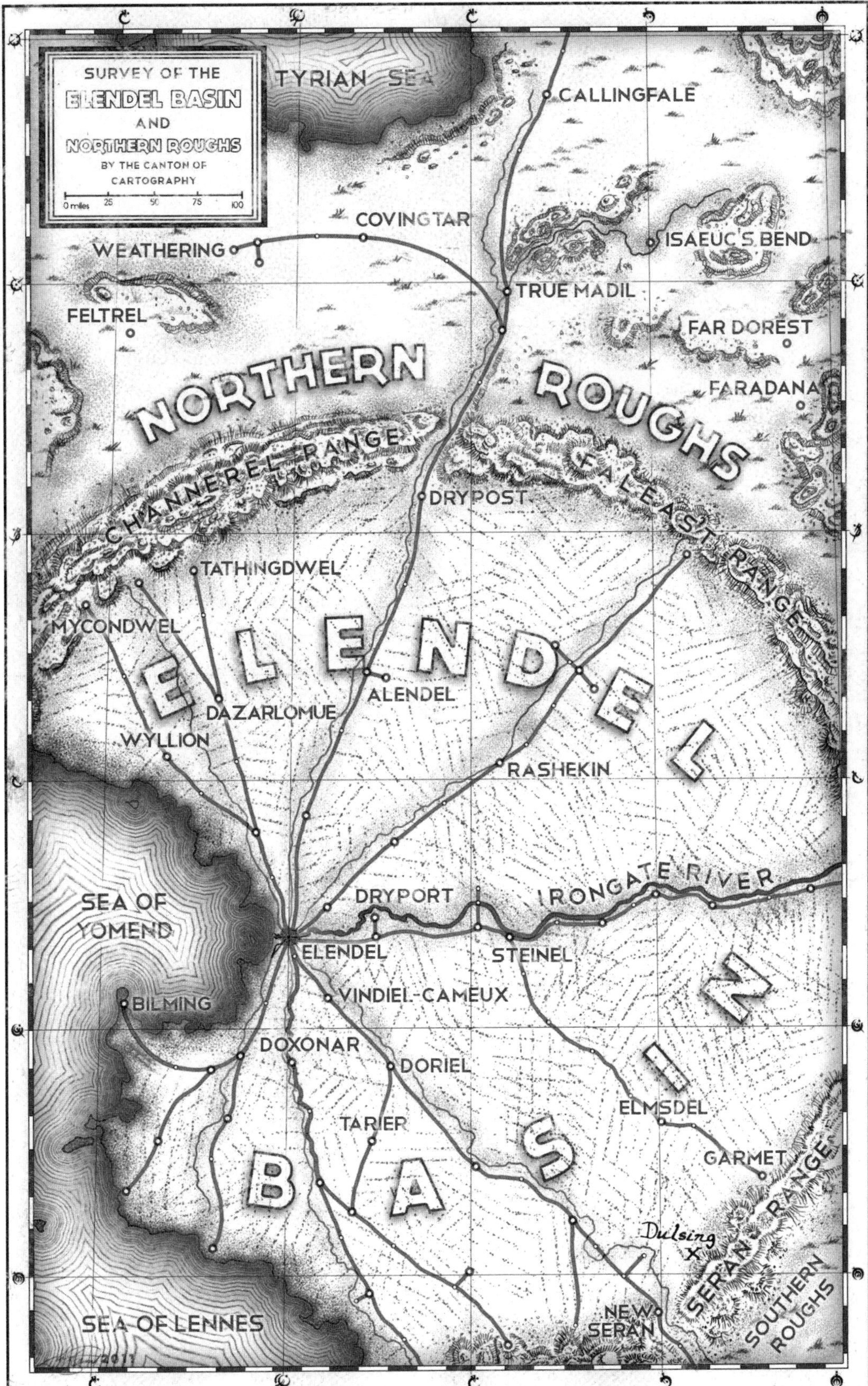

SURVEY OF THE
ELENDEL BASIN
AND
NORTHERN ROUGHS
BY THE CANTON OF
CARTOGRAPHY
0 miles 25 50 75 100
TYRIAN SEA
CALLINGFALE
COVINGTAR
WEATHERING
ISAEUC'S BEND
TRUE MADIL
FELTREL
FAR DOREST
FARADANA
NORTHERN ROUGHS
CHANNEREL RANGE
FALEAST RANGE
DRYPOST
TATHINGDWEL
MYCONDWEL
ELENDEL BASIN
ALENDEL
DAZARLOMUE
WYLLION
RASHEKIN
IRONGATE RIVER
DRYPORT
SEA OF YOMEND
ELENDEL
STEINEL
VINDIEL-CAMEUX
BILMING
DOXONAR
DORIEL
ELMSDEL
TARIER
GARMET
Dulsing
SERAN RANGE
SOUTHERN ROUGHS
NEW SERAN
SEA OF LENNES

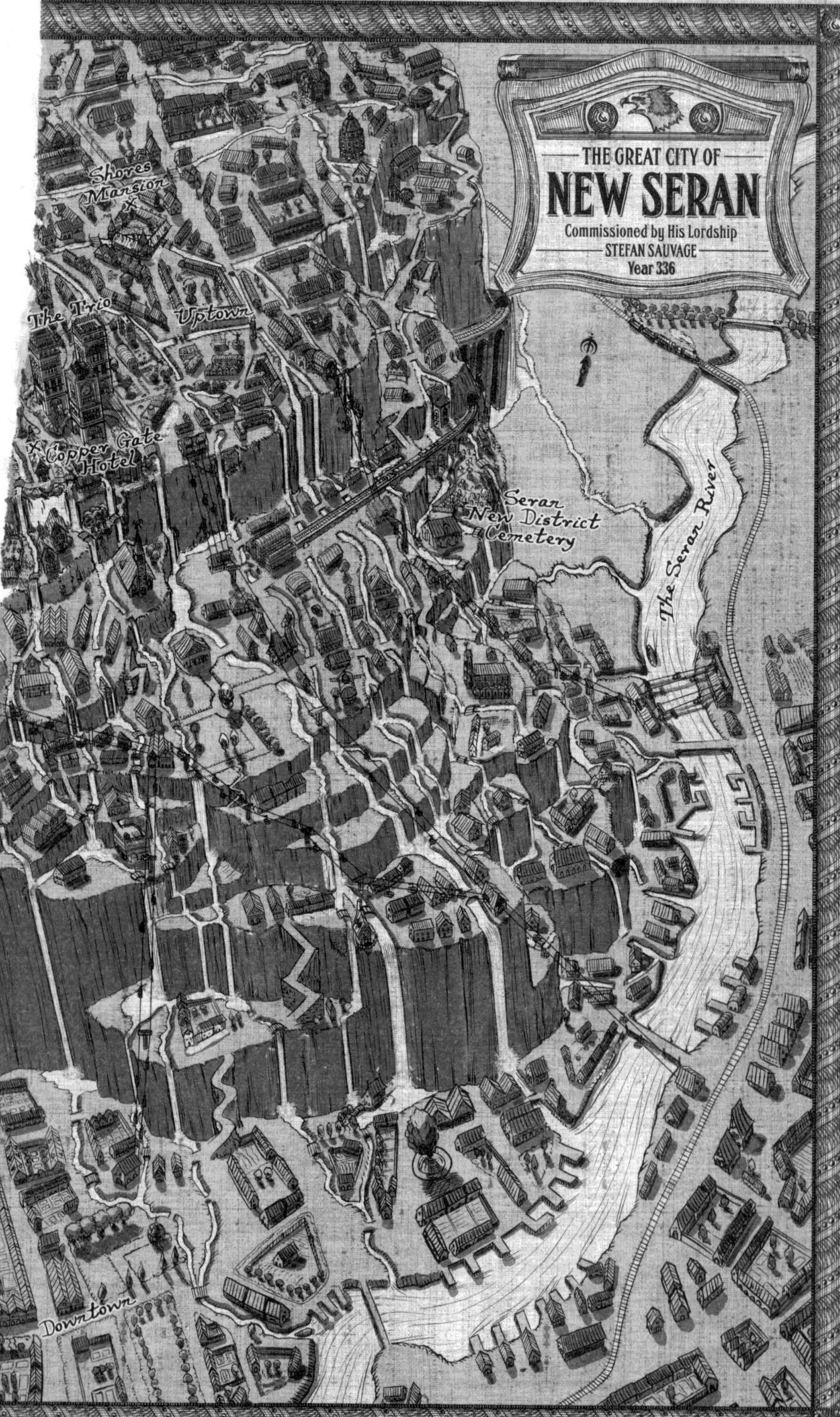

THE GREAT CITY OF
NEW SERAN
Commissioned by His Lordship
STEFAN SAUVAGE
Year 336
Shores Mansion
The Trio
Uptown
Copper Gate Hotel
Seran New District Cemetery
The Seran River
Downtown

THE BANDS OF MOURNING

PROLOGUE

"Telsin!" Waxillium hissed as he crept out of the training hut.

Glancing back, Telsin winced and crouched lower. At sixteen, Waxillium's sister was one year older than he was. Her long dark hair framed a button nose and prim lips, and colorful V shapes ran up the front of her traditional Terris robes. Those always seemed to fit her in a way his never did. On Telsin, they were elegant. Waxillium felt like he was wearing a sack.

"Go away, Asinthew," she said, inching around the side of the hut.

"You're going to miss evening recitation."

"They won't notice I'm gone. They never check."

Inside the hut, Master Tellingdwar droned on about proper Terris attitudes. Submission, meekness, and what they called "respectful dignity." He was speaking to the younger students; the older ones, like Waxillium and his sister, were supposed to be meditating.

Telsin scrambled away, moving through the forested area of Elendel referred to simply as the Village. Waxillium fretted, then hurried after his sister.

"You're going to get into trouble," he said once he caught up. He followed her around the trunk of an enormous oak tree. "You're going to get *me* into trouble."

"So?" she said. "What is it with you and rules anyway?"

"Nothing," he said. "I just—"

She stalked off into the forest. He sighed and trailed after her, and eventually they met up with three other Terris youths: two girls and a tall boy. Kwashim, one of the girls, looked Waxillium up and down. She was dark-skinned and slender. "You brought *him*?"

"He followed me," Telsin said.

Waxillium smiled at Kwashim hopefully, then at Idashwy, the other girl. She had wide-set eyes and was his own age. And Harmony . . . she was gorgeous. She noticed his attention on her and blinked a few times, then glanced away, a demure smile on her lips.

"He'll tell on us," Kwashim said, drawing his attention away from the other girl. "You know he will."

"I won't," Waxillium snapped.

Kwashim gave Waxillium a glare. "You might miss evening class. Who'll answer all the questions? It will be rusting quiet in the classroom with nobody to fawn over the teacher."

Forch, the tall boy, stood just inside the shadows. Waxillium didn't look at Forch, didn't meet his eyes. *He doesn't know, right? He can't know.* Forch was the oldest of them, but rarely said much.

He was Twinborn, like Waxillium. Not that either of them used their Allomancy much these days. In the Village, it was their Terris side—their Feruchemy—that was lauded. The fact that both he and Forch were Coinshots didn't matter to the Terris.

"Let's go," Telsin said. "No more arguing. We probably don't have much time. If my brother wants to tag along, then fine."

They followed her beneath the canopy, feet crackling on leaves. With this much foliage, you could easily forget you were in the middle of an enormous city. The sounds of shouting men and iron-shod hooves on cobbles were distant, and you couldn't see or smell the smoke in here. The Terris worked hard to keep their section of the city tranquil, quiet, peaceful.

Waxillium should have loved it here.

The group of five youths soon approached the Synod's Lodge, where the ranking Terris elders had their offices. Telsin waved for the group of them to wait while she hurried up to a particular window to listen. Waxillium found himself looking about, anxious. Evening was approaching, the forest growing dim, but *anyone* could walk along and find them.

Don't worry so much, he told himself. He needed to join in their antics like his sister did. Then they'd see him as one of them. Right?

Sweat trickled down the sides of his face. Nearby, Kwashim leaned against a tree, completely unconcerned, a smirk growing on her lips as she noticed how nervous he was. Forch stood in the shadows, not crouching, but *rusts*—he could have been one of the trees, for all the emotion he showed. Waxillium glanced at Idashwy, with her large eyes, and she blushed, looking away.

Telsin snuck back to them. "She's in there."

"That's our grandmother's office," Waxillium said.

"Of course it is," Telsin said. "And she got called into her office for an emergency. Right, Idashwy?"

The quiet girl nodded. "I saw Elder Vwafendal running past my meditation room."

Kwashim grinned. "So she won't be watching."

"Watching what?" Waxillium asked.

"The Tin Gate," Kwashim said. "We can get out into the city. This is going to be even easier than usual!"

"Usual?" Waxillium said, looking in horror from Kwashim to his sister. "You've done this *before*?"

"Sure," Telsin said. "Hard to get a good drink in the Village. Great pubs two streets over though."

"You're an *outsider,*" Forch said to him as he stepped up. He spoke slowly, deliberately, as if each word required separate consideration. "Why should you care if we leave? Look, you're shaking. What are you afraid of? You lived most of your life out there."

You're an outsider, they said. Why was his sister always able to worm her way into any group? Why did he always have to stand on the outside?

"I'm not shaking," Waxillium said to Forch. "I just don't want to get into trouble."

"He's *going* to turn us in," Kwashim said.

"I'm not." *Not for this anyway,* Waxillium thought.

"Let's go," Telsin said, leading the pack through the forest to the Tin Gate, which was a fancy name for something that was really just another street—though granted, it had a stone archway etched with ancient Terris symbols for the sixteen metals.

Beyond it lay a different world. Glowing gas lamps marching along streets, newsboys trudging home for the night with unsold broadsheets tucked under their arms. Workers heading to the rowdy pubs for a drink. He'd never really known that world; he'd grown up in a lavish mansion stuffed with fine clothes, caviar, and wine.

Something about that simple life called to him. Perhaps he'd find *it* there. The thing he'd never found. The thing everyone else seemed to have, but he couldn't even put a name to.

The other four youths scuttled out, passing the building with shadowed windows where Waxillium and Telsin's grandmother would usually be sitting and reading this time of night. The Terris didn't employ guards at the entrances to their domain, but they *did* watch.

Waxillium didn't leave, not yet. He looked down, pulling back the sleeves of his robe to expose the metalmind bracers he wore there.

"You coming?" Telsin called to him.

He didn't respond.

"Of course you're not. You never want to risk trouble."

She led Forch and Kwashim away. Surprisingly though, Idashwy lingered. The quiet girl looked back at him questioningly.

I can do this, Waxillium thought. *It's nothing big.* His sister's taunt ringing in his ears, he forced himself forward and joined Idashwy. He felt sick, but he fell in beside her, enjoying her shy smile.

"So, what was the emergency?" he asked Idashwy.

"Huh?"

"The emergency that called Grandmother away?"

Idashwy shrugged, pulling off her Terris robe, briefly shocking him until he saw that she wore a conventional skirt and blouse underneath. She tossed the robe into the bushes. "I don't know much.

I saw your grandmother running to the Synod Lodge, and overheard Tathed asking about it. Some kind of crisis. We were planning to slip out tonight, so I figured, you know, this would be a good time."

"But the emergency . . ." Waxillium said, looking over his shoulder.

"Something about a constable captain coming to question her," Idashwy said.

A *constable*?

"Let's go, Asinthew," she said, taking his hand. "Your grandmother is likely to make short work of the outsider. She could be on her way here already!"

He'd frozen in place.

Idashwy looked at him. Those lively brown eyes made it hard for him to think. "Come on," she urged. "Sneaking out is hardly even an infraction. Didn't you *live* out here for fourteen years?"

Rusts.

"I need to go," he said, turning back to run toward the forest.

Idashwy stood in place as he left her. Waxillium entered the woods, sprinting for the Synod Lodge. *You know she's going to think you're a coward now,* part of him observed. *They all will.*

Waxillium skidded to the ground outside his grandmother's office window, heart thumping. He pressed against the wall, and yes, he *could* hear something through the open window.

"We police ourselves, constable," Grandmother Vwafendal said from inside. "You know this."

Waxillium dared to push himself up, peeking in the window to see Grandmother seated at her desk, a picture of Terris rectitude, with her hair in a braid and her robes immaculate.

The man standing across the desk from her held his constable's hat under his arm as a sign of respect. He was an older man with drooping mustaches, and the insignia on his breast marked him as a captain and a detective. High rank. Important.

Yes! Waxillium thought, fiddling in his pocket for his notes.

"The Terris police themselves," the constable said, "because they rarely need policing."

"They don't need it now."

"My informant—"

"So now you have an informant?" Grandmother asked. "I thought it was an anonymous tip."

"Anonymous, yes," the constable said, laying a sheet of paper on the desk. "But I consider this more than just a 'tip.'"

Waxillium's grandmother picked up the sheet. Waxillium knew what it said. He'd sent it, along with a letter, to the constables in the first place.

A shirt that smells of smoke, hanging behind his door.

Muddied boots that match the size of the prints left outside the burned building.

Flasks of oil in the chest beneath his bed.

The list contained a dozen clues pointing to Forch as the one who'd burned the dining lodge to the ground earlier in the month. It thrilled Waxillium to see that the constables had taken his findings seriously.

"Disturbing," Grandmother said, "but I don't see anything on this list that gives you the right to intrude upon our domain, Captain."

The constable leaned down to rest his hands on the edge of her desk, confronting her. "You weren't so quick to reject our help when we sent a fire brigade to extinguish that blaze."

"I will always accept help saving lives," Grandmother said. "But I need no help in locking them away. Thank you."

"Is it because this Forch is Twinborn? Are you frightened of his powers?"

She gave him a scornful look.

"Elder," he said, taking a deep breath. "You have a criminal among you—"

"*If* we do," she said, "we will deal with the individual ourselves. I have visited the houses of sorrow and destruction you outsiders call prisons, Captain. I will not see one of my own immured there based on hearsay and anonymous fancies sent via post."

The constable breathed out and stood up straight again. He set something new down on the desk with a snap. Waxillium squinted to see, but the constable was covering the object with his hand.

"Do you know much about arson, Elder?" the constable asked softly. "It's often what we call a companion crime. You find it used to cover a burglary, to perpetrate fraud, or as an act of initial aggression. In a case like this, the fire is commonly just a harbinger. At best you have a firebug who is waiting to burn again. At worst . . . well, something bigger is coming, Elder. Something you'll all regret."

Grandmother drew her lips to a line. The constable removed his hand, revealing what he'd put on the desk. A bullet.

"What is this?" Grandmother said.

"A reminder."

Grandmother slapped it off the table, sending it snapping against the wall near where Waxillium hid. He jumped back and crouched lower, heart pounding.

"Do not bring your instruments of death into this place," Grandmother hissed.

Waxillium got back to the window in time to see the constable settling his hat on his head. "When that boy burns something again," he said softly, "send for me. Hopefully it won't be too late. Good evening."

He left without a further word. Waxillium huddled against the side of the building, worried the constable would look back and see him. It didn't happen. The man marched out along the path, disappearing into the evening shadows.

But Grandmother . . . she hadn't believed. Couldn't she see? Forch had committed a crime. They were just going to leave him alone? Why—

"Asinthew," Grandmother said, using Waxillium's Terris name as she always did. "Would you please join me?"

He felt an immediate spike of alarm, followed by shame. He stood up. "How did you know?" he said through the window.

"Reflection on my mirror, child," she said, holding a cup of tea in both hands, not looking toward him. "Obey. If you please."

Sullenly, he trudged around the building and through the front doors of the wooden lodge. The whole place smelled of the wood stain he'd recently helped apply. He still had the stuff under his fingernails.

He stepped into the room and shut the door. "Why did you—"

"Please sit down, Asinthew," she said softly.

He walked to the desk, but didn't take the guest seat. He remained standing, right where the constable had.

"Your handwriting," Grandmother said, brushing at the paper the constable had left. "Did I not tell you that the matter of Forch was under control?"

"You say a lot of things, Grandmother. I believe when I see proof."

Vwafendal leaned forward, steam rising from the cup in her hands. "Oh, Asinthew," she said. "I thought you were determined to fit in here."

"I am."

"Then why are you listening at my window instead of doing evening meditations?"

He looked away, blushing.

"The Terris way is about *order,* child," Grandmother said. "We have rules for a reason."

"And burning down buildings isn't against the rules?"

"Of *course* it is," Grandmother said. "But Forch is not your responsibility. We've spoken to him. He's penitent. His crime was that of a misguided youth who spends too much time alone. I've asked some of the others to befriend him. He *will* do penance for his crime, in our way. Would you rather see him rot in prison?"

Waxillium hesitated, then sighed, dropping into the chair before his grandmother's desk. "I want to find out what is right," he whispered, "and do it. Why is that so hard?"

Grandmother frowned. "It's easy to discover what is right and wrong, child. I will admit that always *choosing* to follow what you know you should do is—"

"No," Waxillium said. Then he winced. It wasn't wise to interrupt Grandmother V. She never yelled, but her disapproval could be sensed as surely as an imminent thunderstorm. He continued more softly. "No, Grandmother. Finding out what's right *isn't* easy."

"It is written in our ways. It is taught every day in your lessons."

"That's one voice," Waxillium said, "one philosophy. There are so many. . . ."

Grandmother reached across the desk and put her hand on his. Her skin was warm from holding the teacup. "Ah, Asinthew," she said. "I understand how hard it must be for you. A child of two worlds."

Two worlds, he thought immediately, *but no home.*

"But you must heed what you are taught," Grandmother continued. "You promised me you would obey our rules while you were here."

"I've been trying."

"I know. I hear good reports from Tellingdwar and your other instructors. They say you learn the material better than anyone—that it's as if you've lived here all your life! I'm proud of your effort."

"The other kids don't accept me. I've tried to do as you say—to be *more* Terris than anyone, to *prove* my blood to them. But the kids . . . I'll never be one of them, Grandmother."

"'Never' is a word youths often use," Grandmother said, sipping her tea, "but rarely understand. Let the rules become your guide. In them, you will find peace. If some are resentful because of your zeal, let them be. Eventually, through meditation, they will make peace with such emotions."

"Could you . . . maybe order a few of the others to befriend me?" he found himself asking, ashamed of how weak it sounded to say the words. "Like you did with Forch?"

"I will see," Grandmother said. "Now, off with you. I will not report this indiscretion, Asinthew, but please promise me you will set aside this obsession with Forch and leave the punishment of others to the Synod."

Waxillium moved to stand up, and his foot slipped on something. He reached down. *The bullet.*

"Asinthew?" Grandmother asked.

He trapped the bullet in his fist as he straightened, then hurried out the door.

"Metal is your life," Tellingdwar said from the front of the hut, moving into the final parts of the evening recitation.

Waxillium knelt in meditation, listening to the words. Around him, rows of peaceful Terris were similarly bowed in reverence, offering praise to Preservation, the ancient god of their faith.

"Metal is your soul," Tellingdwar said.

So much was perfect in this quiet world. Why did Waxillium sometimes feel like he was dragging dirt in solely by being here? That they were all part of one big white canvas, and he a smudge at the bottom?

"You preserve us," Tellingdwar said, "and so we will be yours."

A bullet, Waxillium thought, the bit of metal still clenched in his palm. *Why did he leave a bullet as a reminder? What does it mean?* It seemed an odd symbol.

Recitation complete, the youths, children, and adults alike rose and stretched. There was some jovial interaction, but curfew had nearly arrived, which meant that the younger set had to be on their way to their homes—or in Waxillium's case, the dormitories. He remained kneeling anyway.

Tellingdwar started gathering up the mats people had used for kneeling. He kept his head shaved; his robes were bright yellows and oranges. Arms laden with mats, he paused as he noticed Waxillium hadn't left with the others. "Asinthew? Are you well?"

Waxillium nodded tiredly, climbing to his feet, legs numb from kneeling so long. He plodded toward the exit, where he paused. "Tellingdwar?"

"Yes, Asinthew?"

"Has there ever been a violent crime in the Village?"

The short steward froze, his grip tightening on the load of mats. "What makes you ask?"

"Curiosity."

"You needn't worry. That was long ago."

"*What* was long ago?"

Tellingdwar retrieved the remaining mats, moving more quickly than before. Perhaps someone else would have avoided the question, but Tellingdwar was as candid as they came. A classic Terris virtue—in his eyes, avoiding a question would be as bad as lying.

"I'm not surprised they're still whispering about it," Tellingdwar said. "Fifteen years can't wash away that blood, I suppose. The rumors are wrong, however. Only one person was killed. A woman, by her husband's hand. Both Terris." He hesitated. "I knew them."

"How did he kill her?"

"Must you know this?"

"Well, the rumors . . ."

Tellingdwar sighed. "A gun. An outsider weapon. We don't know where he got it." Tellingdwar shook his head, dropping the mats into a stack at the side of the room. "I guess we shouldn't be surprised. Men are the same everywhere, Asinthew. You must remember this. Do not think yourself better than another because you wear the robe."

Trust Tellingdwar to turn any conversation into a lesson. Waxillium nodded to him and slipped out into the night. The sky rumbled above, foretelling rain, but there was no mist yet.

Men are the same everywhere, Asinthew. . . . What was the purpose, then, of everything they taught in here? If it couldn't prevent men from acting like monsters?

He reached the boys' dorm, which was quiet. It was just after curfew, and Waxillium had to bow his head to the dormmaster in apology before rushing down the hallway and into his room on the ground floor. Waxillium's father had insisted he be given a room to himself, because of his noble heritage. That had only served to set him apart from the others.

He shucked off his robe and threw open his wardrobe. His old clothing hung there. Rain began to patter against his window as he threw on some trousers and a buttoning shirt, which he found more comfortable than those rusting robes. He trimmed his lamp and sat back on his cot, opening a book for some evening reading.

Outside, the sky rumbled like an empty stomach. Waxillium tried to read for a few minutes, then tossed the book aside—nearly knocking over his lamp—and threw himself to his feet. He walked to the window, watching the water stream down. It fell in patches and columns, because of the thick canopy of leaves. He reached over and extinguished the lamp.

He stared at the rain, thoughts tumbling in his head. He'd have to make a decision soon. The agreement between his grandmother and his parents required Waxillium to spend one year in the Village, and only a month of that remained. After that, it would be his choice whether to stay or to leave.

What awaited him outside? White tablecloths, posturing people with nasal accents, and politics.

What awaited him here? Quiet rooms, meditation, and boredom.

A life he detested or a life of mind-numbing repetition. Day after day after day . . . and . . .

Was that someone moving through the trees?

Waxillium perked up, pressing against the cool glass. That *was* someone trudging through the wet forest, a shadowed figure with a familiar height and posture, stooped and carrying a sack over his shoulder. Forch glanced toward the dormitory, but then continued on into the night.

So they were back. That was faster than he'd expected. What was Telsin's plan for getting into the dorms? Slip in through the windows, then claim they'd come home before curfew and the dormmaster just hadn't seen them?

Waxillium waited, wondering if he'd spot the three girls as well, but saw nothing. Only Forch, disappearing into the shadows. Where was he going?

Another fire, Waxillium thought immediately. But Forch wouldn't do it in this rain, would he?

Waxillium glanced at the clock ticking quietly on his wall. An hour after curfew. He hadn't realized he'd spent so much time staring at the rain.

Forch is not my problem, he told himself firmly. He walked back to lie on his bed, but soon found himself pacing instead. Listening to the rain, anxious, unable to stop his body from moving.

Curfew . . .

Let the rules become your guide. In them find peace.

He stopped beside the window. Then he pushed it open and leaped out, bare feet sinking into the wet, rubbery ground. He scrambled forward, streams of water spraying across his head, trickling down the back of his shirt. Which way had Forch gone?

He took his best guess, passing enormous trees like hewn monoliths, the rush of rain and streaming water drowning out all else. A boot print in the mud near a tree trunk hinted he was on the right track, but he had to lean down low to see it. Rusts! It was getting dark out here.

Where next? Waxillium turned about. *There,* he thought. *Storage hall.* An old dormitory, now unoccupied, where the Terris kept extra furniture and rugs. That would be a perfect target for arson, right? Plenty of stuff inside to burn, and nobody would expect it in this rain.

But Grandmother spoke to him, Waxillium thought, scrambling through the rain, feet cold as he kicked up fallen leaves and moss. *They'll know it was him.* Didn't he care? Was he *trying* to get into trouble?

Waxillium stepped up to the old dormitory, a three-story mass of blackness in the already dark night, showers of water streaming off its eaves. Waxillium tested the door, and it was unlocked of course—this was the Village. He slipped inside.

There. A pool of water on the floor. Someone *had* entered here recently. He followed in a crouch, touching the footprints one after another, until he reached the stairwell. Up one flight, then another. What was up here? He reached the top floor and saw a light ahead. Waxillium crept through a hallway with a rug down the center, approaching what turned out to be a flickering candle set on a table in a small room cluttered with furniture and with dark, heavy drapes on the walls.

Waxillium stepped up to the candle. It shivered, frail and alone. Why had Forch left it here? What was—

Something heavy smashed across Waxillium's back. He gasped in pain, thrown forward by the blow, stumbling into a pair of chairs stacked atop one another. Boots thumped on the floor behind him. Waxillium managed to throw himself to the side, rolling to the floor as Forch smashed an old wooden post into the chairs, cracking them.

Waxillium scrambled to his feet, his shoulders throbbing. Forch turned toward him, face all in shadow.

Waxillium backed away. "Forch! It's all right. I just want to talk." He winced as his back hit the wall. "You don't have to—"

Forch came at him swinging. Waxillium yelped and ducked into the hallway. "Help!" he shouted as Forch followed him. *"Help!"*

Waxillium had meant to scramble toward the stairs, but he'd gotten turned around. Instead he was running away from them. He slammed his shoulder against the door at the end of the hallway. That would lead to the upper meeting room, if the dormitory here had the same layout as his own. And maybe another set of steps?

Waxillium pushed through the door and into a brighter room. Old tables stacked atop one another surrounded an open space at the center, like an audience and a stage.

There, in the middle and lit by a dozen candles, a young boy of maybe five lay tied to a wooden plank that stretched between two tables. His shirt had been cut off and lay on the floor. His cries were muffled by a gag, and he struggled weakly against his bonds.

Waxillium stumbled to a halt, taking in the boy, the line of gleaming knives set out on a table nearby, the trails of blood from cuts on the boy's chest.

"Oh, hell," Waxillium whispered.

Forch entered behind him, then closed the door with a click.

"Oh, *hell,*" Waxillium said, turning, wide-eyed. "Forch, what is wrong with you?"

"Don't know," the young man said softly. "I've just got to see what's inside. You know?"

"You went with the girls," Waxillium said, "so you'd have an alibi.

If your room is found empty, you'll say you were with them. A lesser infraction to hide your true crime. Rusts! My sister and the others don't know that you slipped back, do they? They're out there drunk, and they won't even remember that you were gone. They'll swear you were—"

Waxillium cut off as Forch looked up, eyes reflecting candlelight, face expressionless. He held up a handful of nails.

That's right. Forch is a—

Waxillium shouted, throwing himself toward a pile of furniture as nails zipped from Forch's hand, Pushed by his Allomancy. They hit like hail, snapping against wooden tables, chair legs, and the floor. A sudden pain struck Wax in the arm as he scuttled backward.

He cried out, grabbing his arm as he got behind cover. One of the nails had ripped off a chunk of his flesh near the elbow.

Metal. He needed *metal.*

It had been months since he'd burned steel. Grandmother wanted him to embrace his Terris side. He raised his arms, and found them bare. His bracers . . .

In your room, idiot, Waxillium thought. He fished in his trouser pocket. He always used to keep . . .

A pouch of metal flakes. He dug it out as he scrambled away from Forch, who threw aside tables and chairs to get to him. In the background, the captive child whimpered.

Waxillium's fingers trembled as he tried to get the packet of metal flakes open, but it suddenly leaped from his fingers and shot across the room. He spun on Forch, desperate, just in time to see the man slide a metal bar off a table and toss it.

Waxillium tried to duck. Too slow. The Steelpushed bar slammed against his chest, throwing him backward. Forch grunted, stumbling. He wasn't practiced with his Allomancy, and hadn't properly braced himself. His Push threw him backward as much as it tossed Waxillium.

Still, Waxillium hit the wall with a grunt, and he felt something *crack* inside of him. He gasped, his vision blackening as he dropped to his knees. The room wavered.

The pouch. Get the pouch!

He searched the floor around him, frantic, barely able to think. He needed that metal! His fingers, bloodied, brushed it. Eager, he snatched the pouch and pulled open the cloth top. He tipped back his head to dump the flakes in.

A shadow thundered over to him and kicked him in the stomach. The broken bone inside of Waxillium gave, and he screamed, having gotten barely a pinch of metal into his mouth. Forch slapped the pouch out of his hand, scattering the flakes, then picked him up.

The youth looked bulkier than he should have. Tapping a metalmind. A frenzied part of Waxillium's brain tried to Push on the man's bracers, but Feruchemical metalminds were infamously difficult to affect with Allomancy. His Push wasn't strong enough.

Forch shoved Waxillium out the open window, dangling him by his neck. Rain washed over Waxillium, and he struggled for breath. "Please . . . Forch . . ."

Forch dropped him.

Waxillium fell with the rain.

Three stories down, through the branches of a maple tree, scattering wet leaves.

Steel burned to life inside of him, spraying blue lines from his chest to nearby sources of metal. All above, none below. Nothing to Push on to save himself.

Except one bit in his trouser pocket.

Waxillium Pushed on it, desperate, as he tumbled in the air. It shot through his pocket, down along his leg, cutting a line in the side of his foot before being propelled down into the ground by his weight. Waxillium jerked in the air, slowing as soon as the bit of metal hit the ground.

He crashed onto the sodden pathway feet-first, pain jolting up his legs. He fell back to the ground, and found himself dazed but alive. His Push had saved him.

Rain fell on his face. He waited, but Forch didn't come down to finish him off. The youth had slammed the shutters, perhaps worried someone would see the light of his candles.

Every part of Waxillium ached. Shoulders from the first blow, legs from the fall, chest from the bar—how many ribs had he broken? He lay there in the rain, coughing, before finally rolling over to find the bit of metal that had saved his life. He found it easily by following its Allomantic line, and dug in the mud, pulling out something and holding it up.

The constable's bullet. Rain washed his hand, cleansing the metal. He didn't even remember stuffing it into his pocket.

In a case like this, the fire is often just a harbinger. . . .

He should go get help. But that boy above was already bleeding. The knives were out.

Something bigger is coming, Elder. Something you'll all regret.

Suddenly Waxillium hated Forch. This place was perfect, serene. Beautiful. Darkness shouldn't exist here. If Waxillium was a smudge on the white canvas, this man was a pit of pure blackness.

Waxillium shouted, climbing to his feet and throwing himself through the back door and into the old building. He climbed two flights in a haze of stumbling pain before slamming open the door into the meeting room. Forch stood above the weeping child, a bloody knife in his hand. He turned his head slowly, showing Waxillium one eye, half of his face.

Waxillium threw the single bullet up between them, its casing glittering in candlelight, then *Pushed* with everything he had. Forch turned and Pushed back.

The reaction was immediate. The bullet stopped in midair, inches from Forch's face. Both men were thrown backward, but Forch caught himself on a group of tables, staying steady. Waxillium was slammed against the wall beside the doorway.

Forch smiled, and his muscles swelled, strength drawn from his metalmind. He pulled his bar from the table of knives and threw it at Waxillium, who cried out, Pushing against it to stop it from smashing him.

He wasn't strong enough. Forch continued to *Push,* and Waxillium had so little steel. The bar slipped forward in the air, pressing against Waxillium's chest, pushing him against the wall.

Time froze. One bullet hanging just before Forch, their main fight over the bar which—bit by bit—crushed Waxillium. His chest flared in pain, and a scream slipped from his lips.

He was going to die here.

I just want to do what is right. Why is that so hard?

Forch stepped forward, grinning.

Waxillium's eyes fixed on that bullet, glittering golden. He couldn't breathe. But that bullet . . .

Metal is your life.

A bullet. Three parts metal. The tip.

Metal is your soul.

The casing.

You preserve us . . .

And the knob at the back. The spot the hammer would hit.

In that moment, to Waxillium's eyes, they split into three lines, three parts. He took them all in at once. And then, as the bar crushed him, he let go of two bits.

And *shoved* on that knob at the back.

The bullet exploded. The casing flipped backward into the air, Pushed by Forch's Allomancy, while the bullet itself zipped forward, untouched, before drilling into Forch's skull.

Waxillium dropped to the ground, the bar propelled away. He collapsed in a heap, gasping for breath, rainwater streaming from his face to the wooden floor.

In a daze, he heard voices below. People finally responding to the shouts, then the sound of gunfire. He forced himself to his feet and limped through the room, ignoring the voices of Terrismen and women who climbed the steps. He reached the child and ripped off the bonds, freeing him. Instead of running in fear, however, the little boy grabbed Waxillium's leg and held on tight, weeping.

People poured into the room. Waxillium leaned down, picking up the bullet casing off the wet floor, then stood up straight and faced them. Tellingdwar. His grandmother. The elders. He registered their horror, and knew in that moment they would hate him because he had brought violence into their village.

Hate him because he had been right.

He stood beside Forch's corpse and closed one hand around the bullet casing, resting his other on the head of the trembling child.

"I will find my own way," he whispered.

TWENTY-EIGHT YEARS LATER

The hideout door slammed against the other wall, shedding a burst of dust. A wall of mist fell in around the man who had kicked it open, outlining his silhouette: a mistcoat, tassels flaring from motion, a combat shotgun held up to the side.

"Fire!" Migs cried.

The lads unloaded. Eight men, armed to their teeth, fired at the shadowy figure from behind their barricade inside the old pub. Bullets swarmed like insects, but *parted* around this man in the long coat. They pelted the wall, drilling holes in the door and splintering the doorframe. They cut trails through the encroaching mist, but the lawman, all black in the gloom, didn't so much as flinch.

Migs fired shot after shot, despairing. He emptied one pistol, then a second, then shouldered his rifle and fired as quickly as he could cock it. How had they gotten here? Rusts, how had this *happened*? It wasn't supposed to have gone like this.

"It's useless!" one of the lads cried. "He's gonna kill us all, Migs!"

"Why're you just standin' there?" Migs shouted at the lawman. "Be at it already!" He fired twice more. "What's wrong with you?"

"Maybe he's distracting us," one of the lads said, "so his pal can sneak up behind us."

"Hey, that's . . ." Migs hesitated, looking toward the one who had spoken. Round face. Simple, round coachman's hat, like a bowler, but flatter on top. Who was that man again? He counted his crew.

Nine?

The lad next to Migs smiled, tipped his hat, then decked him in the face.

It was over blurringly quick. The fellow in the coachman's cap laid out Slink and Guillian in an eyeblink. Then suddenly he was closer to the two on the far side, slapping them down with a pair of dueling canes. As Migs turned—fumbling for the gun he'd dropped—the lawman leaped over the barricade with tassels flying and kicked Drawers in the chin. The lawman spun, leveling his shotgun at the men on the other side.

They dropped their guns. Migs knelt, sweating, beside an overturned table. He waited for the gunshots.

They didn't come.

"Ready for you, Captain!" the lawman shouted. A pile of constables rushed through the doorway, disturbing the mists. Outside, morning light was starting to dispel those anyway. Rusts. Had they really holed up in here all night?

The lawman swung his gun down toward Migs. "You might want to drop that gun, friend," he said in a conversational tone.

Migs hesitated. "Just shoot me, lawman. I'm in too deep."

"You shot two constables," the man said, finger on the trigger. "But they'll live, son. You won't hang, if I have my way. Drop the gun."

They'd called those same words before, from outside. This time, Migs found himself believing them. "Why?" he asked. "You coulda killed us all without breaking a sweat. *Why?*"

"Because," the lawman said, "frankly, you're not worth killing." He smiled in a friendly-type way. "I've got enough on my conscience already. Drop the gun. We'll get this sorted out."

Migs dropped the gun and stood, then waved down Drawers, who was climbing up with his gun in hand. The man reluctantly dropped his weapon too.

The lawman turned, cresting the barricade with an Allomantic leap, and slammed his shortened shotgun into a holster on his leg. The younger man in the coachman's hat joined him, whistling softly. He appeared to have swiped Guillian's favorite knife; the ivory hilt was sticking out of his pocket.

"They're yours, Captain," the lawman said.

"Not staying for the booking, Wax?" the constable captain asked, turning.

“Unfortunately, no,” the lawman said. “I have to get to a wedding.”

“Whose?”

“Mine, I’m afraid.”

“You came on a raid the morning of your *wedding*?” the captain asked.

The lawman, Waxillium Ladrian, stopped in the doorway. “In my defense, it wasn’t my idea.” He nodded one more time to the assembled constables and gang members, then strode out into the mists.

PART ONE

1

Waxillium Ladrian hurried down the steps outside the bar-turned-hideout, passing constables in brown who bustled this way and that. The mists were already evaporating, dawn heralding the end of their vigil. He checked his arm, where a bullet had ripped a sizable hole through the cuff of his shirt and out the side of his jacket. He'd felt that one pass.

"Oi," Wayne said, hustling up beside him. "A good plan that one was, eh?"

"It was the same plan you always have," Wax said. "The one where I get to be the decoy."

"Ain't my fault people like to shoot at you, mate," Wayne said as they reached the coach. "You should be happy; you're usin' your talents, like me granners always said a man should do."

"I'd rather not have 'shootability' be my talent."

"Well, you gotta use what you have," Wayne said, leaning against the side of the carriage as Cob the coachman opened the door for Wax. "Same reason I always have bits of rat in my stew."

Wax looked into the carriage, with its fine cushions and rich upholstery, but didn't climb in.

"You gonna be all right?" Wayne asked.

"Of course I am," Wax said. "This is my second marriage. I'm an old hand at the practice by now."

Wayne grinned. "Oh, is that how it works? 'Cuz in my experience, marryin' is the one thing people seem to get worse at the more they do it. Well, that and bein' alive."

"Wayne, that was almost profound."

"Damn. I was aimin' for insightful."

Wax stood still, looking into the carriage. The coachman cleared his throat, still standing and holding the door open for him.

"Right pretty noose, that is," Wayne noted.

"Don't be melodramatic," Wax said, leaning to climb in.

"Lord Ladrian!" a voice called from behind.

Wax glanced over his shoulder, noting a tall man in a dark brown suit and bow tie pushing between a pair of constables. "Lord Ladrian," the man said, "could I have a moment, please?"

"Take them all," Wax said. "But do it without me."

"But—"

"I'll meet you there," Wax said, nodding to Wayne. He dropped a spent bullet shell, then Pushed himself into the air. Why waste time on a carriage?

Steel at a comfortable burn inside his stomach, he shoved on a nearby electric streetlight—still shining, though morning had arrived—and soared higher into the air. Elendel spread before him, a soot-stained marvel of a city, leaking smoke from a hundred thousand different homes and factories. Wax shoved off the steel frame of a half-finished building nearby, then sent himself in a series of leaping bounds across the Fourth Octant.

He passed over a field of carriages for hire, rows of vehicles waiting quietly in ranks, early morning workers looking up at him as he passed. One pointed; perhaps the mistcoat had drawn his attention. Coinshot couriers weren't an uncommon sight in Elendel, and men soaring through the air were rarely a point of interest.

A few more leaps took him over a series of warehouses in huddled rows. Wax thrilled in each jump. It was amazing how this could still feel so wonderful to him. The breeze in his face, the little moment of weightlessness when he hung at the very top of an arc.

All too soon, however, both gravity and duty reasserted themselves. He left the industrial district and crossed finer roadways, paved with pitch and gravel to create a smoother surface than cobbles for all those blasted motorcars. He spotted the Survivorist church easily, with its large glass and steel dome. Back in Weathering a simple wooden chapel had been sufficient, but that wasn't nearly grand enough for Elendel.

The design was to allow those who worshipped full view of the mists at night. Wax figured if they wanted to see the mists, they'd do better just stepping outside. But perhaps he was being cynical. After all, the dome—which was made of segments of glass between steel supports, making it look like the sections of an orange—was able to open inward and let the mist pour down for special occasions.

He landed on a rooftop water tower across from the church. Perhaps when it had been built, the church's dome had been tall enough to overshadow the surrounding buildings. It would have provided a nice profile. Now, buildings were rising taller and taller, and the church was dwarfed by its surroundings. Wayne would find a metaphor in that. Probably a crude one.

He perched on the water tower, looming over the church. So he was here, finally. He felt his eye begin to twitch, and an ache rose within him.

I think I loved you even on that day. So ridiculous, but so earnest. . . .

Six months ago, he'd pulled the trigger. He could still hear the gunshot.

Standing up, he pulled himself together. He'd healed this wound once. He could do so again. And if that left his heart crusted with scar tissue, then perhaps that was what he needed. He leaped off the water tower, then slowed by dropping and Pushing on a shell casing.

He hit the street and strode past a long line of carriages. Guests were already in attendance—Survivorist tenets called for weddings either very early in the morning or late at night. Wax nodded to several people he passed, and couldn't help slipping his shotgun out of its holster and resting it on his shoulder as he hopped up the steps and shoved the door open before him with a Steelpush.

Steris paced in the foyer, wearing a sleek white dress that had been chosen because the magazines said it was fashionable. With her hair braided and her makeup done by a professional for the occasion, she was actually quite pretty.

He smiled when he saw her. His stress, his nervousness, melted away a little.

Steris looked up as soon as he entered, then hurried to his side. "And?"

"I didn't get killed," he said, "so there's that."

She glanced at the clock. "You're late," she said, "but not very late."

"I'm . . . sorry?" She'd insisted he go on the raid. She'd planned for it, in fact. Such was life with Steris.

"I'm sure you did your best," Steris said, taking his arm. She was warm, and even trembling. Steris might be reserved, but unlike what some assumed, she wasn't emotionless.

"The raid?" she asked.

"Went well. No casualties." He walked with her to a side chamber, where Drewton—his valet—waited beside a table spread with Wax's white wedding suit. "You realize that by going on a raid on the morning of my wedding, I'll only reinforce this image that society has of me."

"Which image?"

"That of a ruffian," he said, taking off his mistcoat and handing it to Drewton. "A barely civilized lout from the Roughs who curses in church and goes to parties armed."

She glanced at his shotgun, which he'd tossed onto the sofa. "You enjoy playing with people's perceptions of you, don't you? You seek to make them uncomfortable, so they'll be off balance."

"It's one of the simple joys I have left, Steris." He smiled as Drewton unbuttoned his waistcoat. Then he pulled off both that and his shirt, leaving him bare-chested.

"I see I'm included in those you try to make uncomfortable," Steris said.

"I work with what I have," Wax said.

"Which is why you always have bits of rat in your stew?"

Wax hesitated in handing his clothing to Drewton. "He said that to you too?"

"Yes. I'm increasingly convinced he tries the lines out on me." She folded her arms. "The little mongrel."

"Not going to leave as I change?" Wax asked, amused.

"We're to be married in less than an hour, Lord Waxillium," she said. "I think I can stand to see you bare-chested. As a side note, *you're* the Pathian. Prudishness is part of your belief system, not mine. I've read of Kelsier. From what I've studied, I doubt he'd care if—"

Wax undid the wooden buttons on his trousers. Steris blushed, before turning around and finally putting her back to him. She continued speaking a moment later, sounding flustered. "Well, at least you agreed to a proper ceremony."

Wax smiled, settling down in his undershorts and letting Drewton give his face a quick shave. Steris remained in place, listening. Finally, as Drewton was wiping the cream from Wax's face, she asked, "You have the pendants?"

"Gave them to Wayne."

"You . . . *What?*"

"I thought you wanted some disturbances at the wedding," Wax said, standing and taking the new set of trousers from Drewton. He slipped them on. He hadn't worn white much since returning from the Roughs. It was harder to keep clean out there, which had made it worth wearing. "I figured this would work."

"I wanted *planned* disturbances, Lord Waxillium," Steris snapped. "It's not upsetting if it's understood, prepared for, and controlled. Wayne is rather the opposite of those things, wouldn't you say?"

Wax did up his buttons and Drewton took his shirt off the hanger nearby. Steris turned around immediately upon hearing the sound, arms still folded, and didn't miss a beat—refusing to acknowledge that she'd been embarrassed. "I'm glad I had copies made."

"You made *copies* of our wedding pendants?"

"Yes." She chewed her lip a moment. "Six sets."

"*Six?*"

"The other four didn't arrive in time."

Wax grinned, doing up the buttons on his shirt, then letting his valet handle the cuffs. "You're one of a kind, Steris."

"Technically, so is Wayne—and actually so was Ruin, for that matter. If you consider it, that's not much of a compliment."

Wax strapped on suspenders, then let Drewton fuss with his collar. "I don't get it, Steris," he said, standing stiffly as the valet worked. "You prepare so thoroughly for things to go wrong—like you know and expect that life is unpredictable."

"Yes, and?"

"And life *is* unpredictable. So the only thing you do by preparing for disturbances is ensure that something *else* is going to go wrong."

"That's a rather fatalistic viewpoint."

"Living in the Roughs does that to a fellow." He eyed her, standing resplendent in her dress, arms crossed, tapping her left arm with her right index finger.

"I just . . . feel better when I try," Steris finally said. "It's like, if everything goes wrong, at least I *tried*. Does that make any sense?"

"As a matter of fact, I think it does."

Drewton stepped back, satisfied. The suit came with a very nice black cravat and vest. Traditional, which Wax preferred. Bow ties were for salesmen. He slid on the jacket, tails brushing the backs of his legs. Then, after a moment's hesitation, he strapped on his gunbelt and slid Vindication into her holster. He'd worn a gun to his last wedding, so why not this one? Steris nodded in approval.

Shoes went last. A new pair. They'd be hideously uncomfortable. "Are we late enough yet?" he asked Steris.

She checked the clock in the corner. "I planned for us to go in two minutes from now."

"Ah, delightful," he said, taking her arm. "That means we can be spontaneous and arrive early. Well, late-early."

She clung to his arm, letting him steer her down the side chamber toward the entrance to the dome, and the church proper. Drewton followed behind.

"Are you . . . certain you wish to proceed?" Steris asked, stopping him before they entered the walkway to the dome.

"Having second thoughts?"

"Absolutely not," Steris said immediately. "This union is quite beneficial to my house and status." She took Wax's left hand in both of hers. "But Lord Waxillium," she said softly, "I don't want you to feel trapped, particularly after what happened to you earlier this year. If you wish to back out, I will accept it as your will."

The way she clutched his hand as she said those words sent a very different message. But she didn't seem to notice. Looking at her, Wax found himself wondering. When he'd first agreed to the marriage, he'd done so out of duty to his house.

Now, he felt his emotions shifting. The way she'd been there for him these last months as he'd grieved . . . The way she looked at him right now . . .

Rust and Ruin. He was actually *fond* of Steris. It wasn't love, but he doubted he would love again. This would do.

"No, Steris," he said. "I would not back out. That . . . wouldn't be fair to your house, and the money you have spent."

"The money doesn't—"

"It's all right," Wax said, giving her hand a little squeeze. "I have recovered enough from my ordeal. I'm strong enough to do this."

Steris opened her mouth to reply, but a knock at the door heralded Marasi sticking her head in to check on them. With dark hair and softer, rounder features than Steris, Marasi wore bright red lipstick and a progressive lady's attire—a pleated skirt, with a tight buttoned jacket.

"Finally," she said. "Crowd is getting fidgety. Wax, there's a man here wanting to see you. I've been trying to send him away, but . . . well . . ."

She came into the room and held the door open, revealing the same slender man in the brown suit and bow tie from before, standing with the ash girls in the antechamber that led to the dome proper.

"You," Wax said. "How did you get here before Wayne?"

"I don't believe your friend is coming," the man said. He stepped in beside Marasi and nodded to her, then closed the doors, shutting out the ash girls. He turned and tossed Wax a wadded-up ball of paper.

When Wax caught it, it clinked. Unfolding it revealed the two wedding pendants. Scrawled on the paper were the words: *Gonna go get smashed till I can't piss straight. Happy weddings 'n stuff.*

"Such beautiful imagery," Steris observed, taking Wax's wedding pendant in a white-gloved hand as Marasi looked over his shoulder to read the note. "At least he didn't forget these."

"Thank you," Wax said to the man in brown, "but as you can see, I'm quite busy *getting married*. Whatever you need from me can—"

The man's face turned translucent, displaying the bones of his skull and spine beneath.

Steris stiffened. "Holy One," she whispered.

"Holy pain," Wax said. "Tell Harmony to get someone else this time. I'm busy."

"Tell . . . *Harmony* . . ." Steris mumbled, her eyes wide.

"Unfortunately, this is part of the problem," the man in brown said, his skin returning to normal. "Harmony has been distracted as of late."

"How can God be distracted?" Marasi asked.

"We're not sure, but it has us worried. I need you, Waxillium Ladrian. I have a job you'll find of interest. I realize you're off to the ceremony, but afterward, if I could have a moment of your time . . ."

"No," Wax said.

"But—"

"No."

Wax pulled Steris by the arm, shoving open the doors, striding past Marasi, leaving the kandra. It had been six months since those creatures had manipulated him, played him, and lied to him. The result? A dead woman in his arms.

Bastards.

"Was that really one of the *Faceless Immortals*?" Steris said, looking over her shoulder.

"Yes, and for obvious reasons I want nothing to do with them."

"Peace," she said, holding his arm. "Do you need a moment?"

"No."

"You're sure?"

Wax stopped in place. She waited, and he breathed in and out, banishing from his mind that awful, *awful* scene when he'd knelt on a bridge alone, holding Lessie. A woman he realized he'd never actually known.

"I'm all right," he said to Steris through clenched teeth. "But God should have known not to come for me. Particularly not today."

"Your life is . . . decidedly odd, Lord Waxillium."

"I know," he said, moving again, stepping with her beside the last door before they entered the dome. "Ready?"

"Yes, thank you." Was she . . . teary-eyed? It was an expression of emotion he'd never seen from her.

"Are *you* all right?" he asked.

"Yes," she said. "Forgive me. It's just . . . more wonderful than I'd imagined."

They pushed open the doors, revealing the glistening dome, sunlight streaming through it and upon the waiting crowd. Acquaintances. Distant family members. Seamstresses and forgeworkers from his house. Wax sought out Wayne, and was surprised when he didn't find the man, despite the note. He was the only real family Wax had.

The ash girls scampered out, sprinkling small handfuls of ash on the carpeted walkway that ringed the perimeter of the dome. Wax and Steris started forward in a stately walk, presenting themselves for those in attendance. There was no music at a Survivorist ceremony, but a few crackling braziers with green leaves on top let smoke trail upward to represent the mist.

Smoke ascends while ash falls, he thought, remembering the priest's words from his youth, back when he'd attended Survivorist ceremonies. They walked all the way around the crowd. At least

Steris's family had made a decent showing, her father included—the red-faced man gave Waxillium an enthusiastic fist-raise as they passed.

Wax found himself smiling. This was what Lessie had wanted. They'd joked time and time again about their simple Pathian ceremony, finalized on *horseback* to escape a mob. She said that someday, she'd make him do it proper.

Sparkling crystal. A hushed crowd. Footsteps on scrunching carpet dappled with grey ash. His smile widened, and he looked to the side.

But of course, the wrong woman was there.

He almost stumbled. *Idiot man,* he thought. *Focus.* This day was important to Steris; the least he could do was not ruin it. Or rather, not ruin it in a way she hadn't expected. Whatever that meant.

Unfortunately, as they walked the remaining distance around the rotunda, his discomfort increased. He felt nauseous. Sweaty. Sick, like the feeling he had gotten the few times he had been forced to run from a killer and leave innocents in danger.

It all forced him, finally, to acknowledge a difficult fact. He wasn't ready. It wasn't Steris, it wasn't the setting. He just wasn't *ready* for this.

This marriage meant letting go of Lessie.

But he was trapped, and he *had* to be strong. He set his jaw and stepped with Steris onto the dais, where the priest stood between two stands topped with crystal vases of Marewill flowers. The ceremony was drawn from ancient Larsta beliefs, from Harmony's *Beliefs Reborn,* a volume in the Words of Founding.

The priest spoke the words, but Wax couldn't listen. All was numbness to him, teeth clenched, eyes straight ahead, muscles tense. They'd found a priest murdered in this very church. Killed by Lessie as she went mad. Couldn't they have done something for her, instead of setting him on the hunt? Couldn't they have *told* him?

Strength. He would *not* flee. He would *not* be a coward.

He held Steris's hands, but couldn't look at her. Instead, he turned his face upward to look out the glass dome toward the sky. Most of it was crowded out by the buildings. Skyscrapers on two sides, windows glistening in the morning sun. That water tower certainly did block the view, though as he watched, it shifted. . . .

Shifted?

Wax watched in horror as the legs under the enormous metal cylinder bent, as if to kneel, ponderously tipping their burden on its side. The top of the thing sheared off, spilling tons of water in a foaming wave.

He yanked Steris to him, arm firmly around her waist, then ripped off the second button down on his waistcoat and dropped it. He Pushed against this single metal button, launching himself and Steris away from the dais as the priest yelped in surprise.

Water *crashed* against the dome, which strained for the briefest of seconds before a section of it snapped open, hinges giving way inward to the water.

2

"Are you certain you're all right, my lord?" Wax asked, helping Lord Drapen, constable-general of the Sixth Octant, down the steps toward his carriage. Water trickled beside them in little streams, joining a small river in the gutters.

"Ruined my best pistol, you realize," Drapen said. "I'll have to send the thing to be cleaned and oiled!"

"Bill me the expense, my lord," Wax said, ignoring the fact that a good pistol would hardly be ruined by a little—or, well, a *lot* of—water. Wax turned the aging gentleman over to his coachman, sharing a resigned look, before turning and climbing back up the steps into the church. The carpet squished when he stepped on it. Or maybe that was his shoes.

He passed the priest bickering with the Erikell insurance assessor—come to do an initial report for when the church demanded payment on their policy—and entered the main dome. The one open section of glass still swung on its hinges up above, and the tipped water tower—its legs on the other side had kept it from crashing down completely—still blocked out much of the sky.

He passed overturned benches, discarded Marewill petals, and general refuse. Water dripped, the room's only sound other than the echoing voice of the priest. Wax squished his way up to the dais. Steris sat on its edge, wet dress plastered to her body, strands of hair that had escaped from her wedding braids sticking to the sides of her face. She sat with arms crossed on her knees, staring at the floor.

Wax sat down next to her. "So, next time a flood is dumped on our heads, I'll try to remember that jumping *upward* is a bad idea." He pulled his handkerchief from his pocket and squeezed it out.

"You tried to get us backward too. It merely wasn't fast enough, Lord Waxillium."

He grunted. "Looks like simple structural failure. If it *was* instead some kind of assassination attempt . . . well, it was an incompetent one. There wasn't enough water in there to be truly dangerous. The worst injury was to Lord Steming, who fell and knocked his head when scrambling off his seat."

"No more than an accident then," Steris said. She flopped backward onto the dais, the carpet letting out a soft squish.

"I'm sorry."

"It's not your fault." She sighed. "Do you ever wonder if perhaps the cosmere is out to overwhelm you, Lord Waxillium?"

"The cosmere? You mean Harmony?"

"No, not Him," Steris said. "Just cosmic chance rolling the dice anytime I pass, and always hitting all ones. There seems to be a poetry to it all." She closed her eyes. "Of *course* the wedding would fall apart. Several tons of water falling through the roof? Why wouldn't I have seen that? It's so utterly outlandish it *had* to happen. At least the priest didn't get murdered this time."

"Steris," Wax said, resting a hand on her arm. "We'll fix this. It will be all right."

She opened her eyes, looking toward him. "Thank you, Lord Waxillium."

"For what, exactly?" he asked.

"For being nice. For being willing to subject yourself to, well, me. I understand that it is not a pleasant concept."

"Steris . . ."

"Do not think me self-deprecating, Lord Waxillium," she said, sitting up and taking a deep breath, "and please do not assume I'm being morose. I am what I am, and I accept it. But I am under no illusions as to how my company is regarded. Thank you. For not making me feel as others have."

He hesitated. How did one respond to something like *that*? "It's not as you say, Steris. I think you're delightful."

"And the fact that you were gritting your teeth as the ceremony started, hands gripping as tightly as a man dangling for his life from the side of a bridge?"

"I . . ."

"Are you saddened at the fact that our wedding is delayed? Can you truly say it, and be honest as a lawman, Lord Waxillium?"

Damn. He floundered. He knew a few simple words could defuse or sidestep the question, but he couldn't find them, despite searching for what was an awkwardly long time—until saying anything would have sounded condescending.

"Perhaps," he said, smiling, "I'll just have to try something to relax me next time we attempt this."

"I doubt going to the ceremony drunk would be productive."

"I didn't say I'd drink. Perhaps some Terris meditation beforehand."

She eyed him. "You're still willing to move forward?"

"Of course." As long as it didn't have to be today. "I assume you have a backup dress?"

"Two," she admitted, letting him help her to her feet. "And I did reserve another date for a wedding two months from now. Different church—in case this one exploded."

He grunted. "You sound like Wayne."

"Well, things *do* tend to explode around you, Lord Waxillium." She looked up at the dome. "Considering that, getting drenched must be rather novel."

Marasi trailed around the outside of the flooded church, hands clasped behind her back, notebook a familiar weight in her jacket pocket. A few constables—all corporals—stood about looking as if they were in charge. That sort of thing was important in a crisis; statistics showed that if a uniformed authority figure was nearby, people were less likely to panic.

Of course, there was also a smaller percentage who were *more* likely to panic if an authority figure was nearby. Because people were people, and if there was one thing you could count on, it was that some of them would be weird. Or rather that *all* of them would be weird when circumstances happened to align with their own individual brand of insanity.

That said, today she hunted a very special kind of insane. She'd tried the nearby pubs first, but that was too obvious. Next she checked the gutters, one soup kitchen, and—against her better judgment—a purveyor of "novelties." No luck, though her backside did get *three* separate compliments, so there was that.

Finally, running out of ideas, she went to check if he'd decided to steal the forks from the wedding breakfast. There, in a dining hall across the street from the church, she found Wayne in the kitchens wearing a white jacket and a chef's hat. He was scolding several assistant cooks as they furiously decorated tarts with fruit glaze.

Marasi leaned against the doorway and watched, tapping her notebook with her pencil. Wayne sounded utterly unlike himself, instead using a sharp, nasal voice with an accent she couldn't quite place. Easterner, perhaps? Some of the outer cities there had thick accents.

The assistant cooks didn't question him. They jumped at what he said, bearing his condemnation as he tasted a chilled soup and swore at their incompetence. If he noticed Marasi, he didn't show it, instead wiping his hands on a cloth and demanding to see the produce the delivery boys had brought that morning.

Eventually, Marasi strolled into the kitchen, dodging a short assistant chef bearing a pot almost as big as she was, and stepped up to Wayne.

"I've seen crisper lettuce in the garbage heap!" he was saying to a cringing delivery boy. "And you call these grapes? These are so overripe, they're practically fermenting! And—oh, 'ello, Marasi." He said the last line in his normal, jovial voice.

The delivery boy scrambled away.

"What are you doing?" Marasi asked.

"Makin' soup," Wayne said, holding up a wooden spoon to show her. Nearby, several of the assistant cooks stopped in place, looking at him with shocked expressions.

"Out with you!" he said to them in the chef's voice. "I must have time to prepare! Shoo, shoo, go!"

They scampered away, leaving him grinning.

"You do realize the wedding breakfast is canceled," Marasi said, leaning back against a table.

"Sure do."

"So why . . ."

She trailed off as he stuffed an entire tart in his mouth and grinned. "Hadda make sure they didn't welch on their promif an' not make anyfing to eat," he said around chewing, crumbs cascading from his lips. "We paid for this stuff. Well, Wax did. 'Sides, wedding being canceled is no reason not to celebrate, right?"

"Depends on what you're celebrating," Marasi said, flipping open her notebook. "Bolts securing the water tower in place were definitely loosened. Road below was conspicuously empty, some ruffians—from another octant entirely, I might add—having stopped traffic by starting a fistfight in the middle of the rusting street."

Wayne grunted, searching in a cupboard. "Hate that little notebook of yours sometimes."

Marasi groaned, closing her eyes. "Someone could have been hurt, Wayne."

"Now, that ain't right at all. Someone *was* hurt. That fat fellow what has no hair."

She massaged her temples. "You realize I'm a constable now, Wayne. I can't turn a blind eye toward *wanton* property damage."

"Ah, 's not so bad," Wayne said, still rummaging. "Wax'll pay for it."

"And if someone had been hurt? Seriously, I mean?"

Wayne kept searching. "The lads got a little carried away. 'See that the church is flooded,' I told them. Meant for the priest to open the place in the morning and find his plumbing had gotten a little case of the 'being all busted up and leaking all over the rusting place.' But the lads, they got a little excited is all."

"The 'lads'?"

"Just some friends."

"Saboteurs."

"Nah," Wayne said. "You think they could pronounce that?"

"Wayne . . ."

"I slapped 'em around already, Marasi," Wayne said. "Promise I did."

"He's going to figure it out," Marasi said. "What will you do then?"

"Nah, you're wrong," Wayne said, finally coming out of the cupboard with a large glass jug. "Wax has a blind spot for things like this. In the back of his noggin, he'll be relieved that I stopped the wedding. He'll figure it was me, deep in his subcontinence, and will pay for the damages—no matter what the assessor says. And he won't say anything, won't even investigate. Watch."

"I don't know. . . ."

Wayne hopped up onto the kitchen counter, then patted the spot beside him. She regarded him for a moment, then sighed and settled onto the counter there.

He offered her the jug.

"That's cooking sherry, Wayne."

"Yeah," he said, "pubs don't serve anything this hour but beer. A fellow has to get creative."

"I'm sure we could find some wine around—"

He took a swig.

"Never mind," Marasi said.

He lowered the jug and pulled off his chef's hat, tossing it onto the counter. "What're you so uptight for today, anyway? I figured you'd be whooping for joy and runnin' around the street pickin' flowers and stuff. He's not marrying her. Not yet, anyway. You still got a chance."

"I don't *want* a chance, Wayne. He's made his decision."

"Now, what kinda talk is that?" he demanded. "You've given up? Is that how the Ascendant Warrior was? Huh?"

"No, in fact," Marasi said. "She walked up to the man she wanted, slapped the book out of his hand, and kissed him."

"See, there's how it is!"

"Though the Ascendant Warrior also went on and murdered the woman Elend was planning to marry."

"What, really?"

"Yeah."

"Gruesome," Wayne said in an approving tone, then took another swig of sherry.

"That's not the half of it," Marasi said, leaning back on the counter, hands behind her. "You want gruesome? She also supposedly ripped out the Lord Ruler's insides. I've seen it depicted in several illuminated manuscripts."

"Kind of graphic for a religious-type story."

"Actually, they're all like that. I think they have to put in lots of exciting bits to make people read the rest."

"Huh." He seemed disbelieving.

"Wayne, haven't you ever *read* any religious texts?"

"Sure I have."

"Really?"

"Yeah, lots of the things I read have religious texts in them. 'Damn.' 'Hell.' 'Flatulent, arse-licking git.'"

She gave him a flat stare.

"That last one is in the Testimony of Hammond. Promise. Least, all the letters are." Another swig. Wayne could outdrink anyone she knew. Of course, that was mostly because he could tap his metalmind, heal himself, and burn away the alcohol's effects in an eyeblink—then start over.

"Here now," he continued, "that's what you've gotta do. Be like the Lady Mistborn. Get your murderin' on, see. Don't back down. He should be yours, and you gotta let people know."

"My . . . murderin' on?"

"Sure."

"Against my sister."

"You could be polite about it," Wayne said. "Like, give her the first stab or whatnot."

"No, thank you."

"It doesn't have to be *real* murderin', Marasi," Wayne said, hopping off the counter. "It can be figurative and all. But you should *fight*. Don't let him marry her."

Marasi leaned her head back, looking up at the set of ladles swinging above the counter. "I'm not the Ascendant Warrior, Wayne," she said. "And I don't particularly care to be. I don't want someone I have to convince, someone I have to rope into submission. That sort of thing is for the courtroom, not the bedroom."

"Now, see, I think some people would say—"

"Careful."

"—that's a right enlightened way to think of things." He took a swig of sherry.

"I'm not some tortured, abandoned creature, Wayne," Marasi said, finding herself smiling at her distorted reflection in a ladle. "I'm not sitting around pining and dreaming for someone else to decide if I should be happy. There's nothing there. Whether that's due to actual lack of affection on his part, or more to stubbornness, I don't care. I've moved on."

She looked down, meeting Wayne's eyes. He cocked his head. "Huh. You're serious, aren't you?"

"Damn right."

"Moved on . . ." he said. "Rusted nuts! You can *do* that?"

"Certainly."

"Huh. You think . . . I should . . . you know . . . Ranette . . ."

"Wayne, if ever someone should have taken a hint, it was you. Yes. Move on. Really."

"Oh, I took the hint," he said, taking a swig of sherry. "Just can't remember which jacket I left it in." He looked down at the jug. "You sure?"

"She has a *girl*friend, Wayne."

“’S only a phase,” he mumbled. “One what lasted fifteen years. . . .” He set the jug down, then sighed and reached into the cupboard from before, taking out a bottle of wine.

“Oh, for *Preservation’s* sake,” Marasi said. “That was in there all along?”

“Tastes better iffen you drink something what tastes like dishwater first,” Wayne said, then pulled the cork out with his teeth, which *was* kind of impressive, she had to admit. He poured her a cup, then one for himself. “To moving on?” he asked.

“Sure. To moving on.” She raised her cup, and saw reflected in the wine someone standing behind her.

She gasped, spinning, reaching for her purse. Wayne just raised his cup to the newcomer, who rounded the counter with a slow step. It was the man in the brown suit and bow tie. No, not the man. The *kandra*.

“If you’re here to persuade me to persuade him,” Wayne said, “you should know that he doesn’t ever listen to me unless he’s pretty drunk at the time.” He downed the wine. “’S probably why he’s lived so long.”

“Actually,” the kandra said, “I’m not here for you.” He turned to Marasi, then tipped his head. “My first choice for this endeavor has rejected my request. I hope you don’t take offense at being my second.”

Marasi found her heart thumping quickly. “What do you want?”

The kandra smiled broadly. “Tell me, Miss Colms. What do you know about the nature of Investiture and Identity?”

3

Wax, at least, had a change of clothing that wasn't wet—the suit he had worn on the raid. So he was pleasantly dry as his carriage pulled up to Ladrian Mansion. Steris had returned to her father's house to recover.

Wax put aside his broadsheet and waited for Cob, the new coachman, to hop down and yank open the carriage door. There was a frantic eagerness to the little man's motions, as if he knew that Wax only used a coach for propriety's sake. Leaping home on lines of steel would have been far faster, but just as a lord couldn't walk everywhere, Steelpushing around town too much in the daytime when not chasing criminals made members of his house uncomfortable. It simply wasn't what a house lord did.

Wax nodded to Cob and handed him the broadsheet. Cob grinned; he loved the things. "Take the rest of the day off," Wax told him. "I know you were looking forward to the wedding festivities."

Cob's grin widened, then he bobbed his head and climbed back onto the coach to see it, and the horses, cared for before leaving. He'd likely spend the day at the races.

Wax sighed, climbing the steps to the mansion. It was one of the finest in the city—luxurious with carved stonework and deep hardwood, with tasteful marble accents. That didn't stop it from being a prison. It was just a very nice one.

Wax didn't enter. Instead, he stood on the steps for a while before turning around and sitting on them. Closing his eyes, he let it all settle on him.

He was good at hiding his scars. He'd been shot almost a dozen times now, a few of those wounds quite bad. Out in the Roughs, he'd learned to pick himself up and keep on going, no matter what happened.

At the same time, it felt like things back then had been simple. Not always easy, but simple. And some scars continued to ache. Seemed to get worse with time.

He rose with a groan, leg stiff, and continued up the steps. Nobody opened the door for him or took his coat as he entered. He maintained a small staff in the house, but only what he considered necessary. Too many servants, and they'd hover and worry when he did anything on his own. It was as if the idea of him being capable drove them into feeling vestigial. . . .

Wax frowned, then slipped Vindication from his hip holster and raised her beside his head. He couldn't say, precisely, what had set him off. Footsteps up above, when he'd given the housekeepers the day off. A cup on a side table with a bit of wine in the bottom.

He flicked a little vial from his belt and downed the contents: steel flakes suspended in whiskey. The metal burned a familiar warmth inside of him, radiating from his stomach, and blue lines sprang into existence around him. They moved with him as he crept forward, as if he were tied with a thousand tiny threads.

He leaped and Pushed on the inlays in the marble floor, soaring up alongside the stairs to the second-story viewing balcony above the grand entryway. He slipped easily over the banister, landing with gun at the ready. The door to his study quivered, then opened.

Wax tiptoed forward.

"Just a moment, I—" The man in the light brown suit froze as he found Wax's gun pressed against his temple.

"You," Wax said.

"I'm quite fond of this skull," the kandra remarked. "It's sixth-century anteverdant, the head of a metal merchant from Urteau whose grave was shifted and protected as a side effect of Harmony's rebuilding. An antique, if you will. If you make a hole in it, I'll be *rather* put out."

"I told you I wasn't interested," Wax growled.

"Yes. I took that to heart, Lord Ladrian."

"Then why are you here?"

"Because I was invited," the kandra said. He reached up and grasped the barrel of Wax's gun between two fingers, then pushed it gently to the side. "We needed a place to converse. Your associate suggested it, as—I'm told—the servants are away."

"My associate?" At that point, he heard laughter from ahead. "Wayne." He eyed the kandra, then sighed and slipped his gun into its holster. "Which one are you? TenSoon, is that you?"

"Me?" the kandra asked, laughing. "TenSoon? What, do you hear me panting?" He chuckled, gesturing for Wax to enter his own study, as if he were doing Wax some grand courtesy. "I am VenDell, of the Sixth. Pleased to meet you, Lord Ladrian. If you must shoot me, please do it in the left leg, as I've no particular fondness for those bones."

"I'm not going to shoot you," Wax said, shoving past the kandra and entering the room. The blinds had been drawn and the thick curtains left to droop down, plunging the room into almost complete darkness, save for two small new electric lamps. Why the closed curtains? Was the kandra that concerned about being seen?

Wayne lounged in Wax's easy chair, feet up on the cocktail table, helping himself to a bowl of walnuts. A woman stretched out in a similar posture in the companion chair, wearing tight trousers and a loose blouse, eyes closed as she leaned back in the chair, hands behind her head. She wore a different body from last time Wax had seen her, but the posture—and the height—gave him good clues that this was MeLaan.

Marasi was inspecting some odd equipment set up on a pedestal at the back of the room. It was a box with small lenses on the front.

She stood up straight as soon as she saw him, and—being Marasi—blushed deeply.

"Sorry about this," she said. "We were going to go to my flat to talk, but Wayne insisted. . . ."

"Needed some nuts," Wayne said around a mouthful of walnuts. "When you invited me to stay here, you *did* say to make myself at home, mate."

"I'm still unclear as to why you *needed* a place to talk," Wax said. "I said I wasn't going to help."

"Quite so," VenDell said from the doorway. "As you were unavailable, of necessity I turned to other options. Lady Colms has been so kind as to listen to my proposition."

"Marasi?" Wax asked. "You went to Marasi?"

"What?" VenDell asked. "That's surprising to you? She *was* instrumental in the defeat of Miles Hundredlives. Not to mention her help during the riots Paalm instigated."

Wax looked at the kandra. "You're trying to get to me through another route, aren't you?"

"Look who's full of himself," MeLaan said from her chair.

"He's always full of himself," Wayne said, cracking a walnut. "Mostly on account of him eatin' his own fingernails. I seen him do it."

"Is it so ridiculous," Marasi said, "that they'd actually want my help?"

"I'm sorry, I didn't mean it that way," Wax said, turning to her.

"Then what way *did* you mean it?"

Wax sighed. "I don't know, Marasi. It's been a long day. I got shot at, got a water tower dumped on my head, and had my wedding fall apart. Now Wayne is dropping broken walnut shells all over my chair. Honestly, I think I just need a drink."

He walked toward the bar at the back of the room. Marasi eyed him, and as he passed, she muttered, "Will you get me one too? Because this is all making me go a little crazy."

He smiled, digging out some single-malt whiskey, pouring for himself and for Marasi. VenDell disappeared out the door, but returned a few minutes later with some piece of equipment that he hooked to the strange device. He ran a wire from the device to one of the wall lamps, pulling out the bulb and screwing in the end of the wire instead.

Leaving would feel childish, so Wax leaned against the wall and sipped his whiskey, saying nothing as VenDell turned on his machine. An image appeared on the wall.

Wax froze. It was a *picture,* similar to an evanotype—only on the wall and quite large. It displayed the Field of Rebirth in the center of Elendel, where the tombs of Vin and Elend Venture were to be found. He'd never seen anything like that image. It seemed to have been created entirely by light.

Marasi gasped.

Wayne threw a walnut at it.

"What?" he said as the others glared at him. "Wanted to see if it was real." He hesitated, then threw another walnut. The nut made a shadow on the image where it moved between the device and the wall. So it *was* light.

"Image projector," VenDell said. "They call it an evanoscope. By next year these will be commonplace, I should think." He paused. "Harmony implies that if we find this wondrous, it will *really* burn our metals when the images start moving."

"Moving?" Wax said, stepping forward. "How would they do that?"

"We don't know," MeLaan said with a grimace. "He accidentally let it slip, but won't say anything more."

"How does God," Marasi asked, still staring at the image, "*accidentally* let something slip?"

"As I said," VenDell said, "He has been distracted lately. We've tried to tease out more regarding moving images, but so far no luck. He's often like this—says it's vital that we discover things on our own."

"Like a chick breaking out of its shell," MeLaan said. "He says that if we don't struggle and learn on our own, we won't be strong enough to survive what is coming."

She left the words hanging in the room, and Wax shared a look with Marasi.

"Well . . ." Marasi said slowly, "*that's* ominous. Has He said anything more about Trell?"

Wax folded his arms. Trell. It was a god from the old records, long before the Catacendre—indeed, long before the Lord Ruler. Harmony had memorized this religion, with many others, during his days as a mortal.

Marasi had an obsession with the god, and one that was not unwarranted. Wax wasn't certain whether her claim was true or not that the worship of Trell was involved in what had happened to Lessie, but the spikes they'd discovered . . . they didn't seem to have been made of any metal known to man.

The kandra had confiscated those. Wax had been so deep in his sorrows that by the time he'd started to recover, they'd already been taken.

"No," VenDell said. "And I have no update on the spikes, if that's what you're wondering. But this task I have for you, Miss Colms, might provide insight. Suffice it to say, we're worried about the possible intrusion of another god upon this domain."

"Hey," MeLaan said, "what's a girl gotta do to get some of that whiskey?"

"Sister," VenDell said, twisting something on his machine, making the image brighter, "you are a representative of Harmony and His enlightenment."

"Yup," MeLaan said, "and I'm a tragically *sober* one."

Wax brought her a glass, and she grinned at him in thanks.

"Chivalry," she said, raising it.

"Manipulation," VenDell said. "Miss Colms, I spoke to you earlier of Investiture and Identity. I promised you an explanation. Here." He flipped something on his machine, changing the image on the wall to a list of Feruchemical metals, their attributes, and their natures. It wasn't the pretty, artistic rendition that Wax often saw in popular lore—it was far less fancy, but much more detailed.

"The basic physical abilities of Feruchemy are well understood," VenDell said, walking forward and using a long reed to point at a section of the projected chart. "Terris tradition and heritage has explored them for at least fifteen hundred years. Harmony left detailed explanations in the Words of Founding.

"Likewise, the abilities in the so-called mental quadrant of the chart have been outlined and discussed, tested and defined. Our understanding doesn't reach as far here—we don't know why memories stored in a metalmind degrade the way they do when removed, or why tapping mental speed tends to make one hungry, of all things—but still, we have a great deal of experience in this area."

He paused, and circled his pointer around a group of metals and abilities at the bottom: Fortune, Investiture, Identity, and Connection. Wax leaned forward. They'd spoken of these during his year living in the Village, but only as part of the catechisms of Feruchemy and Terris belief. None of those specified what the powers actually *did*. They were considered beyond understanding, like God, or time.

"Chromium," VenDell said, "nicrosil, aluminum, duralumin. These aren't metals that most ancients knew. Only in recent times have modern metallurgical processes allowed them to become commonplace."

"Commonplace?" Wayne said. "With a single aluminum bullet, mate, I could buy you an outfit that don't look so stupid *and* have money left over for a nice hat or two."

"Be that as it may," VenDell said, "compared to the amount of aluminum in the world before the Catacendre, the metal *is* now common. Bauxite refining, modern chemical processes, these have given us access to metals on a level that was never before possible. Why, the Last Obligator's autobiography explains that early aluminum was harvested from the inside of the Ashmounts!"

Wax stepped forward along the cone of light emanating from the machine. "So what do they do?"

"Research is ongoing," VenDell said. "Ferrings with these abilities are very, very rare—and it is only in the last few decades that we've had access to enough of these metals to begin experimenting. Rebuilding society has been a . . . wearisome process."

"You were alive before," Marasi said. "In the days of the Ascendant Warrior."

VenDell turned, raising his eyebrows. "Indeed, though I never met her. Only TenSoon did."

"What was life like?" Marasi asked.

"Hard," VenDell said. "It was . . . hard."

"There are holes in our memories," MeLaan added softly. "From when our spikes were removed. It took a piece out of us. There are things we'll never get back."

Wax took a drink. There was a *weight* that came from speaking to the kandra, in realizing that most of them had already been alive for hundreds of years when the World of Ash had ended. These were *ancient* beings. Perhaps Wax should not be surprised by their presumption. To them, he—indeed, everyone else alive—was little more than a child.

"Identity," VenDell said, slapping his reed against the wall, casting a shadow on the image. "Lord Ladrian, could another Feruchemist use your metalminds?"

"Of course not," Wax said. "Everyone knows that."

"Why?"

"Well . . . because. They're mine."

Feruchemy was simple, elegant. Fill your metalmind with an attribute for an hour—like Wax's weight, or Wayne's health and healing—and you could draw out an hour's worth of that attribute later on. Alternatively, you could draw out a burst of power that was extremely intense but lasted only a moment.

"The raw power of both Allomancy and Feruchemy," VenDell said, "is something we call Investiture. This is very important, as in Feruchemy, an individual's Investiture is keyed specifically to them. To what we call Identity."

"You've made me curious," Wax said, looking at the wall as VenDell leisurely walked back to his machine. "How does it know? My metalminds . . . do they *recognize* me?"

"After a fashion," VenDell said, changing the image to one of a Feruchemist tapping strength. The woman's muscles had grown to several times their normal size as she lifted a horse above her head. "Each man or woman has a Spiritual aspect, a piece of themselves that exists in another Realm entirely. You might call it your soul. Your Investiture is keyed to your soul—indeed, it might be a *part* of your soul, much as your blood is a part of your body."

"So if a person could store their Identity," Marasi said, "as Waxillium does with his weight . . ."

"They'd be without it for a time," VenDell said. "A blank slate, so to speak."

"So they could use *anyone's* metalmind?" Marasi asked.

"Possibly," VenDell said. He cycled through pictures of several more Feruchemists using their abilities before coming to rest on an image of a set of bracers. Simple metal bands, like wide bracelets, meant to be worn on the upper arms beneath clothing. It was impossible to tell the type of metal without color, but they had ancient Terris markings engraved on them.

"Some have been experimenting with your idea," VenDell said, "and early results are promising. However, having a Feruchemist who can use anyone's metalminds is intriguing, but not particularly life-changing. Our society is strewn with individuals who have extraordinary abilities—this would simply be one more variety. No, what interests me is the *opposite,* Miss Colms. What if a Feruchemist were to divest himself of all Identity, then fill *another* metalmind with an attribute. Say, strength. What would it do?"

"Create an unkeyed metalmind?" Marasi asked. "One that another Feruchemist could access?"

"Possibly," VenDell said. "Or is there another possibility? Most people living right now have at least some Feruchemist blood in them. Could it be that such a metalmind as I describe, one that is keyed to no single individual, might be usable by *anyone*?"

Understanding settled on Wax like a slowly burned metal. From the chair beside the image device, Wayne whistled slowly.

"Anyone could be a Feruchemist," Wax said.

VenDell nodded. "Investiture—the innate ability to burn metals or tap metalminds—is also one of the things Feruchemy can store. Lord Waxillium . . . these are arts we are only beginning to comprehend. But the secrets they contain could change the world.

"In the ancient days, the Last Emperor discovered a metal that transformed him into a Mistborn. A metal anyone could burn, it is said. This whispers of a hidden possibility, something lesser, but still incredible. What if one could somehow manipulate Identity and Investiture to create a set of bracers which imparted Feruchemical *or* Allomantic ability upon the person wearing them? One could make any person a Mistborn, or a Feruchemist, or *both at once*."

The room fell silent.

A walnut bounced off VenDell's head.

He immediately turned to glare at Wayne.

"Sorry," Wayne said. "Just had trouble believing someone could be so melodramatic, so I figured you might not be real. Hadda check, ya know?"

VenDell rubbed his forehead, breathing out sharply in annoyance.

"This is all fascinating," Wax admitted. "But unfortunately, it's also impossible."

"And why is that?" VenDell asked.

"You don't even know how, or if, this would work," Wax said, waving toward the screen. "And even if you could figure it out, you'd need a Full Feruchemist. Someone with at least *two* Feruchemical powers, as they'd need to be able to store their Identity in a metalmind along with another Feruchemical attribute. Rusts! To do what you proposed a moment ago, and create Allomancers too, you'd basically need someone who was already both Mistborn and Full Feruchemist."

"This is true," VenDell said.

"And how long has it been since a Full Feruchemist was born?"

"A very, very long time," VenDell said. "But, being *born* a Feruchemist isn't the only way to make this happen."

Wax hesitated, then shared a look with Marasi. She nodded, and he strode across the room to pull back the wooden panel hiding his wall safe. He did the combination and removed the book that Ironeyes had sent him. He turned, raising it. "Hemalurgy? Harmony hates it. I've *read* what the Lord Mistborn had to say on the topic."

"Yes," VenDell said. "Hemalurgy is . . . problematic."

"In part because we wouldn't exist without it," MeLaan said. "That's not a particularly fun thing to know—that people had to be murdered in order to bring you to sapience."

"Creating new spikes is a horrid practice," VenDell agreed. "We have no intentions of doing such a thing to experiment with Identity. Instead, we're waiting. A Full Feruchemist is bound to be born among mankind eventually—particularly with the Terris elite working so hard to preserve and condense their bloodlines. Unfortunately, our . . . restraint will not be shared by everyone. There are those who are growing very close to understanding how all this works."

My uncle, Wax thought, looking down at the book in his fingers. So far as he could tell, Edwarn—the man known as Mister Suit—was trying to breed Allomancers. What would he do with Hemalurgy, if he knew about it?

"We need to stay ahead of those who might use this for ill purposes," VenDell said. "We need to experiment and determine how these Identity-free metalminds would work."

"Doing so will be dangerous," Wax said. "Mixing the powers is *incredibly* dangerous."

"Says the Twinborn," MeLaan said.

"I'm safe," Wax said, glancing at her. "My powers don't compound—they're from different metals."

"They may not compound," VenDell said, "but they're still fascinating, Lord Waxillium. *Any* mixing of Allomancy and Feruchemy has unanticipated effects."

"What is it about you," Wax said, "that makes me want to punch you, even when you're saying something helpful?"

"None of us have been able to figure it out," MeLaan said, waving for Wayne to toss her a walnut. "One of the cosmere's great mysteries."

"Now, now, Lord Ladrian," VenDell said, holding up his hands. "Is that the way to speak to someone who bears your ancestor's hands?"

"His . . . hands?" Wax said. "Are you speaking metaphorically?"

"Ah, no," VenDell said. "Breeze *did* say I could have them after he died. Excellent metacarpals. I bring them out for special occasions."

Wax stood still for a moment, holding the book in his hand, trying to digest what the kandra had just said. His ancestor, the first Lord Ladrian, Counselor of Gods . . . had given this creature his hands.

In a way, Wax had shaken hands with Breeze's corpse. He stared at his glass, surprised to find it empty, and poured some more whiskey.

"This has been a very enlightening lesson," Marasi said. "But pardon, Your Holiness, you still haven't explained what you need from me."

VenDell changed the picture to one of an illustration. A man with long dark hair and a bare chest, wearing a cloak that extended behind him into eternity. His arms, crossed before him, were wrapped with intricate bracers in a fanciful design. Wax recognized the iconography, if not the specific image. Rashek. The First Emperor.

The Lord Ruler.

"What do you know of the Bands of Mourning, Miss Colms?" VenDell asked.

"The Lord Ruler's metalminds," Marasi said with a shrug. "Relics from mythology, like the Lady Mistborn's knives, or the Lance of the Fountains."

"There are four individuals," VenDell said, "who, to our knowledge, have held the power of Ascension. Rashek, the Survivor, the Ascendant Warrior, and Lord Harmony Himself. Harmony's Ascension granted Him a precise and in-depth knowledge of the Metallic Arts. It stands to reason that the Lord Ruler gained the same information. He understood Identity as a Feruchemical ability, and knew the hidden metals. Indeed, he gave aluminum to his Inquisitors."

VenDell flipped the image to a more detailed illustration of those arms wrapped in bands of metal. "Curiously, nobody knows exactly what happened to the Bands of Mourning. Back when the Lord Ruler fell, TenSoon had not yet joined the Ascendant Warrior, and though he swears he heard them mentioned, the holes in his memory prevent him from saying how or when.

"The mythology surrounding the Bands is *quite* extensive. You can find myths about them dating back to before the Catacendre, and you can find someone telling new ones in a pub around the corner, invented on the spot for your amusement. But a theme runs through them all—if you held the Lord Ruler's bracers, you supposedly gained his powers."

"That's just fancy," Wax said. "It's a natural thing to wish for, to make stories about. It doesn't mean anything."

"Doesn't it?" VenDell asked. "Lore says the Bands have the *very power* that science has only now determined is plausible to assemble?"

"Coincidence," Wax said. "And just because he *might* have created something doesn't mean he did, and just because you *think* Identity works like you say, doesn't mean you're right. Besides, the Bands would have been destroyed when Harmony remade the world. And that's not even considering that it would be foolish for the Lord Ruler to create weapons someone else could use against him."

VenDell clicked his machine. The image changed to another evanotype, this one of a mural on a wall. It depicted a room with a central dais in the shape of a truncated pyramid. Set upon a pedestal on the dais was a pair of bracers made of delicate, curling metal, shaped in spirals.

Only a mural. But it did seem like it was depicting the Bands of Mourning.

"What is that?" Marasi asked.

"One of our brothers," MeLaan said, sitting up in her chair, "a kandra named ReLuur, took this image."

"The Bands of Mourning fascinated him," VenDell said. "ReLuur spent the last two centuries chasing them. He recently returned to Elendel bearing an evanotype camera in his pack and these pictures." VenDell clicked to the next image, a picture of a large metal plate set into a wall and inscribed with a strange script.

Wax narrowed his eyes. "I don't know that language."

"Nobody does," VenDell said. "It's completely alien to us, unrelated to any Terris, Imperial, or other root. Even the old languages in Harmony's records bear no resemblance to this script."

Wax felt a chill as the images continued. Another shot of the strange language. A statue that resembled the Lord Ruler, bearing a long spear. This appeared to be covered in frost. Another shot of the mural, more detailed, which depicted bracers with many different metals twining together. Not bracers for a Ferring like Wax, but bracers for a Full Feruchemist.

Only a mural, yes. But it was compelling.

"ReLuur believed in the Bands," VenDell said. "He claims to have seen them, though his camera bore no image of the actual relics. I'm inclined to trust his words."

VenDell showed another image, of a different mural. It depicted a man standing atop a peak, hands raised above him and a glowing spear hovering there, just beyond his touch. A corpse slumped at his feet. Wax went forward, walking into the stream of light until he was standing right in front of the image, looking up at the portion he wasn't blocking. The face of the man in the mosaic had eyes upturned and lips parted as if in awe at what he held.

He wore the bracers on his arms.

Wax turned around, but standing in the stream of light he couldn't see anything in the room. "You mean to tell me your brother, this ReLuur, actually *found* the Bands of Mourning?"

"He found something," VenDell said.

"Where?"

"He doesn't know," VenDell said softly.

Wax stepped out of the light, frowning. He looked from VenDell to MeLaan. "What?" he asked them.

"He's missing a spike," MeLaan said. "Best we could determine, he was accosted before he could return here from the mountains near the Southern Roughs."

"We can't get any straight answers out of him," VenDell said. "A kandra with a missing spike . . . well, they aren't quite sane any longer. As you well know."

Wax shivered, a pit of emptiness shifting inside him. "Yes."

"So, Miss Colms," VenDell said, stepping away from his machine. "This is where you come in. ReLuur was . . . is . . . one of our finest. Of the Third Generation, he is an explorer, an expert at bodies, and a genius. Losing him would be a great blow to us."

"We can't reproduce," MeLaan said. "Our numbers are set. The Thirds like ReLuur . . . they're our parents, our exemplars. Our leaders. He is precious."

"We would like you to recover his spike," VenDell said. "From whoever took it. This will restore his sanity, and hopefully his memories."

"The longer he goes without it, the bigger the holes will be," MeLaan said.

"So perhaps you can understand our urgency," VenDell said. "And why I found it prudent to interrupt Lord Ladrian, even on what was obviously an important day. When ReLuur returned to us, he was missing an entire arm and half his chest. Though he will not—or cannot—speak of where he got these pictures, he is able to recall being attacked in New Seran. We believe someone ambushed him there, on his return, and stole the artifacts he had discovered."

"They have his spike," MeLaan said, voice tense. "It's still there. It *has* to be."

"Wait, wait," Marasi said. "Why not give him another spike? You've got enough of them lying around to make earrings, like the one you gave Waxillium."

The two kandra looked at her as if she were mad, but Wax couldn't see why. He thought the question was an excellent one.

"You are misunderstanding the nature of these spikes," VenDell all but sputtered. "First, we do not have kandra Blessings 'lying around.' The earrings you mention are crafted from old Inquisitor spikes, and have barely any potency to them. One might have been good enough for Lord Waxillium's little stunt six months ago, but they would *hardly* be enough to restore a kandra."

"Yeah," MeLaan said. "If that worked, we'd have already used all those spikes to make new children. We can't; a kandra Blessing must be created very specifically."

"We *did* try something akin to what you suggest," VenDell admitted. "TenSoon . . . relinquished one of his own spikes to give our fallen brother a few moments of lucidity. It was very painful for TenSoon, and—unfortunately—accomplished nothing. ReLuur only screamed, begging for his spike. He spat out TenSoon's a moment later. Trying to use someone else's spikes when you don't have your own already can provoke radical changes in personality, memory, and temperament."

"Lessie," Wax said, voice hoarse. "She . . . she changed spikes frequently."

"And each was a spike created specifically for her," VenDell said. "Not one that had been used by another kandra. And besides, would you call her particularly stable, Lord Waxillium? You must trust us on this; we have done what we can. Here, at least.

"MeLaan will be traveling to New Seran to investigate and retrieve ReLuur's missing spike. Miss Colms, we would like you to join her and help recover our brother's mind. We can intervene with your superiors in the constable precinct, and make certain you are assigned field duty working for the government in a clandestine fashion. If you can restore ReLuur's spike, we will be able to find answers."

VenDell eyed Wax. "This will not be a wild hunt for some impossible artifact. All we want is our friend back. Of course, any clues you can discover regarding where he went on his quest, and where he got these pictures, would be appreciated. There are some people of interest in New Seran, nobility that ReLuur is fixated upon for reasons we can't get out of him."

Wax studied the last image for a time longer. It was tempting. Mystical artifacts were all well and good, but someone attacking—and nearly killing—one of the Faceless Immortals? *That* was interesting.

"I'll go," Marasi said from behind him. "I'll do it. But . . . I wouldn't mind help. Waxillium?"

A part of him longed to go. Escape the parties and the dances, the political engagements and business meetings. The kandra would know that; Harmony would know that.

Anger simmered deep within him at the thought. He'd hunted Lessie, and they *hadn't told him*.

"This sounds like the perfect challenge for your skills, Marasi," he found himself saying. "I doubt you need me. You are perfectly capable, and I feel a fool for having implied otherwise, even accidentally. If you do want company, however, perhaps Wayne would be willing to provide some extra protection. I'm afraid that I, however, must—"

The image on the wall flickered to a shot of a city with grand waterfalls. New Seran? He'd never been there. The streets were overgrown with foliage, and people promenaded about in clothing of striped brown suits and soft white dresses.

"Ah, I forgot," VenDell said. "There *was* one other image in ReLuur's belongings. We discovered it last, as the others were packed carefully away to await development. We suspect this image was taken in New Seran, just before the attack."

"And why should I care?" Wax said. "It . . ."

He trailed off, feeling an icy shock as he recognized someone in the picture. He stepped back into the stream of light, pressing his hand against the white wall, trying—fruitlessly—to feel the image. "Impossible."

She stood between two men who held to her arms tightly, as if pulling her forward against her will. Keeping her prisoner even in broad daylight. She had glanced over her shoulder toward the camera as the evanotype was taken. It must be one of the new models he'd been hearing about, that didn't require the subject to stand still for the image to set.

The woman was in her forties, lean but solid, with long dark hair framing a face that—despite their years apart—Wax knew very, very well.

Telsin. His sister.

4

Two hours after the strange meeting, Wayne puttered through Wax's mansion, peeking behind pictures, lifting up vases. Where did he keep the *good* stuff?

"It *is* her, Steris," Wax was saying in the ground-floor sitting room not far away. "And that man with his back turned, holding her by the arm, that could be my uncle. They're involved in this. I *have* to go."

It had always seemed funny to Wayne how rich folk got to decide what was valuable. He inspected a picture frame that was likely pure gold. Why did anyone care about this shiny stuff? Gold could do some fun things with Feruchemy, but it was pure rubbish when it came to Allomancy.

Well, rich folk liked it. So they paid a lot for it, and that made it valuable. No other reason.

How did they decide what was valuable? Did they all just gather together, sit around in their suits and gowns, and say, "Oi. Let's start eatin' fish eggs, and make the stuff real expensive. That'll rust their brains, it will." Then they'd have a nice round of rich folks' laughter and throw some servants off the top of a building to see what kind of splats they'd make when they hit.

Wayne put the picture back. He refused to play by rich people's rules. He'd decide for himself what something was worth. And that frame was ugly. Didn't help none that Steris's cousins, who were depicted in the evanotype it held, looked like fish.

"Then you should most certainly go, Lord Waxillium," Steris said. "Why the concern? We can make arrangements to postpone other duties."

"It's infuriating, Steris!" Even from out in the hall, Wayne could hear the *I'm pacing* in his tone. "Not a word of apology, from them or Harmony regarding what they did to me. VenDell made offhanded comments—referring to me shooting Lessie as a 'stunt.' They *used* me. Lessie was only trying, in a broken way, to free me from them. Now they saunter back, no mention of what I lost, and expect me to just pick up and do their bidding again."

Poor Wax. That had busted him up right good, it had. And Wayne could see why. Still, an apology? Did people what got killed in a flood expect an apology from God? God did as God wished. You simply hoped to not get on His worse side. Kinda like the bouncer at the club with the pretty sister.

Harmony wasn't the only god, anyway. And that was what Wayne was about today.

After some silence, Wax continued, more softly. "I have to go. Even after what they did, if my uncle is really involved in this . . . if I can free Telsin . . . I have to go. Tomorrow night, there will be a gathering of the outer cities political elite in New Seran. Governor Aradel is rightly concerned, and was going to send a representative anyway. It gives me a plausible excuse to be in the city. Marasi can look for the lost spike; I can hunt down my uncle."

"It is decided, then," Steris said. "Will we be leaving immediately?"

Wax was silent for a moment. "We?"

"I assumed . . . I mean, if you are taking my sister, it would look very odd if I were not accompanying you." Wayne felt like he could hear her blush. "I don't mean to be presumptuous. You may, of course, do as you wish, but—"

"No," he said. "You're right. It would look odd to go alone. The gathering will include a reception, after all. I don't want to imply . . . I mean . . ."

"I can go, but stay out of your way."

"It could be dangerous. I can't ask it of you."

"If this is what you feel you must do, then I will be happy to take the risk."

"I . . ."

Rusts. Those two were as awkward as a man suddenly splitting his cheeks in church. Wayne shook his head, picking up one of the vases in the entryway. Good pottery, with a nice swirly-dirly pattern. Maybe that would do for his offering.

Someone knocked on the door, and Wayne put the vase back. It didn't feel right. He took one of the flowers though, and traded it for an extra sock from his back pocket. Huh. He had a silverware set in his other pocket. From the wedding breakfast? Yeah, that was right. They'd put out a place setting for him, had his name and everything. That meant the silverware had been his.

He put the fork, knife, and spoon back in his pocket and tucked the flower behind his ear, then walked to the door, reaching it right before that butler did. He gave the man a glare—it was only a matter of time before he cracked and tried to kill them all—then pulled open the door.

That kandra bloke stood on the other side. His suit now was an even *lighter* shade of tan. "You," Wayne said, pointing. "We just got ridda you!" It had only been . . . what, two hours since he left?

"Good afternoon, young lad," the kandra said. "Are the adults home?"

Darriance quite politely pushed Wayne aside and gestured for VenDell to enter. "You are expected, sir."

"He is?" Wayne said.

"Master Ladrian said to send you in," the butler said, pointing toward the sitting room.

"Thank you," VenDell said, striding toward the room.

Wayne caught up with him quickly.

"Nice flower," the kandra said. "Can I have your skeleton when you're dead?"

"My . . ." Wayne felt at his head.

"You're a Bloodmaker, correct? Can heal yourself? Bloodmaker bones tend to be particularly interesting, as your time spent weak and sickly creates oddities in your joints and bones that can be quite distinctive. I'd love to have your skeleton. If you don't mind."

Taken aback by this request, Wayne stopped in place. Then he ran past him, pushing into the room where Wax and Steris were talking. "Wax," he complained, pointing, "the immortal bloke is being creepy again."

"Greetings, Lord Ladrian," VenDell said, walking in and holding up a folder. "Your tickets, along with transcripts of everything we've been able to pry out of ReLuur. I warn you, most of it isn't terribly lucid."

Wayne glanced at Wax's liquor cabinet. Maybe something in there would work for what he needed for his offering.

"I haven't said that I'd go," Wax told the immortal. "You're roping me into this, sure as sheep in a pen."

"Yes," the immortal said. He held out the folder again. "In here is a list of people ReLuur mentions. You'll find it interesting that he lists several, including the woman holding the party I'm sending you to, as having had interactions with your uncle."

Wax sighed, then accepted it. He gestured to Steris, who had risen to curtsy. "My fiancée. We were debating whether she should accompany me or not."

"We have made provisions for whatever you decide," VenDell said. "Though it *will* look less suspicious if you go too, Lady Harms, I cannot guarantee your safety."

"It might be helpful if *you* accompanied us, VenDell," Wax said. "We could use an extra Metalborn."

VenDell's eyes bulged, and he turned white, like he'd been told his baby had been born with two noses. "Go out into the field? *Me?* Lord Ladrian, I assure you, that's not what you want."

"Why not?" Wax asked, leaning back against the wall. "You're practically impossible to kill, and you can change your rusting shape into anything you want."

"Wait," Wayne said, turning away from the liquor cabinet. "You can turn into anything? Like a bunny?"

"Very small animals are extremely difficult, as we need a certain mass to hold our cognitive functions and—"

"Bunny," Wayne said. "Can you be a *bunny*."

"If absolutely necessary."

"So *that's* what that damn book was about."

VenDell sighed, looking toward Wax. "MeLaan can perform any transformations you might need. *I* honor the First Contract, Lord Ladrian. Besides, the outside doesn't suit me. There's too much . . ." He waved his hands in front of him.

"Too much what?" Wax asked, frowning.

"*Everything,*" VenDell said—though Wayne didn't miss that the rusting bunny glanced at him when he said it.

Wayne shook his head, trying the liquor cabinet. It was locked, unfortunately. What a fine heap of trust Wax showed in him.

"My sister will meet you at the station," VenDell said. "Track seventeen, in four hours."

"*Four hours?*" Steris said. "I need to send for the maids! And the valet! And . . ." She raised a hand to her head, looking faint. "And I need to make a *list*."

"We'll be there, VenDell," Wax said.

"Excellent," the kandra fellow said, fishing in his pocket. Wayne got interested, until he came out with a dull old bent earring, simple, old-style. "I brought you one of these."

"No thanks."

"But, if you need to—"

"*No thanks,*" Wax said.

The look between the two of them grew real uncomfortable, like each was accusing the other of having made an unpersonable stench of some sort. "Good, good," Wayne said, drifting toward the door. "Meet you all at the station."

"Aren't you going to pack?" Steris called after him.

"Sack's in my room," Wayne called back. "Under my bed. I'm always packed and ready to go, mate. Never can tell when a misunderstandin' will crop up." He turned away, popped his hat off the rack, flipped it onto his head, and ducked out the front door.

Leave them to their discussing and their arguing and their creepy immortal bunnies. He had things that needed to be done. Well, one thing at least.

Wayne had a *quest*.

He whistled as he danced down the steps. A simple tune, easy and familiar, with an accompanying beat playing in his mind. Ba-bum, ba-bum, ba-bum. Quick, energetic. He strolled down the street, but found himself less and less pleased with his flower. It was not the proper offering for the god with whom he must meet. Too obvious, too soft.

He spun it in his fingers, thoughtful, softly whistling his tune. No better ideas came to him. This area was too fancy, with mansions and gardens and men clipping hedges. The streets didn't even stink of horse dung. It was hard to think in a place like this; everyone knew the *best* thinking happened in alleyways and slums. Places where the brain had to be alert, even panicked—where the bugger knew that if it didn't perk up and get some geniusing done, you were likely to get yourself stabbed, and then where would it be?

Holding your brain hostage against your own stupidity—*that* was how to get stuff done. Wayne made his way to a nearby canal, and searched out a gondola man who looked bored.

"My good man," Wayne said to himself. "My *good* man." Yeah, that was it. Speak like you couldn't breathe right—high First Octant accent, with a little Terris stirred in. Rich accent. Very rich.

"You, boatman!" Wayne called, waving. "Hey! Oh, do hurry. I haven't the time!"

The boatman poled over.

"Quickly now, quickly, my good man!" Wayne shouted. "Tell me. How much for the day?"

"The day?" the boatman said.

"Yes, yes," Wayne said, hopping into the boat. "I have need of your services for the entire day." Wayne settled himself without waiting for a response. "Onward, now. Up the Fourth-Fifth Canal, turn right around the Hub, then east up the Irongate. First stop is in the Third Octant. She's counting on me, you know."

"The whole day," the boatman said, eager. "Yes, sir, um . . . my lord. . . ."

"Ladrian," Wayne said. "Waxillium Ladrian. We aren't moving. Why aren't we moving?"

The boatman began poling, so gleeful at the prospect of many hours of employment that he forgot to ask for any money up front.

"Fifty," the man finally said.

"Hmm?"

"Fifty. For the whole day."

"Yes, yes, fine," Wayne said. *Dirty thief,* he thought. *Trying to cheat an upstanding citizen, and a house lord at that, merely because he acted a little distracted?* What was this world coming to? When his grandfather Ladrian had been house lord, men had *known* how to be respectful. Why, a boatman in those days would have dunked himself in the canal before taking a wuzing more than he was due!

"If you don't mind me asking, my lord," the boatman said. "And I mean no offense . . . but your clothing."

"Yes?" Wayne asked, straightening his Roughs coat.

"Is something wrong with it?"

"*Wrong* with it?" Wayne said, stuffing his accent so full of noble indignation it was practically bleeding. "Wrong with it? Man, do you not follow fashion?"

"I—"

"Thomton Delacour himself designed these clothes!" Wayne said. "Northern outlands inspiration. It's the height, I tell you! The height. A *Coinshot* couldn't get higher!"

"Sorry. Sorry, my lord. I said I didn't want to offend!"

"You can't just *say* 'don't be offended' and then say something offensive, man! That's not how it works." Wayne settled back, arms folded.

The boatman, wisely, said nothing more to him. After about ten minutes of travel, the time had arrived.

"Now," Wayne said, as if to himself, "we'll need to stop at Glimmering Point docks. And then a skid along Stansel Belt."

He let his accent shift, a little of the Knobs—a slum—slipping in. Dull accent, like a mouth filled with cotton. The folks there used the word "skid" for practically anything. Distinctive word, that. Skiiiid. Sounded like it should be something dirty.

"Um, my lord?"

"Hm?" Wayne said. "Oh, just going over my errands. My nephew is getting married—you might have heard of the wedding, it's all the talk of the city. So many errands. Yes indeed, the day will be quite the skid."

That was a ruffian's accent, but just a hint, like the lemon in a good hot toddy. He slipped it in under the highborn accent.

The boatman started to get uncomfortable. "You said the Stansel Belt? Not a nice area, that."

"Need to hire some workers," Wayne said absently.

The boatman continued poling, but he was nervous now. Tapping his foot, moving the pole more quickly, ignoring calls from colleagues they passed. Something was *wrong*. Like the scent of a meat pie left under the sofa for a few days. A whole day's hiring? An outrageous sum? It might instead be a setup. Pretend to be a lord, then lure him into the slums to be robbed. . . .

"My lord!" the man said. "I just realized. Gotta get back. Can't be hired for the whole day. My mother, she'll need me."

"What nonsense is this?" Wayne demanded. "I haven't the time for your prattle, man! And catching another boat will waste my precious time. I'll double your fee."

Now, the man was *really* anxious. "Sorry, my lord," he said, poling to the side of the canal. "Very sorry. Can't do it."

"At least take me to Stansel—"

"No!" the man yelped. "Nope, can't do it. Gotta go."

"Well," Wayne huffed, climbing out. "I've never been treated in such a manner! And we're not even halfway down portway!"

"Sorry, my lord!" the man said, poling away as quickly as he could. "Sorry!"

Wayne cocked his hat, grinned, and checked the sign hanging from the streetlamp. Exactly where he'd wanted to go, and not a clip paid. He started whistling and strolled along the canal, keeping an eye out for a better offering. What would the god want?

Maybe that? he wondered, eyeing a line of people waiting at Old Dent's roadside cart, wanting to buy some of his fried potatoes. Seemed a good bet.

Wayne wandered over. "Need some help, Dent?"

The old man looked up and wiped his brow. "Five clips a small pouch, eight for a large, Wayne. And don't eat none of the stock, or I'll fry your fingers."

Wayne grinned, slipping behind the cart as the man turned back to his brazier and stirred a batch that was frying. Wayne took the customers' money—and didn't eat much of the stock—until the last man in line arrived, a fancy-looking fellow in a doorman's jacket. Probably worked at one of the hotels down the lane. Good tips at those jobs.

"Three large," the man said.

Wayne got his potatoes, took the man's money, then hesitated. "Actually," Wayne said, holding up a note, "do you have change? We got too many large bills."

"I suppose," the man said, digging in his nice eelskin wallet.

"Great, here's a twenty."

"I've got two fives and ten ones," the man said, putting them down.

"Thanks." Wayne took them, then hesitated. "Actually, I've got plenty of ones. Could I get that ten I saw in your wallet?"

"Fine."

Wayne gave him a handful of coins and took the ten.

"Hey," the man said, "there are only seven here."

"Whoops!" Wayne said.

"What are you doing, Wayne?" Old Dent said. "There's more change in the box under there."

"Really?" Wayne glanced. "Rusts. Okay, how about you just give me my twenty back?" He counted the man back thirteen and poured the coins and bills into his hand.

The man sighed, and gave Wayne the twenty. "Can I just get some sauce for my chips?"

"Sure, sure," Wayne said, squeezing some sauce onto the pouches, beside the potatoes. "That's a nice wallet. Whaddaya want for it?"

The man hesitated, looking at his wallet.

"I'll give you this," Wayne said, plucking the flower off his ear and holding it out with a banknote worth ten.

The man shrugged and handed over the empty wallet, taking the bill and stuffing it in his pocket. He threw the flower away. "Idiot," the man said, marching off with his potatoes.

Wayne tossed the wallet up and caught it again.

"Did you shortchange that man, Wayne?" Old Dent asked.

"What's that?"

"You got him to give you fifty, and you gave him back forty."

"What?" Wayne said, stuffing the wallet in his back pocket. "You know I can't count that high, Dent. 'Sides, gave him ten extra at the end."

"For his wallet."

"Nah," Wayne said. "The flower was for the wallet. The bill was 'cuz I somehow ended up with an extra ten completely on accident, very innocent-like." He smiled, helped himself to a pouch of chips, and went wandering off.

That wallet was nice. His god would like that. Everyone needed wallets, right? He got it out and opened and closed it repeatedly, until he noticed that one side was worn.

Rusts. He'd been cheated! This wouldn't work at all for an offering. He shook his head, walking along the canal promenade. A pair of urchins sat on one side, hands out for coins. The melancholy sound of a busker rose from a little farther down the path. Wayne was near the Breakouts, a nice slum, and he caught whiffs of their distinctive odor. Fortunately the aroma wafting from a nearby bakery overwhelmed most of it.

"Here's the thing," he said to one of the urchins, a girl not seven. He settled down on his haunches. "I ain't travailed enough."

". . . Sir?" the girl asked.

"In the old stories of quests, you gotta *travail*. That's like traveling, but with an *ailment* stapled on. Headaches and the like; maybe a sore backside too."

"Can . . . can I have a coin, sir?"

"Ain't got no coins," Wayne said, thinking. "Damn. In the stories they always tip the urchins, don't they? Lets ya know they're the heroes and such. Hold here for a sec."

He stood up and burst into the bakery, real heroic-like. A woman behind the counter was just pulling a rack of meat buns out of the oven. Wayne slammed his fork down onto the plain wooden countertop, leaving it flourished there like a rusting legendary sword.

"How many buns'll you give me for this?" he asked.

The baker frowned, looking at him, then taking the fork. She turned it over in her fingers. "Mister," she said, "this is *silver*."

"So . . . how many?" Wayne asked.

"A bunch."

"A bunch'll do, fair merchant."

A moment later he emerged from the bakery holding three large paper sacks filled with a dozen buns each. He dropped a handful of change the baker had insisted on giving him into the urchins' hands, then held up a finger as their jaws dropped.

"You," he said, "must *earn* this."

"How, sir?"

"Take these," he said, dropping the sacks. "Go give the stuff inside away."

"To who?" the girl asked.

"Anyone who needs them," Wayne said. "But see here, now. Don't eat more than four yourselves, all right?"

"*Four?*" the girl said. "All for me?"

"Well, five, but you bargain hard. Little cheat." He left them stunned and danced along the edge of the canal, passing the busker, who sat strumming an old guitar.

"Something lively, minstrel!" Wayne called, tossing the silver spoon into the man's overturned hat, which awaited tips.

"Here now," the man said. "What's this?" He squinted. "A spoon?"

"Merchants are apparently desperate for the things!" Wayne called. "They'll give you half a hunnerd meat buns for one, with change to boot. Now, give me 'The Last Breath,' minstrel!"

The man shrugged, and started plucking the song from Wayne's mind. Ba-bum, ba-bum, ba-bum. Quick, energetic. Wayne rocked back and forth, eyes closed. *The end of an era,* he thought. *A god to be appeased.*

He heard the two urchins laughing, and opened his eyes to see them tossing meat buns at the people they passed. Wayne smiled, then kicked himself in a smooth skid along the edge of the canal, which was slippery with a coating of slime. He managed to go a good ten feet before losing his balance and slipping.

Which, of course, plunged him right into the canal.

Coughing, he pulled himself up onto the side. Well, maybe this would count as a travail. If not, it was probably poetry, considering what he'd done to Wax this morning.

He fished out his hat, then put his back to the canal. That was the way to go. Eyes forward, back turned toward the past. No sense getting your nose stuck in things that don't matter anymore. He continued on his way, trailing water and spinning the last of the silverware—the knife—in his fingers. This was *not* the right offering for his quest. He was pretty sure of it. But what was?

He stopped at the next canal bridge, then stepped back. A short man in a uniform he didn't recognize was walking down a nearby street with a little book in hand. Motorcars were parked here in various positions, most partly up onto the sidewalks. The man in the uniform stopped at each one, writing something down in his book.

Wayne followed after him. "Here now," he asked the man. "What're you doing?"

The little man in the uniform glanced at him, then back at his notebook. "New city ordinance about the parking of motorcars requires them to be left in an orderly manner, not up on the side-walks like this."

"So . . ."

"So I'm writing down the registry numbers of each one," the man said. "And we'll track down the owners and charge them a fine."

Wayne whistled softly. "That's *evil*."

"Nonsense," the man said. "It's the law."

"So you're a conner?"

"Fine enforcement officer," the man said. "Spent most of my time inspecting kitchens before last month. This is a lot more productive, I'll tell you. It—"

"That's great," Wayne said. "Whaddaya want for the book?"

The man regarded him. "It's not for trade."

"I've got this here nice wallet," Wayne said, holding it up, water dripping out the side. "Recently cleaned."

"Move along, sir," the man said. "I am not—"

"How 'bout this?" Wayne said, yanking out the knife.

The man jumped back in alarm, dropping his notebook. Wayne snatched it, dropping the knife.

"Great trade. Thanks. Bye." He took off at a dash.

"Hey!" the man shouted, chasing after him. "Hey!"

"No tradebacks!" Wayne shouted, hand on his wet hat, running for all he was worth.

"Come back here!"

Wayne dashed out onto the main street along the canal, passing a couple of old men sitting on a tenement's steps near the entrance to the slums.

"That's Edip's boy," one of them said. "Always gettin' himself into trouble, that one is."

The man got hit in the face by a meat bun a second later.

Wayne ignored that, holding his hat to his head and running all-out. The conner was a determined one. Followed Wayne a good ten streets before slowing, then stopping, hands on his knees. Wayne grinned and ducked around one last corner before slamming his back against the bricks of a building, beside a window. He was pretty winded himself.

He'll probably file a report, Wayne thought. *Hope the fine they make Wax pay ain't too large.*

He ought to find something to bring back as an apology. Maybe Wax needed a wallet.

Wayne heard something beside him, and turned to see a woman with spectacles leaning out the window to look at him curiously. She was holding a pen, and just inside the window a half-finished letter lay on the desk in front of her. Perfect.

Wayne tipped his hat, snatching the pen from her hand. "Thanks," he said, opening the notebook and scribbling some words. As she cried out, he tossed the pen back to her, then continued on his way.

The final destination, the god's dwelling, was not far now. He veered down a street lined with trees and quaint smaller townhomes. He counted them off, then turned to the right and stood facing it. The god's new temple. She'd moved here a few months ago.

He took a deep breath, banishing the music in his head. This had to be *quiet.* He crept carefully up the long walk to the front door. There, he quietly tucked the book into the spot between the doorknob and the door. He didn't dare knock. Ranette was a jealous god, known for shooting people—for her, it was practically a governmental mandate. If the constables didn't find a few corpses on her doorstep every week, they'd start to wonder if she wasn't feeling well.

Wayne slipped away. He smiled, imagining Ranette's reaction when she opened the door, and was so distracted that he almost ran right into *Ranette herself* walking up the path to her house.

Wayne stumbled back. Perfect brown hair, pulled back to expose a gorgeous face, weathered from her time in the Roughs. A fantastic figure, round in all the right places. Tall. Taller than Wayne. So he had something to look up to.

"Wayne! What were you doing at my door?"

"I—"

"Idiot," she said, shoving past him. "You'd better not have broken in. Tell Wax I delivered those cords to him just now. He needn't have sent someone to check on me."

"Cords?" Wayne asked. What cords?

She ignored the question, muttering. "I swear, I *am* going to shoot you, you little maggot."

He watched her go, smiled to himself, then turned and continued walking away.

"What's this?" she said from behind him.

He kept walking.

"Wayne!" she shouted at him. "I'll shoot you, right now. I swear I will. Tell me what you've done."

He turned around. "It's just a gift, Ranette."

"A notebook?" she asked, flipping the pages.

He shoved his hands into his trouser pockets and shrugged. "Writin' book," he said. "You're always writin' stuff down, thinkin' about things. Figured if there's one thing you could always use more of, it's a writin' book. All those ideas you have must get pretty crowded up there. Makes sense you'd need places to store them."

"Why's it damp?"

"Sorry," he said. "Forgot and stuck it in my pocket for a moment. But I got it right back out. I fought ten constables for that, I'll have you know."

She flipped through it, eyes narrowed in suspicion, until she reached the last page. "What's this?" She held it up close and read the words he'd scrawled on the back page. " 'Thank you and goodbye'? What's wrong with you?"

"Nothin's wrong," Wayne said. "I just figured it was time."

"You're leaving?"

"For a little, but that's not what the words mean. I'm sure we'll see each other again. Perhaps frequently and such. I'll see you . . . but I won't be *seein'* you again. See?"

She looked at him for a long moment, then seemed to relax. "You mean it?"

"Yeah."

"Finally."

"Gotta grow up sometime, right? I've found that . . . well, a man wantin' something don't make it true, you know?"

Ranette smiled. Seemed an awful long time since he'd seen her do that. She walked to him, and he didn't even flinch when she extended her hand. He was proud of that.

He took her hand, and she raised his, then kissed it on the back. "Thank you, Wayne."

He smiled, let go, and turned to leave. One step into it, though, he hesitated, then shifted his weight to his other foot and leaned toward her again. "Marasi says you're courtin' another girl."

". . . I am."

Wayne nodded. "Now, I don't want to go wrong, seein' as I'm being so gentlemanly and grown-up and the like. But you can't blame a man for gettin' ideas when hearing something such as that. So . . . I don't suppose that there's a chance for the *three* of us to—"

"Wayne."

"I don't mind none if she's fat, Ranette. I likes a girl what has something to hold on to."

"Wayne."

He looked back at her, noting the storm in her expression. "Right," he said. "Right. Okay. Yeah. I don't suppose, when we're lookin' fondly on this conversationalizing and our memorable farewell, we could both just forget I said that last part?"

"I'll do my best."

He smiled, took off his hat, and gave her a deep bow he'd learned off a sixth-generation doorman greeter at Lady ZoBell's ballroom in the Fourth Octant. Then he stood up straight, replaced his hat, and put his back toward her. He found himself whistling as he went on his way.

"What is that song?" she called after him. "I know it."

"'The Last Breath,'" he said without turning back. "The pianoforte was playin' it when we first met."

He turned the corner, and didn't look back. Didn't even check if she'd sighted on him with a rifle or something. Feeling a spring in his step, he made his way to the nearest busy intersection and tossed the empty wallet into the gutter. It wasn't long before a carriage-for-hire pulled up, and its coachman glanced to the side, saw the wallet, and scrambled down to grab it.

Dashing out from an alley, Wayne beat the man to it, diving for the wallet and rolling on the ground. "It's mine!" he said. "I seen it first!"

"Nonsense," the coachman said, swatting Wayne with his horse reed. "I dropped it, you ruffian. It's mine!"

"Oh, is that so?" Wayne said. "How much is innit?"

"I need not answer to you."

Wayne grinned, holding up the wallet. "I tells you what. You can have it and everything that's inside. But you take me to the Fourth Octant west train station."

The coachman eyed him, then held out his hand.

Half an hour later, the coach rolled up to the rail station—a bleak-looking building with peaked towers and tiny windows, as if to taunt those trapped inside with a scant view of the sky. Wayne sat on the back footman's stand, legs swinging over the side. Trains steamed nearby, rolling up to platforms to gorge themselves on a new round of passengers.

Wayne hopped down, tipped his hat to the grumbling coachman—who seemed well aware he'd been had—and strolled in through the open doors. He shoved his hands in his pockets and looked about until he found Wax, Marasi, and Steris standing amid a small hill of suitcases, with servants waiting at the ready to carry them.

"Finally!" Wax snapped. "Wayne, our train is nearly boarding. Where have you been?"

"Makin' an offering to a beautiful god," Wayne said, looking up toward the building's high ceiling. "Why do you suppose they made this place so big? Ain't like the trains ever come in here, eh?"

"Wayne?" Steris asked, wrinkling her nose. "Are you drunk?"

He put a bit of a slur into his speech. "Course not. Why . . . why'd I be drunk at this hour?" He looked at her lazily.

“You’re insufferable,” she said, waving to her lady’s maid. “I can’t believe you risked being late for a little liquor.”

“Wasn’t a *little,*” Wayne said.

When the train arrived, he joined the others in climbing aboard—Steris and Wax had ordered an entire *car* set aside for the lot of them. Unfortunately, the last-minute hiring meant it had to be hitched all the way at the back, and Wayne had to share a room with Herve the footman. Bugger that. He knew for a fact the man snored. He’d find someplace else to sleep, or else just stay up. The train to New Seran wasn’t going to take *that* long. They’d arrive before sunrise.

In fact, as the thing finally started to chug into motion, he swung out his compartment’s window—much to Herve’s consternation—and climbed up onto the roof. He sat there whistling softly, watching Elendel pass for a time, wind ruffling his hair. A simple tune, easy and familiar, and the accompanying beat played on the tracks below. Ba-bum, ba-bum, ba-bum. Quick . . . energetic.

He lay down then, staring at the sky, the clouds, the sun.

Eyes forward, back turned toward the past.

PART TWO

5

Watching the passing scenes, Wax was immediately struck by how *populated* the land was south of Elendel.

It was easy to forget how many people lived in cities other than the capital. The railway rolled along beside a river wide enough to swallow whole towns up in the Roughs. Villages, towns, and even cities sprinkled the route, so common that the train barely went five minutes without passing another one. Between the towns, orchards stretched into the distance. Fields of wheat bowed and danced. Everything was green and vibrant, refreshed on evenings when the mists came out.

Wax turned from the window and dug into the package Ranette had sent him. Inside, in a fitted, plush-lined case, was a large double-barreled shotgun. Beside it, in their own indentations, were three spheres each wrapped with a thin cord.

The spheres and cords he'd expected. The shotgun was a treat.

Experimenting with extra-powerful loads, a note read, *and enormous slugs, for stopping Thugs or full-blooded koloss. Please test. Will require increased weight on your part to fire. Recoil should be exceptional.*

Rust and Ruin, the shells for this thing were almost as wide as a man's wrist. It was like a cannon. He held one up as the train slowed into a station. It wasn't quite dark yet, but windows in the town were bright with electricity.

Electric lights. He lowered the shell, studying them. The outer cities had electricity?

Of course they do, idiot, he immediately thought to himself. Why wouldn't they? He'd fallen into the same trap he'd once mocked others for. He'd started to assume that anything important, trendy, or exciting happened inside Elendel. That sort of attitude had annoyed him when he'd lived in the Roughs.

The train yielded a handful of passengers and picked up fewer, which surprised Wax, considering the crowded platform. Were they waiting for another train? He leaned to the side to get a better look out the window. No . . . the people were clumped together, listening to one of their number shout something Wax couldn't hear. As he strained to read a sign one of the people carried, someone threw an egg and it *splatted* right beside his window.

He pulled back. The train started up again, having waited only a fraction of the time it normally did at a stop. As it eased out of the station, more eggs flew toward it. Wax finally got a good look at the sign. END ELENDEL OPPRESSION!

Oppression? He frowned, leaning as the train turned a bend, letting him watch the crowd of people on the platform. A few hopped onto the tracks and shook fists.

"Steris?" he asked, packing away Ranette's box. "Have you paid attention to the outer cities situation?"

No reply came. He glanced toward his fiancée, who still sat across the compartment from him, huddled in her seat with a blanket around her shoulders. She didn't appear to have noticed the stop or the eggs; her face was stuck so far into her book that snapping it closed would have caught her nose.

Landre, the lady's maid, had gone to ready Steris's bed, and Wayne was doing who knows what. So the two of them were alone in the room.

"Steris?"

No reply. Wax cocked his head, trying to read the spine and make out what had her so fascinated, but she'd wrapped the volume in a cloth cover. He inched to the side, and saw that her eyes were wide as she read. She turned the page quickly.

Wax frowned, rising and leaning across to get a view of one of the pages. Steris saw him, jumped, and snapped the book closed. "Oh!" she said. "Did you say something?"

"What are you reading?"

"History of New Seran," Steris said, tucking the book under her arm.

"You looked shocked as you read."

"Well, I don't know if you realize it, but the name Seran has a very disturbing history. What did you want to ask me?"

Wax settled back. "I saw a crowd on the train platform. They seemed angry about Elendel."

"Oh, hum, yes. Let's see. Outer cities . . . political situation." She seemed to need a moment to compose herself. What *had* she read in that history that was so disconcerting? "Well, I'm not surprised to hear of it. They aren't happy, for obvious reasons."

"You mean the taxation issues? They're *that* upset?" He looked out the window, but they were too far away now for him to make out the crowd. "We only tax them a little, to maintain infrastructure and government."

"Well, they would argue that they don't need our government, as they have their own city administrations. Waxillium, many in the Basin feel that Elendel is trying to act as if our governor were some kind of emperor—something that was supposed to have ended when the Lord Mistborn stepped down after his century of rule."

"But our taxes don't pay Governor Aradel," Wax said. "They pay for things like constables to police the docks and the maintenance of the railway lines."

"Technically that is correct," Steris said. "But then all goods are *also* taxed when they enter Elendel using the very railway lines and rivers we maintain. Have you noticed that there are almost no railway lines traveling directly from city to city outside of Elendel? Other than the interchange at Doriel, everyone wishing to go from one outer city to another must go *toward* Elendel. Want to ship something from Elmsdel to Rashekin? Have to pass through Elendel. Want to sell metals in Tathingdwel? Have to pass through Elendel."

"A hub system makes perfect sense," Wax said.

"And it also lets us tax practically all goods shipped throughout the entire Basin," Steris said. "By outer cities arguments, that means we're taxing them *twice*. First by our levies to maintain the railway lines, then a second time by making them pass everything through us. They've lobbied for years to get some direct lines running around the Basin in a loop, and have always been denied."

"Huh," Wax said, settling back.

"The rivers are just as bad," Steris said. "We don't control where they were placed, of course. But they do all flow toward Elendel, so we control water traffic. There are roadways between towns, but they're horribly inefficient compared to water or rail travel, so Elendel tariffs basically set prices around the Basin. We can be certain that any goods produced in the city are never undercut, and can provide incentives for things we *don't* produce to be sold at a discount in the city."

Wax nodded slowly. He'd had an inkling, and had heard about the outer cities' complaints. But he'd always read Elendel broadsheets on the matter; to hear it spelled out so directly by Steris made him marvel at his own shortsightedness.

"I should have paid more attention. Perhaps I should talk to Aradel about this."

"Well, there are reasons Elendel does as it has." Steris set her book aside and stood to get down a piece of luggage. Wax eyed the book, noting that she'd marked her page. He reached toward it, but a sudden jerk by the train sent Steris sitting back down with a thump, and she set her suitcase on the book. "Lord Waxillium?"

"Sorry. Continue."

"Well, the governor and Senate are trying to maintain a single unified nation in the Basin, rather than letting it fracture into a bunch of city-states. They're using the economics to push the outer cities to accept centralized rule in exchange for lowered tariffs. Even Aradel, as a moderate liberal, has accepted that this is good for the Basin as a whole. Of course, the noble houses don't care so much about unity as reaping the benefits of a stranglehold on trade."

"And I assume I've benefited from these policies?"

"Benefited?" Steris said. "You practically thrive on them, Lord Waxillium. Your textiles and metalworks would be undercut dramatically without these tariffs. You've voted for maintaining them twice and for *raising* them once."

"I . . . have?"

"Well, I have," Steris said. "You did tell me to see to your house's interests in voting at—"

"Yes, I know," Wax said, sighing.

The train rocked on its tracks, rhythmic thumps sounding from below. Wax turned back to the window, but they weren't passing a town at the moment, and everything was growing dark. No mist tonight.

"Is something wrong, Lord Waxillium?" Steris asked. "Whenever we speak of politics or house finances, you grow distant."

"It's because I'm a child sometimes, Steris," Wax said. "Please, continue your instruction. These are things I need to learn. Don't let my foolishness discourage you."

Steris leaned forward and rested her hand on his arm. "These last six months have been difficult. You can be excused for letting your attention toward politics lapse."

He continued looking out the window. Following Lessie's first death, he'd lost himself. He'd determined not to react that way again, and had thrown his attention into working with the constables. Anything to keep him occupied, and to prevent him from lapsing into the same melancholy inactivity that had struck him when he'd first lost her.

"I've still been a fool. And maybe there's more. Steris, I've never had a mind for politics, even when I was trying to do my duty. It might be beyond me."

"In our months together, I've come to see you as a fiercely intelligent person. The puzzles I've seen you solve, the answers I've seen you tease out . . . Why, they're nothing short of remarkable. You are most certainly capable of caring for your house. Begging your pardon, I'd say it is not your mind, but what you mind, that is the issue."

Wax smiled, looking toward her. "Steris, you're a delight. How could anyone ever think you dull?"

"But I *am* dull."

"Nonsense."

"And when I asked you to help me review my list of preparations for the trip?"

That list had been *twenty-seven* pages long. "I still can't believe you got all those things into our bags."

"All of—" Steris blinked. "Lord Waxillium, I didn't *bring* all of those things."

"But you made a list."

"To think of everything we *might* need. I feel better when something goes wrong if I've contemplated that it might. At least this way, if we run into something we've forgotten, I can feel good knowing I figured we might need it."

"But if you didn't bring all of that stuff, then what is in all those boxes? I saw Herve struggling to lug a few of them up to the train."

"Oh," Steris said, opening the suitcase she'd gotten down. "Why, our house finances, of course."

Indeed, inside was a large stack of ledgers.

"This trip was unplanned," Steris explained, "and I have to prepare an accountability report for the banks by next month. House Ladrian has recovered for the most part from your uncle's spending—but we need to maintain strict books in order to convince lenders we're solvent, so they will be willing to work with us."

"We have accountants, Steris," Wax said.

"Yes, this is their work," she said. "I need to check it over—you can't simply *turn in* someone else's work without making certain the work was done properly. Besides, they're off three clips in this quarter's financials."

"Three clips?" Wax said. "Out of how much money?"

"Five million."

"They're off three hundredths of a boxing," Wax said, "out of five *million*. I'd say that's not bad."

"Well, it's within the thresholds the banks demand," Steris said, "but it's still sloppy! These financials are how we represent ourselves to the world, Lord Waxillium. If you want to overcome the impression people have of House Ladrian and its indulgences, you must agree that we have a responsibility to present ourselves— You're doing it again."

Wax started, sitting up straighter. "Excuse me."

"Distant look in your eyes," Steris noted. "Aren't you the one who is always talking about the responsibility men have to uphold the law?"

"Different thing entirely."

"But your responsibility to your house—"

"—is why I'm here, Steris," Wax said. "Why I came back in the first place. I recognize it. I acknowledge it."

"You just don't like it."

"A man doesn't have to like his duty. He just has to do it."

She clasped her hands in her lap, studying him. "Here, let me show you something." She rose, reaching for another suitcase on the rack above her seat.

Wax took her moment of distraction as a chance to slip the book she'd been reading out from its hiding place. He flipped forward to the page she'd marked, curious to discover exactly what about New Seran had captivated her so.

He was completely shocked, then, when the page didn't contain a historical description, but instead *anatomy* sketches. Along with long descriptions explaining . . . human reproduction?

The room grew very still. Wax glanced up to find Steris staring at him with a look of horror on her face. She went beet red and dropped to her seat, covering her face with her hands and groaning loudly.

"Um . . ." Wax said. "I guess . . . hm . . ."

"I think I'm going to throw up," Steris said.

"I didn't mean to pry, Steris. You were just acting so *odd,* and so fascinated by what was in the book—"

She groaned again.

Wax sat, awkward in the shaking train car, searching for words. "So . . . you don't have any . . . experience in these matters, I assume."

"I keep asking for details," Steris said, slumping back into her seat and leaning her head back against the wall, looking up at the ceiling. "But nobody will tell me anything. 'You'll figure it out,' they say with a wink and a grin. 'The body knows what to do.' But what if mine *doesn't*? What if I do it *wrong*?"

"You could have asked me."

"Because *that* wouldn't be embarrassing," Steris said, closing her eyes. "I know the basics; I'm not an idiot. But I *need* to provide an heir. It's vital. How am I supposed to do this properly if I don't have any information? I tried to interview some prostitutes about it—"

"Wait. You did?"

"Yes. A trio of very nice young ladies; met them for tea, but they clammed up the moment they discovered who I was—they even got strangely protective, and wouldn't give me any details *either.* I get the impression they thought I was cute. What about being a spinster could possibly be cute? Do you realize I'm almost *thirty*?"

"One foot in the grave, obviously," Wax said.

"It's easy to joke when you're a man," she snapped. "You're not on a deadline to provide something useful to this arrangement."

"You're worth more than your ability to bear children, Steris."

"That's right. There's my money too."

"And all *I* am to this arrangement is a title," Wax said. "It goes both ways."

Steris settled back, breathing in and out through her teeth for a few moments. Finally she cracked one eye. "You can shoot things too."

"What every proper lady needs in a man."

"Murdering is very traditional. Goes all the way back."

Wax smiled. "Actually, if you want to be *strictly* traditional—going back to the Imperial Pair—it was the lady in the relationship who did the murdering."

"Either way, I apologize for my tirade. It was completely uncalled for. I shall endeavor to be firmer with myself following our union."

"Don't be silly," Wax said. "I like seeing moments like this from you."

"You like it when ladies are in distress?"

"I like it when you show me something new. It's good to remember that people have different sides."

"Well," she said, taking the book, "I can continue my research at another point. Our wedding has been delayed, after all."

This was to be the night, he realized. *Our first night of marriage.* He'd known, of course, but thinking about it made him feel . . . what? Relieved? Sad? Both?

"If it eases your mind," Wax said as she tucked the book into her suitcase, "we won't need to be . . . involved with any real frequency, particularly once a child is provided. I don't imagine your research will be necessary for more than a dozen or so occasions."

As he said it she wilted, shoulders slumping, head bowing. She was still facing away from him, digging in her suitcase, but he spotted it immediately.

Damn. That had been a stupid thing to say, hadn't it? If Lessie had been here, she'd have stomped on his toe for that one. He felt sick, then cleared his throat. "That was injudicious of me, Steris. I'm sorry."

"The truth should never be the wrong thing to say, Lord Waxillium," she said, straightening and looking toward him, composed once again. "This is exactly as our arrangement was to be, as I know full well. I *did* write the contract."

Wax crossed the train car, then sat next to her, resting his hand on hers. "I don't like this talk from you. Or from me. It's become a habit for us to pretend this relationship is nothing more than titles and money. But Steris, when Lessie died . . ." He choked off, then took a deep breath before continuing. "Everyone wanted to talk to me. Speak at me. *Blather* about how they knew what I was feeling. But you just let me weep. Which was what I needed more than anything. Thank you."

She met his eyes, then squeezed his hand.

"What we are together," Wax said to her, "and what we make of our future need not be spelled out by a piece of paper." Or, well, a large stack of them. "The contract need not set our bounds."

"Pardon. But I thought that was exactly the purpose of a contract. To define and set bounds."

"And the purpose of life is to push our bounds," Wax said, "to shatter them, escape them."

"An odd position," Steris said, cocking her head, "for a lawman."

"Not at all," Wax said. He thought for a moment, then crossed to his side of the chamber again and dug into Ranette's box, getting out one of the metal spheres wound with a long cord. "Do you recognize this?"

"I noticed you looking at it earlier."

Wax nodded. "Third version of her hook device, like the one we used to climb ZoBell Tower. Watch."

He burned steel and Pushed on the sphere. It leaped from his fingers, streaking toward the bar on the luggage rack, trailing the cord behind—which he held in his hand. As the sphere reached the rack, Wax Pushed on a specific thin blue line revealed by his Allomantic senses. It pointed to a latch hidden inside the sphere, like the one inside Vindication that turned off the safety.

A hidden set of hooks deployed from the sphere. He tugged the cord, and was pleased to find that it locked into place, catching on the luggage rack.

Way more handy than the other designs, Wax thought, impressed. He Pushed on the switch a second time, and the mechanism disengaged, retracting the hooks with a snap. The ball fell to the couch beside Steris, and Wax pulled it into his hand by the cord.

"Clever," Steris said. "And this relates to the conversation how?"

Wax Pushed on the sphere again, but this time didn't engage the mechanism. Instead he held the cord tight, giving the sphere about three feet of line. It jerked to a stop in midair, hovering. He kept Pushing, upward and away from him at an angle—but also held the cord, and that kept the sphere from falling.

"People," Wax said, "are like cords, Steris. We snake out, striking this way and that, always looking for something new. That's human nature, to discover what is hidden. There's so much we can do, so many places we can go." He shifted in his seat, changing his center of gravity, which caused the sphere to rotate upward on its tether.

"But if there aren't any boundaries," he said, "we'd get tangled up. Imagine a thousand of these cords, zipping through the room. The law is there to keep us from ruining everyone else's ability to explore. Without law, there's no freedom. That's why I am what I am."

"And the hunt?" Steris asked, genuinely curious. "That doesn't interest you?"

"Sure it does," Wax said, smiling. "That's part of the discovery, part of the *search*. Find who did it. Find the secrets, the answers."

There was, of course, another part—the part Miles had forced Wax to admit. There was a certain perverse anger that lawmen directed at those who broke the law, almost a *jealousy*. How dare these people escape? How dare they go the places nobody else was allowed to?

He let the sphere drop, and Steris picked it up, looking it over with a meticulous eye. "You talk about answers, secrets, and the search. Why is it you hate politics so much?"

"Well, it might be because sitting in a stuffy room and listening to people complain is the *opposite* of discovery."

"No!" Steris said. "Every meeting is a mystery, Lord Waxillium. What are their motives? What quiet lies are they telling, and what truths can you discover?" She tossed his sphere back to him, then took her suitcase and set it on the small cocktail table in the center of the cabin. "House finances are the same."

"House finances," he said, flatly.

"Yes!" Steris said. She fished in the suitcase, getting out a ledger. "See, look." She flipped it open and pointed at an account.

He looked at the page, then up at her. *Such excitement,* he thought. But . . . ledgers?

"Three clips," he said. "The tables are different by three clips. I'm sorry, Steris, it's a meaningless amount. I don't see—"

"It's *not* meaningless," she said, scooting over to sit beside him. "Don't you see? The answer is *here* somewhere, in this book. Aren't you even curious? The mystery of where they went?" She nodded to him, excited.

"Well, I suppose you could show me how to look," he said. He dreaded the idea, but then, she looked so happy.

"Here," she said, handing him a ledger, then fishing out another. "Look at goods received. Compare the dates and the payouts to the ledger! I'm going to study maintenance."

He glanced toward the window in their door, half expecting Wayne to be out there in the hallway, snickering himself senseless at the prank. But Wayne was not there. This was no prank. Steris grabbed her own ledgers and attacked them with as much ferocity as a hungry man might a good steak.

Wax sighed, sat back, and started looking through the numbers.

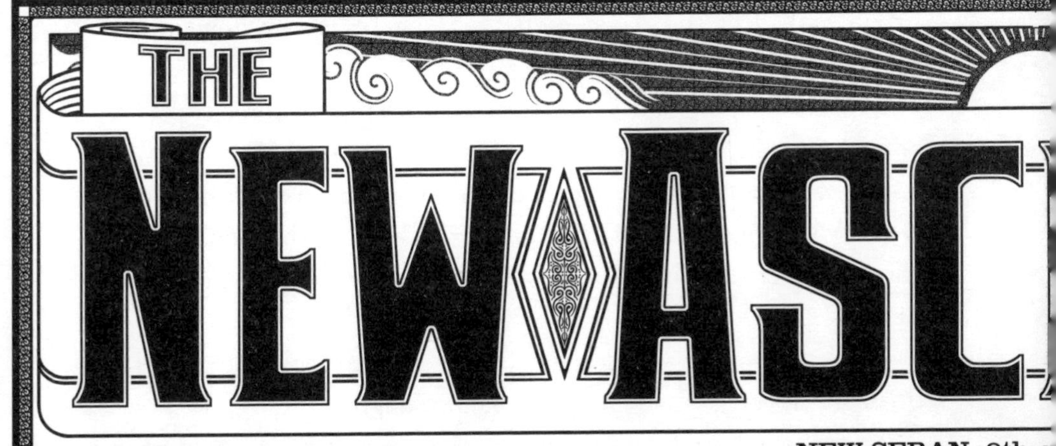

Vol. 6, No.220 NEW SERAN, 8th o

Nicki Savage, Paranatural Detective in...

The Constructs of Antiquity

When a thief steals a large map of New Seran, Ms. Savage is on the case. The map's secret pocket contains her father's parting gift to her, the location of a tribe of metal beings—the kalkis—lost creations of the Lord Ruler. Currently the only one keeping our daring debutante from the secrets of the Unknown Constructs of Antiquity is the magical burglar she calls the Haunted Man!

Part Two "The Ghastly Gondola!"

I arrived just as the gondola doors slammed shut and the whole conveyance lurched away. Behind the glass doors, the haunted man smiled, the green glow of his devices lighting him from below.

I ran alongside the car, matching pace with it while at the same time digging out my trusty little bottle of chromium for a quick swig. Warmth rose from my stomach to my throat, and so did my confidence.

As the car slid away from the dock, I leapt into the air.

(Continued below the fold!)

BILMING'S NE 'AMUSE' ELEND

A week ago, Bilming's Lord Mayor Bastien Severington stood at the city's impressive harbor and greeted high-ranking officials and noblepersons of the Elendel Senate. Like the peaceable tortoise—symbol of Bilming's great city—Governor Severington's gracious invitation to Elendel's elite has been seen as a gesture of friendship and unity.

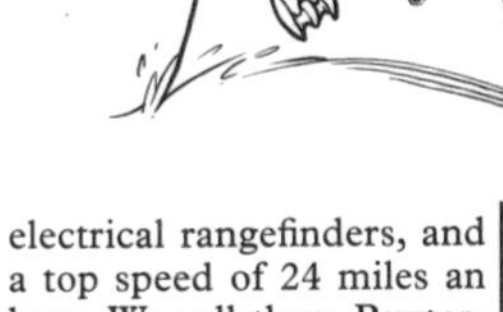

More impressive than the harbor are the rows of ships docked there. Most are the usual familiar clippers and cargo ships, but among them float metal beasts like sharks among turtles. These are the warships developed by Lord Mayor Severington and the late Dr. Florin Malin, predecessor to the Basin's current Minister of Science and Technology.

"Each ship carries eight 12-inch twin guns with each turret having a range of sixteen miles," said Severington. "Other improvements include reinfoced armor hulls, electrical rangefinders, and a top speed of 24 miles an hour. We call them Pewternauts."

But some members of Elendel's delegation were not impressed.

"What an amusing display of toys," said Senator Inis Julien. "Why do we need warships? The Basin is alone on land and on the seas. From whom do we need protection?"

(Continued on back.)

Broken Gondola Strands Passengers

An unidentified disturbance halted the Zinc Line yesterday evening about sunset, according to the New Seran Transportation Authority. The NSTA carried passengers home the old-fashioned way, on donkeys and rickshaws down the switchbacks. We see this as proof for the need of a back-up

The Ghastly Gondola!

The monks of Baz-Kor had trained me well, their practiced moves designed to get a leecher close enough to touch another Allomancer and drain them of their re-

6

Marasi stopped on the image of the monster.

It was evening; people chatted softly around her in the dining car, and the train rolled around a picturesque bend, but for a moment she was transfixed by that image. A sketch of violent, rough lines that somehow conveyed a terrible dread. Most of the pages in the stack VenDell had delivered contained transcripts of questions answered—or, more often, not answered—by the wounded kandra.

This was different. A wild sketch using two colors of pencil to depict a terrible visage. A burning red face, a distorted mouth, horns and spikes streaking out along the rim. But black eyes, drawn like voids on the red skin. It looked like a childhood terror ripped right out of a nightmare.

The bottom of the page had a caption. *ReLuur's sketch of the creature described on* 8/7/342. Yesterday.

The next page was an interview.

VenDell: Describe to us again the thing you saw.

ReLuur: The beast.

VenDell: Yes, the beast. It guarded the bracers?

ReLuur: No. No! It was before. Fallen from the sky.

VenDell: The sky?

ReLuur: The darkness above. It is of the void. It has no eyes. It looks at me! It's looking at me now!

Further questioning was delayed for an hour as ReLuur whimpered in the corner, inconsolable. When he became responsive again, he drew this sketch without prompting, muttering about the thing *he had seen. Something is wrong with the eyes of the creature. Perhaps spikes?*

Spikes. Marasi pulled her purse from under the table, digging into it as the couple at the table behind her laughed loudly, calling for more wine. Marasi pushed aside the two-shot pistol she had tucked inside and took out a thin book, a copy of the one that Ironeyes had given to Waxillium.

Inside it she found the description she wanted, words written by the Lord Mistborn, Lestibournes. *So far as I've been able to figure out, Hemalurgy can create practically anything by rewriting its Spiritual aspect. But hell, even the Lord Ruler had trouble getting it right. His koloss were great soldiers—I mean, they could eat* dirt *and stuff to stay alive—but they basically spent all day killing each other on a whim, and resented no longer being human. The kandra are better, but they turn to piles of goop if they don't have spikes—and they can't reproduce on their own.*

I guess what I'm saying is that you shouldn't experiment too much with this aspect of Hemalurgy. It's basically useless; there are a million ways to mess up for every one way there is to get a good result. Stick to transferring powers and you'll be better off. Trust me.

It was so *odd* to read the Lord Mistborn's words and have them sound so casual. This was the Survivor of the Flames, the governor who had ruled mankind in benevolence for a century, guiding them on the difficult path to rebuild civilization. He sounded so *normal.* He even admitted in one section to having Breeze, Counselor of Gods, write most of his speeches for him. So all of the famous words, quotes, and inscriptions attributed to the Lord Mistborn were fabrications.

Not that he was a fool. No, the book was full of insight. Disturbing insight. The Lord Mistborn advocated gathering the Metalborn who were elderly or terminally ill, then asking them to sacrifice themselves to make these . . . spikes, which could in turn be used to create individuals of great power.

He made a good argument in the book. It wouldn't have been so disturbing if it had been easy to dismiss.

She studied the descriptions of Hemalurgic experiments in the book, trying to ignore the loud couple behind her. Could this drawing be of a new kind of Hemalurgic monster, like those Wax had encountered under Elendel? Designed by the Set, or perhaps the result of a failed experiment? Or was this instead related to the continually ephemeral Trell, the god with an unknown metal?

She eventually put them aside and focused on her primary task. How to find ReLuur's spike? He'd been wounded in some kind of explosion that had ripped off part of his body, and he'd been forced to flee, leaving the flesh—and the spike—behind.

Kandra flesh remained in its humanlike state once cut free of the body, so those cleaning up after the explosion would have simply disposed of it, right? She needed to see if they'd created some kind of mass grave for people killed in that explosion. Of course, if the Set knew what to look for in a kandra's corpse, they might have recovered the spike. The pictures—and the possibility they were experimenting with Hemalurgy—made that more plausible. So that was another potential lead. And . . .

And was that Wayne's voice? Marasi turned to look at the laughing couple behind her. Sure enough, Wayne had joined them, and was chatting amicably with the drunk pair, who wore fine evening attire. Wayne, as usual, was in Roughs trousers and suspenders, duster hung on the peg beside the table.

He saw Marasi and grinned, drinking a cup of the couple's wine before bidding them farewell. The train hit a sharp bump, causing plates to rattle on tables as Wayne slid into the seat across from Marasi, his face full of grin.

"Mooching wine?" Marasi asked.

"Nah," he said. "They're drinking bubbly. Can barely stand the stuff. *I'm* mooching accents. Those folks, they're from New Seran. Gotta get a feel for how people talk there."

"Ah. You do realize it's proper to remove your hat indoors, correct?"

"Sure do." He tipped his hat at her, then leaned back in his chair and somehow got his booted feet up on the small table. "What're *you* doin' in here?" he asked.

"The dining car?" Marasi asked. "I just wanted a place to spread out."

"Wax rented us out an entire *train car,* woman," Wayne said, pointing at a passing waiter, then pointing at his mouth and making a tipping motion. "We've got like six rooms or somethin' all to ourselves."

"Maybe I simply wanted to be around people."

"And we ain't people?"

"That is subject to some dispute in your case."

He grinned, then winked at her as the waiter finally stepped over.

"You wanted—" the waiter began.

"Liquor," Wayne said.

"Would you care to be a little more specific, sir?"

"*Lots* of liquor."

The waiter sighed, then glanced at Marasi, and she shook her head. "Nothing for me."

He moved off to obey. "No bubbly!" Wayne shouted after him, earning him more than one glare from the car's other occupants. He then turned to eye Marasi. "So? Gonna answer my question? What're you hidin' from, Marasi?"

She sat for a moment, feeling the rhythmic rattle of the train's motion. "Does it ever bother you to be in his shadow, Wayne?"

"Who? Wax? I mean, he's been putting on weight, but he's not *that* fat yet, is he?" He grinned, though that faded when she didn't smile back. And, in an uncharacteristic moment of solemnity, he slid his boots off the table and rested one elbow on it instead, leaning toward her.

"Nah," he said after some thought. "Nah, it doesn't. But I don't care much if people look at me or not. Sometimes my life is easier if they *ain't* looking at me, ya know? I like listening." He eyed her. "You're sore that he thought you couldn't do this on your own?"

"No," she said. "But . . . I don't know, Wayne. I studied law in the first place—studied famous lawkeepers—because I wanted to become something others thought I couldn't. I got the job at the precinct, and thought I'd accomplished something, but Aradel later admitted he was first interested in hiring me because he wanted someone who could get close to, and keep an eye on, Waxillium.

"We both know the kandra wanted him on this mission, and they arranged the meeting with me to try to hook him. At the precinct, when I accomplish something, everyone assumes I had Waxillium's help. Sometimes it's like I'm no more than an *appendage*."

"You're not that at all, Marasi," Wayne said. "You're important. You help out a lot. Plus you smell nice, and not all bloody and stuff."

"Great. I have no idea what you just said."

"Appendages don't smell nice," Wayne said. "And they're kinda gross. I cut one outta a fellow once."

"You mean an appendix?"

"Sure." He hesitated. "So . . ."

"Not the same thing."

"Right. Thought you was makin' a metaphor, since people don't need one of those and all."

Marasi sighed, leaning back and rubbing her eyes with the heels of her hands. Why was she discussing this with *Wayne* again?

"I understand," he said. "I know what you're feeling, Mara. Wax . . . he's kind of overwhelming, eh?"

"It's hard to fault him," Marasi said. "He's effective, and I don't think he even knows that he's being overbearing. He fixes things—why should I be upset about that? Rusts, Wayne, I *studied* his life, admiring what he did. I should feel lucky to be part of it. And I do, mostly."

Wayne nodded. "But you want to be your own person."

"Exactly!"

"Nobody's forcing you to stay with us," Wayne noted. "As I recall, Wax spent a lot of effort at first trying to keep you from always gettin' involved."

"I know, I know. I just . . . Well, this once I was thinking for a time that I might be able to do something important on my own." She took a deep breath, then let it out. "It's stupid, I know, but it still feels frustrating. We'll do all this work, find that spike, and get back to the kandra—then they'll thank Waxillium."

Wayne nodded thoughtfully. "I knew this fellow once," he said, leaning back again, feet on the table, "who thought it would be a good idea to take people huntin'. City folk, you know? Who ain't never seen an animal larger than a rat what ate too much? Out in the Roughs, we got lions. Fierce things, with lotsa teeth an—"

"I know what a lion is, Wayne."

"Right. Well, Chip—that's his name—he got some broadsheets printed up, but borrowed some notes from his girl in order to do it. And so she thought she should get a piece of the money once he got people to pay for this trip. Well, the first money came in, and they got in a fight and she ended up stabbing him right in his holster, if you know what I mean. So he stumbles out into the street all bleedin', and that's where the constables found him and told him you can't be killin' no lions. There's a law about it, see, as they're some kind of noble natural treasure, or some such.

"Anyway, they took Chip and stuffed him in jail, where they slammed the bars—by accident—on his rusting fingers. Broke his hand up right good, and he can't bend the tips of his fingers no more."

His drink arrived—a bottle of whiskey and a small cup. He took it, telling the waiter to charge Waxillium, then poured some and settled back.

"Is that the end?" Marasi asked.

"What?" Wayne said. "You want *more* to happen to the poor fellow? Right sadistic of you, Marasi. Right sadistic."

"I didn't mean . . ." She took a deep breath. "Did that have any relevance to the situation I'm in?"

"Not really," Wayne said, taking a drink, then removing a little wooden box from his pocket and getting out a ball of gum. "But I tell ya, Chip, he has it *really* bad. Whenever I'm thinkin' my life is miserable, I remember him, and tell myself, 'Well, Wayne. At least you ain't a broke, dickless feller what can't even pick his own nose properly.' And I feels better."

He winked at her, popped the gum in his mouth, then slipped away from the table. He waved to MeLaan, who was wearing a fine lace gown and oversized hat. A normal woman would have needed *quite* the corset to pull off the outfit, but the kandra had probably just sculpted her body to fit. Which was horribly unfair.

Marasi stared at the notes. Wayne had left her feeling confused, which was not unusual, but perhaps there was wisdom in what he said. She dug back into the research, but it wasn't too long before she started to droop. It was getting late, the sun having fully set outside, and they wouldn't arrive for another few hours. So she packed up the stack of pages inside their large folder.

As she did, something slipped out of the folder. Marasi frowned, holding it up. A small cloth pouch. Opening it revealed a small Pathian earring and a note.

Just in case, Waxillium.

She yawned, tucking it away, and pushed out of the dining car. The private car Waxillium had hired for them was two cars back, at the tail end of the train. She held tight to the sheets as she stepped onto the open-air platform between cars, wind whipping at her. A short railman stood here, and eyed her as she crossed to the next car. He didn't say anything this time, though last time he'd tried to encourage her not to move between cars, insisting that he'd bring her food if she wished.

The next car over was first-class, with a row of private rooms on one side. Marasi passed electric lights glowing on the walls as she crossed the car. Last time she'd been on a train, those had been gas, with bright, steady mantles. She liked progress, but these seemed much less reliable—they'd waver when the train slowed, for example.

She crossed to the final car, then passed her own room and walked toward the room where Waxillium and Steris had taken dinner, to check on them. Both were still there, surprisingly. Waxillium she had expected, but late nights were not Steris's thing.

Marasi slid open the door, peeking in. "Waxillium?"

The man knelt on the floor, his seat covered in ledgers and sheets of paper. Eyes intent on one of them, he held up his hand toward her in a quieting gesture as she started to ask what he was doing.

Marasi frowned. Why—

"Aha!" Waxillium proclaimed, standing up. "I found it!"

"What?" Steris said. "Where?"

"Tips."

"I looked in tips."

"One of the dockworkers turned the request in late," Waxillium said, grabbing a sheet and spinning it toward Steris. "He tipped a dock boy four clips to run a message for him, and asked for reimbursement. Dockmaster gave it to him, and filed a note, but he wrote the four like a three and the accountants recorded it that way."

Steris looked it over with wide eyes. "You bastard," she said, causing Marasi to blink. She'd *never* heard language like that from Steris. "How did you figure this out?"

Waxillium grinned, folding his arms. "Wayne would say it's because I'm brilliant."

"Wayne has the mental capacity of a fruit fly," Steris said. "In comparison to him, anyone is brilliant. I . . ." She trailed off, noticing Marasi for the first time. She blinked, and her expression became more reserved. "Marasi. Welcome. Would you like to sit?"

"On what?" Marasi asked. Every surface was covered in ledgers and pages. "The luggage rack? Are those house *finances*?"

"I found a lost clip," Waxillium said. "The last one, I should add, which gives me two for the evening, while Steris found one."

Marasi stared at Steris, who started clearing a place for her to sit. She looked to Waxillium, who stood beaming with the sheet in his hand, looking it over again as if it were some lost metal he'd rescued from a labyrinth.

"A lost clip," Marasi said. "Great. Maybe you can find something in these." She held up the pages VenDell had given her. "I'm heading to bed for a few hours."

"Hmm?" Waxillium said. "Oh, sure. Thanks." He set down the page with some reluctance, taking the folder.

"Be sure to look at the drawings of monsters," Marasi said, yawning. "Oh, and this was in there." She tossed him the pouch with the earring and walked back into the hallway.

She walked toward her room, feeling the train slow once more. Another town? Or were there sheep crossing the tracks again? They were supposed to be getting into the part of the route that was the prettiest. Too bad it would be so dark out.

She walked back to her door, first of those in their car, and glanced out the front window toward the rest of the train, which she was surprised to see moving off into the distance. She gaped for a moment, and then the door at the other end of the car burst open.

The man standing on the platform beyond leveled a gun down the corridor and fired.

7

Well, I think you showed a real talent for this, Lord Waxillium, as I believe *I* suggested—"

Wax stopped listening to Steris.

Train slowing.

Chugging sounds retreating.

Door opening.

Wax burned steel.

Steris continued talking, and he nodded absently, part of him going through the motions as the rest of him came alert. He heard a click and Pushed to his left and held it, Pushing to the right against the frame of the train car to keep himself from moving.

As the bullet passed in the hallway outside, his Push—already in place—slammed it sideways into the wall.

Go. His Push had shoved open the door. He dropped the earring—damn that VenDell—and Pushed to the right, on the train car's metal window frame. This launched him out to the left, streaking into the hallway. He rammed into the wall where he'd Pushed the bullet, Vindication in hand, and drilled the surprised man at the end of the hallway in the forehead.

Marasi clipped off a scream. Steris stuck her head out into the hallway, wide-eyed. Not the smartest move, but she'd rarely been in gunfights.

"Thanks," Marasi said.

He nodded curtly. "Get your sister behind some cover." He slipped past her and stepped out onto the small platform between train cars—only, their car had been unhooked and left to drift. A group of three shocked-looking men on horses rode alongside the slowing car.

Horses? Wax thought. *Really?*

By the starlight—which was bright tonight, with no clouds and the Red Rip low on the horizon—he could see they wore vests over their shirts and sturdy trousers. A larger crowd of them galloped alongside the train ahead. This wasn't a specific attack on just his car, but a full-blown armed robbery.

That meant he had to be quick.

He shoved on the platform beneath him and decreased his weight. The three robbers nearby started firing, but Wax's Push flung him into the air above their shots and his decreased weight meant that the wind resistance pushed him backward, onto the train car. He landed, increased his weight, and picked one man off his horse.

The remaining bandits took off forward, kicking their horses and chasing after the others, yelling, "Allomancer! Allomancer!"

Blast, Wax thought, dropping one of the men as the other dodged his horse into a stand of trees. He was out of pistol range in a moment, and would soon catch his fellows.

Wax dropped onto the platform and rushed down the hallway. The room he'd shared with Steris was empty, but he spotted quivering blue lines in the one next door. Marasi had wisely piled everyone into the servants' compartment.

"Robbery," Wax said as he threw open the door, startling the servants, Marasi, and Steris. Most of them sat on the floor, though Marasi was by the window, peeking out. And Steris was on the built-in seat, remarkably composed.

"Robbers?" Steris asked. "Really, Lord Waxillium, *must* you bring your hobbies with you everywhere we go?"

"They're going after the rest of the train," Wax said, pointing. "The first thieves must have recognized this car as a private one, probably lush with riches to plunder, and so they uncoupled it. But something is wrong."

"Other than people trying to kill us?" Marasi asked.

"No," Steris said, "in my experience, that's quite normal."

"What's *wrong,*" Wax said, "is that they're riding horses."

The others stared at him.

"Horseback train robberies," Wax said, "are something out of the story magazines. Nobody *actually* does that. What good does it do to board a moving train, risking your life, when you can just stop the vehicle like the Vanishers did?"

"So our bad guys . . ." Marasi said.

"New to this," Wax said. "Or they've been reading too much cheap fiction. Either way, they're still going to be dangerous. I can't risk leaving you here, in case they come back for you. So keep your heads down and *hang on.*"

"Hang on?" Herve said. "Why—"

Wax ducked back out into the hallway and ran to the back end of the car. After checking out the doorway, he jumped onto the tracks behind the private car, which was finally rolling to a stop. Then he tapped his metalminds and increased his weight.

A lot.

The gravel sank under his feet as his body became increasingly heavy. He gritted his teeth, flared his metal, and *Pushed.*

The car lurched in place as if another train had crashed into it. His Push sent it rattling along the tracks, and Wax let out his breath. His muscles didn't hurt, but he felt as if he'd slammed into a wall.

He released his metalmind, returning his weight to normal, and Pushed on the rails to pull himself out of the gravel. He almost lost a boot in the process.

He Pushed against the tracks once more, sending himself chasing after the moving car. *Not nearly fast enough,* he thought as he dropped to the ground and increased his weight again. The car rocked as he shoved it, then he hopped and followed, repeating the process three more times to get it up to speed. Then finally he Pushed himself all the way up to it, jamming his shoulder against the back wall and using Allomancy on the tracks behind to sustain and increase the momentum.

Ground passed behind in a blur, rows and rows of wooden ties, the steel rails with a continuous stream of metal lines that pointed toward Wax's chest. He groaned, and moved so his back was toward the wall. Still, the Pushing threatened to crush him, as he couldn't increase his weight here much or risk ripping up the tracks.

They shot past a group of horses with a few youths guarding them—the bandits' extra mounts. Wax raised Vindication and fired a few shots into the air, but the horses were too well trained to spook at the sound.

He redoubled his Push as he thought he heard gunfire ahead of him. A moment later, his car slammed into the train proper. Wax let go, dropping to the platform, his back aching. The couplers had engaged, however, and the car remained attached to the rest of the train.

He peeked into the car, then ducked in, passing the room where the others were hiding. In his own compartment, he dropped Vindication into her holster, then yanked his gun case off the top rack.

"Waxillium?" Marasi said, slipping into the room.

"You seen Wayne?" Wax asked.

"He was in the dining car a little bit ago."

"He'll be fighting already. If you see him, let him know I'm going to hit the front of the train, then sweep backward." Wax snapped one Sterrion closed, now loaded, then reached for the second.

"Got it," Marasi said. She hesitated. "You're worried."

"No masks."

"No . . ."

"Robbers wear masks," Wax said. He clicked the second Sterrion closed, then buckled on his gunbelt. Vindication, after a reload, went back into his shoulder holster.

"And men who don't wear masks?"

"They don't care if they're seen." He looked over and met her eyes. "They're already outlaws, and don't have anything to lose. Men like that kill easily. What's more, it's obvious to me that they've never tried a train robbery before. Either they are very, very desperate—or someone put them up to this."

She paled. "You don't think the attack is a coincidence."

"If it is, I'll eat Wayne's hat." He eyed the shotgun Ranette had given him, then tied on his thigh holster and slipped it in. Then he hung two of her cord-and-sphere contraptions from his gunbelt. Finally, he reached up and took a rifle bag off the top shelf and tossed it to Marasi.

"Watch Steris," he said. "See if you can find Wayne; check on the next car or two, but don't worry about advancing farther if you meet resistance. Just hold your ground and protect these people."

"Right."

He moved toward the hallway, but as soon as he stepped out a hail of gunfire drove him back again. He cursed. All it would take was one aluminum bullet—which he couldn't Push on—and he'd be dead.

He took a deep breath, then glanced out quickly while Pushing, and counted four bandits on the rear platform of the next car forward.

They fired again. He ducked back and watched the blue lines of bullets as they flew, taking chunks of wood paneling off the wall and splintering his doorframe. It didn't appear that any of the bullets were aluminum.

"Distraction?" Marasi asked.

"Yes, please," Wax said, increasing his weight and Pushing on the window frame, launching it out of the side of the car and against a passing tree. "Fire a few times as I leave, then give me a count of twenty, followed by a distraction."

"Will do."

Wax threw himself out the window. Immediately he fired Vindication downward, burying a bullet in the ground and giving him something to Push on to launch himself upward. Marasi fired a few quick shots inside, and hopefully the robbers would assume his shot had been inside as well.

Soaring high, wind whipping at his hair and suit coat, he shot a second bullet into the ground, but farther out, and used it to nudge himself to the right—placing him above the train.

He didn't let himself touch down, instead using a Push on the nails in the train roof to keep flying forward. He soared over his own car and the one the robbers were in, finally landing on the dining car, which was third from the back.

As he turned to face the rear, his mental count hit twenty. A second later, he heard a spray of gunfire coming from Marasi. That was his mark; Wax dropped between the dining car and the robbers' car.

He fell practically on top of one of the robbers, who was backing out of the second car from the end—which he hadn't expected. Wax leveled his gun, but the surprised man punched him in the gut.

Wax grunted, increasing his weight. The platform beneath him strained, but when he shoved the robber with his shoulder, it sent the man tumbling toward the tracks. The robber had kindly left the door open for him, and he had a clean shot at the backs of his fellows at the far end, who were focused on Marasi in the last train car beyond.

Wax didn't shoot; he just Pushed on the metal they were carrying. The men flipped off the rear platform, dropping into the space between cars. One caught the railing. Wax shot him in the arm, then turned, leveling his gun toward the dining car.

People cringed inside, hiding under tables, whimpering. Rusts . . . Without bandanas or identifying marks to watch for, he'd have trouble spotting the bandits. He set up his steel bubble, a faint Push away from himself in all directions that excluded his own weapons. It was far from perfect—he'd been shot several times while using it—but it did help.

He turned and strode into the second car from the back, the one the robbers had been using, checking for hostiles at each door, his steel bubble rattling doorknobs. First-class passengers were hiding here, and none appeared hurt.

In Wax's car, Marasi ducked out of the room, carrying one of Wax's favorite hats. She shrugged apologetically at its numerous holes.

"If I find Wayne, I'll send him to you," he told her, reaching to his gunbelt for a metal vial. He came up with wet fingers, and his belt clinked with broken glass.

Damn. The robber who'd slugged him had broken his vials. He hurriedly hopped over the space between cars, entering their private car again. "I need metal," he explained at Marasi's inquisitive look.

He stepped up to his room, then hesitated as a hand stuck out of the next room down, holding a small vial.

"Steris?" he said, walking to her. She was still sitting on the plush train bench—though her face was paler than before. "Steel flakes in suspension," she said, wiggling the vial.

"Since when have you carried one of these?" Wax asked, taking it from her.

"Since about six months ago. I put one into my purse in case you might need it." She raised her other hand, displaying two more. "I carry the other two because I'm neurotic."

He grinned, taking all three. He downed the first one, then nearly choked. "What the hell is in this?"

"Other than steel?" Steris asked. "Cod-liver oil."

He looked at her, gaping.

"Whiskey is bad for you, Lord Waxillium. A wife *must* look out for her husband's health."

He sighed and drank one more, then tucked the last into his gunbelt. "Stay safe. I'm going to scout the train." He left and threw himself out the end door, Pushing on the tracks and launching himself in a high arc upward.

The land spread before him, bathed in starlight. The southern end of the Basin, approaching the Seran mountain range, was far more varied in geography than the northern portion. Here, hills rolled across the land, which slowly increased in elevation.

The Seran River cut a strikingly straight path through the hills, often having carved out gorges and canyons. The train line stayed up higher, hugging the tops of hillsides, though its path required it to cut two or three times across the river on large latticework bridges.

The train consisted of eight passenger cars, several cargo cars, and a dining car. He let himself drop, focusing on a specific car near the front where gunshots sounded. As he landed just behind that car, someone stumbled out onto the platform, holding his face.

Armed bank guard, he thought, noting the man's uniform. The train was bringing a payroll shipment inside a courier car disguised as if carrying a more mundane cargo. What was that scent in the air? Formaldehyde? The guard was gasping, and soon another stumbled out after him.

Both fell a moment later to gunfire from inside the courier car. Wax dropped down onto the platform beside the fallen men, checking on them. One was still moving; Wax knelt and moved the man's hand to cover the hole in his shoulder. "Press hard," he said over the sounds of the thumping track. "I'll be back for you."

The man nodded weakly. Wax took a deep breath and stepped into the courier car, where his eyes immediately started burning. Men moved inside, wearing strange masks and working at a large safe in the center. Half a dozen dead guards lay strewn across the floor of the car.

Wax started shooting, flooring several of the robbers, then Pushed himself out again, then upward as the others took cover and started firing back. He landed on the car behind the courier car, holstered Vindication—who was out of bullets—and brought out a Sterrion.

He prepared to drop down to try picking off more robbers, but an explosion inside the courier car interrupted him. It was a small blast, as explosions went, but it still left Wax's ears ringing. He winced and dropped to the platform, noticing figures moving in the smoke, stooping beside the safe, removing its contents. Others started firing at him.

He ducked to the side, then Pushed the door to the courier car closed, blocking the gunfire with the reinforced metal door. He grabbed the wounded guard under the arms and pulled him backward over the small gap between platforms and into the passenger car behind. This was another car with private compartments, though second-class, where those rooms had been filled with larger groups.

It was currently empty; the passengers, hearing the gunfire in the next car, had fled down the train. He checked each room anyway. Afterward, he propped the wounded man against the wall inside one of the rooms and tied a handkerchief around the wound, pulling it tight.

"The money . . ." the guard said.

"They've got the money," Wax replied. "Stopping them isn't worth risking any more lives."

"But . . ."

"I got a good look at several of them," Wax said, "and hopefully so did you. We'll give descriptions, chase them down, set a trap on *our* terms. Besides, if they leave now, there might be time to help a few of your friends in there."

The guard nodded weakly. "Couldn't stop them. They threw bottles through the windows. . . . And then the doors ripped off. Steel doors, Pushed into the room, twisted off their hinges like they were paper . . ."

Wax felt a chill. So the bandits had Metalborn too. Wax peeked around the wall back toward the courier car, and found the door he'd closed open again. A thin man stood on the platform, wearing a long coat and supporting himself on a cane. He gestured, speaking urgently and motioning for another bandit to lumber toward Wax's car—a hulking brute who had to be almost seven feet tall.

Wonderful. "Get in here," Wax said to the guard, pulling open the luggage compartment in the room's floor. "Keep your head down."

The guard crawled into the compartment, which was cramped and shallow, but large enough for a person, even with a few pieces of luggage in it. Wax pulled out both Sterrions, crouching in the doorway of the private room. The train continued to rock, going around a bend. The thing hadn't stopped. Did the engineer not know about the attack, or was he hoping to get to the next town?

Rusts, the courier car changed all of Wax's assessments. Maybe this *wasn't* about him. But why not simply stop the train and raid it in the wilderness? Too many questions, and no time to answer them. He had a bandit to kill. He'd have to jump out and surprise the brute, bring him down quick. If he was the Metalborn, surprise would be—

Something bounced down the hallway and came to a rest on the floor beside Wax, just outside the doorway in which he crouched. A small metal cube. He jumped back, fearing an explosive, but nothing happened. What had that been?

And then he realized with a deep, bone-chilling horror that he was no longer burning metal. There was nothing inside of him *to* burn.

His steel reserves had—somehow—vanished.

Marasi fired three shots with the rifle, driving the bandits in the next car back under cover. *Impressive,* she thought, absently handing the weapon to Steris for reloading. She'd always used a target rifle before. You took one shot at a time with those, cocking between, but Waxillium's rifle had a wheel full of cartridges that turned on its own, like a revolver.

Steris handed back the gun, and Marasi took aim again, waiting for any bandit bits to peek out. She hid just inside the door to the servants' compartment, and the bandits hadn't made any serious attempts at advancing on her position.

Someone said something beside her. Marasi glanced into the room, where Drewton was speaking. Marasi pulled out one of her wax earplugs.

"What?" she asked.

"Are those earplugs?" the valet asked.

"What do they look like?" she said, then sighted down the rifle and fired a shot.

Drewton shoved his hands over his ears. Indeed, in the small chamber, the shot was loud enough that she was annoyed he'd made her remove her earplug.

"You carry them with you?" Drewton asked.

"Steris does." Apparently. Marasi had been a little surprised when Steris had pulled out a pair for herself, then—an unconcerned look on her face—handed a pair to Marasi.

"So you *expected* this to happen?"

"More or less," Marasi said, watching for movement from the bandits.

He seemed aghast. "This sort of thing happens *often*?"

"Would you say it happens often, Steris?" Marasi asked.

"Hmm?" Steris said, removing an earplug. "What was that?"

Marasi fired a shot, then looked up. *Think I winged that one.* "The valet wants to know if this sort of thing happens often to us."

"You more than me," Steris said conversationally. "But when Lord Waxillium is around, things *do* tend to pop up."

"Things?" Drewton said. "Pop up? This is a rusting train robbery!"

Steris regarded the valet with a cool expression. "Didn't you inquire about your prospective master before entering Lord Waxillium's employ?"

"Well, I mean, I *knew* he had an interest in the constabulary. Like some lords have an interest in the symphony, or in civic matters. It seemed odd, but not ungentlemanly. I mean, it's not as if he was involved in the *theater*."

They've gone quiet over there, Marasi thought, nervously tapping one finger against the rifle barrel. Were they going to try to cross over onto the top of her car again? One of the holes in the ceiling still dripped blood from the previous attempt.

To the side, Steris clicked her tongue disapprovingly at Drewton's words. He hadn't done his homework, which was a dreadful sin in Steris's eyes. Little could be worse than entering a situation without being *thorough*.

"Is . . . is he going to come back?" Drewton asked.

"Once he's finished," Steris said.

"Finished with what?"

"Killing the rest of them, hopefully," she said.

Marasi found herself surprised at Steris's bloodthirst. Of course, the woman hadn't been *quite* the same since her kidnapping eighteen months back. It wasn't that Steris acted traumatized—but she'd changed.

"They aren't trying to get to us anymore," Drewton said. "Did they retreat?"

"Maybe," Marasi said. *Probably not.*

"Should we go look?" Drewton asked.

"We?"

"Well, you." He tugged at his collar. "Gunfights. I had not actually expected gunfights. Aren't the servants usually left out of such extravagances?"

"Most of the time," Marasi said.

"Except when the house blew up," Steris added.

"Except then."

"And . . . you know," Steris said.

"Best not to mention it."

"Mention what?" Drewton asked.

"Don't worry about it," Marasi said, glaring at Steris. Honestly. If the man couldn't do a little research before taking a job—

"Wait," Drewton said, frowning. "What exactly happened to Lord Ladrian's *previous* valet?"

Motion in the hallway again. Marasi snapped her rifle up, ready to fire. However, the person who moved out into the hallway wasn't one of the bandits, but an older woman in a fine traveling dress. A bandit walked behind her, gun to her head.

Marasi shot him right in the forehead.

She gaped, shocked at herself, and almost dropped the gun. Fortunately the remaining bandit—seeing that the ploy hadn't worked—ran out of the car, fleeing toward the front of the train.

Rusts! Marasi felt sweat trickle down her temple. She'd fired so quickly, without even thinking. The poor hostage stood there, blood from the dead man all over her. Marasi knew what that felt like. Yes, she did.

Beside her, Drewton let out a few oaths that would have made Harmony blush. "What were you thinking?" he demanded of her. "You could have hit the woman."

"Statistics . . . Statistics say . . ." Marasi took a deep breath. "Shut up."

"Huh?"

"Shut up." She stood, holding the gun in nervous hands, and made her way into the next car.

The woman had found her husband—alive, fortunately—and was crying in his arms. Marasi stood over the bandit corpse, then looked back out at the roof of her car, where another one lay. She *hated* this part. A year and a half working with Waxillium hadn't made killing any easier. It was unnerving, and it was such a waste! If you had to shoot a man, society had already failed.

Marasi steeled herself and did a quick check of the rooms of the first-class car, determining that the bandits had well and truly retreated. One of the first-class passengers claimed to have experience with a gun, and she handed him the rifle and set him watching to be certain no bandits returned.

From there she went to the dining car, checking on the passengers, calming them. Gunshots came from farther up the train. Waxillium was doing his job. His effective, *brutal* job. The next car up—fourth from the end—was a second-class car, with packed rooms. She checked on the people here too.

Between the two cars, she found four people who had been shot. One was dead, another seriously wounded, so Marasi went to see if Steris had, by chance, brought any bandages or medical equipment. The chances were slim, but this *was* Steris. Who knew what she had planned for?

Marasi passed Drewton, who sat morosely on a seat in one of the first-class cabins, obviously wondering how an expert cravat-tier had ended up in the middle of a virtual war zone. Steris, however, wasn't in the servants' compartment. Nor was she in the one she had been sharing with Waxillium.

Increasingly frantic, Marasi searched through the first-class rooms. No Steris. Finally, she thought to ask the man she'd posted on guard.

"Her?" he said. "Yes, miss. She went by here a few minutes ago, moving up the train. Should I have stopped her? She seemed very determined about something."

Marasi groaned. Steris must have slipped past while she was checking in the rooms of the second-class car. Frustrated, she took her rifle back and chased after her sister.

Wax's metal reserves were gone.

Wax knelt, completely stunned. This was impossible. How in Harmony's name?

He twisted, discovering that the enormous bandit had stepped into this car. Doors rattled around the man, shaking as if someone were trying violently to get out. Wax ducked into the hallway and lifted his gun, but it was flipped from his fingers by a Push. Immediately after, Wax *himself* was shoved backward by his gunbelts. He slammed into the opposite wall of the car, right next to the closed door leading toward the back of the train.

He groaned in pain. How? How had they . . . ?

He shook his head, then heaved against the wall, using his breakaway buckles to rip free of his gunbelts. He dropped to the floor, leaving his guns and the metal vial stuck to the wall as the brute loped toward him.

Wax dodged under the man's first swing and delivered a punch right into the man's side. It felt like punching a steel wall. He danced backward, but rusts, it had been years since he'd gotten into a real fistfight—and he was slower than he'd once been. The giant's next right hook caught him as he tried to jab for the face.

His vision flashed, and his cheek erupted in pain. The blow shoved him into the side wall. *Rusts!* Where was Wayne? The brute came in again, and Wax dodged to the side, barely, and managed to connect with the man's face. Once, twice, three quick jabs.

The brute smiled. Doors still rattled around him—he was a Coinshot, obviously, Pushing out with a bubble like the one Wax used. It even pressed a little on the metalminds Wax wore on his upper arms, which were resistant to Allomancy.

This man could have ended the fight at any moment by grabbing a bit of metal and shooting it. He *preferred* the hand-to-hand fight. Indeed, the man raised his fists and nodded to Wax, still grinning, inviting him to come in for another round.

To hell with that.

Wax turned and slammed his shoulder against a door into an empty second-class compartment and made for the window.

"Hey!" the man said behind him. *"Hey!"*

Wax leaped at the window and increased his weight. He hit the window shoulder-first, arms covering his face, and smashed through—then barely managed to catch the bottom window frame as he fell outside.

Fingers dripping blood from the broken glass, he pulled himself up, stood on the windowsill, and scaled the outside of the train, finally heaving himself onto the roof. Wind rushed around him, and he was shocked to see that he wasn't alone up here. Ahead about four cars, a group of armed men pressed toward the front of the train, bearing something large and seemingly heavy. What in the name of the lost metal was that?

"Hey!" the large bandit said again as he climbed the side of the car.

Wax sighed, then kicked the man in the face as he tried to pull himself onto the top. The man growled. Wax kicked him again, then stomped on one of his hands. The man glared at Wax, then dropped back down to the window and climbed inside.

You can beat anybody, Wayne always said, *so long as you don't let them fight back properly.*

Wax moved to the center of the train car. He felt he should be chasing down those men up ahead. But he was unarmed now, and the Coinshot below was bound to pester him.

You have what you wanted, he thought at the robbers. *Why are you still fighting?*

The brute's head appeared a moment later, peeking over the lip of the car's roof, near the rear platform, which had a ladder. Wax rushed him, preparing to kick again, but the brute climbed up too quickly. He was holding something.

One of Wax's gunbelts. Damn.

The man grinned, stepping onto the rooftop, pulling Ranette's enormous shotgun out and dropping the gunbelt. Beneath them, the train shot out of the forest and rolled toward an open bridge rising hundreds of feet above the river below.

The brute raised the shotgun as if to fire from the hip.

Excellent.

Wax dove for the rooftop as the brute pulled the trigger, and the massive kick Ranette had built into the gun took him entirely by surprise. The weapon ripped out of his fingers, jerking backward and falling down between the cars. The man howled, cradling his hand.

Wax tackled him in the chest. The man grunted, stumbling backward, but caught himself before he toppled off the train. Wax didn't care.

He was after the gunbelt, which had fallen at the man's feet. He snatched it with fingers still wet with blood. It held Ranette's two cord devices, along with a single, glorious metal vial.

Wax yanked it out, tucking the gunbelt into his waistband. However, the vial lurched in his fingers. He snatched it, holding on tightly, but the brute's Push sent him backward across the train's roof in a skid. He slipped and fell to his knees, catching the side of the train.

The Coinshot kept Pushing. Wax clung to the rooftop with his left hand, but his right arm—which held the metal vial—strained in its socket. The brute smiled and started walking forward. Each step closer let him Push harder.

Wax gritted his teeth. The cuts on his fingers were superficial, though they stung like hell and the blood made his grip slippery. He struggled, trying to pull the vial toward his mouth, but failed.

Ranette's sphere devices. They hung from the gunbelt tucked into his waist. Could he use those? How? Beneath him, the train started across the bridge.

The thug advanced on Wax, rolling his shoulder and trying to make a fist despite his broken thumb. Behind the man something moved on the ladder. A head coming up? Wayne!

No. He saw the tip of a gun wave as the person climbed. Wayne wouldn't have a gun. Marasi?

Steris appeared at the lip of the roof, wind blowing her hair wildly. She looked from the huge robber to Wax, then seemed to gasp—though the wind was too loud for Wax to hear it. She scrambled up and set herself, crouching on one knee, holding Ranette's shotgun.

Oh no.

"Steris!" he shouted.

The brute spun, noticing her as she set the gun at her shoulder, wide-eyed, dress rippling against her body in the wind.

She pulled the trigger. Unsurprisingly, the shot went wild, but it did manage to clip the brute in the arm, spraying blood. The man grunted, releasing his Push on Wax.

Unfortunately, the enormous kick of that gun—intended to be used to fight Allomancers—hurled Steris backward.

And right off the side of the train.

8

Wax leaped off the side of the train and raised the vial to his mouth.

Steris toppled below, falling toward the river. He ripped the cork free with his teeth and turned over in the air, sucking down the contents of the vial. Cod-liver oil and metal flakes washed into his mouth. Swallowing took a precious moment.

Nothing.

Nothing.

Nothing.

Power.

Wax shouted, flaring steel and Pushing on the tracks up above. He shot downward in a blur, slamming into Steris, grabbed her, and Pushed on the shotgun that toppled beneath her.

It hit the water.

They slowed immediately. Water viscosity being what it was, you could Push off something sinking. A second later, the shotgun hit the bottom of the churning river, and that left the two of them hanging about two feet above the water's surface. A faint, solitary blue line led from Wax to the shotgun.

Steris breathed in short, frantic gasps. She clung to him, blinked, then looked down at the river.

"What is *wrong* with that gun!" she said.

"It's meant for me to shoot," Wax said, "when my weight is increased to counteract the kick." He looked up toward the disappearing train. It had crossed the river, but now would have to slow and chug its way down some switchbacks on a hill on the other side, coming out of the highlands to head on toward New Seran.

"Hold this," he told Steris, handing her his gunbelt and removing the two spheres. "What were you thinking? I told you to stay back in the other car."

"As a point of fact," she said, "you did *not*. You told me to stay safe."

"So?"

"So, it has been my experience that the safest place in a gunfight is near you, Lord Waxillium."

He grunted. "Hold your breath."

"What? Why should I—"

She yelped as he Pushed on the steel bridge supports nearby, plunging them down into the river. Ice-cold water surrounded them as Wax kept Pushing, plunging downward until he reached his gun—easily located by its blue line—settled into the muck on the bottom. Ears throbbing from the pressure, he snatched the gun, replacing it with one of Ranette's sphere devices, then Pushed.

They popped back out of the river, trailing water, and Wax Pushed them as high as his anchor would allow and handed Steris the shotgun to hold. From there, he Pushed off one of the support beams below—launching them upward and to the side. A Push on one from the other direction sent them bounding upward the other way, and he was able to work them toward the top of the bridge.

The angle of these Pushes had sent them out away from the tracks, unfortunately. When they soared up past the bridge, he needed to sling Ranette's other sphere device out—getting it into a small gap between bridge struts. He engaged the hooks, so that the

Push from below, combined with the taut cord in his hand, swung him and Steris in an arc.

He landed on the tracks, a soggy Steris in one arm, cord in the other. He could imagine Ranette's grin as he told her how well the thing had worked. He disengaged the hooks and yanked the device back into his hand, though he had to wind the cord manually.

Steris's teeth chattered audibly, and he glanced at her as he finished winding, expecting to see her frightened and miserable. Instead, despite being dripping wet, she had a stupid grin on her face, eyes alight with excitement.

Wax couldn't help smiling himself as he stowed Ranette's sphere and tied on his gunbelt, then shoved his shotgun into the holster. "Remember, you're not supposed to find things like that fun, Steris. You're *supposed* to be boring. I have it on good authority from this woman I know."

"A tone-deaf man," Steris said, "can still enjoy a good choir—even if he could never participate."

"Not buying the act, my dear," Wax said. "Not any longer. You just climbed on top of a moving train car and shot a bandit, rescuing your fiancé."

"It behooves a woman," she said, "to show an interest in her husband's hobbies. Though I suppose I should be outraged, as this is the second dunking you've given me in a very short period of time, Lord Waxillium."

"I thought you said the first one wasn't my fault."

"Yes, but this was twice as cold. So it evens out."

He smiled. "You want to wait here, or join me?"

"Um . . . join you?"

He nodded to the left. Far below, the train hit the end of its switchbacks down the hillside, leveling out to approach the final bend before heading southward. Her eyes opened wider, then she grabbed him in a tight grip.

"When we land," he said, "keep your head down and find a place to hide."

"Got it."

He took a deep breath, then launched them high in a powerful arc through the night air. They sailed across the river, coming down like a bird of prey toward the front of the train.

Wax slowed himself and Steris with a careful Push on the engine, setting down atop the coal tender. Inside the cab right in front of them, a bandit held a gun to the engineer's head. Wax let go of Steris, then spun around and pumped the shotgun—popping the expended shells into the air—and Pushed on the shells, sending them through the back of the engine cab and right into the bandit's head. She dropped, falling on the engine controls.

Wax was nearly thrown off as the train lurched, slowing down. He spun, grabbing Steris by the arm. To his right, the startled engineer grabbed the lever, smoothing out the deceleration. Holding Steris to him, Wax leaped with a short Push into the open rear of the engine, where they landed beside the engineer and the dead bandit.

"What are they doing?" he asked, dropping Steris, then kneeling and taking the dead bandit's pistol.

"They have some device," the engineer said, frantic, pointing. "They're installing it between the coal tender and the first car. Shot my fireman when he tried to defend me, the bastards!"

"Where's the next town?"

"Ironstand! We're getting close. Few more minutes."

"Get us there as quickly as you can, and call for some surgeons and the local constables the moment we arrive."

The man nodded frantically. Wax closed his eyes and took a deep breath to orient himself.

The final push. Here we go.

Halfway through the train, Marasi had reason to curse Waxillium Ladrian. Well, *another* reason. She added it to the list.

Though she was supposed to be finding Steris, she spent most of her time being mobbed by worried passengers who needed soothing.

Apparently the bandits had quickly worked their way through the second- and third-class cars, shaking people down for what little money they had. The people were terrified, upset, and looking for anyone with a hint of authority to comfort them.

Marasi did her best, settling them onto benches, checking to see if any more people were seriously wounded. She helped bandage a young man who had stood up to a bandit, and now bore a shot in the side as a result. He might make it.

Passengers had seen Steris come through here. Marasi tried to contain her worry and peeked into the next car in the line. It was deserted save for one passenger standing calmly at the far end, cane in hand, blocking the passage.

Marasi checked the various rooms as she entered, rifle held at the ready, but spotted no bandits. This was the last car before the cargo cars—which, oddly, were at the front of this train. This car's interior showed its share of bullet holes in the woodwork, suggesting Waxillium had been here.

"Sir?" Marasi asked, hastening to the lone man. He was slender, and younger than she'd expected him to be from behind, considering how his posture slumped, and how he relied upon the cane to keep him upright. "Sir, it's not safe for you here. You should move to the rear cars."

He turned toward her with raised eyebrows. "I am always inclined to obey the wishes of a pretty woman," he said. She could see that he kept one hand stiff at his side, fingers closed as if clutching something. "But what of you, miss? Is there no danger to you?"

"I can care for myself," Marasi said, noting that the next car in line was crowded with corpses. She felt sick.

"Indeed!" the man said. "You look quite capable. Quite capable indeed." He leaned in. "Are you more than you appear, perhaps? A Metalborn?"

Marasi frowned at the odd question. She'd taken a dose of cadmium, of course—for all the good it would do. Her Allomancy was generally something to laugh at; she could slow down time in a bubble around herself, which meant speeding it up for everyone else.

A wonderful power if you were bored and waiting for the play to start. But it wasn't of so much use in combat, where you'd be left frozen in place while your enemies could escape, or just set themselves up to shoot you when the bubble dropped. True, she could make the bubble fairly large, so she could catch others inside of it—but that would still leave her trapped, and likely with hostiles.

The man smiled at her, then abruptly raised his hand, the one that appeared to be clutching something. Marasi started to react, bringing her rifle up. But at that moment, the train unexpectedly lurched, slowing as if someone had leaned on the brake. The man cursed, stumbling and slamming into the wall before falling to the floor. Marasi caught herself, but dropped the rifle.

She looked at the man, who regarded her with wide eyes before maladroitly stumbling to his feet—one of his legs didn't work right—and hastening out of the train car onto the platform, slamming the door behind him.

Marasi stared after him, confused. She'd assumed he was pulling a gun on her, but that hadn't been the case at all. The object had been far too small. She reached for her gun, and beside it on the floor she was surprised to find a small metal cube with bizarre symbols on it.

Gunfire sounded ahead. Marasi tucked the curiosity away and shouldered her rifle, determined to find Waxillium and, hopefully, her stupid sister.

Eyes closed, Wax felt the metal burning. That fire, comfortable and familiar. Metal was his soul. Compared to it, the chill of the river was no more than a raindrop on a bonfire.

He felt the gun in his fingers. A bandit's gun, unfamiliar to him, yet he knew it—knew it by the lines pointing at its barrel, trigger, levers, the bullets inside. Five shots left. He could see them even with his eyes closed.

Go.

He opened his eyes and leaped out of the engine, Pushing himself forward in a rush. He passed over the coal tender, then burst into the first cargo car—laden with mail in heaping sacks—and passed through in a tempest. He skidded out onto its rear platform and Pushed to either side, launching two bandit guards upward and outward, one in each direction.

The train ran up beside the river here. Trees blurred past on the left, water on the right. Wax launched himself upward, onto the top of the second cargo car, noting the bandits with their device here. Another, larger group had gathered on top of the next car, the one they'd robbed.

Wax fired with cold precision, killing the three bandits. He stepped up to the "device" the engineer had mentioned, which was nothing more than a large case of dynamite and a trigger linked to a clock. Wax ripped the detonator off, tossed it aside, then Pushed the entire box away to be sure. It plunged into the river.

Something Pushed his gun out of his hand. He spun, finding the large bandit from before lumbering toward him across the roof. He'd left the larger group of bandits on the next rooftop over.

You again, Wax thought with a growl, dropping his gunbelt, but resting his foot on it to keep it from blowing away. The man came running toward Wax. With the brute very close, Wax knelt and yanked out Ranette's sphere device.

The bandit Pushed on that, of course—causing the sphere to leap backward to the side. Wax kept a firm hold on the cord, wrapping it with a yank around the bandit's leg.

The bandit stared down in confusion.

Wax Pushed, shoving the sphere into a batch of trees, engaging its hooks. "I believe this is your stop."

The large man suddenly *flew* off the train, yanked by the cord—which was now hooked to a tree. Wax picked up his gunbelt and advanced on the larger group of bandits, wind whipping around him on the rooftop.

He was facing down at least a dozen of them—and he had no weapon. Fortunately, the group was busy throwing one of their members off the train.

Wax blinked in surprise. But that was indeed what they were doing—they tossed one of the bandits overboard. It was the man with the cane, who hit the water beside the train with a splash. A group of the others started to follow suit, leaping into the river. One spotted Wax, pointing. Six remaining bandits leveled weapons.

Then froze.

Wax hesitated, the wind at his back. The men didn't move. Didn't flinch. Didn't even blink. Wax hopped across to the next car, then took a cork from his pocket—from one of his vials—and tossed it toward the men.

It hit some invisible barrier and froze there, hanging in the air. Wax grinned, then dropped down between the cars and pushed into the one the men were standing on. There he found Marasi standing atop a bunch of suitcases, her shoulders pressed against the train's ceiling just below the men so she could engage a speed bubble and freeze them all in place.

9

Wax had never shot a doctor before, but he *did* like trying out new experiences. Perhaps today would be the day.

"I'm fine," he growled as the woman dabbed with cotton at the wound on his face, where the massive brute had punched him. His lip had split.

"I'll decide that," she said.

Nearby, the Ironstand constables marched four befuddled bandits along the train platform, which was flooded with light from a few tall arc lamps. Wax sat on a bench near where the other surgeons were attending to the wounded. Farther back, in the shadows of the night, a tarp covered the bodies they'd retrieved. There were far too many of those.

"It looks worse than it is," Wax said.

"You had blood all over your face, my lord."

"I wiped my forehead with a bloody hand." She had wrapped that hand with gauze already, but had agreed that the cuts were superficial.

Finally she stepped back and sighed, nodding. Wax stood up, grabbing his damp suit coat and striding toward the train. He saw Marasi peering out of the front. She shook her head.

No sign of Wayne or MeLaan.

The lump inside Wax's stomach grew two sizes. *Wayne'll be fine,* he told himself. *He can heal from practically anything.* But there *were* ways to kill a Bloodmaker. A shot to the back of the head. Prolonged suffocation. Basically, anything that would have forced Wayne to keep healing until his Feruchemical storages ran out.

And, of course, there was the *other* thing. The strange effect that had somehow stolen Wax's Allomantic powers. If that worked on Feruchemy too . . .

Wax strode onto the train, stepping past Marasi without saying a word, and started his own search. The train was dark, now that it had stopped—and the only lights came from the platform outside. There wasn't much to see by.

"Lord Waxillium?" Constable Matieu said, sticking his head in between two of the cars. The spindly man had a ready smile, which fell off his face as Wax bustled past.

"Busy," Wax said, entering the next car.

Blue lines let him see sources of metal even in the darkness. Wayne would be carrying metal vials and his bracers. *Look for faint sources of metal, hidden behind something.* Perhaps . . . perhaps they'd just knocked him out and stuffed him somewhere.

"Um . . ." the constable said from behind. "I was wondering if any of your other servants will be needing, um, emotional support."

Wax frowned, looking out the window to where Drewton was sitting, surrounded by no fewer than three nurses. He accepted a cup of tea from one while he complained about his ordeal. Wax could hear it even inside the train car.

"No," Wax said. "Thank you."

Matieu followed him through the train. He was the local captain, though from what Wax gathered, this town was small enough that his "big cases" usually were on the order of who had been stealing Mrs. Hutchen's milk off her doorstep. He was glad to have found surgeons. Most of them probably worked half their time on cows, but it was better than nothing.

Not a few younger officers stood on the platform. They'd put away their stupid autograph books, fortunately, though they seemed deflated that their captain wouldn't let them pester Wax.

Where? Wax thought, feeling more and more sick. Marasi arrived a moment later with an oil lamp, her light illuminating the train car for him as he poked through a cargo room full of mail bags.

He won't be in here, Wax thought. This was forward of the car that had been secretly carrying the payroll shipment. Wayne wouldn't have been able to cross through that one; they'd have had it blocked off even before the bandits arrived. Still, he wanted to be careful. He searched this one, then waved to Marasi and picked his way through the wreckage of the car that had been robbed.

Matieu tagged along. "I have to say, Lord Waxillium, that we're *very* lucky you were aboard. The Nightstreet Gang has been growing bolder and bolder, but I never thought they'd try something like this!"

"So this *is* an established gang?" Marasi said.

"Oh, sure," Matieu said. "Everyone in the area knows about the Nightstreets, though mostly they hit cities closer to the Roughs. We figure it's slim pickings out past the mountains, so they have begun to venture inward. But this! A full-on train robbery? And stealing Erikell payroll? That's daring. Those folks make weapons, you know."

"They had at least one Allomancer with them," Wax said, leading the way through the empty courier car, which still smelled faintly of formaldehyde.

"I hadn't heard that," Matieu said. "Even luckier you were along!"

"I didn't stop them from getting away, or from stealing the payroll."

"You killed or captured a good *half* of them, my lord. The ones we've got, they'll give us a lead on the others." He hesitated. "We'll have to put together a posse, my lord. They'll be making for the Roughs. Sure could use your help."

Wax swept this room, focusing on the blue lines. "And the man with the limp?"

"My lord?"

“He seemed to be in charge of them,” Wax said. “A man in a fine suit who walked with a cane. About six feet tall, with a narrow face and dark hair. Who is he?”

“I don’t know that one, my lord. Donny is the leader.”

“Big guy?” Wax asked. “Neck like a stump?”

“No, my lord. Donny is little and feisty. Evilest rusting kig you’ve ever seen.”

Kig. It was slang for a koloss-blooded person. Wax hadn’t seen anyone among the bandits with the proper skin color for that. “Thank you, Captain,” Wax said.

The man seemed to recognize it as a dismissal, but he hesitated. “And can we count on your help, my lord? When we chase down Donny and his gang?”

“I’ll . . . let you know.”

Matieu saluted, which was completely inappropriate—Wax wasn’t part of this jurisdiction—and retreated. Wax continued searching, pulling open a luggage compartment beneath the first passenger car. The metal lines leading into it only pointed at a few pieces of baggage.

“Waxillium,” Marasi said, “you can’t help with their hunt. We have a job already.”

“Might be related.”

“Might not be,” she said. “You heard him, Waxillium. These guys are a known criminal element.”

“Who happened to rob the very train we were on.”

“But at the same time seemed utterly shocked by the presence of an Allomancer gunman in the last car. Instead of tossing dynamite at us and riddling the coach with bullets, they sent a couple men to rob what they assumed would be easy pickings.”

Wax chewed on that, then checked another luggage compartment, bracing himself as he did so. No bodies. He let out a breath.

“I can’t think about this right now,” he said.

She nodded in understanding. They checked the other compartments, and he didn’t see any suspicious lines, so they moved on. Crossing the space between cars, he spotted Steris watching him.

She sat alone on a bench with a blanket around her shoulders, holding a cup of something that steamed. She seemed perfectly calm.

He continued on. Losing friends was part of a lawman's life; it had happened to him more times than he wanted to count. But after what had happened back in the city six months ago . . . well, he wasn't sure what losing Wayne would do to him. He steeled himself, moved to the next car, and opened the first of its luggage compartments, then froze.

Faint steel lines coming from another place in this train car. They were *moving*.

Wax rushed toward them. Marasi followed, suddenly alert, her lamp held high. The lines were coming from the floor inside one of the rooms. Only no luggage was on its racks, and no litter was on its floor. It was a private compartment that hadn't been rented out for the trip.

Wax entered and ripped open the luggage compartment in the floor. Wayne blinked up at him. The younger man had mussed hair, and his shirt was unbuttoned, but he wasn't in any bonds that Wax could see. He didn't seem to have been harmed at all. In fact . . .

Wax crouched down, Marasi's light revealing what had been hidden to him by the overhang of the luggage compartment. MeLaan, shirt completely off, was in the compartment too. She sat up, entirely unashamed of her nudity.

"We've stopped!" she said. "Are we there already?"

"Well how was I supposed to know we'd get rusting attacked?" Wayne exclaimed, now properly clothed, though his hair was still a mess.

Wax sat listening with half an ear. The train officials had opened a room in the station for them to use. He knew he should be angry, but he was mostly just relieved.

"Because we are *us*," Marasi said, arms folded. "Because we're on our way to a dangerous situation. I don't know. You could at *least* have told us what you were doing." She hesitated. "And by the way, what do you *think you were doing*?"

Wayne bowed his head where he sat before her. MeLaan leaned against the wall near the door. She was looking toward the ceiling, as if trying to feign innocence.

"Movin' on," Wayne said, pointing at Marasi. "Like you told me to."

"That wasn't moving on! That was 'Running on at full speed.' It was 'Shooting on forward like a bullet,' Wayne."

"I don't like doin' stuff halfway," he said solemnly, hand over his heart. "It's been a long time since I had me a good neckin' on account of my diligent monogamous idealization of a beauteous but unavailable—"

"And *how,*" Marasi interrupted, "did you *not* hear the fight? There was gunfire, Wayne. Practically *on top of you.*"

"Well, see," he said, growing red, "we was *real* busy. And we were down next to the tracks, which made a lot of noise. We'd wanted a place what was private-like, you know, and . . ." He shrugged.

"Bah!" Marasi said. "Do you *realize* how worried Waxillium was?"

"Don't bring me into this," Wax said, seated with his feet up on the next bench.

"Oh, and you *approve* of this behavior?" Marasi asked, turning on him.

"Heavens, no," Wax said. "If I approved of half the things Wayne does, Harmony would probably strike me dead on the spot. But he's alive, and we're alive, and we can't blame him for getting distracted during what we assumed would be a simple ride."

Marasi eyed him, then sighed and walked back out onto the platform, passing MeLaan without a glance.

Wayne stood and wandered over to him, pulling his box of gum from his pocket and tapping it against his palm to settle the powder inside. "These thieves, did one of them happen to shoot her when you weren't lookin'? 'Cuz she's sure gotten stiff all of a sudden."

"She was just worried about you," Wax said. "I'll talk to her after she's cooled down."

MeLaan left her position by the door. "Was there anything strange about the attack?"

"Plenty of things," Wax said, standing and stretching. Rusts. Was he really getting too old for all this, as Lessie always joked with him? He usually felt exhilarated after a fight.

It's the deaths, he thought. Only one passenger had died, an older man. But they'd lost half a dozen payroll guards, not to mention the many wounded.

"One of the bandits," he said to MeLaan, "he did something that dampened my Allomancy."

"A Leecher?" she asked.

Wax shook his head. "He didn't touch me."

Leechers who burned chromium could blank another Allomancer's metals—but it required touch. "It did feel the same. My steel was there one moment, then gone the next. But MeLaan, there was some kind of device involved. A little metal cube."

"Wait," a voice said. Marasi appeared in the doorway. "A *cube*?"

All three of them looked at her, and she blushed in the harsh electric light. "What?"

"You stalked away," Wayne pointed, "indigenously."

"And now I'm stalking back in," Marasi said, striding toward Wax and fishing in her pocket. "I can be indigen—indig*nant* in here just as easily." She pulled her hand out, holding a small metal cube.

The same cube he'd seen before his steel was drained. Wax plucked it from her palm. "Where'd you get this?"

"The guy with the cane dropped it," Marasi said. "He moved as if to pull a gun on me, and raised this."

Wax turned it toward MeLaan, and she shook her head.

"That's a *real* strange gun," Wayne noted.

"Is there anything in that lore VenDell talked about," Wax said, "that mentions a device that negates Allomancy?"

"Nothing I've heard," MeLaan said.

"I mean," Wayne said, "it ain't even got a barrel."

"But you said you don't pay attention to the research, MeLaan," Marasi said, taking the cube back.

"That's true."

"And if they could shoot the rusting thing," Wayne added, "the bullet would be small as a flea."

Marasi sighed. "Wayne, can't you ever let a joke die?"

"Hon, that joke *started* dead," he said. "I'm just givin' it a proper burial."

"We need another train south," Marasi said, turning to the others.

"These bandits might have information," Wayne said. "Chasin' them down could be useful. 'Sides, I didn't get to stomp none of them, on account of some untimely snogging."

"At least it was *good* snogging," MeLaan added. Then, to Marasi's glare, she added, "What? It was. Poor guy hadn't had a proper snog in years. Had a lot of pent-up energy."

"You're not even human," Marasi said. "You should be ashamed. *Not to mention* that you're six hundred years old."

"I'm young at heart. Really—I copied this one off a sixteen-year-old that I ate a few months back."

The room grew very still.

"Oh . . . was that gauche?" MeLaan said, wincing. "That *was* gauche, wasn't it? She didn't taste very good, if that's anything to you. Hardly rotten at all. And . . . I should stop talking about this. New Seran? Are we going, or staying to chase bandits?"

"Going," Wax said, which earned a nod from Marasi. "If this is connected, we'll run into them later. If it's not, then I'll see what I can do to help once we've dealt with my uncle."

"And how're we going to get to New Seran?" Wayne said. "Doesn't look like our train will be leaving anytime soon."

"Freight train," Wax said, checking the wall lists. "Coming through in an hour. They're going to move our train onto the repair track, so we can flag that one down for a ride. It won't be comfortable, but it will get us there by morning. Go gather your luggage. Hopefully there aren't too many holes in it."

Wayne and MeLaan obeyed, walking out side by side. Maybe there was actually something there between them. If anything, Wayne didn't seem the least bit put out by being reminded just how alien, and just how old, MeLaan was.

Then again, Wayne wasn't known for his taste in women. Or, well, his *taste* at all, really. Wax glanced at Marasi, who had remained behind. She held up the little cube, turning it over in her fingers, inspecting the intricate carvings it bore on its various faces.

"Can I get VenDell's notes back from you?" she said. "Maybe there's something in them about this thing."

"More convinced this wasn't a random train robbery?"

"Maybe a little," Marasi said. "You should talk to my sister."

"She seemed perfectly calm when I checked on her earlier."

"Of course she's calm," Marasi said. "She's Steris. But she's *also* doing needlework."

". . . And that's bad?"

"Steris only does needlework when she has an overwhelming desire to appear normal," Marasi said. "She read somewhere that it's an appropriate hobby for a woman of means. She hates it to death, but won't tell a soul. Trust me. If needlework is involved, she's upset. I could talk to her, but she's never listened to me. She didn't even know about me until we were teenagers. Besides, you'll need to get used to this."

She strode from the room, and Wax—oddly—found himself smiling. Whatever else could be said, Marasi had come a long way since he'd first met her.

He took his jacket off the hook on the wall and slipped it on, then walked back into the night. Marasi was calling for the stationmaster, probably to arrange their passage on the cargo train. Wax strolled along the tracks, passing cold electric lights, until he reached the bench where Steris worked on her needlepoint.

He settled down beside her. "Marasi says you're having a tough time of it."

Steris paused her needlepoint. "You're a very straightforward man, Lord Waxillium."

"Can be."

"But as we both know, it's all an act. You were raised among Elendel's elite. You had tutors and diction coaches. In your youth, you spent your time at parties and balls."

"And then I spent twenty years in the Roughs," Wax said. "The winds out there can weather the strongest granite. Are you surprised they can do the same to a man?"

She turned to him, head cocked to the side.

Wax sighed and leaned back, stretching his legs out, ankles crossed. "Have you ever been somewhere you didn't fit in? A place where everyone else seems to get it immediately? They know what to do. They know what to say. But rusts, you have to *work* to untangle it all?"

"That describes my entire life," Steris said softly.

He put his arm around her, and let her rest her head on his shoulder. "Well, that was how those parties were for me. Social situations were a chore. Everyone laughing, and me just standing there, stressed out of my mind and trying to figure out the right thing to do. I didn't smile a lot back then. Guess I still don't. I'd escape the parties when I could, find my way to a quiet balcony."

"And do what? Read?"

Wax chuckled. "No. I don't mind a book now and then, but Wayne is the real reader."

Steris raised her head, looking surprised.

"I'm serious," Wax said. "Granted, he likes ones with pictures now and then, but he *does* read. Often out loud. You should hear him do the voices to himself. Me . . . I'd just find a balcony that looked out over the city somewhere, and I'd stare. Listen." He smiled. "When I was a boy, more than a few people thought I was slow because I'd sit there staring out a window."

"Then you found your way to the Roughs."

"I was so glad to be away from Elendel and its phoniness. You call me blunt. Well, that's the man I want to be. That's the man I admire. Perhaps I'm only acting like him, but it's a sincere act. Hang me, but it is."

Steris sat quietly for a few moments, head on his shoulder, and Wax stared out into the night. A nice night, all things considered.

"You're wrong," she noted, sounding drowsy. "You do smile. Most often when you're flying on lines of steel. It's the only time I think . . . I think I see . . . pure joy in you. . . ."

He looked down at her, but she'd apparently dozed off, judging by the way she was breathing. He settled back, thinking about what she'd said, until the cargo train finally pulled into the station.

ENDANCY

' CLADENCE 342 2¢

EWEST SHIPS EL OFFICIALS

FARTHING MANSION HIT!

An act of vandalism and thievery has the city's elite on edge. Late last night, someone broke into Farthing Mansion, stole some items, and vandalised the wall with a reverse gold symbol.

Lady Farthing is offering a reward for the return of her jewelry. Please report all information to the Uptown Precinct.

(Continued on back.)

The mark of the vandal

)oes Harmony Have a Metal?

The First Age philosopher ·alabris Menthon meant ·is rhetorically, but even the ord Mistborn thought on this ·hen he famously said, "Hav- ·g the has Sazed a metal?"

From councils to pubs, the ·uestion is still debated. But ·ow, breakthroughs in sci- ·nce have brought us closer · an answer.

(Continued on back.)

part could have avoided this whole debacle, and you wouldn't be hanging fifty feet above death from the threads of a poorly-rendered map. Climb in. Let's come to an agreement."

He reached up as if to take my offer, but something in his hand flashed in the light of the stars. Instinctively, I burnt metal, releasing one hand to touch the device.

It was an everyday hunting

10

Wax started awake to the sound of distant explosions.

He immediately scrambled to his feet, reaching for his metals, bleary-eyed and disoriented. Where was he? Crew cabin of the cargo train. It was large, with some stiff couches in the back for the engineers to catch a nap while their train was waiting to be unloaded. Steris was asleep on one, wrapped in his jacket. Wayne dozed in the corner, hat over his face.

They'd left the servants behind for now; they would come along on the next passenger train. MeLaan had chosen to ride in the back with their luggage—she had wanted to look through her bundles of bones to pick the right body for the night.

Wax downed metals and whipped out Vindication, stumbling forward toward the sounds—which, now fully awake, he wasn't certain were explosions at all. A continuous rumble, like an earthquake, off in the distance. He stepped out into the cab proper of the engine car. This was a newer machine, one of the oil-driven ones, with no need for a coal tender.

Marasi stood near the front with the engineer, a tall fellow with bright eyes and forearms like pistons.

That rumbling . . . Wax frowned, lowering his gun as Marasi

glanced at him. The sky was bright blue; morning had arrived. He stepped into the cabin, and could see that ahead, New Seran rose before them. The city spread across a series of enormous, flat-topped stone terraces. There were at least a dozen of them, and each was split by multiple streams, which crossed them and then dropped off the edge down to the next terrace. The sound wasn't an earthquake or explosion, but that of *waterfalls*.

In places, the drop was just a little ripple—a fall of some five feet or so. But in others, majestic waterfalls plunged fifty feet or more before pounding onto the next stone platform. It looked like a man-made effect, for the various split streams and waterfalls eventually ran back together into the river, which flowed away from the city toward distant Elendel.

Wax slid Vindication into her holster, though it took two tries because he was so mesmerized by the waterfalls. Indeed, the whole city. Buildings sprouted between the rivers, and vibrant green vines draped the cliffs like nature's own tresses. Beyond, the Seran mountains rose, lofty and whited at the tops.

Marasi grinned, leaning out of the cab to get a better look up at the heights of the city. The engineer stood by his levers, valves, and cranks trying to act casual, though he was obviously watching Wax and Marasi for their reactions.

"I often think," the man eventually said, "that Harmony was showing off a little when He made this place."

"I had no idea this was here," Wax said, stepping up beside Marasi. Behind him, Wayne yawned and stumbled to his feet.

"Yeah, well," the engineer said, "people from Elendel often forget there's a whole country out here. No offense, my lord. There's a lot of Elendel to take in, so it makes sense you'd get a little blinded by it."

"You're from New Seran?" Marasi asked.

"Born and raised, Captain Colms."

"Then you can tell us where to find our hotel, perhaps?" Marasi asked. "The Copper Gate?"

"Oh, that's a *nice* one," the engineer said, pointing. "Top terrace, in the waterman district. Look for the big statue of the Lord Mistborn. It's not two blocks from there."

"How close can you get us?" Marasi asked.

"Not close at all, I'm afraid," the engineer said. "We're not a passenger train, and even those can only go to the middle tiers. We'll be down at the bottom. It'll take you a few hours to ride the gondolas up. There are ramps too, if you'd prefer a carriage, but they take longer—and the gondolas have a better view."

Gondolas would have been wonderful, Wax thought, if most of them had had more than a few hours of sleep. With the reception tonight, they'd need to be rested and ready to go.

"Shortcut?" he asked Marasi.

"You realize I'm wearing a skirt."

"I do. What happened to that fancy new constable uniform with the trousers?"

"Packed away. Not everyone likes wearing uniforms when we don't have to, Waxillium."

"Well, you can wait and take the gondolas," Wax said. "Think of me resting peacefully in a soft hotel bed while you blink bleary eyes and droop against—"

"All right, *fine*," Marasi said, stepping up to him. "Just stay away from crowds."

Wax grabbed her around the waist. "I'll be back for the rest of you," he told Wayne, who nodded. "Engineer, have our things sent to the Copper Gate, if you please."

"Yes, my lord."

Wax slid open the side of the cab, took another drink of metal flakes—recovered from the stash in his luggage—then pulled Marasi tight, burned steel, and leaped. A flared Push sent them soaring away from the train, which was slowing as it approached the buildings clustered around the base of New Seran.

They dropped toward these, but a shot from Vindication as they neared the ground gave him something to bounce off of. He sent them upward, past the lower tiers, using metal he found there to keep them aloft.

The homes here were much smaller than those in Elendel. Quaint, even. In Elendel, you could rarely afford to waste space on a single dwelling—even in the slums, towering apartments were the norm. There was a kind of eternal shift going on, where sections of town would fall into disrepair over time, filling with the poor while those able to afford something new moved to other sections. It was fascinating to him that, if you looked at old maps, what were now slums had once been considered prime real estate.

He saw few apartment buildings and only three skyscrapers, confined to a small commercial district on the top terrace. Though the terraces constrained the city's boundaries, they looked large enough to hold the population. Lots of parks and small streams, none deep enough to be navigable like Elendel's canals.

He stayed to the rooftops, rather than the streets, for Marasi's sake—though she didn't have much trouble with her skirt. She'd tucked it around her legs before they started, and the generally upward motion kept it from flaring.

Wax threw the two of them in great leaping arcs over residential areas until they reached the next cliff face, where he found a gondola and used it as an anchor to shoot them up the fifty feet or so toward the top tier of the terraces. He exulted in the moment, the freedom, the beauty of it. There was a majesty about soaring alongside a churning waterfall, with sparkling pools and lush gardens spreading out beneath.

They topped the cliff face, and Wax landed them softly alongside the falls. Marasi let out a held breath as he set her down; he could tell from the tension of her grip that she hadn't enjoyed the flight as much as he had. Steelpushing wasn't natural to her, nor were the heights—she backed away from the cliff as soon as she was free.

"Going to go get the others?" she asked.

"Let's find the hotel first," Wax said, pointing the way toward a statue he'd spotted upon landing. He could still make out the green patina of the statue's head over the tops of the nearby homes. He started in that direction.

Marasi joined him, and they entered a street with a fair amount of foot traffic, papergirls and boys hawking broadsheets at every corner. Fewer horses or carriages than in Elendel—almost none, though he did see a fair number of pedicabs. That made sense, with the layout of the city. He found it interesting that the gondola system wasn't only for getting between terraces; there were also lines crossing the sky above them carting people from one section of this terrace to another.

"Like a shark among minnows," Marasi mumbled.

"What's that?" Wax asked.

"Look at how people swerve around you," Marasi said. "Lord Cimines once did a study comparing constables to sharks, showing how the people in a crowded walkway responded exactly the same way as animals do to a predator moving nearby."

He hadn't noticed, but she was right. People gave him a wide berth—though not because they guessed he was a constable. It was the mistcoat duster, the weapons, and perhaps his height. Everyone seemed a little shorter down here, and he saw over the crowd by several inches.

In Elendel, his clothing had been abnormal—but so was everyone's. That city was a mishmash, like an old barrel full of spent cartridges. All different calibers represented.

Here, the people wore lighter clothing than in Elendel. Pastel dresses for the ladies, striped white suits and boater hats for the men. Compared to them, he was a bullet hole in a stained-glass window.

"Never been good at blending in anyway," he said.

"Fair enough," Marasi said. "I've been meaning to ask. Do you need Wayne tonight?"

"At the party?" Wax asked, amused. "I have trouble imagining a situation where he doesn't end up drunk in the punch bowl."

"Then I'll borrow him," Marasi said. "I want to check the graveyards for ReLuur's spike."

Wax grunted. "That will be dirty work."

"Which *is* why I asked for Wayne."

"Noted. What do you think the chances are you'll find the thing buried in a grave?"

Marasi shrugged. "I figure we'll start with the most obvious and easiest method."

"Grave robbing is the easiest method?"

"It is with proper preparation," Marasi said. "I don't intend to do the digging, after all. . . ."

Wax stopped listening.

The chatter of the crowd faded as he froze in place, staring at a broadsheet held up by a papergirl on a nearby corner. That symbol, the jagged reverse *mah* . . . he knew that symbol all too well. He left Marasi midsentence, pushing through the crowd to the girl and snatching the paper.

That symbol. Impossible. FARTHING MANSION HIT, the headline read. He fished out a few clips for the girl. "Farthing Mansion? Where is it?"

"Just up Blossom Way," the girl said, pointing with her chin and making the coins in his palm disappear.

"Come on," he said, interrupting Marasi as she started saying something.

People did make way for him, which was convenient. He could have taken to the sky, but he found the mansion without difficulty, partially because of the people crowded outside and pointing. The symbol was painted in red, exactly like the one he'd known back in the Roughs, but this time it marred the wall of a fine, three-story stone mansion instead of a stagecoach.

"Waxillium, for the love of sanity," Marasi said, catching up to him. "What has gotten into you?"

He pointed at the symbol.

"I recognize that," Marasi said. "Why would I recognize that?"

"You read the accounts of my time in the Roughs," Wax said. "It's in there—that's the symbol of Ape Manton, one of my old nemeses."

"Ape Manton!" Marasi said. "Didn't he—"

"Yes," Wax said, remembering the nights of torture. "He hunts Allomancers."

But why would he be here? Wax had put him away, and not just in some minor village. He'd been locked up in True Madil, biggest town in the Northern Roughs, with a jail like a vise. How in Harmony's True Name had he gotten all the way down to New Seran?

Robbery wouldn't be the end of Manton's activities here. He always had a motive behind the thefts, a goal. *I have to figure out what he took, and why he—*

No.

No, not right now. "Let's get to the hotel," Wax said, ripping himself away from the sight of that red symbol.

"Rusts," Marasi said, hurrying after him. "Could he be involved somehow?"

"With the Set? Not a chance. He hates Allomancers."

"Enemy of my enemy . . ."

"Not the Ape," Wax said. "He wouldn't take the hand of a Metalborn trying to save him from slipping to his death."

"So . . ."

"So he's not part of this," Wax said. "We ignore him. I'm here for my uncle."

Marasi nodded, but seemed disturbed. They passed a Lurcher juggler, dropping balls and tugging them back up into the air—along with the occasional object from among the amused crowd of watchers. A waste of Allomantic abilities. And all these people. Suffocating. He had hoped that in leaving Elendel, he would escape crowded streets. He nearly pulled out his gun and fired a shot to clear them all away.

"Wax . . ." Marasi said, taking his arm.

"What."

"*What?* Rusts, your stare could nail a person's head to the wall right now!"

"I'm fine," he said, pulling his arm away from her.

"This vendetta against your uncle is—"

"It's not a vendetta." Wax picked up his pace, striding through the crowd, mistcoat tassels flaring behind him. "You know what he's doing."

"No, and neither do you," Marasi said.

"He's breeding Allomancers," Wax said. "Maybe Feruchemists. I don't need to know his exact plan to know how bad that is. What if he's making an army of Thugs and Coinshots? Twinborn. *Compounders.*"

"That might be true," Marasi admitted. "But you aren't chasing him because of any of that, are you? He beat you. In the Hundredlives case, Mister Suit *got the best of you*. Now you're going to win the war where you lost the battle."

He stopped in place, turning on her. "How petty do you think I am?"

"Considering what I just told you," she said, "I'd say I consider you precisely *that* petty. It's not wrong to be angry at Suit, Waxillium. He's holding your sister. But rusts, please don't let it cloud your judgment."

He took a deep breath, then gestured toward the mansion up the street. "You want me to go chasing after the Ape instead?"

"No," Marasi said, then blushed. "I agree that we need to stay focused on getting back the spike."

"You're here for the spike, Marasi," Wax said. "I'm here to find Suit." He nodded down the street, toward a discreet hotel sign, barely visible on the front of a building. "You go check us in. I'm going to fetch the others."

"With this suite and the others, you'll basically have the entire top floor to yourselves." The hotel owner—who insisted upon being called Aunt Gin—beamed as she said it.

Wayne yawned, rubbing his eyes as he poked through the lavish room's bar. "Great. Lovely. Can I have your hat?"

"My . . . hat?" The elderly woman looked up at the oversized hat. The sides drooped magnificently, and the thing was *festooned* with flowers. Like, oodles of them. Silk, he figured, but they were really good replicas.

"You have a lady friend?" Aunt Gin asked. "You wish to give her the hat?"

"Nah," Wayne said. "I need to wear it next time I'm an old lady."

"The next time you *what*?" Aunt Gin grew pale, but that was probably on account of the fact that Wax went stomping by, wearing his full rusting mistcoat. That man never could figure out how to blend in.

"Do these windows open?" Wax asked, pointing toward the penthouse suite's enormous bay windows. He stepped up onto one of the sofas and shoved on the window.

"Well, they used to open," Aunt Gin said. "But they rattled in the breezes, so we painted them shut and sealed the latches. Never could stand the thought of someone—"

Wax shoved one of them open, breaking off the latch and making a sharp cracking sound as the paint outside was ripped, perhaps some of the wood splintering.

"Lord Ladrian!" Aunt Gin said with a gasp.

"I'll pay for the repairs," Wax said, hopping off the couch. "I need that to open in case I have to jump out."

"Jump—"

"Aha!" Wayne said, pulling open the bar's bottom cabinet.

"Alcohol?" Marasi asked, walking by.

"Peanuts," Wayne said, spitting out his gum and then popping a handful of nuts into his mouth. "I ain't had nothin' to eat since I swiped that fruit in Steris's luggage."

"What are you babbling about?" Steris asked from the couch, where she was writing in her notebook.

"I left you one of my shoes in trade," Wayne said, then dug in his duster's pocket, pulling out the other shoe. "Speaking of that, Gin, will you swap me your hat for this one?"

"Your *shoe*?" Aunt Gin asked, turning back toward him, then jumping as Wax forced open another window.

"Sure," Wayne said. "They're both clothes, right?"

"What would I do with a man's shoe?"

"Wear it next time you gotta be a fellow," Wayne said. "You've got the perfect face for it. Good shoulders, too."

"Well, I—"

"Please ignore him," Steris said, rising and walking over. "Here,

I've prepared for you a list of possible scenarios that might transpire during our residence here."

"Steris . . ." Wax said, forcing open the third and final window.

"What?" she demanded. "I will not have the staff unprepared. Their safety is our concern."

"Fire?" Aunt Gin asked, reading the list. "Shoot-outs. Robbery. Hostage situations. *Explosions?*"

"That one is completely unfair," Wax said. "You've been listening to Wayne."

"Things *do* explode around you, mate," Wayne said, munching peanuts. Nice bit of salt on these.

"He's right, unfortunately," Steris said. "I've accounted for seventeen explosions involving you. That's a huge statistical anomaly, even considering your profession."

"You're kidding. Seventeen?"

"Afraid so."

"Huh." He had the decency to look proud of it, at least.

"A pastry shop once blew up while we was in it," Wayne said, leaning in to Aunt Gin. "Dynamite in a cake. Big mess." He held out some peanuts toward her. "How about I throw in these peanuts with the shoe?"

"Those are *my* peanuts! From this very room!"

"But they're worth more now," Wayne said. "On account of my being *real* hungry."

"I told you to ignore him," Steris said, tapping on the notebook she'd handed Aunt Gin. "Look, you only read the table of contents. The rest of the pages contain explanations of the possible scenarios I've outlined, and suggested responses to them. I've sorted the list by potential for property damage."

Wax leaped into the center of the room, then thrust his hand forward. The door quivered.

"What . . . what is he doing?" Aunt Gin asked.

"Checking to see where the best places in the room are for slamming the door with his mind," Wayne said. "In case someone bursts in on us."

"Just read the notebook, all right?" Steris requested in a pleasant tone.

Aunt Gin looked toward her, seeming bewildered. "Are these things . . . threats?"

"No, of course not!" Steris said. "I only want you to be prepared."

"She's thorough," Wayne said.

"I like to be thorough."

"Usually that means if you ask her to kill a fly, she'll burn down the house just to be extra sure it gets done."

"Wayne," Steris said, "you're needlessly making the lady concerned."

"Flooding from a diverted waterfall," Aunt Gin said, reading from the book again. "Koloss attack. *Cattle stampede through the lobby?*"

"That one is highly unlikely," Steris said, "but it never hurts to be prepared!"

"But—"

The door to the adjoining suite slammed open. "Hello, humans," MeLaan said, stepping into the doorway wearing nothing more than a tight pair of shorts and a cloth wrapped around her chest. "I need to put on something appropriate for tonight. What do you think? Large breasts? Small breasts? *Extra*-large breasts?"

Everybody in the room paused, then turned toward her.

"What?" MeLaan said. "Picking a proper bust size is vital to a lady's evening preparations!"

Silence.

"That's . . . kind of an improper question, MeLaan," Steris finally said.

"You're just jealous because you can't take yours off to go for a run," MeLaan said. "Hey, where is that bellboy with my things? I swear, if he drops my bags and cracks any of my skulls, there will be *fury* in this room!" She stalked away.

"Did she say *skulls*?" Aunt Gin said.

The door slammed.

"Aha!" Wax said, lowering his hand. "There it is."

Marasi approached and wrapped her arm around the elderly

lady's shoulders, leading her away. "Don't worry. It won't be nearly as bad as they make it seem. Likely nothing will happen to you or your hotel."

"Other than Wax rippin' your windows apart," Wayne noted.

"Other than that," Marasi said, giving him a glare.

"Young lady," Aunt Gin said under her breath, "you need to get away from these people."

"They're fine," Marasi said, reaching the door. "We've just had a long night."

Aunt Gin nodded hesitantly.

"Good," Marasi said. "Now, when you get down below, would you please send someone to the trade bureau for me? Have them collect the names of each and every person who works at the local graveyards."

"Graveyards?"

"It's vitally important," Marasi said, then pushed the woman out and shut the door.

"Graveyards?" MeLaan said, sticking her head into the room. She was now completely bald. "Reminds me. Would you order me something to eat? A nice hunk of aged meat."

"Rotting, you mean," Wax said.

"Nothing like the odor of a nice flank after a day in the sun," MeLaan said, ducking back into her room as a knock came at the other door. "Ah! My bags. Excellent. What? No, of course there aren't corpses in these. Why would I need bones with the flesh still on them? Thank you. Bye."

Wayne popped the last of the peanuts into his mouth. "I dunno about you all, but *I'm* gonna find a place to snore for a few hours."

"Sleeping arrangements, Waxillium?" Marasi asked.

"You and Steris in the suite across the hall," Wax said, "Wayne and I in here. MeLaan gets her own room. She probably wants to, um . . ."

"Melt?" Marasi offered.

". . . on her own."

"I'm good, really," MeLaan called from the next room. A second later she opened the door again. She wore the same bones and build, but this time she was completely bare-chested.

It wasn't a woman's chest.

"I solved the problem," MeLaan said. "I'll go as a fellow. That will probably be more covert anyway. Just have to choose the right bones."

Wayne cocked his head. She'd sculpted her face too, giving herself masculine features. Steris's eyes were bulging. At least that was worth seeing.

"You're . . ." Steris said. "You'll become a . . ."

"A man?" MeLaan asked. "Yeah. It'll look better when I've decided on the right body. Need to settle on a voice, too." She looked around the room. "Um, is this a problem?"

Everyone looked at Wayne for some reason. He thought for a moment, then shrugged. Maybe he should have given his shoes to *her.*

"You don't *mind*?" Steris demanded of him.

"It's still her."

"But she looks like a man!"

"So does the lady what runs this house," Wayne said, "but she has kids, so someone still decided to take her an—"

"It will do, MeLaan," Wax said, resting a hand on Steris's arm. "Assuming you can get into the party."

"Don't worry about that," she said, spinning around. "I will get in, and be ready to give you support. But this is your play, Ladrian, not mine. You're the detective; I'm just around for the punchy-punchy, stabby-stabby."

She closed the door. Wayne shook his head. *Now that, that's a situation a man don't rightly encounter all that often. . . .* Well, he'd found occasion to be an old lady now and then, so it made sense to him. It was probably good for a woman to be a fellow once in a while, if only to offer some perspective. Easier to piss too. Couldn't discount that.

"She assumes," Wax said, "that our detective style isn't *normally* the punchy-punchy, stabby-stabby type."

"To be fair," Wayne said, "it's usually a more shooty-shooty, whacky-whacky type."

Marasi rubbed her forehead. "Why are we having this conversation?"

"Because we're tired," Wax said. "Get some sleep, everyone. Wayne, you're going to go with Marasi tonight and dig up some graves." He took a deep breath. "And I, unfortunately, am going to a party."

11

Wearing a formal cravat and jacket reminded Wax of the year after he'd left the Village. A year when his uncle had gleefully wrapped him in the packaging of a young nobleman and presented him to the city's elite, feeling he'd won some kind of war when Wax was expelled from Terris society.

Wax had moved back in with his parents, of course. But it had been his uncle who had overseen his education, grooming him specifically as heir to the house. After that time in the Village, Wax's life had grown to be less and less about his immediate family—he'd barely seen his parents during that year, despite living with them.

That was when his uncle's grip had really started to strangle him. Wax tapped his fingers on the armrest of his carriage, remembering those parties. How much were his memories of them colored by his uncle's presence?

The carriage eventually pulled up before a resplendent mansion with stained-glass windows and limelights burning outside. A classical style of lighting, though the interior had little in common with the ancient keeps of lore it was meant to evoke—as he well knew from the floor plans he'd memorized earlier today, while the others were sleeping.

This mansion was more sprawling than imposing, with a multi-peaked roof design, like the profile of a mountain range. A line of carriages waited to pull through the coach portico and drop off their occupants.

"You're nervous," Steris said, laying her hand on his arm. She wore white lace gloves, and her dress—which she'd fretted over for at least an hour—was one of the filmy and gauzy ones that the most fashionable ladies in Elendel were wearing this year. The skirt was more full and cloudlike than the more traditional gowns Steris usually favored.

He'd been surprised when she'd chosen it. Most of her wardrobe, especially on this trip, was chosen for utility. Why wear this now?

"I'm not nervous," Wax said, "I'm contemplative."

"Shall we go over the plan?"

"What plan?" Wax said.

ReLuur, in his ravings, had directed them toward this party of Kelesina Shores, who was a lady of some prestige in New Seran—and who he implied was connected to all this. She was their best lead, though ReLuur's notebook had also listed five other families he thought were of interest.

The problem was, none of those notes mentioned *why* they were of interest—or what it was ReLuur thought they knew. Why would a group of lords and ladies of the outer cities elite have anything to do with an ancient archaeological relic? True, some noblemen liked to consider themselves "gentlemen adventurers." But those types mostly sat around smoking cigars and talking. At least that fop Jak actually left his rusting house.

Time wore on, as carriages moved up the drive with all the speed of a line of cows on a hot day. Finally, Wax kicked open his door. "Let's walk."

"Oh dear," Steris said with a sigh. "Again?"

"Don't tell me you didn't plan for this."

"I did. But this line isn't that long, Lord Waxillium. Don't you think this time maybe we should wait?"

"I can see the rusting front doors," Wax said, pointing. "We can walk to them in thirty seconds. Or we can sit here and wait as pompous people waddle out of their seats and fuss with their scarves."

"I see the night is starting off on the right foot," Steris said. Wax hopped down, ignoring the footman's offered hand. He waved the man back, and helped Steris from the vehicle himself. "Go ahead and park," he called to the coachman. "We'll call for you when we're done." He hesitated. "If you hear gunshots, go back to the hotel. We'll make our own way."

The coachman started, but nodded. Wax held his arm out for Steris, and the two strolled along the path into the mansion grounds, passing carriages full of people who seemed to be trying to glare at them without actually looking in their direction.

"I've prepared a list for you," Steris said.

"I'm so surprised."

"Now, no complaining, Waxillium. It will help. I've put the list in this little book," Steris said, producing a palm-sized notebook, "for ease of reference. Each page contains a conversation opener, indexed to the people it will likely work best upon. The numbers below list ways you could segue the conversation into useful areas and perhaps figure out what our targets are up to, and what their connection is to the Bands of Mourning."

"I'm not socially incompetent, Steris," Wax said. "I can make small talk."

"I know that," Steris said, "but I'd rather avoid an incident like the Cett party. . . ."

"Which Cett party?"

"The one where you head-butted someone."

He cocked his head. "Oh, right. That smarmy little man with the ridiculous mustache."

"Lord Westweather Cett," Steris said. "Heir to the house fortune."

"Right, right . . ." Wax said. "Stupid Cetts. In my defense, he did call me out. Demanding to duel a Coinshot. I probably saved his life."

"By breaking his nose." She held up her hand. "I am not requesting justifications or explanations, Lord Waxillium. I merely thought I'd do what I could to help."

He grumbled, but took the book, flipping through it by lamplight as they walked across the grounds. At the back of the book were descriptions of the various people likely to be at the party. He'd memorized some descriptions VenDell had sent, but this list was far more extensive.

As usual, Steris had done her research. He smiled, tucking the book into his jacket pocket. Where had she found the time? They continued up the path, though Wax froze as he heard rustling in the shrubbery nearby. He burned steel instantly, noticing some moving points of metal, and his hand went to the pistol under his jacket.

A dirty face peered out and grinned. The eyes were milky white. "Clips for the poor, good sir," the beggar said, stretching out a hand and exposing long, unkempt fingernails and a ragged shirt.

Wax kept his hand on his weapon, studying the man.

Steris cocked her head. "Are you wearing cologne, beggar?"

Wax nodded as he too smelled it, faintly.

The beggar started, as if surprised, then grinned. "It's got a good kick to it, my lady."

"You've been *drinking* cologne?" Steris asked. "Well, that can't be healthy."

"You should be away from here, beggar," Wax said, eyeing the cluster of attendants and coachmen closer to the building's entrance. "These are private grounds."

"Oh, my lord, I know it, I do." The beggar laughed. "I own the place, technically. Now, regarding those coins for old Hoid, my *good* lord . . ." He pushed his hand forward farther, eyes staring sightlessly.

Wax dug in his pocket. "Here." He tossed the man a banknote. "Get off the grounds and find yourself a proper drink."

"A generous lord indeed!" the beggar said, dropping to his knees and fishing for the banknote. "But too much! Far too much!"

Wax took Steris's arm again, walking her toward the imposing front doors.

"My lord!" the beggar screeched. "Your change!"

He saw the blue line moving and reacted immediately, spinning and catching the coin, which had been hurled with exacting accuracy at his head. So, not blind after all. Wax snorted, pocketing the coin as a passing groundsman saw the beggar and shouted, "Not you again!"

The beggar cackled and disappeared back into the shrubs.

"What was *that* about?" Steris asked.

"Damned if I know," Wax said. "Shall we?"

They proceeded down the row of waiting carriages, and though the line had sped up during their stroll, they still reached the front doors before they otherwise would have. Wax tipped his head toward a large woman who barely fit through the door of her carriage, then strode up the steps with Steris on his arm.

He presented his card at the door, though they would know to watch for him. This was no simple reception; this was about politics. There would probably be only one official speech—that of the host to the attendees—but everyone knew why they were here. To mingle, share ideas, and likely be invited to donate to one of many causes reflecting outer cities interests.

Wax passed the doorkeeper, who cleared his throat and pointed toward an alcove in the side of the entryway. There, servants were taking hats, coats, and shawls.

"We've nothing to check," Wax said, "thank you."

The man took Wax's arm gently as he tried to proceed. "The lady of the house has asked that all attendees be unburdened of items of a vulgar nature, my lord. For the safety of all parties attending."

Wax blinked, then finally got it. "We have to check weapons? You're kidding."

The tall man said nothing.

"I don't think he's the joking type," Steris noted.

"You realize," Wax said, "that I'm a Coinshot. I could kill a dozen people with your cufflinks."

"We'd appreciate it if you didn't," the doorkeeper said. "If you please, Lord Ladrian, there are to be *no* exceptions. Do we need to call the house Lurcher to make certain you are being honest with us?"

"No," Wax said, pulling his arm free. "But if something goes wrong tonight, you're going to wish we'd never had this conversation." He walked with Steris to the counter where white-gloved servants were taking hats in exchange for tickets. He reluctantly took Vindication from the holster under his arm and set her on the counter.

"Is that all, my lord?" the woman there asked.

He hesitated, then sighed and knelt, pulling his backup gun—a tiny two-shotter—from the holster on his calf. He dropped it onto the counter.

"Might we have a look in the lady's purse?" the servant asked.

Steris submitted.

"You realize," Wax said, "that I'm a deputized constable. If anyone should be armed, it's me."

The servants said nothing, though they seemed embarrassed as they handed back Steris's purse and gave Wax a ticket for his weapons.

"Let's go," he said, pocketing the pasteboard and trying—unsuccessfully—to hide his annoyance. Together they approached the ballroom.

Wayne liked how banks worked. They had *style*. Many people, they'd keep their money out of sight, hidden under beds and some such. What was the fun of that? But a bank . . . a bank was a target. Building a place like this, then stuffing it full of cash, was like climbing atop a hill and daring anyone who approached to try to knock you off.

He figured that must be the point. The sport of it. Why else would they put so much valuable stuff together in one place? It was supposed to be a message, proof to the little people that some folks were so rich, they could use their money to build a house for their money and *still* have enough money left to *fill* that house.

Robbing such a place was suicide. So all that potential thieves could do was stand outside and salivate, thinking of the stuff inside. Really, a bank was like a giant sign erected to say "rust off" to everyone who passed by.

Which was magnificent.

He and Marasi stopped on the long flight of steps up to the front, which was set with stained-glass windows and banners, after the classical cantonesque style of architecture. Marasi wanted to come here before the graveyards. Something about the bank records leading them to the right location.

"All right, see," Wayne said, "I've got it figured out. I'm gonna be a rich fellow. Made loads off of the sweat and blood o' lesser men. Only I won't say it like that, 'cuz I'll be in *character,* you see."

"Is that so?" Marasi said, starting up the steps.

"Yup," Wayne said, joining her. "Even brought me fancy hat." He held up a top hat and spun it on his finger.

"That hat belongs to Waxillium."

"No it don't," Wayne said, putting it on. "I gave 'im a rat for it."

"A . . . rat?"

"Minus the tail," Wayne said. "On account of this hat bein' kinda dusty when I took it. Anyway, I'll be the rich fellow. You be my younger brother's daughter."

"I'm not young enough to be your niece," Marasi said. "At least not one who . . ." She trailed off as Wayne scrunched his face up good, emphasizing wrinkles, and brought out his fake mustache. ". . . Right," she added. "I'd forgotten about that."

"Now, my dear," Wayne said, "while I am distracting the employees of this fine establishment with a depository request, you shall steal into their records room and acquaint yourself with the requisite information. It shouldn't test your skills, as I shall regale them with descriptions of my wealth and prestige, which should draw the attention of most who are still working at this late hour."

"Wonderful," Marasi said.

"As an aside, my dear," Wayne added, "I am not fond at all of your dalliance with that farmhand upon our estate. He is far beneath you in stature, and your indiscretion will surely besmirch our good name."

"Oh please."

"Plus he has warts," Wayne added as they reached the top of the steps. "And is prone to extreme bouts of flatulence. And—"

"Are you going to talk about this the entire time?"

"Of course! The bank's employees need to know how I toil with the next generation and its woefully inadequate ability to make decisions *my* generation found simple and obvious."

"Grand," Marasi said, pushing through the bank's broad glass doors.

A banker immediately rushed up to them. "I'm sorry. We're *very* near closing."

"My good man!" Wayne began. "I'm certain you can make time for the investment opportunity you will soon find present in—"

"We're from the Elendel Constabulary," Marasi interrupted, taking out her engraved credential plate and holding it up. "Captain Marasi Colms. I'd like to look over some of your deposit records. Shouldn't take but a few minutes, and I'll be out of your hair."

Wayne floundered, then gaped at her as the banker—a squat, swarthy man who had a gut like a cannonball and a head to match—took her certification and looked it over. That . . . that was *cheating*!

"What records do you need?" the banker asked guardedly.

"Do any of these people have accounts with you?" Marasi asked, proffering a paper.

"I suppose I can check . . ." the banker said. He sighed and walked farther into the building to where a clerk sat going over ledgers. He slid through a door behind the desk, and Wayne could hear him muttering to himself in the room beyond.

"Now I've gotta say," Wayne said, pulling off the top hat, "that was the *worst* example of actin' I've ever seen. Who would believe that the rich uncle has a *constable* for a niece, anyway?"

"There's no need to lie when the truth will work just as well, Wayne."

"No need . . . Of *course* there's need! Why, what happens when we have to thump some people, then run off with their ledgers? They're gonna *know* it was us, and Wax'll have to pay a big heap of compensatory fines."

"Fortunately, we're not going to be thumping anyone."

"But—"

"No thumping."

Wayne sighed. Fat lot of fun this was going to be.

"I'll have you know that we take the privacy of our patrons very seriously," the banker explained, hand protectively on the ledgers he'd retrieved from the records room. They sat in his office now, and he had a little desk plaque that named him MR. ERIOLA. Neither of the others seemed to grasp why Wayne snickered when he read that.

"I understand," Marasi said, "but I have a healthy suspicion one of these men is a criminal. Certainly you don't want to abet their activities."

"I don't want to violate their trust in me either," the banker said. "What makes you so certain these men are criminals? Do you have any proof?"

"The proof," Marasi said, "will be in the numbers." She leaned forward. "Do you know how many crimes can be proven by looking at statistics?"

"Considering the question, I'm going to assume it's a nontrivial number," the banker said, leaning back in his chair and lacing his hands on his ample belly.

"Er, yes," Marasi said. "Most crimes can be traced to either passion or wealth. Where wealth is involved, numbers come into play—and where numbers come into play, forensic accounting gives us answers."

The banker didn't seem convinced—but then, in Wayne's estimation, he didn't seem completely human either. He was at least part dolphin. The man continued plying Marasi with questions, obviously stalling for some reason. That made Wayne uncomfortable. Usually when people stalled like that, it was so their mates could have time to arrive and administer a proper beating.

He bided his time playing with objects on the banker's desk, trying to build a tower of them, but he kept his eyes on the door. If someone *did* arrive to attack them, he'd have to toss Marasi out the window to get away.

A moment later the door swung open. Wayne grabbed for Marasi, his other hand going for one of his dueling canes, but it was only the clerk from outside. She bustled over to the banker—so Wayne didn't feel a bit guilty admiring her bustle, so to speak—and handed him a half sheet of paper.

"What's that?" Marasi asked as the woman left.

"Telegram," Wayne guessed, relaxing. "Checkin' up on us, are you?"

The banker hesitated, then turned the paper around. It contained a description of Wayne and Marasi, followed by the words, *They are indeed constables under my command. Please afford them every courtesy and liberty in your establishment—though do keep an eye on the short man, and check your till after he leaves.*

"Here, now," Wayne said. "That's right unfair. Those things cost a clip every five words to send, they do. Old Reddi wasted good money libelin' me."

"Technically, it's defamation," Marasi said.

"Yup," Wayne said, "manure, through and through."

"Def*amation,* Wayne, not . . . Oh, never mind." She met the eyes of the banker. "Are you satisfied?"

"I suppose," he said, then slid the ledgers over to her.

"Numbers," Marasi said, digging in her purse for a moment. She brought out a small book and tapped it with one finger. "This contains a list of the common wages for workers in the cemetery business, by the job they do." She pulled open the ledgers. "Now, looking at the deposits by our men in question, we can find patterns. Who is putting more money in the bank than their payroll would reasonably account for?"

"Surely this isn't enough to convict a man," the banker said.

"We're not looking to convict," Marasi said, looking through the first ledger. "I just need a little direction. . . ."

In the minutes that followed, Wayne got his tower to balance with six separate items, *including* the stapler, which left him feeling rather proud. Eventually, Marasi tapped on one of the ledgers.

"Well?" the banker asked. "Did you find your culprit?"

"Yes," Marasi said, sounding disturbed. "All of them."

". . . All of them."

"Every rotten one," Marasi said. "No pun intended." She took a deep breath, then slapped the ledger closed. "I guess I could have picked one at random, Mister Eriola. But still, it is good to know."

"To know what?"

"That they're all crooked," she said, and started fishing in her purse again. "I should have guessed. Most corpses are buried with *something* valuable, if only the clothing. No use letting that all rot away."

The banker paled. "They're selling the *clothing* off the *dead people*."

"That," Marasi said, slipping a small bottle of Syles brandy out of her purse and setting it on the table, "and perhaps any jewelry or other personal effects buried with the bodies."

"Hey," Wayne said. "I'm right dry in the throat, I am. That would sure hit me well, like a morning piss after a nine-pinter the night afore."

"That's horrible!" the banker said.

"Yes," Marasi said, "but if you think about it, not *too* horrifying. The only crimes being perpetrated here are against the dead, and their legal rights are questionable."

Wayne fished in his pocket a moment, then brought out a silver letter opener. Where did he get that? He set it on the table and took the drink, downing it in one shot.

"Thank you for your time, Mister Eriola," Marasi continued, taking the letter opener and sliding it toward the banker. "You've been very helpful."

The banker looked at the letter opener with a start, then checked his desk drawer. "Hey, that's *mine*," he said, reaching into the desk and pulling out something that looked like a piece of cord. "Is this . . . a rat's tail?"

"Longest I ever seen," Wayne said. "Quite a prize. Lucky man, you are."

"How in the world did you . . ." The banker looked from Wayne to Marasi, then rubbed his head. "Are we finished here?"

"Yes," Marasi said, standing. "Let's go, Wayne."

"Off to make an arrest?" the banker said, dropping the tail into the wastebasket, which was a crime in and of itself. The thing was almost two hands long!

"Arrest?" Marasi asked. "Nonsense, Mister Eriola. We aren't here to arrest anyone."

"Then what was the point of all that?"

"Why," Marasi said, "I had to know whom to employ, of course. Come along, Wayne."

12

So little had changed since Wax's youth. Oh, the people at this party wore slightly different clothing: formal waistcoats had grown stouter, and hemlines had risen to midcalf while necklines had plunged, with mere bits of gauze draping across the neck and down the shoulders.

The people, though, were the same. They weighed him, calculating his worth, hiding daggers behind ready smiles. He met their condescending nods, and didn't miss his guns as much as he would have thought. Those were not the right weapons for this fight.

"I used to be so nervous at these things," Wax said softly to Steris. "When I was a kid. That was when I still cared about their opinions, I guess. Before I learned how much power over a situation you gain when you decide that you don't care what others think of you."

Steris eyed a couple of passing ladies in their completely laceless gowns. "I'm not certain I agree. How you are perceived *is* important. For example, I'm regretting my choice of gown. I was shooting for fashionable, but fashion is different down here. I'm not in style; I'm avant-garde."

"I like it," Wax said. "It stands out."

"So does a pimple," Steris said. "Why don't you get us some drinks, and I'll take stock of the room and figure out where our targets are?"

Wax nodded in agreement. The grand ballroom was carpeted and adorned with golden chandeliers—though their candleholders glowed with electric lights. The ceiling wasn't terribly high, but the walls were colorfully decorated with false archways that each held a mural. Classical pieces, like the Ascendant Warrior rising above a flock of ravens—the typical depiction of the Lord Ruler's wraiths, of whom only Death himself remained.

Though nobody approached him, they also didn't avoid him. If anything they remained determinedly in his path, refusing to budge—then acted like they hadn't noticed him as he wove around them. He was from Elendel, their political enemy, and in not moving they made a statement.

Rusts, he hated these games.

The bar covered almost the entire length of the far wall, and was serviced by at least two dozen bartenders, so as to make absolutely certain none of the very important guests had to wait. He ordered wine for Steris and a simple gin and tonic for himself, which got him a raised eyebrow. Apparently that wasn't fancy enough. Should have ordered straight-up whiskey.

He turned and scanned the room as the bartender prepared the drinks. Soft music by a harpist helped cover the many conversations. It made him uncomfortable to admit that some of the casual discussions in a room like this could do more to affect the lives of the Basin's people than putting any criminal—no matter how vile—in prison.

Marasi is always talking about things like that, he thought. *How the lawkeeping of the future will be about statistics, not shotguns.* He tried to imagine a world where murders were prevented by careful civic planning, and found himself unable to see it. People would always kill.

Still, sometimes it was hard not to feel like the one chandelier in the room that still required candles.

"Your order, my lord," the bartender said, setting the drinks down on fancy cloth napkins, each embroidered with the date of the party. Those would be for the attendees to take as keepsakes.

Wax fished a coin from his pocket for a tip and slid it to the bartender. He grabbed his drinks to head back to Steris, but the bartender cleared his throat. The man held up the coin, and it was not a fivespin as Wax had meant to give him. In fact, it was unlike any coin Wax had ever seen.

"Was this a mistake, my lord?" the man asked. "I don't mean to be ungrateful, but I'd hate to take something that looks like a memento."

The symbols on that coin . . . Wax thought, stepping back to the bar. *They're the same ones as on the walls in the pictures ReLuur took.* He nearly overturned the wineglass of another guest in his haste to grab the coin back. He absently shoved the bartender another tip and held up the coin.

Those *were* the same symbols, or very similar. And it had a face on the back, that of a man looking straight outward, one eye pierced by a spike. The large coin was made of two different metals, an outside ring and an inner one.

The coin certainly didn't seem old. Was it new, or merely well-preserved? Rust and Ruin . . . how had this gotten into his pocket?

The beggar tossed it to me, Wax thought. But where had *he* gotten it? Were there more of these in circulation?

Troubled, he struck out to find Steris. As he walked, he passed Lady Kelesina, the party's hostess and the woman who was his eventual target. The older woman stood resplendent in a gown of black and silver, holding miniature court before a group of people asking after one of her civic projects.

Wax listened in for a moment, but didn't want to confront the woman yet. He eventually located Steris standing beside a tall, thin table near the corner. There weren't any chairs in the ballroom. No dancing either, though there was a dance floor raised an inch or two in the center of the chamber.

Wax set the coin on the table and slid it to Steris.

"What's this?" she asked.

"The coin that the beggar threw at me. Those symbols look similar to the ones in the pictures ReLuur took."

Steris pursed her lips, then turned the coin over and looked at the other side. "A face with one eye spiked through. Does it mean something?"

"No idea," Wax said. "I'm more interested in how that beggar got it—and why he threw it at me. It has to be a relic ReLuur found at that temple. Could he have lost it, or traded it to someone, in the city?"

He tapped the table with one finger, certain now that beggar had been something more than he pretended. He was equally certain that if he went hunting now, he'd find that the man had vanished.

Eventually, Wax pocketed the coin. "We have to hope that the answers are in this room somewhere. Assuming Kelesina really is involved."

"Then it's time get to work."

"I passed her back there. Shall we?"

"Not yet. See that couple over there? The man has on a maroon waistcoat."

Wax followed her nod. The couple she indicated were young, well-dressed, and smug. Great.

"That is Lord Gave Entrone," Steris said. "Your houses have had some minor business dealings—he's in textiles—which should give you an opening to speak with him."

"I've heard of him," Wax said. "I courted a cousin of his once. It went poorly."

"Well, he's *also* on the list your mad kandra made in his notebook, so he might know something. He's young, dynamic, and well-regarded—but not terribly important, so he'll work nicely as a first try."

"Right," Wax said, eyeing Entrone, who had drawn a crowd of several more young women as he told a story that involved lots of gesturing. He took a deep breath. "You want to take the lead?"

"It should be you."

"You sure? I can't help feeling I'd be better put to use with Marasi and Wayne, digging in graves—while you are comfortable here. You're good at these things, Steris. You really are—and *don't* give me any more of your rhetoric about being 'boring.'"

Her expression grew distant. "In this case, it's not that I'm boring, it's more that . . . I'm off. I've learned to fake being normal, but lists of prepared comments and jokes can only take me so far. People can sense that I'm not being authentic—that I don't like the things they like or think the way they do. Sometimes it amazes me that people like Wayne, or even those kandra, can be so startlingly human when I feel so alien."

He wished he could figure out how to keep her from saying things like that. He didn't know the right words; every time he tried to argue the point, it only seemed to make her withdraw.

Steris held out an arm to him. He took it, and together they crossed the room toward Lord Gave and the small crowd he had drawn. Wax had worried about how to break into the conversation, but as soon as he neared, the people talking to Gave stepped back and made room for him. His reputation and status preceded him, apparently.

"Why, Lord Waxillium!" Gave said with a knowing smile. "I was *delighted* when I heard that you were going to attend our little gathering! I've wanted to meet you for years."

Wax nodded to him, then to his date and a couple he'd been chatting with. Those two didn't retreat.

"How are you finding New Seran, my lord?" one of the ladies asked him.

"Seems mighty inconvenient to get around," Wax said. "Nice otherwise, though."

They laughed at that, as if he'd said something humorous. He frowned. What had he missed?

"I'm afraid," Gave said, "you won't find much to interest you here. New Seran is a quiet city."

"Oh, but what are you saying, Lord Gave!" the other young man said. "Don't misrepresent our town. The nightlife here is fantastic,

Lord Waxillium! And the symphony has been given a citation of excellence by two of your previous governors."

"Yes," Gave said, "but there aren't many shoot-outs."

The others gave him blank stares.

"I was a lawman," Wax told them, "in the Roughs."

"A . . ." one of the ladies said. "You oversaw a city's constable precinct?"

"No, he was a *real lawman,*" Gave said. "The 'ride a horse and shoot bandits' type. You should read the accounts—they're all the rage in the Elendel broadsheets."

The three others regarded him with bemused expressions. "How . . . unique," one of the ladies finally said.

"The accounts are exaggerated," Steris said quickly. "Lord Waxillium has only been *directly* responsible for the deaths of around a hundred people. Unless you include those who died of infection after he shot them—I'm still not sure how to count those."

"It was a difficult life," Wax said, looking toward Gave, who smiled behind his cup of wine, eyes twinkling. For a man like him, Wax and Steris were obviously good sport. "But that is behind me now. Lord Gave, I wanted to thank you for our years of mutually profitable trade."

"Oh, don't bring business into it, Lord Waxillium!" Gave said, with a tip of his wine. "This is a *party.*"

The others laughed. Again, Wax had no idea why.

Damn, he thought, looking between them. *I* am *rusty.* He'd complained, dragged his feet, but he hadn't expected to be *this* clumsy.

Focus. Gave knew something about the Bands of Mourning, or at least ReLuur had thought he did.

"Do you have any hobbies, Lord Gave?" Wax asked, earning an eager nod from Steris at the comment.

"Nothing of real note," Gave said.

"He *loves* archaeology!" his date said at the same time though. He gave her a dry look.

"Archaeology!" Wax said. "That's hardly unnotable, Lord Gave."

"He loves relics!" the lady said. "Spends hours at the auction house, snatching up anything he—"

"I like *history,*" Gave interjected. "Artwork from times past inspires me. But you, dear, are making me sound too much like one of those gentlemen adventurers." He sneered at the term. "I'm sure you saw the type up in the Roughs, Lord Waxillium. Men who'd spent their lives in society, but suddenly decided to go off seeking some kind of thrill or another where they don't belong."

Steris stiffened. Wax met the man's gaze levelly. The insult, veiled though it was, was similar to those he'd suffered in Elendel society.

"Better they try something new," Wax said, "as opposed to wasting their lives in the same old activities."

"My Lord Waxillium!" Gave said. "Disappointing one's family is *hardly* original! People have been doing it since the days of the Last Emperor."

Wax made a fist at his side. He was accustomed to insults, but this one still got under his skin. Perhaps it was because he was on edge, or perhaps it was because of his worry about his sister.

He pushed down his anger, Steris squeezing his arm, and tried another tactic. "Is your cousin well?"

"Valette? Most certainly. We are all pleased with her new marriage. I'm sorry your relationship didn't work out, but the man who courted her after you was *dreadful.* When titles are part of a union, it's always unpleasant to see what crawls out from the mists looking for a bone."

He didn't look at Steris as he said it. He didn't need to. That sly smile, so self-satisfied as he sipped his wine.

"You rat," Wax growled. "You rusting, spineless rat." He reached for his gun, which—fortunately—wasn't there.

The other three young nobles looked to him, shocked. Gave grinned in a cocky way before adopting an expression of outrage. "Excuse me," he said, turning his date by the arm and striding away. The others scuttled after.

Wax sighed, lowering his arm, still angry. "He did that *deliberately,*" he muttered. "Didn't he? He wanted an excuse to leave the conversation, so he insulted me. When that didn't work, he flung one at you, knowing I'd overreact."

"Hmmm . . ." Steris said. "Yes, you have the right of it." Steris nodded. Other people nearby made conversation, but they left an open space around Wax and Steris.

"I'm sorry," Wax said. "I let him get to me."

"That's why we tried him first," Steris said. "Good practice. And we *did* learn something. The archaeology comment prodded too close to something he didn't want to discuss. He turned to veiled insults to distract us."

Wax took a deep breath, shoving away his annoyance at this entire situation. "What now? Do we try another one?"

"No," Steris said, thoughtful. "We don't want our targets to know that we're approaching them specifically. If you interact with unaffiliated people in between, our pattern will be more difficult to spot."

"Right," Wax said, looking through the busy hall as the harpist retreated and a full band, with brass—something you'd never see at a party in Elendel—began setting up instruments in her place.

He and Steris sipped drinks as the music started. Though it was slow enough to encourage dancing with a partner, there was a pep to it Wax hadn't expected. He found he quite liked it. It seemed to be able to beat out his frustration, turn it to something more excited instead.

"Why don't you go there next?" Steris said, nodding toward a distinguished older woman with her grey hair in a bun. "That's Lady Felise Demoux, accompanied by her nephew. You've had business dealings with her; she's exactly the sort of person you'd be expected to seek out. I'll refill our drinks."

"Get me a seltzer," Wax said. "I'll need my mind clear for this."

Steris nodded, moving off through the crowd as people made way for dancing in the center of the room. Wax approached Lady Demoux and introduced himself with a card given to her nephew, then requested a dance, which was accepted.

Small talk. He could do small talk. *What is wrong with you, Wax?*

he thought at himself as he accompanied Lady Demoux to the dance floor. *You can interrogate a criminal without trouble. Why do you dread simple conversation?*

Part of him wanted to dismiss it as mere laziness. But that was his response to everything he didn't want to do—an excuse. What was it really? Why was he so reluctant?

It's because these are their rules. If I play by them, I accept their games. It felt like he was accepting their collar.

He turned to raise his hand to the side for Lady Demoux to take. However, as he did, a *different* woman slid into place and grasped his hand, towing him into the dancing and away from the perimeter. He was so surprised that he let it happen.

"Excuse me?" Wax said.

"No excuses necessary," the woman said, "I won't take but a moment of your time." She looked to be Terris, judging by her dark skin—though hers was darker than most he'd seen. Her hair was in tight braids, streaked with grey, and her face bore full, luscious lips. She took the lead in the dance, causing him to stumble.

"You realize," she said, "that you are a very rare specimen. Crasher: a Coinshot and a Skimmer."

"Neither are that rare," Wax said, "in terms of Metalborn."

"Ah, but any Twinborn combination is rare indeed. Mistings are one in a thousand; most Ferrings even more unusual, and their bloodlines constrained. To arrive at any specific combination of two is highly improbable. You are one of only three Crashers ever born, Lord Waxillium."

"What, really?"

"I cannot, of course, be one hundred percent certain of that figure. Infant mortality on Scadrial is not as bad as some regions, but still shockingly high. Tell me, have you ever tried increasing your weight while in midair?"

"Who are you?" Wax said, stepping into the dance and seizing back control, twisting her to his right.

"Nobody important," she said.

"Did my uncle send you?"

"I have little interest in your local politics, Lord Waxillium," she replied. "If you would kindly answer my questions, I will let you be."

He turned with her to the music. They danced more quickly than he was accustomed to, though the steps were familiar. The constant intrusion of those brass instruments drove the song, made his steps seem to spring. Why had he mentioned his uncle? Sloppy.

"I've increased my weight while moving," he said slowly. "It doesn't do anything—all things fall at the same speed, regardless of how heavy they are."

"Yes, the uniformity of gravitation," the woman said. "That's not what I'm curious about. What if you're soaring through the air on a Steelpush and you suddenly make yourself heavier. What happens?"

"I slow down—I'm so much heavier that it's harder to Push myself forward."

"Ahh . . ." the woman said softly. "So it is true."

"What?"

"Conservation of momentum," she said. "Lord Waxillium, when you store weight, are you storing mass, or are you changing the planet's ability to recognize you as something to attract? Is there a difference? Your answer gives me a clue. If you *slow* when you become heavier midflight, then that is not likely due to you having trouble Pushing, but due to the laws of physics."

She stepped back from him in the middle of the dance, releasing his hands and sidestepping another couple, who gave them a glare for interfering with the flow of the dance. She produced a card and handed it toward him. "Please experiment with this further and send me word. Thank you. Now, if I can just figure out why there's no redshift involved in speed bubbles . . ."

With that she wandered off the floor, leaving him befuddled in the middle of the dancing. Suddenly conscious of how many stares he was drawing, he lifted his chin and sauntered off the dance floor, where he found Lady Demoux and apologized to her profusely for the interruption. She allowed him to have the next dance, which passed without incident, save for Wax having to hear a protracted description of Lady Demoux's prize-winning hounds.

Once done, he tried to find the strange woman with the braids, even going so far as to approach the doorkeeper and ask after her. The card had an address in Elendel, but no name.

The doorman claimed he hadn't admitted anyone by that description, which left Wax even more troubled. His uncle *was* trying to breed Allomancers. A woman asking after the specifics of Allomantic powers couldn't be a coincidence, could it?

He did pass MeLaan. Square-chinned, standing over six feet tall, her masculine body bulged with muscles beneath her tuxedo, and she'd drawn a gaggle of interested young ladies. She winked at Wax as he passed, but he gave her no response.

Steris had a drink waiting for him at the table, where she was flipping through pages of her notebook and mumbling. As Wax neared, he noticed a young man approach and try to engage her in conversation, but she dismissed him with a wiggle of her fingers, not even looking up. The man, deflated, drifted away.

Wax stepped up to the table. "Not interested in dancing?"

"What would be the point?" she said.

"Well, I'm going out and dancing, so maybe you could too."

"You are lord of your house," Steris said absently, still reading. "You have political and economic obligations. Anyone who would want to do the same with me is simply trying to get to you, something for which I have no time."

"Either that," Wax said, "or he thought you were pretty."

Steris looked up from her notes and cocked her head, as if the thought hadn't even occurred to her. "I'm engaged."

"We're new here," Wax said, "largely unknown save to those who pay attention to Elendel politics. The lad probably didn't know who you were."

Steris blinked very pointedly. She actually seemed *troubled* by the idea that someone unknown might find her attractive. Wax smiled, reaching for the cup she'd set out for him. "What is this?"

"Soda water," she said.

He held it up to the light. "It's *yellow.*"

"All the rage here, apparently," Steris said. "With lemon flavoring."

Wax took a drink, then nearly choked.

"What?" Steris asked, alarmed. "Poison?"

"Sugar," Wax said. "About seven cups of it."

Steris took a sip, then pulled back. "How odd. It's like champagne, only . . . not."

Wax shook his head. What was wrong with people in this city?

"I've decided upon our next target," Steris said, pointing toward a man across the room leaning against the archway near some tanks of exotic fish. In his thirties, he wore his jacket unbuttoned with a kind of purposeful sloppiness. Occasionally, someone else would approach and talk to him for a short time, then move back out into the crowd.

"They're reporting to him?" Wax asked.

"Devlin Airs," Steris said with a nod. "Informant. You'll find his sort at any party. He's either one of the least important people in the room or one of the most important, depending upon the secrets you're interested in discovering. He was also on ReLuur's list."

Wax studied the man for a time, and when he looked back toward Steris, half of his fizzy yellow drink was gone. She looked innocently in the other direction.

"Probably best," she said, "if you approach him alone. His type doesn't like an audience."

"All right," Wax said, taking a deep breath.

"You can do this, Lord Waxillium."

He nodded.

"I mean it," Steris said, resting her hand on his. "Lord Waxillium, this is exactly what you've been doing for the last twenty years, in the Roughs."

"I could shoot people there, Steris."

"Could you really? Is that how you solved things? You couldn't get answers, so you shot somebody?"

"Well, I'd usually just punch them."

She gave him a raised eyebrow.

"To be honest, no, I didn't have to shoot—or punch—all that often.

But the rules *were* different. Hell, I could *make* the rules, if I needed to."

"Same goes here," Steris said. "These people know things that you need to know. You need to either trick them or trade with them. As you've always done."

"Perhaps you're right."

"Thank you. Besides, who knows? Maybe he'll pull a knife on you, and you'll get an excuse to punch him anyway."

"Don't get my hopes up," he said, then gave her a nod, and walked across the room.

The gates to the Seran New District Cemetery were topped with a crouching statue of the Survivor, scarred arms spread wide and gripping the metalwork arch on either side. Marasi felt dwarfed by the statue's looming intensity—brass cloak tassels spreading out in a radial flare behind him, his metallic face glaring down at those who entered. A spear through his back pierced the front of his chest, the polished tip emerging to hang a foot below the center of the arch.

When she and Wayne passed beneath it, Marasi felt as if it should drip blood upon her. She shivered, but didn't slow her step. She refused to be intimidated by the Survivor's glare. She'd been raised Survivorist, so the gruesome imagery associated with the religion was familiar to her.

It was just that every time she saw a depiction of the Survivor, his posture seemed so demanding. It was like he *wanted* people to recognize the contradiction in his religion. He commanded that people survive, yet the death imagery associated with him was a cruel reminder that they'd eventually fail in that task. Survivorism therefore was not about winning, but about lasting as long as you could before you lost.

The Survivor himself, of course, broke the rules. He always had. Doctrine explained he was not dead, but surviving—and planning to return in their time of greatest need. But if the end of the world hadn't been enough to get him to return in his glory, then what could *possibly* do so?

They wound through the graveyard, seeking the caretaker's building. Evening had fallen, and the mists had decided to come out tonight. She tried not to take that as any kind of sign, but it *did* make the place look extra creepy. Gravestones and statues were shadowed in the churning mists. Some nights, she saw the mists as playful. Tonight their unpredictable motions seemed more a crowd of shifting spirits, watching her and Wayne, angered at their intrusion.

Wayne started whistling. That sent another shiver up Marasi's spine. Fortunately, the gravekeeper's building was now only a short distance up the path—she could see its lights creating a bubble of yellow in the mists.

She stuck close to Wayne, *not* because she felt more comfortable having him beside her. "Our target is a man named Dechamp," she said. "Should be the night gravekeeper, and one of those whose ledger entries show regular upticks in income. He's grave robbing for sure. In fact, this cemetery showed the highest frequency of that, *and* the ledgers listed it as the place the city pays to take care of unidentified bodies. I'm reasonably certain the kandra's remains ended up here; we just need to find this man and get him to dig for us."

Wayne nodded.

"This won't be like with the banker," Marasi said. "Who was reluctant, but ultimately helpful."

"Really?" Wayne said. "Because I thought he was kind of a tit. . . ."

"Focus, Wayne. We'll have to use the full weight of the law here, to push this man. I suspect we'll have to offer clemency to get him to help us."

"Wait, wait," Wayne said, stopping on the path, tendrils of mist curling around his brow, "you're gonna flash your goods at him *too*?"

"I really wish you wouldn't phrase it that way."

"Now, listen," Wayne said softly, "you were right 'bout the banker. You did damn good work in there, Marasi, and I'm not too proud to admit it. But authority works different out here in the world of regular men. You bring out your credentials with this fellow, and I guarantee he's gonna react like a rabbit. Find the nearest hole, hunker down, not say a word."

"Good interrogation techniques—"

"Ain't worth beans if you're in a hurry," Wayne said, "which we are. I'm puttin' my foot down." He hesitated. "'Sides, I already lifted your credentials."

"You . . ." Marasi started, then rummaged through her purse and discovered that the small, engraved plate that held her constable's credentials was gone, replaced with an empty bottle of Syles brandy. "Oh please. This isn't worth *nearly* the same as those credentials."

"I know I gave you a good deal," Wayne said. "'Cuz yours is only a bit of useless metal—which is about what it'd be worth here, in this cemetery."

"You *will* give the credentials back after we're done."

"Sure. If you fill that bottle in trade."

"But you said—"

"Convenience fee," Wayne said, then looked up the path toward the gravekeeper's building. He took his top hat off and stomped on it.

Marasi stepped back, hand to her breast, as Wayne ground the hat beneath his heel, then brought it up and twisted it the other way. Finally, after inspecting it critically, he pulled a knife off his metal-belt and cut a hole in the hat's side. He tossed aside his duster and cut off one of the straps of his suspenders.

When the top hat went back on his head, he looked shockingly like a vagrant. Of course, he was always one step from *that*, but it was still surprising how much of a difference two little changes could make. He spun the knife in his hand and inspected Marasi with a critical eye. The sun had set completely, but with the light of the city diffusing through the mists, it could actually be brighter on a night like this than on one without any mist.

"What?" Marasi said, uncomfortable.

"You look too fancy," Wayne said.

Marasi glanced down at herself. She wore a simple, sky-blue day dress, hem at midcalf, laced up the sleeves and neck. "This is pretty ordinary, Wayne."

"Not for what we'll be doin'."

"I can be your employer or something."

"Men like this don't open up none if there's someone respectable about." He spun the knife in his hand, then reached for her chest.

"Wayne!" she said.

"Don't be so stiff. You want this done right, right?"

She sighed. "Don't get too frisky."

"Sooner get frisky with a lion, Mara. That I would."

He cut the opaque lace window out of her bodice, leaving her with a plunging neckline. Her sleeves went next, shortened by a good foot to above the elbow. He took the lace there and tied it like a ribbon around her dress right beneath her breasts, then pulled the laces on the back of the dress more tightly. That lifted and thrust her upper chest outward in a decidedly scandalous way.

From there, he made a few choice slits on the skirt before rubbing dirt on the bottom parts. He stepped back, tapping his cheek thoughtfully, and nodded.

Marasi looked down, inspecting his handiwork, and was actually impressed. Beyond enhancing the bust, he'd cut along seams, pulling out threads, and the effect wasn't so much *ruined* as *used*.

"Everyone looks at the chest first," Wayne said, "even women, which is kinda strange, but that's the way it is. Like this, nobody will care that the dirt looks too fresh and the rest of the dress ain't aged properly."

"Wayne, I'm shocked," she said. "You're an *excellent* seamstress."

"Clothes is fun to play with. Ain't no reason that can't be manly." His eyes lingered on her chest.

"Wayne."

"Sorry, sorry. Just gettin' into character, you know." He waved for her to follow, and they headed up the path. As they did, Marasi realized something.

She wasn't blushing.

Well, that's a first, she thought, growing strangely confident.

“Try not to open your mouth much,” Wayne advised as they approached the hut. “On account of you normally soundin’ way too smart.”

“I’ll see what I can do.”

He snapped a branch off a tree they passed, spun it around his finger, then held it down before himself like a gnarled cane. Together they approached the glowing building: a small, thatched structure that had a few weathered mistwraith statues sticking up from its mossy yard. The statues—made in the form of skeletons with skin pulled tight across the skulls—were traditionally thought to ward away the real things, as mistwraiths could be very territorial. Marasi suspected the creatures could tell the difference between real and stone members of their species—but of course, scientists claimed that the mistwraiths hadn’t even survived the Catacendre in the first place. So the question was probably moot.

A greasy little man with a blond ponytail whistled to himself beside the hut, sharpening his shovel with a whetstone. *Who sharpens a shovel?* Marasi thought as Wayne presented himself, chest thrust out, improvised cane before him as if he were some grand attendee at a ball.

“And are you,” Wayne said, “bein’ the one called Dezchamp?”

“Dechamp,” the man said, looking up lazily. “Now, now. Did I leave that gate open again? I am supposed to be closin’ the thing each night. I’ll have to be askin’ you to leave this premises, sir.”

“I’ll make my way out, then,” Wayne said, pointing with his cane-stick, yet not moving. “But afore I go, I would like to make you aware of a special business proposition regardin’ you and me.”

Wayne had exaggerated his accent to the point that Marasi had to pay strict attention to make out what he was saying. Beyond that, there was a more staccato sense to it. More stressed syllables, more of a rhythm to the sentences. It was, she realized, very similar to the accent the gravekeeper was using.

“I’m a honest man, I am,” Dechamp said, drawing his whetstone along his shovel. “I don’t have no business I needs to discuss, particularly not at a time of night like this one here.”

"Oh, I've heard of your honesty," Wayne said, rolling back on his heels, hands on his cane before him. "Heard it spoken of from one street to the next. Everyone's talkin' 'bout your honesty, Dechamp. It's a right *keen* topic of interest."

"If everyone's sayin' so much," Dechamp replied, "then you'll know I already got plenty of people with whom to share my honesty. I'm . . . gainfully contracted."

"That don't matter none for our business."

"I do think it might."

"See, it won't," Wayne said, "on account of my needin' only one special little item, that nobody else would find of interest."

Dechamp looked Wayne up and down. Then he eyed Marasi, and his eyes lingered as Wayne had said they would. Finally Dechamp smiled and stood, calling into the hut. "Boy? Boy!"

A child scrambled out into the mists, bleary-eyed and wearing a dirty smock and trousers. "Sir?"

"Go and kindly do a round of the yard," Dechamp said. "Make sure we ain't disturbed."

The boy grew wide-eyed, then nodded and scampered off into the mists. Dechamp rested his shovel on his shoulder, pocketing the whetstone. "Now, what can I be callin' you, good sir?"

"Mister Coins will do," Wayne said. "And I'll be callin' you Mister Smart Man, for the decision you just made right here and now."

He was changing his accent. It was subtle, but Marasi could tell he'd shifted it faintly.

"Nothing is set as of yet," Dechamp said. "I just like to give that boy some exercise now and then. Keeps his health."

"Of course," Wayne said. "And I understand completely that nothing has been promised. But I tell you, this thing I want, ain't *nobody* else goin' to give you a clip for it."

"If that's so, then why are you so keen for it?"

"Sentimental value," Wayne said. "It belonged to a friend, and it was really hard for him to part with it."

Marasi snorted in surprise at that one, drawing Dechamp's attention.

"Are you the friend?"

"I don't speak skaa," she said in the ancient Terris language. *"Could you perhaps talk in Terris, please?"*

Wayne winked at her. "No use, Dechamp. I can't get her to speak proper, no matter how much I try. But she's fine to look at, ain't she?"

He nodded slowly. "Iffen this item be under my watchful care, where might it be found?"

"There was a right tragic incident in town a few weeks back," Wayne said. "Explosives. People dead. I hear they brought the pieces to you."

"Bilmy runs the day shift," Dechamp said. "He brought 'em in. The ones what weren't claimed, the city put in a nice little grave. They was mostly beggars and whores."

"And right undeservin' of death," Wayne said, taking off his hat and putting it over his breast. "Let's go see them."

"You want to go *tonight*?"

"Iffen it ain't too much a sweat."

"Not much sweat, Mister Coins," Dechamp said, "but your name had better match your intentions."

Wayne promptly got out a few banknotes and waved them. Dechamp snatched them, sniffed them for some reason, then shoved them in his pocket. "Well, those ain't coins, but they'll do. Come on, then."

He took out an oil lantern, then led them into the mists.

"You changed your accent," Marasi whispered to Wayne as they followed a short distance behind.

"Aged it back a tad," Wayne explained softly. "Used the accent of a generation past."

"There's a difference?"

He looked shocked. "Of *course* there is, woman. Made me sound older, like his parents. More authority." He shook his head, as if he couldn't believe she'd even asked.

Dechamp's lantern reflected off the mists as they walked, and that actually made it harder to see in the night, but he'd probably need it when digging. It did little to dispel the eeriness of gravestones broken by the occasional twisted mistwraith image. She understood, logically, why the tradition would have grown up. If there was one place you wanted to keep scavengers away from, it would be the graveyard. Except that the place had its own set of human scavengers, so the statues weren't working.

"Now," Dechamp said, and Wayne caught up to listen, "I'll have you know that I *am* an honest man."

"Of course," Wayne said.

"But I'm also a thrifty man."

"Ain't we all," Wayne said. "I never buys the fancy beer, even when it's last call and the bartender halves it to empty the barrel."

"You're a man after my own heart, then," Dechamp said. "Thrifty. What's the good of lettin' things rot and waste away, I says. The Survivor, he didn't waste nothing useful."

"Except noblemen," Wayne said. "Wasted a fair number o' them."

"Wasn't a waste," Dechamp said, chuckling. "That there was *weapons* testing. Gotta make sure your knives is workin'."

"Indeed," Wayne said. "Why, sometimes the sharp ends on mine need *lotsa* testin'. To make sure they don't break down in the middle of a good killin'."

They shared a laugh, and Marasi shook her head. Wayne was in his element—he could talk about stabbing rich people all day long. Never mind that he himself was wealthier, now, than most of Elendel.

She didn't much care to listen to them as they continued to laugh and joke, but unfortunately she also didn't want to get too far away in this darkness. Yes, the mists were supposed to belong to the Survivor, but *rusts,* every second tombstone looked like a figure stumbling toward her in the night.

Eventually the gravekeeper led them to a freshly filled grave tucked away behind a few larger mausoleums. It was unmarked save for the sign of the spear, carved in stone and set into the dirt. Nearby, a few other new graves—these open—awaited corpses.

"You might want to grab a seat," Dechamp said, hefting his shovel. "This'll go fast, since the grave is upturned, but not *that* fast. And you might tell the lady to watch the other way. There's no tellin' what bits I might toss up."

"Grab a seat . . ." Wayne said, looking around at the field of tombstones. "Where, my good man?"

"Anywhere," Dechamp said, starting to dig. "They don't care none. That's the motto of the gravekeeper, you know. Just remember, they don't care none. . . ."

And he set to it.

13

I *have to accept their rules,* Wax thought, crossing the room to the informant. *They're different, no matter what Steris says. But I* do *know them.*

He'd decided to stay in the Basin and do what he could here. He'd seen the dangers on the streets of Elendel, and had worked to fight them. But those were a lesser wound—it was like patching the cut while the rot festered up the arm.

Chasing down the Set's lesser minions . . . they probably *wanted* him doing those things. If he was going to protect the people, he was going to have to gun for more important targets. That meant keeping his temper, and it meant dancing and playing nice. It meant doing all the things his parents, and even his uncle, had tried to teach him.

Wax stopped near the alcove the informant, Devlin, occupied. The man was watching the nearby fish tank, which stood beneath a depiction of Tindwyl, Mother of Terris, perched on the walls during her last stand against the darkness. In the tank, tiny octopuses moved across the glass.

After a moment's waiting, the informant nodded toward him. Wax approached and rested his arm against the glass of the tank beside

Devlin, a short, handsome man with a hint of hair on his upper lip and chin.

"I expected you to be arrogant," Devlin noted.

"What makes you think that I'm not?"

"You waited," Devlin said.

"An arrogant man can still be polite," Wax said.

Devlin smiled. "I suppose he can be, Lord Waxillium." One of the little octopuses seized a passing fish in its tentacles and dropped from the side of the tank, holding the squirming fish and pulling it up toward its beak.

"They don't feed them," Devlin noted, "for a week or so before a party. They like the show they provide."

"Brutal," Wax said.

"Lady Kelesina imagines herself the predator," he said, "and we all her fish, invited in to swim and perhaps be consumed." Devlin smiled. "Of course, she doesn't see that she's in a cage as well."

"You know something about that cage?" Wax asked.

"It's the cage we're all in, Lord Waxillium! This Basin that Harmony created for us. So perfect, so *lush*. Nobody leaves."

"I did."

"To the Roughs," Devlin said, dismissive. "What's *beyond* them, Waxillium? Beyond the deserts? Across the seas? Nobody cares."

"I've heard it asked before."

"And has anyone put up the money to find the answers?"

Wax shook his head.

"People can ask questions," Devlin said, "but where there is no money, there are no answers."

Wax found himself chuckling, to which Devlin responded with a modest nod. He had developed a subtle way of explaining that he needed to be paid to give information. Oddly, despite the immediate—and somewhat crass—demand, Wax found himself more comfortable here than he'd been with Lord Gave.

Wax fished in his pocket and held out the strange coin. "Money," he said. "I have an interest in money."

Devlin took it, then cocked an eyebrow.

"If someone could tell me how this could be spent," Wax noted, "I would be enriched. Really, we all would be."

Devlin turned it over in his fingers. "Though I've never seen the exact image on this one, coins like these have been moving with some regularity through black-market antiquities auctions. I've been baffled as to why. There is no reason to keep them secret, and it would not be illegal to sell them in the open." He flipped the coin back to Wax.

He caught it with surprise.

"You didn't expect me to answer so frankly," Devlin said. "Why do people so often ask questions when they're not expecting answers?"

"Do you know anything else?" Wax asked.

"Gave bought a few," Devlin said, "then immediately stopped, and the pieces he purchased are no longer on display in his home."

Wax nodded thoughtfully and dug into his pocket for some money to offer the informant.

"Not here," Devlin said, rolling his eyes. "One hundred. Send a note of transfer to your bank and have them move it to my account."

"You'd trust me?" Wax asked.

"Lord Waxillium, it's my *job* to know whom to trust."

"It will be done, then. Assuming you have a little more for me."

"Whatever is being covered up," Devlin said, looking back toward the fish tank, "a good quarter of the nobility in the city is embroiled in it. First I was curious; now I'm terrified. It involves a massive building project to the northeast of here."

"What kind of building project?" Wax asked.

"No way of knowing," Devlin said. "Some farmers have seen it. Claimed Allomancers were involved. News died before it got here. Quashed. Smothered. Everything's been strange in New Seran lately. A murderer from the Roughs showing up, attacking the homes of rich Metalborn, then *you* come to a party . . ."

"This project to the northeast," Wax said. "Allomancers?"

"I don't have anything more on it," Devlin said, then tapped the fish tank, trying to frighten one of the little octopuses.

"What about the explosion a few weeks back?" Wax asked. "The one in the city?"

"An attack by this murderer from the Roughs, they say."

"Do you believe them?"

"It didn't kill any Metalborn," Devlin said.

None that you know of, Wax thought. Where did Hemalurgy fit into all of this?

Devlin stood and nodded to Wax, extending a hand as if in farewell.

"That's it?" Wax asked.

"Yes."

"Steep price for so little," Wax said, taking the hand.

Devlin leaned in, speaking softly, "Then let me give you a bit more. What you're involved in is dangerous, more than you can imagine. Get out. That's what I'm doing."

"I can't," Wax said as Devlin pulled back.

"I know you, lawman," Devlin said. "And I can tell you, the group you chase, you don't need to worry about them. They won't be a danger for decades, perhaps centuries. You're ignoring the bigger threat."

"Which is?" Wax asked.

"The rest of the people in this room," Devlin said, "the ones not involved in your little conspiracy—the ones who care only about how their cities are being treated."

"Pardon," Wax said, "but they don't seem like nearly the same level of danger to me."

"Then you aren't paying attention," Devlin said. "Personally, I'm curious to find out how many lives the Basin's first civil war claims. Good day, Lord Ladrian." He walked away, snapping his fingers as he passed a few people. One of them scuttled off to follow him.

Wax found himself growling softly. First that woman during the dancing, now this fellow. Wax felt like he was being jerked around on the end of someone's string. What had he even found out? Confirmation that artifacts were being sold? So someone else had found the place that ReLuur had evanotyped?

A building project, Wax thought. *Allomancers.*

Civil war.

Feeling cold, Wax moved back through the crowd. He rounded a group of people, noting that Steris was gone from their table—though she'd finished his cup of sweetened soda water before leaving. He turned and started through the crowd, looking for her.

That, by chance, brought him unexpectedly face-to-face with a statuesque woman with her hair in a bun and a ring on each finger. "Why, Lord Waxillium," Kelesina said, waving for her companions to withdraw, leaving her alone with Wax. "I was hoping to get a chance to speak with you."

He felt an immediate spike of panic—which he shot in the head and dumped in a lake. He would *not* be intimidated by one of Suit's lackies, no matter how wealthy or influential. "Lady Shores," he said, taking her hand and shaking it rather than kissing it. He might not be in the Roughs, but he didn't intend to take his eyes off his enemy.

"I hope you've been enjoying the party," she said. "The main address is about a half hour away; you might find it of note. We've invited the mayor of Bilming himself to speak. I'll be certain to get you a transcript to bring back to your peasant governor, so that you needn't worry about memorizing the details."

"That's very courteous of you."

"I—" she began.

Rusts, he was *tired* of letting someone else steer his conversation tonight.

"Have you seen Lord Gave?" Wax interrupted. "I insulted him by accident earlier. I wish to make amends."

"Gave?" Kelesina said. "Don't mind him, Waxillium. He's hardly worth the bother."

"Still," Wax said. "I feel like I'm wearing blocks of concrete on my feet and trying to dance! Every step I take, I smash *somebody's* toes. Rusts, I'd hoped that people down here wouldn't be as touchy as they are in Elendel."

She smiled. The words seemed to put her at ease, as if she were getting from him exactly what she expected.

Use that, Wax told himself. But how? This woman had decades' worth of experience moving in social circles. Steris could opine all she wanted about his virtues, but he'd spent years doing target practice instead of attending parties. How could he expect to match these people at their own game?

"I'm sorry to see you didn't bring your associate," Kelesina said.

"Wayne?" Wax asked, genuinely incredulous.

"Yes. I've had letters regarding him from friends in Elendel. He seems so colorful!"

"That's one way to put it," Wax said. "Pardon, Lady Kelesina, but I'd sooner bring my *horse* to a party. It's better behaved."

She laughed. "You are a charmer, Lord Waxillium."

This woman was guilty as sin, and he knew it. He could feel it. He did the next part by instinct. He pulled the coin from his pocket and held it up.

"Maybe you can answer something for me," he said, and realized he'd started to let a Roughs accent slip into his voice. *Thanks for that, Wayne.* "I was given this outside, by mistake I think. I asked some folks in here about it, and some of them got so pale in the face, I'd have thought they'd been shot."

Kelesina froze.

"Now personally," Wax said, flipping it over, "I think it has to do with those rumors of what's happenin' out northeast. Big dig in the ground, I'll bet? Well, I figure this must be from that. Relic from the old days. Mighty interesting, eh?"

"Don't be taken in by those rumors, Lord Waxillium," she said. "After stories circulated, people began coining things like those in the city to sell to the gullible."

"Is that so?" Wax said, trying to sound disappointed. "That's a shame. It sounded really interesting to me." He pocketed the coin as the band started another song. "Care for a dance?"

"Actually," she said, "I promised the next one already. Can I find you later, Lord Waxillium?"

"Sure, sure," he said, then gave her a nod as she withdrew. He stepped back to his table, watching her move pointedly through the crowd with frightened motions.

"Was that Lady *Kelesina*?" Steris said, joining him, holding another cup of the sweetened yellow drink.

"Yup," Wax said.

"I wasn't planning to talk to her until after the speech," Steris said, huffing. "You've thrown off my entire timeline."

"Sorry."

"It will have to do. What did you discover from her?"

"Nothing," Wax said, still watching Lady Kelesina as she met with some men in suits nearby. She kept her face calm, but the curt way she motioned . . . yes, she sure was agitated. "I told her what I'd discovered."

"You *what*?"

"I tipped her off that I was on to them," Wax said, "though I tried to act stupid. I don't know if she bought that part. Wayne's far better than I am at it. He's a natural, you see."

"You've ruined it then?"

"Maybe," Wax said. "But then, if this were the Roughs and I were confronting a criminal—but had no evidence—this is what I'd do. Let it slip that I was suspicious of them, then watch where they go."

Lady Kelesina stalked from the hall, leaving one of the other men to give apologies. Wax could almost hear them. *The lady has a matter of some urgency to take care of at the moment. She will return shortly.*

Steris followed his gaze.

"Ten notes says she's gone to contact Suit," Wax said, "and let him know that I'm on to them."

"Ah," Steris said.

He nodded. "I figured I couldn't outtalk her, no matter how hard I tried. But she's not used to being chased by the law. She will make simple mistakes, ones that even a rookie stagecoach robber would never make."

"We'll need to follow her somehow."

"That would be the plan," Wax said, drumming his fingers on the table. "I may have to start a fight and get thrown out."

"Lord Waxillium!" Steris said, then started fishing in her purse.

"I'm sorry. I'm having trouble thinking of something else." It was a weak plan though. Getting thrown out would likely alert Kelesina. "We need a distraction, an excuse to leave. Something believable, but not *too* disconcerting . . . What is that?"

Steris had removed a small vial of something from her purse. "Syrup of ipecac and saltroot," she said. "To induce vomiting."

He blinked in shock. "But why . . ."

"I had assumed they might try to poison us," Steris said. "Though I considered it only a small possibility, it's best to be prepared." She laughed uncomfortably.

Then she downed the whole thing.

Wax reached for her arm, but too late. He watched in horror as she stoppered the empty vial and tucked it into her purse. "You might want to get out of the splash radius, so to speak."

"But . . . Steris!" he said. "You'll end up humiliating yourself."

She closed her eyes. "Dear Lord Waxillium. Earlier, you spoke of the power of not caring about what others thought of you. Do you remember?"

"Yes."

"Well, you see," she said, opening her eyes and smiling, "I'm trying to practice that skill."

She proceeded to vomit all over the table.

The digging continued, and Marasi passed the time reading inscriptions on gravestones. Wayne, for his part, had settled down on a grave with his back to the stone, as if it were the most natural thing in the world. As she passed to check on the progress, she found him rummaging in his pocket. A moment later, he pulled a *sandwich* out and started eating. When he saw Marasi staring at him, he held it toward her, wagging it to see if she wanted a bite.

Feeling sick, she turned away from him and sought out more grave inscriptions. This was obviously the poorer section of the yard; plots were close together, and the markers were small and simple. The mist wove between them, curling around her as she knelt beside a stone, wiped off the moss, and read the memorial left for the child buried here. *Eliza Marin. 308–310. Ascend and be free.*

The steady sound of the gravedigger's shovel accompanied her as she moved between the graves. Soon she was too far from the light to make out the inscriptions. She sighed, turning, and found someone standing in the mists nearby.

She practically jumped out of her shoes, but the shifting mists—and the figure's too-steady posture—soon revealed this to be a statue. Marasi approached, frowning. Who had paid for a statue to be placed in the paupers' section of the graveyard? It was old, having sunken a foot or so on the right side as the ground shifted, tipping the statue askew. It was also masterly, an extraordinary figure cut of gorgeous black marble standing some eight feet tall and resplendent in a sweeping mistcloak.

Marasi rounded it, and was not surprised to find a feminine figure with short hair and a petite, heart-shaped face. The Ascendant Warrior was here, settled among the graves of the impoverished and the forgotten. Unlike Kelsier's statue, which had loomed over those who passed beneath his gaze, this one seemed about to take flight, one leg raised, eyes toward the sky.

"For years, I wanted to be you," Marasi whispered. "Every girl does, I suppose. Who wouldn't, after hearing the stories?" She'd even gone so far as to join the ladies' target club because she figured if she couldn't Push bits of metal around, a gun was the closest she could get.

"Were you ever insecure?" Marasi asked. "Or did you always know what to do? Did you get jealous? Frightened? Angry?"

If Vin had been an ordinary person at any point, the stories and songs had forgotten. They proclaimed her the Ascendant Warrior, the woman who had slain the Lord Ruler. A Mistborn and a legend who had carried the world itself upon her arms while Harmony prepared for divinity. She'd been able to kill with a glare, tease out secrets nobody else knew, and fight off armies of enraged koloss all on her own.

Extraordinary in every way. It was probably a good thing, or the world wouldn't have survived the War of Ash. But rusts . . . she left a hell of a reputation for the rest of them to try to live up to.

Marasi turned from the statue and crossed the springy ground back to Wayne and Dechamp. As she approached, the gravedigger climbed out and stuck his shovel into the earth, digging a flask from his pack and taking a protracted swig.

Marasi peeked into the grave. He had made good time—the earth had been dug out of the hole four feet deep.

"Wanna share that with a fellow?" Wayne asked Dechamp, standing.

Dechamp shook his head, screwing the lid back on his flask. "My gramps always said, never share your booze with a man who ain't shared his with you."

"But that way, nobody'd share their booze with anybody!"

"No," Dechamp said. "It just means I get twice as much." He rested his hand on his shovel, looking into the grave. Without the steady rhythm of his work, the graveyard was silent.

They had to be close to the bodies now. The next part would be unpleasant—sorting through the corpses for one that was in pieces, then checking that to see if it contained a spike. Her stomach churned at the thought. Wayne took another bite of his sandwich, hesitated, and cocked his head.

Then he grabbed Marasi under the arm and heaved, flipping her into the grave. The impact knocked the breath out of her.

Gunfire sounded above a moment later.

14

Marasi gasped as Wayne slid into the shallow grave, flopping down square on top of her. It knocked the wind out of her *again*.

Wayne grunted, and the gunshots stopped a moment later. Still trying to recover, Marasi stared up at the black sky and swirling mist. It took her a moment to realize that the mist was frozen in place.

"Speed bubble?" she asked.

"Yeah," Wayne said, then groaned, twisting to the side and putting his back to the earthen wall so he wasn't lying directly on her. His shoulder glistened with something wet.

"You've been hit."

"Three times," Wayne said, then winced as he turned his leg. "No, four." He sighed, then took a bite of his sandwich.

"So . . ."

"Give me a sec," he said.

She twisted in the grave and peeked up over the earthen lip. Nearby, Dechamp fell slowly—as if through molasses—toward the ground, blood spraying from several gunshot wounds, droplets hanging in the air. A vanishing muzzle flash from the darkness revealed the origin of the gunfire: a group of figures on the path, shadowed and nearly invisible. Bullets zipped through the mist, leaving trails.

"How'd you know?" she asked.

"They made the crickets stop," Wayne said. "Dechamp musta sold us out. I'd bet Wax's hat that he sent that boy to fetch these fellows."

"The Set was here first," Marasi said, her stomach sinking.

"Yeah." Wayne poked at one of the holes in his shirt, wiggling it around to check that the wound had healed. With his other hand, he stuffed the last bite of sandwich into his mouth, then joined her in peeking up over the lip of the grave. Above, a lethargically moving bullet hit the invisible edge of Wayne's speed bubble. In an eyeblink, it zipped across the air—barely a foot over Marasi's head—before hitting the other side, where it slowed down again.

She cringed belatedly. Anytime something entered a speed bubble, it was refracted, changing trajectory. While it was unlikely one would get bounced so radically that it would point downward toward them, it *was* possible. Beyond that, Wayne's bendalloy burned extremely quickly. He'd have to drop the bubble before too long.

"Plan?" Marasi asked.

"Not dyin'."

"Anything more detailed than that?"

"Not dyin' . . . today?"

She gave him a pointed look. Another pair of bullets zipped overhead while, outside the speed bubble, Dechamp's body hit the ground.

"We've gotta get close to them," Wayne said, slipping one of his dueling canes out from the loop on his belt.

"That's going to be hard," Marasi said. "I think they're scared of you."

"Yeah?" Wayne asked, sounding encouraged. "You really think?"

"They're unloading enough ammunition to take down a small army," Marasi said, ducking as a bullet entered the speed bubble, "and they opened fire even though Dechamp was caught in the barrage. While I doubt he meant much to them, it indicates they were scared enough that they didn't dare waste a moment to wait for him to climb back into the grave."

Wayne nodded slowly, grinning. "How 'bout that. I gots me a *reputation*. I wonder . . ."

Marasi glanced behind them. This grave was near several others that had been left open earlier, waiting for occupants. "Can you get your speed bubble big enough to include one of those other graves from in here?"

He followed her gaze, then rubbed his chin. "The closest one maybe, if I drop this bubble and move to the back of this grave before makin' another." He couldn't move a bubble once it was in place, and couldn't leave its confines without it dissipating.

"So we have to get them to come check on our corpses," Marasi said. "Which might be hard, if they're really that scared of you."

"Nah," Wayne said, "might actually be easy."

"How—"

"Runnin' outta time," Wayne said. "You still got that little popgun in your purse?"

She pulled out the small pistol. "It has terrible range," she said, "and only two shots."

"Don't matter none," Wayne said. "Once I drop this, fire it at the fellows. Then be ready to move."

She nodded.

"Here we go," Wayne said.

The bubble dropped.

Mists leaped back into motion, swirling above, and the sudden sound of gunfire pervaded the graveyard. Dechamp twitched, and he gasped, eyes going glassy in the lanternlight. Marasi waited until the assailants stopped shooting, the cracks of their guns echoing in the night. Then she leveled her little gun and squeezed off two shots toward the shadows.

She ducked back down, uncertain what that was supposed to have accomplished. "You realize we're now trapped *and* unarmed, Wayne."

“Yup,” he said. “But if those fellows are really bothered by my fearsome reputation . . .”

“What?” Marasi asked, glancing toward him as he peeked over the edge. A few cracks sounded as the dark figures fired back, but it wasn’t as frantic as before. What was . . .

“There!” Wayne said, leaping toward the back of the grave and then popping up a speed bubble. “Ha! They came prepared, they did. Good men.”

Marasi risked peeking up again. She came almost face-to-face with a spinning piece of dynamite frozen in the air, the wick spraying sparks and smoke that mixed with the mists. She yelped, scrambling back. It was almost to the speed bubble.

“Across we go,” Wayne said, taking off his top hat and tossing it out of their grave toward the next one. He scrambled after it. Marasi joined him, staying low and hoping that the attackers wouldn’t notice. Wayne’s speed bubble would make them blurs to the eyes of the men, but it was dark and the mists would help obscure things.

She slid across and down into the other grave, which was deeper than the first. Wayne nodded to her, then dropped the bubble.

Marasi pressed her back to the side of the grave, squeezed her eyes shut, plugged her ears, and counted in her head. She only reached two before an explosion shook the ground and dropped a wave of dirt into their grave. Rusts! People must have heard that halfway across the city.

She glanced at Wayne, who took out his other dueling cane and twirled one in each hand. She heard footsteps scraping outside, and imagined the shadowy attackers cautiously creeping up to check on people they’d supposedly killed.

Can you beat them on your own? Marasi half whispered, half mouthed at Wayne.

He grinned and mouthed back, *Does a guy wif no hands got itchy balls?* He grabbed the side of the grave and hauled himself out. The mists above froze a moment later as Marasi was caught in a speed bubble—Wayne, putting one up and trapping half the men nearby in it with him.

She was accustomed, by now, to the sound of wood on a man's skull, but it still made her wince. The speed bubble dropped as someone managed to get a shot off, but more groaning and cursing followed.

A short time later Wayne appeared at the top of the grave, backlit by the flickering lantern in the mists. He shoved his dueling canes into their loops, then knelt and held out his hand.

Marasi reached up to accept his help from the grave.

"Actually," Wayne said, not taking her hand, "I was hopin' you'd hand me my hat."

"We'll send for your carriage, Lord Waxillium," said the assistant house steward. "We're terribly sorry about the unfortunate occasion of your lady's distress. You're certain she ate nothing here that might disagree with her?"

"She had only drinks," Wax said, "and few of those at that."

The cook relaxed visibly. She towed one of the maids away by the arm as soon as she saw that Wax had noticed her. He stood in the doorway of a guest chamber, and behind him Steris lay on the bed, eyes closed.

The assistant steward—an aged Terriswoman in the proper robes—clicked her tongue softly, looking over her shoulder toward the vanishing cook and maid. Despite her displeasure, Wax could tell that she too was relieved to hear that the food at the party couldn't be blamed. No need for the other guests to worry.

A piercing voice echoed down the hallway. Someone—a man with a high-pitched tone—was announcing the reception's speaker. Wax could hear easily; the introducer was assisted by electric amplifiers. It seemed the Tarcsel girl's devices had spread even to New Seran. The assistant steward took an unconscious step back toward the ballroom.

"Feel free to go," Wax told her. "We'll wait here for a half hour or so to be certain my lady is well rested, and by then our carriage will certainly be waiting."

"If you're certain. . . ."

"I am," Wax said. "Just see to it that we're not disturbed. Miss Harms grows most discomforted by noises when she's ill."

The steward bowed and retreated down the hallway toward the ballroom. Wax clicked the door closed, then approached the bed where Steris lay. She cracked an eye open, then glanced at the door to be sure it was closed.

"How do you feel?" Wax asked.

"Nauseated," Steris said, half propping herself on one elbow. "That was a tad hasty on my part, wasn't it?"

"Haste was appreciated," Wax said, checking the wall clock. "I'll give it a few minutes to make sure the hall is clear, then duck out. I'm not certain how long Kelesina will be away, but I'll need to move quickly to learn anything."

Steris nodded. "Do you think they might have her here? Your sister, I mean."

"Unlikely," Wax said. "But anything is possible. I'll settle for a lead of any sort."

"What's she like?"

"She seemed like your average full-of-herself noblewoman. Certain that—"

"Not Lady Kelesina, Waxillium. Your sister."

"I . . ." Wax swallowed, checking the clock. "I haven't seen her in decades, Steris."

"But you work so eagerly to rescue her."

He sighed, settling down beside Steris. "She was always the bold one, when we were kids. I was careful, earnest, trying so hard to figure out what to do. And Telsin . . . she seemed to have it all in hand. Until I left the Village and she stayed."

"More Terris than you, then."

"Maybe. I always thought she hated the place, considering how often she found excuses to escape. Then she stayed." He shook his head. "I never knew her, Steris. Not as I should have. I was too focused on myself. I can't help feeling that I failed everyone—Mother, Father, Telsin herself—by not remaining close to her when I was out in the Roughs. And I'm failing them again by leaving her under my uncle's control."

Steris, still lying on the bed, squeezed his hand.

"I'll find her," Wax said. "I'll make it right. I ran to the Roughs, thinking I didn't need any of them. But as the years pass, Steris, I find I want less and less to be alone. I can't explain it, I guess. She's my *family*. My only family."

Outside, a new voice started talking. Introduction done, Lord Severington had begun his speech. Wax glanced at the clock, then stood. "All right. I need to go and explore while everyone else is distracted by the speech."

Steris nodded, then swung her feet over the side of the bed and took a deep breath.

"You should wait here," Wax said. "This could be dangerous."

"Have you forgotten what I said last night?" she asked.

"The safest place to be is most certainly *not* near me, Steris," Wax said.

"Regardless, you may need to escape quickly. There won't be time to come back for me. And if you're spotted, someone will wonder why you are alone—but if we're together, we can say we were just leaving, and were looking for the way to our carriage."

Those were good arguments. He reluctantly nodded, motioning for her to follow. She did so with alacrity, waiting beside the door as he opened it and peeked out. He could hear Lord Severington's voice even better.

". . . time to show those in Elendel that their tyranny is not only unjust, it is against the will of the Survivor, who died in the name of freedom. . . ."

The hallway was empty. Wax stepped out, Steris at his side. "Try not to look like you're sneaking," he suggested softly.

She nodded, and together they moved down a long hallway set with brass gas lamps that had been converted to electricity. According to the mansion layout he had memorized, the ballroom and these small guest quarters were in their own wing to the east. If they moved west along this hallway, took this corner . . .

They passed under an archway into the mansion's central atrium, where a stream ran through the center of the mansion—diverted from one of the waterfalls, then cascading down a set of arranged rocks covered in chimes. Only a few lights glowed on the walls, giving the atrium a dusklike feeling.

"That humidity must be awful for the mansion's woodwork," Steris noted. "What practical reason could they have to run a *river* through the middle of their house?"

"I'm sure the reasons aren't practical at all," Wax said. Nearby, a maid passed in from another doorway. She saw him and froze.

Wax glared at her, standing up straight, putting as much nobleman sneer into his expression as he could muster. The young woman didn't challenge them, but ducked her head and scuttled away, carrying her stack of linens.

They picked their way through the dim atrium. Above, broad glass windows would have given a view of the sky—but instead mist spun and swirled. Wax raised his fingers in greeting toward the distant mists, but stopped himself.

Harmony watched through those mists. Harmony the impotent, Harmony the meaningless. He set his jaw and turned away from the windows, leading Steris along a path in the indoor garden, which was set with small rocks and plants. From his maps, he guessed that Kelesina would be up on the second floor somewhere. As they followed the path northward, walking along the stream, he spotted a second-floor balcony.

"Honestly," Steris muttered, "how can they even know if the water is *sanitary*? A river running through their gardens wasn't enough? It has to go through the house itself?"

Wax smiled, studying that balcony. "I'm going to scout ahead up there. Speak loudly if someone confronts you. That will warn me, and I'll sneak back."

"Very well," Steris said.

He dug in his pocket for a few coins, feeling old-fashioned as he burned steel and prepared to jump.

"Do you want something more substantial?" Steris asked.

He glanced at her, then down at her purse. "They searched your purse."

"That they did," she said, then took the hem of her skirt, lifting it up to the side and revealing a small handgun strapped to her thigh. "I worried they'd do something like that. So I made other plans."

Wax grinned. "I could get used to having you around, Steris."

She blushed in the dim light. "I might, uh, need your help getting the thing off."

He knelt down, realizing that she'd used approximately seven rolls of tape to strap the gun in place. Also, being Steris, she'd worn shorts under the dress—in case she had to do what she was doing. Two pairs, judging by the bit of cloth he saw peeking out from under the top one.

Wax set to work extricating the gun. "I see you didn't want this coming off accidentally."

"I kept imagining it falling out and firing," Steris said, "mid-dance."

Wax grunted, working at her thigh beneath her dress. "You realize that if this were a play, this is exactly the point where someone would walk in on us."

"Lord Waxillium!" Steris said. "What kind of theater have you been attending?"

"The kind you find in the Roughs," Wax said, yanking the gun free. It proved to be one of his Riotings, a .22 six-shot he kept in his gun case but rarely used. It would do. He stood up, letting Steris settle her skirt back down. "Nice work."

"I tried a shotgun first," she said, blushing. "You should have seen me try to walk with one of those on my leg!"

"Stay out of sight, if you can," he told her, then dropped a coin and launched himself toward the upper balcony.

Marasi stepped into the gravekeeper's shack, clicking the door closed behind her. Wayne looked up from breaking the legs off a chair.

"Is that necessary?" Marasi asked.

"Dunno," he said, snapping off another one. "It's fun, though. How are our toughs?"

Marasi glanced out the window toward where a group of the local constables were carting away the last of the thugs. It turned out that setting off dynamite in the middle of the city was a fine way to get the attention of the authorities.

"They don't know anything," she said. "Hired muscle, paid and sent to do the hit. The ones who hired them mentioned your name, which turns out to have been a mistake."

"I'm famous," Wayne said happily, snapping another leg off. The hut had been thoroughly ransacked, drawers ripped out, cushions slit, furniture in shambles. Wayne looked at the chair leg he'd broken, apparently checking to see if it was hollow, then tossed it over his shoulder.

"We can try to follow the payments to those men," Marasi continued, "but I suspect that Suit was too careful for this to be traced. And there's no sign of the runner boy."

Wayne grunted, stomping on the floor in one section, then taking a few steps and stomping again.

"The police brought an Allomancer," Marasi continued. "And there's no metal in that grave, so if the spike was ever there, it isn't now." She sighed, leaning back against the wall. "Rust and Ruin . . . I hope Waxillium is having more luck than we are."

Wayne kicked a hole in the floor with the heel of his boot. Marasi perked up, then walked over as he fished around in a compartment he'd found.

"Aha!" he exclaimed.

"What is it?" Marasi asked.

Wayne brought out a bottle. "Dechamp's hidden booze stash."

"That's all?"

"All? It's great! A fellow like that hides his booze well. Too many other workers around to swipe the stuff."

"So we're at a dead end."

"Well, there's an account book on the desk there that I found under a false bottom in the drawer," Wayne noted, taking a swig of the dark liquid he'd found. "Lists everybody what paid the people here for a grave robbin' in the last few years."

Marasi started. "When did you find that?"

"First," Wayne said. "Hardly had to search for it. The booze though, that they hid well. Good priorities, these folks."

Marasi stepped over some stuffing from one of the sofas and picked up the ledger. It didn't belong to Dechamp, but to the graveyard as a whole. It listed plots, what had been found in them, and to whom it had been sold.

It's so the boss of the place can keep track of what they've sold and what they haven't, Marasi thought. And to keep track of his minions, to be certain they didn't get any ideas about making their own side business of grave robbing.

Next to an entry from a few days back was a note from the manager. *If anyone comes looking to investigate this plot, send to me immediately.*

Marasi closed the book, then fished from her pocket the paper that listed workers at the graveyard. "Come on," she said to Wayne. "We have one more stop to make tonight."

I ran alongside the car, matching pace with it while

the dock, I leapt into the air. (Continued below the fold!)

“Other improvements include reinfoced armor hulls,

protection?” (Continued on back.)

Broken Gondola Strands Passengers

An unidentified disturbance halted the Zinc Line yesterday evening about sunset, according to the New Seran Transportation Authority. The NSTA carried passengers home the old-fashioned way, on donkeys and rickshaws down the switchbacks. We see this as proof for the need of a back-up emergency transport system.

(Continued on back.)

NOW PLAYING! at the Uptown Trio Theater

THE DEN OF THE SURVIVOR!

A crew of freedom fighters

RISE UP AGAINST OPRESSION

and

OVERTHROW A CORRUPT GOV'T

Starring Javier DaLeuc and Penelope Portreau.

See the timeless story on stage until the end of next month!

Drink to the Health of Elendel!

Brand Whiskey has been grown and distilled exclusively in the Outer Cities. It's not sold in Elendel, so it never passes through the Lion's Den and is therefore never taxed. It tastes better than anything Central, and because it's made local, you can rest easy knowing that your coin hasn't lined any tyrant's pocket. Long live brand!

Looking for Adventure?

Basin Bill is looking for —YOU!—

Hundreds of cities were lost at the Final Ascension. Magical Artifacts, Riches, and Fame can be yours! Apply in person at Basin Bill's Old Time Pub & Playhouse.

Do Your Metal Tools Speak to You?

HELLO!

Your neighbors probably don't want to hear about it. But WE do! Visit 27 Ralen Place. Ask for K or N. Bring the talking metal with you.

Potential Allomancers Needed to Test New Metal Alloys—latest scientific breakthrough has created an ENTIRELY SAFE method of discovering new Allomantic abilities. Unlock your latent potential! Apply at Tenement 1447, Crate District, around the corner from Meprisable's Animal Rendering.

Write Scientific Fantasies!—B. Sablerfils, playwright of *A Hero for All Ages*, shows you how! Inquire at the University of New Seran.

THE RAVAGING LION OF ELENDEL

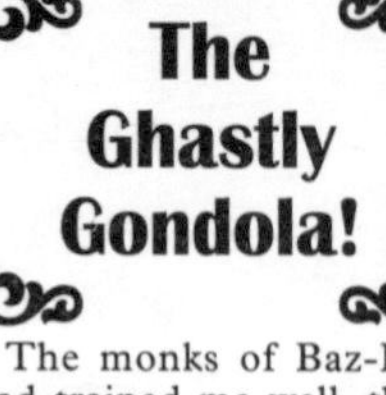

The Ghastly Gondola!

The monks of Baz-K
had trained me well, the
practiced moves designed
get a leecher close enou
to touch another Alloman
and drain them of their r
serves. But it was the bal
lessons that enabled my ju
from the platform onto t
moving gondola.

I landed perfectly on t
small ridge surrounding t
bottom of the car and ma
aged a firm grip on the ou
door handles. I was safe
the moment, but the rid
I'd landed on was only a f
inches wide. If I didn't fin
way inside the gondola so
even my ballet-enhanced
strength would fail, droppi
me almost a hundred feet
the city below, where ro
tops glowed in the failing s
like boxings in an open pur

Ethereal light emanat
from inside the car, casti
the haunted man's shad
against the windows. Ea
burst showed him striving
ready some arcane devi
presumably to provide
escape.

From my satchel, I retriev
the device I had stolen fr
him when last we grappl
Covered in strange symb
and weirdly warm to t
touch, it was much heav
than it appeared, and I h
no clue how to operate it.

But ignorance is no mat
for invention. I slammed
rod of metal into the d
glass, shattering it.

An uncanny explosion a
swered me, and my Baz-K
reflexes pulled me abrup
to the side as a bolt how
past. It was neither an arr
nor a bullet, but a blast
pure energy shaped lik
ghost. Its entirely too-hum
scream made the hairs on
neck stand on end, and
frame of the broken d
rusted and crumbled in
wake of its passing. W
manner of man could h
ness the powers of the de
If the energy had envelop
me as well, would I also h
disintegrated in an insta
I breathed deep and rus
into the car.

Strange mechanical devi
littered the floor, and ab

15

Templeton Fig smoothed the feathers of his dead white crow. He knew for a fact that this animal was an authentic albino, not some knockoff crafted by an opportunist who had heard of his collection. By now, he had seen enough dead animals bleached white to spot a fake.

He had stuffed this bird himself, prize of his collection, and set it looking over its shoulder with a small strip of rabbit skin in its beak. Such a magnificent creature. People always found it striking, as its coloring was the opposite of what they expected. Things like cats and dogs sometimes had white coloring naturally, and so his albino specimens of those weren't as spectacular.

He replaced the glass dome over the crow, then stepped back and clasped his hands, looking at the white animals in a row. Frozen in death. Perfection. Only . . . the suckling boar. Had it been moved to the side? The housekeeper had better not have decided to dust his collection again.

He stepped up, twisting the glass jar that held the boar. Behind him, fire crackled in his hearth, though it wasn't particularly cold outside. He even had the window open. He liked the contrast—warmth from the fire, a cool breeze from outside. As he was trying to get the boar just right, the door to his study creaked.

"Templeton?" a quiet voice asked, peeking in. Destra had bags under her eyes, hair frazzled. Her nightgown seemed to have swallowed her. The woman had lost more weight. Soon she would be positively skeletal. "Are you coming to bed?"

"Later," he said, looking back to his boar. There.

"*When* later?"

"Later."

She winced at his tone and pulled the door closed behind her. The woman should know better than to disturb him. Sleep. How could he sleep until he knew what had happened at the graveyard? One did not disappoint the men with whom he had been dealing. They asked for something to be done, and you saw it done.

He would know soon. He stepped forward, moving his albino squirrel to the end of the line. Did it look better that way? He reached up and wiped the sweat from his brow, then moved the squirrel back. No, that wasn't right either. Then how was he to—

His fire stopped crackling.

Templeton's breath caught. He turned slowly in place, fishing in his vest pocket for his handkerchief. The fire was still there, but it was *motionless*. Trell's soul! What could have frozen the flames?

Something thumped on his door. Templeton backed away, fingers clawing at his pocket, still seeking that handkerchief. The door thumped again, and his back hit the shelf where he kept his collection. He tried to whisper an inquiry, but he was having trouble breathing.

The door burst open and the gravedigger Dechamp—eyes staring sightlessly, blood covering his shirt—fell into the room.

Templeton screamed then, scuttling away from the door, and put his back to the far wall of his small den. His fingers found the windowsill, gripping it for strength as he stared at the corpse lying in the doorway.

Something tapped on his window.

Templeton squeezed his eyes shut, not wanting to look. Frozen fire. A body on his floor. He was dreaming. It was a nightmare. It wasn't possible. . . .

Tap. Tap. Tap.

He found his handkerchief finally and clutched it, his eyes squeezed shut.

"Templeton." The rasping voice drifted in through the window.

Templeton turned slowly and faced the window. He opened his eyes.

Death stood outside.

Cloaked in black, Death's face was hidden beneath the hood—but two metal spikes protruded from the cowl, catching the firelight on their heads.

"I'm dead," Templeton whispered.

"No," Death whispered. "You can die when I say. Not before."

"Oh, *Harmony*."

"You are not His," Death whispered, standing in the darkness outside. "You are mine."

"What do you want from me? Please!" Templeton slumped to his knees. He forced himself to glance back toward Dechamp. Would that body rise? Would it come for him?

"You have something of mine, Templeton," Death whispered. "A spike." He raised his arms, letting the cloak shift back and expose white skin. A spike was stuck through one arm. The other arm was bare, save for a bloody hole.

"It wasn't my fault!" Templeton screamed. "They insisted! I don't have it!"

"Where."

"Sent by courier!" Templeton said. "To Dulsing! I don't know more. Oh, please. Please! They demanded I recover the spike for them. I didn't know it was yours! It was just a rusting piece of metal. I'm innocent! I'm . . ."

He trailed off, realizing that the fire had started crackling again. He blinked, focusing again on the window. It was empty. A . . . a dream after all? He turned and found Dechamp's corpse still leaking blood on the floor.

Templeton whimpered and huddled down. He was honestly relieved when the constables burst into the room a short time later.

Wayne shucked the awful, heavy cloak and held up his arm, healing his wounds. Not much left in his metalmind. He was going to have to be sparing after this. Those bullet wounds earlier had taken a lot out of him.

"You didn't need to *actually* cut holes in your arm, Wayne," Marasi said, joining him in the garden—he'd trampled some very nice petunias to get to the window.

"Course I did," Wayne replied, wiping away the blood. "You've gotta be *authentic*." He scratched at his head, and shifted the wires that held two half spikes hovering in front of his eyes.

"Take that thing off," Marasi said. "It looks ridiculous."

"He didn't think so," Wayne said. Inside the house, the constables dragged Templeton Fig away. The information in the ledger Wayne had found should be enough to see him well and truly incarcerated. Poor chap. He didn't really do anything *wrong*. You can't steal from a person that's already dead. But then, people were strange about their stuff. Wayne had given up on trying to figure out all their little rules.

He'd send the fellow some fruit in prison. Might make him feel better. "How was the accent?" he asked.

"Worked well enough."

"I wasn't sure how Death 'imself would sound, you know? I figured all important-like, like Wax when he's tellin' me to take my feet off the furniture. Mixed with some real *old*-soundin' tones, like a grandfather's grandfather. And grindy, like a man what is choking to death."

"In fact," Marasi said, "he's quite articulate, and not at all 'grindy.' And the accent is strange—not like anything I've heard before."

Wayne grunted, taking off his head spikes. "Can you do it for me?"

"What? The accent?"

Wayne nodded eagerly.

"No. Not a chance."

"Well, next time you meet that guy, tell 'im he's gotta come talk to me. I need to hear what he sounds like."

"What does it matter?"

"I gotta hear," Wayne said. "For next time."

"Next time? How often do you expect you'll be imitating Death?"

Wayne shrugged. "This is the fourth so far. So you never can tell." He took the last swig of Dechamp's brandy, then slung his cloak over his shoulder and started through the mists back toward the road.

"Dulsing," Marasi said.

"You know it?"

"It's a little farming settlement," Marasi said. "Maybe fifty miles northeast of New Seran. I read about it in my textbooks—there was a landmark water rights case there—but it's isolated and tiny, barely worth anyone's time. What in the world does the Set want with it?"

"Maybe they like their tomatoes real fresh," Wayne said. "I know I do."

Marasi grew silent, obviously deep in thought, worried for some reason. Wayne left her to it, digging out his tin of gum, tapping it, then flipping it open and selecting one of the soft, powder-covered balls to chew. So far as he was concerned, this had been a bang-up night. Dynamite, a nice brawl, free brandy, and getting to scare the piss out of someone.

It was the simple things that made his life worth living.

Wax had little luck with the first set of rooms he scouted. Though they supposedly belonged to Kelesina, they proved to be empty. He was tempted to ransack them for information, but decided that would take too long—and would be too incriminating at the moment. Being discovered lost in a hallway was excusable; being discovered going through a lady's desk drawers was another thing entirely.

He prowled back to the atrium and checked on Steris, gave her a wave, then continued down another hallway. This one bordered the outer wall and had windows open to the mists, which streamed in with their own miniature waterfalls. Likely some servant had the duty to close those windows on a misty night, but had gotten distracted by the party.

He listened at a set of doors, and heard nothing other than a voice drifting in from the window—the voice of Lord Severington, still plowing through his speech in the ballroom. With the amplification devices, Wax could make out a word here and there.

". . . suffer the rule . . . new Lord Ruler? . . . improper taxation . . . era must end . . ."

I will have to give that more attention, Wax thought, prowling through the hallway toward the next set of rooms. Severington was mayor of Bilming, the port city west of Elendel. It was the only major one in the Basin besides Elendel itself—and was an industrial powerhouse. If conflict *did* come, they'd be spearheading it.

They're spearheading it now, Wax realized as more words drifted up to him.

He continued down the hallway, listening at the next set of doors. He was about to turn away, when he heard a voice. There was someone inside. Wax crouched down, ear to the door, wishing he had a Tineye along to listen for him. That voice . . .

That was his uncle.

Wax pressed his ear up against the door, heedless of how he'd look to someone entering the hallway. Rusts . . . he couldn't make out much. A half word here and there. But it *was* Edwarn. Another voice spoke, and that was almost certainly Kelesina.

The gap under the door was dark. Wax put his hand to his pocket and the handgun secreted there, then turned the door's knob and eased it open. Beyond was some kind of study, completely dark but for the thin strip of light under the door on the far side. Wax slipped inside, closed the door behind him, and scuttled through the room—stifling a curse as he smacked his arm on an end table. Heart thumping, he put his back to the wall beside the other door.

"Never mind that," his uncle was saying. His voice was muffled, as if he were speaking through a cloth or a mask or something. "Why have you interrupted me? You know the importance of my work."

"Waxillium knows about the project," Kelesina said. "And he's found one of the coins. He's acting stupid, but he *knows*."

"The diversions?"

"He's not biting."

"You're not trying hard enough then," Suit said. "Kidnap one of his friends and leave a letter, purportedly from one of his old enemies. Challenge his wits, draw him into an investigation. Waxillium cannot resist a personal grudge. It will work."

"The train robbery didn't," Kelesina said. "What of that, Suit? We wasted vital resources, important connections I had spent years cultivating, on that attack. You promised that if we attacked while he was on board, he wouldn't be able to resist investigating. Yet he ignored it. Left Ironstand that same night."

Wax felt a chill as a whole set of assumptions shifted within him. The train robbery . . . had it been a *distraction,* intended to draw his attention away from pursuing the Set?

"Recovering the device," Suit said, "was worth the risk."

"You mean the device Irich immediately lost?" Kelesina demanded. "That one shouldn't be trusted with important missions. He's too eager. You should have let me recover the item once Waxillium was off the train."

"There was a good chance he'd take the bait," Edwarn said. "I know my nephew; he's probably still itching to go after those bandits. If he's at your party instead, then you aren't doing your duty properly. I haven't time to hold your hand on this, Kelesina. I need to be off to the second site."

Wax frowned. The train hadn't been just a distraction, it seemed. But the words left him with a deeper sense of worry. He'd chased half a dozen leads during the last year, anticipating that he was close on the heels of his uncle. How many of those had been plants? And how many of his other cases had been intentional distractions? And Ape Manton? Was he really even in New Seran? Likely not.

Edwarn spoke a truth. He knew Wax well. Too well, for a man he'd barely seen in the last twenty years.

"Well," Suit said, "you have your chance now to recover the device, as you promised you could. How is that going?"

"It wasn't in the things he checked at the party," Kelesina said. "We snuck a spy among the hotel staff, and she will search for it in his rooms. I'm telling you, Irich—"

"Irich was punished," Suit said. Why did his voice sound so much smaller than Kelesina's? "That is all you need know. Recover it for me, and other mistakes might be forgiven. It is only a matter of time before they accidentally use Allomancy near it."

"And *then* will we see this 'miracle' you keep promising, Suit?" she demanded. "A few more speeches like this one, and Severington will have the entirety of the Basin whipped into a frenzy. Completely ignoring that Elendel has us outmanned and outgunned."

"Patience!" Suit said, sounding amused.

"*You* try to be patient. They're bleeding us dry. You promised to crush that city, provide an army, and—"

"Patience," Suit repeated softly. "Stop Waxillium. That is your part of the bargain now. Keep him in the city; keep him distracted."

"That's *not* going to work, Suit," Kelesina said. "He knows too much already. That damn shapeshifter must have told him—"

"You let it escape?"

Kelesina was silent.

"I thought," Suit said, voice growing cold, "that you had disposed of the creature. You presented its spike to me, claiming the other had been destroyed."

"We . . . may have assumed too quickly."

"I see," Suit said.

The two did not speak for a protracted moment. Wax raised his gun beside his head, sweat trickling down his brow in the dark room. He toyed with breaking in right then. He had evidence on Kelesina in the form of the wounded kandra and his own testimony. Several people died in that blast. Murder.

But did he have enough against Edwarn? Would his uncle just slip away again? Rusts, an army? They spoke of destroying Elendel.

Dared he wait? If he took her and Suit right now, she might break, testify against him—

Footsteps.

They came from the hallway outside. As they approached the door, he made a snap decision, dropping a coin—it wasn't the special one, he had that in a different pocket—and Pushing.

Light from the hallway poured into the room as the door opened, revealing the steward from before. She crossed the room in a rush, and blessedly didn't turn on the room's lights—instead walking straight to the doorway that Wax had been listening at.

She didn't look up and see Wax pressed to the ceiling above her, Pushing against a coin she walked right over in her haste to knock on the door. Kelesina called for her to enter.

"My lady," the steward said in an urgent tone. "Burl sent me word while watching the party for Allomancers. He sensed someone using metals in this direction."

"Where is Waxillium?"

"His fiancée was sick," the steward said. "We brought her to a guest room to recover."

"Curious," Uncle Edwarn said. "And where is he now?"

Wax dropped to the floor with a thump, leveling his gun at the people inside the room. "He's right here."

The steward spun, gasping. Kelesina rose from her seat, eyes wide. And Uncle Edwarn . . .

Uncle Edwarn wasn't in the room. The only thing there was a boxy device on the table in front of Kelesina.

16

Why, Waxillium!" the box said, projecting his uncle's voice. "So good to hear your dulcet tones. I presume your entrance was properly dramatic?"

"It's a telegraph for voices," Wax said, stepping forward. He kept his gun on Kelesina, who backed up to the wall of the small room. She'd gone completely pale.

"Something like that," Edwarn said, his voice sounding small. The electric mechanism didn't reproduce it exactly. "How is Lady Harms? I hope her ailment was nothing too distressing."

"She's fine," Wax snapped, "no thanks to the fact that you tried to have us all killed on that train."

"Now, now," Edwarn said. "That wasn't the point. Why, killing you was an afterthought. Tell me, did you look into the casualties on the train? One passenger killed, I believe. Who was he?"

"You're trying to distract me," Wax said.

"Yes, I am. But that doesn't mean I'm lying. In fact, I've found that telling you the truth is a far better method in general. You should look into the dead man. You'll be impressed by what you find."

No. Stay focused. "Where are you?" Wax demanded.

"Away," Suit said, "on matters of *great* import. I do apologize for not being able to meet you in person. I offer up Lady Kelesina as a measure of my condolences."

"Kelesina can go to hell," Wax said, grabbing the box and lifting it, nearly yanking the wires in the back from the wall. "Where is my sister!"

"So many impatient people in the world," Edwarn's voice said. "You really should have focused on your own city, Nephew, and kept your attention on the little crimes fed to you. I've tried being reasonable. I fear I'm going to have to do something drastic. Something that will be certain to divert you."

Wax felt cold. "What are you going to do, Suit?"

"It's not about what I'm going to do, Nephew. It's about what I'm *doing*."

Wax glanced toward Kelesina, who had been reaching for the pocket of her dress. She raised her hands, frightened, right as something enormous *smashed* into Wax. He stumbled against the table, overturning it.

Wax blinked in shock. The steward! She'd grown to incredible strength, arms bulging beneath her robes, neck thick as a man's thigh. Wax cursed, raising his gun, which the steward immediately slapped from his hand.

His wrist screamed in pain and he winced, *Pushing* on the nails in the wall to throw himself in a roll across the floor away from the steward. He came up fishing in his pocket for coins, but the steward wasn't focused on him. She grabbed Wax's gun off the floor, then turned toward Kelesina, who screamed.

Oh no . . .

The shot left his ears ringing. Kelesina fell limp to the floor, blood dribbling from the hole in her forehead.

"He killed her!" a voice screamed from the doorway outside. Wax spun to find the maid he'd seen earlier standing there, hands to her face. "Lord Ladrian *killed* our lady!" The woman ran away screaming the words over and over, although she'd obviously had a clear view of the room.

"You bastard!" Wax shouted toward the box.

"Now, now," the box said. "That's patently false, Waxillium. You have a very clear understanding of my parentage."

The steward walked over to Kelesina, fishing at something on Kelesina's body. Then, for some reason, the steward shot the dead woman again.

Either way, this gave Wax a chance to seize the box, which had fallen from the table near him.

"You'd better be careful, Nephew," the box said. "I've told them to kill you if they can. In this case, a dead scapegoat will work as well as a living one."

Wax roared, ripping the box free of the wall and Pushing it out the doorway, into the next room. He brought his hand up and Pushed back on the gun in the steward's hand as she tried to aim it at him.

She cursed in Terris. Wax turned and scrambled from the smaller room into the one beyond, where he'd first hidden from the steward. He kicked the door shut to give himself some cover, then Pushed on his coin from before and leaped over a couch, soaring through the room. He scooped up the box communication device and skidded out into the hallway.

Half a dozen men in black coats and white gloves were advancing down the hallway toward him. They froze in place, then leveled their weapons.

Rusts!

Wax Pushed on the frames of the windows and reentered the room as the men opened fire. The inner door into the room that had held the telegraph opened, and Wax Allomantically shoved it back, cracking it into the steward's face.

Another way out. Servants' corridors? Blue lines pointed all around him and he looked for one out of place . . . there! He Pushed on it, opening a hidden door in the wall which led into a small passage, lit with dangling lightbulbs, that servants used. Still carting the telegraph box, he leaped through it as men piled into the sitting room behind him.

The weaving maze of passages let him keep ahead of them, though he did have to spend a coin taking one of them out as they got too close. That drove the others back, but notably, he couldn't sense any metal on their bodies. Aluminum weapons. This was one of Suit's kill squads, likely contacted and sent into action the moment Kelesina had telegraphed him.

Wax burst out of the passageways into a room that he hoped would let him circle back toward the atrium. If they'd found Steris . . .

He dashed through a conservatory, lit by several dim electric lights and lined with maps on the walls, and entered one of the hallways he'd explored earlier. Excellent. He charged toward the central atrium, but as soon as he reached the balcony's stairway down, something leaped from the shadows and blindsided him.

The Terriswoman, face bleeding from where the slammed door had broken her nose, growled and grabbed him around the neck. He Pushed a coin up at her, but it didn't have time to gain momentum. It hit her in the chest, then stayed there as he Pushed on it, trying to push her off. He strained, his vision growing dark, until a fist punched the Terriswoman across the face.

She let go, stumbling back and shaking. Wax gasped for breath, looking up at MeLaan looming over him.

"Rusts!" she said with a deep bass voice. "You *did* start without me."

The Terriswoman came charging in again, and Wax rolled to the side, fishing for coins. He brought up his last three in a handful as the steward punched MeLaan across the face. Something cracked audibly, and Wax hesitated as the steward stumbled back, clutching her mangled hand, the knuckles apparently shattered, the thumb ripped almost free.

MeLaan grinned. Her face had split where she'd been struck, revealing a gleaming metal skull underneath. "You really should be careful what you punch."

The Terriswoman lurched to her feet, and MeLaan casually grabbed her own left forearm in her right hand and *ripped* it off, revealing a long, thin metal blade attached to the arm at the stump. As the Terriswoman came for her, MeLaan thrust the weapon through the woman's chest. The steward gasped and collapsed to her knees, then deflated like a punctured wineskin.

"Harmony, I love this body," MeLaan said, glancing toward Wax with a goofy grin on her face. "How did I ever consider wearing another?"

"Is that whole thing aluminum?" Wax asked.

"Yup!"

"It must be worth a fortune," Wax said, standing and putting his back to the wall. The balcony was in front of him, the hallway he'd come down to his left. The kill squad would be following soon.

"Conveniently, I've had a few hundred years to save up," MeLaan said. "It—"

Wax pulled her to cover beside the wall with him; she was actually lighter than he had anticipated, considering that she had metal bones.

"What?" she asked softly.

Wax raised a coin, listening for footfalls. On the balcony before him, the Terriswoman twitched. When he heard the footstep he increased his weight a fraction, then spun around the corner and grabbed the first man's gun in one hand, twisting it toward the floor. It fired ineffectively, and Wax pressed his other hand against the man's chest and Pushed on the coin there.

Man and coin went flying back down the hallway toward his fellows, who leaped to the side. Wax was left with the aluminum gun, which he flipped in the air and caught, squeezing off four shots. The first pulled a little left, hitting the enemy in the arm, but he was able to place the next shots right in their chests.

All three dropped. The fourth man groaned from the floor where Wax had Pushed him.

"Damn," MeLaan said.

"Says the woman who just ripped half her arm off."

"It goes back on," MeLaan said, picking up her forearm, which she slid back over the blade. Blood dribbled from where she'd broken the skin. "See? Good as new."

Wax snorted, tucking the stolen aluminum gun into his waistband. "You can get out on your own?"

She nodded. "Want me to recover the guns you checked?"

"Can you?"

"Probably."

"That would be wonderful." Wax walked to the Terriswoman and checked to see that she was dead, then fished in her pockets until he came up with the gun she'd used to kill Kelesina. There was something else in her pocket as well. A metal bracelet of pure gold.

The Terriswoman took this off Kelesina, Wax thought, turning it over in his fingers as he remembered the moment earlier, when the murderer had knelt beside Kelesina's body.

He burned steel, and his hunch proved correct. While he could sense the bracelet, the line was much thinner than it should have been. This was a metalmind, and one heavily Invested with healing power.

"Was Kelesina Terris?"

"How should I know?" MeLaan asked.

He pocketed the bracelet and grabbed the box telegraph device—which he wanted to send to Elendel for inspection—and tossed it to MeLaan. "Bring that, if you don't mind, and meet us at the hotel. Be ready to leave the city. I doubt we're staying the night."

"And you were so certain we'd be out of here without a fight."

"I never said that. I said it wouldn't get so bad that I needed Wayne. And it didn't."

"A semantic technicality."

"I'm a nobleman. Might as well learn *something* from my peers." He saluted her with the small gun, then dropped off the balcony and used a coin to slow himself. "Steris?"

She crawled from a nearby shrub. "How did it go?"

"Poorly," Wax said, looking up toward the ceiling, then removing his dinner jacket. "I may have accidentally let them implicate us in Lady Kelesina's murder."

"Bother," Steris said.

"Their evidence will depend on whether they can trace the bullets back to me," Wax said, "and whether they recover any of my prints from the area. Either way, they'll be producing fake witnesses to try to make it look like I came down here *specifically* to assassinate Kelesina. Grab on."

Steris grabbed him with, he noted, no small amount of eagerness. She really did enjoy this part. He took the bullets from his .22 and held them in one hand, then launched off the coin below to shoot them toward the ceiling. He flung the bullets toward the skylights and Pushed them in a spray to weaken a window, then raised his arm—wrapped in his jacket—over his head and crashed them through the glass and out into the swirling mists.

They landed on the roof as Wax got his bearings. Out in the mists, he felt better almost immediately, and his hand—which had been smarting where the Terriswoman smacked his gun away—stopped throbbing.

"Did you learn anything useful?" Steris asked.

"Not sure," Wax said. "Most of what I overheard was about a rebellion against Elendel. I know Edwarn is heading somewhere important. He called it the second site? And he said something about what I think is that little cube Marasi found."

He pulled her tight again, then sent them in a Push upward through the mists in the direction of their hotel. She held to him tightly, but watched the lights of the city beneath with awe.

"He had Kelesina murdered," Wax said. "I should have seen it. Should have anticipated."

"At least," Steris said over the sound of the passing wind, "the mists are out. They'll have trouble tracking us."

"You did well tonight, Steris. Very well. Thank you."

"It was engaging," she said as he dropped them onto a rooftop. Her smile, which she let out readily, warmed him. She was proof that, despite his dislike of the politics in the Basin, it had good people. Genuine people. Strikingly, he had been forced to realize something almost exactly like that about the Roughs after first moving there.

She was gorgeous. Like an uncut emerald sitting in the middle of a pile of fakes cut to sparkle, but really just glass. Her enthusiasm balanced, somewhat, his concern over what had happened. Missing Suit. Being implicated. Lessie would say . . .

No. He didn't need to think of Lessie right now. He smiled back at Steris, then pulled her tighter and Pushed, launching them straight up. Higher, up away from this district. The city's taller buildings were visible only as lines of lights in the night, pointing upward through the mists. He launched up off a rooftop, then passed a shaking gondola, moving by electricity and carrying a group of gawking passengers. It rocked as Wax launched them sideways from it toward the skyscrapers.

Two were near enough one another, and with a quick series of furious Pushes, he was able to throw himself and Steris up through the swirling mists in a succession of arcs, first one way, then the other. He crested the tops and Pushed off one, sending them up a little farther. He had hoped that with the elevation of this highest terrace of the city—

Yes. They burst from the mists into a realm seen by very few. The Ascendant's Field, Coinshots called it: the top of the mists at night. White stretched in all directions, churning like an ocean's surface, bathed in starlight.

Steris gasped, and Wax managed to hold them in place by Pushing against the tips of the two skyscrapers below. Without a third, he wasn't certain how long he could balance, but for the moment they remained steady.

"So beautiful . . ." Steris said, clinging to him.

"Thank you again," Wax said to her. "I still can't believe you snuck a gun into the party."

"It's only appropriate," Steris said, "that you would make a smuggler out of me."

"Just as you try to make a gentleman out of me."

"You're already a gentleman," Steris said.

Wax looked down at her as she held to him while trying to stare in every direction at once. He suddenly found something burning in him, like a metal. A protectiveness for this woman in his arms, so full of logic and yet so full of wonder at the same time. And a powerful affection.

So he let himself kiss her. She was surprised by it, but melted into the embrace. They started to drift sideways and arc downward as he lost his balance on his anchors, but he held on to the kiss, letting them slip back down into the churning mists.

Wayne put his feet up on the table in their hotel suite, a new book open in front of him. He'd picked it up earlier, when poking through the city.

"You oughtta read this thing, Mara," he called to Marasi, who paced back and forth behind his couch. "Strangest thing you ever heard. These blokes, they build this ship, right? Only it's meant to go *up*. Uses a big explosion or some such to send it to the stars. These other blokes steal it, right, and there's seven of them, all convicts. They go lookin' for plunder, but end up on this star what has no—"

"How can you read?" Marasi asked, still pacing.

"Well, I'm not right sure," Wayne said. "By all accounts, I should be dumber than a sack full o' noodles."

"I mean, aren't you nervous?" Marasi asked.

"Why should I be?"

"Something could go wrong."

"Nah," Wayne said. "I'm not along. Wax can only get into so much trouble without me to—"

Something hit the window, causing Marasi to jump. Wayne turned to see Wax clinging to one of the windowsills, Steris tucked under one arm like a sack of potatoes—well, a sack of potatoes that had a very nice rack, anyway. Wax pulled open the window, set Steris inside, then swung in himself.

Wayne popped a peanut into his mouth. "How'd it go?"

"Eh," Wax said. He had lost his dinner jacket somewhere, and blood—hopefully not his own—covered one arm of his shirt. His cravat drooped, half tied.

"We figured out where Suit and his people are likely holed up," Wayne said as Marasi ran over to check on her sister, who looked flustered, but alive and such.

"You're kidding," Wax said.

"Nope," Wayne said, then grinned and popped a peanut. "What'd you find?"

"Clues about Marasi's cube," Wax said, pulling off his cravat. "And something about a building project, and a potential army. Suit's timetable seems to be more advanced than I'd thought."

"Cheery," Wayne said. "So . . ."

Wax sighed, then pulled out his billfold and tossed a note at Wayne. "You win."

"You had a *bet*?" Marasi demanded.

"Friendly wager," Wayne said, making the note disappear. "Can I bring these peanuts when we go?"

"Go?" Marasi said, standing up.

Wayne thumbed toward Wax, who had pulled out his travel bag. "We're leaving. Marasi, Steris, I'd suggest packing lightly. You have about fifteen minutes."

"I'm already packed," Steris said, standing up.

"I—" Marasi looked from him to her, seeming baffled. "What did you *do* at that party?"

"Hopefully," Wax said, "not start a war. But I can't say for certain."

Marasi groaned. "You let him do this," she accused Steris.

Steris blushed. Wayne always found that expression odd from her, seeing as how she had the emotions of a rock and all.

What followed was an energetic bout of motion as Wax and Marasi both ran to pack things. Wayne sidled up to Steris and popped a peanut in his mouth. "You got that preparin'-your-bags-early thing from me, didn't you?"

"I . . . Well, yes, actually."

"What will you trade me for it, then?" Wayne said. "Gotta have a good trade when you take stuff."

"I'll think about it," Steris said.

Fifteen minutes later, the four of them piled into a carriage driven by MeLaan in her male body. A bedraggled Aunt Gin stood on the doorstep of her hotel watching them. She held a wad of cash in her hand—a wad that included the money Wayne had won off Wax.

He'd left it as a tip on account of him putting his boots up on the furniture.

A furiously loud set of bells sounded in the distance, and it drew closer. "Is that the constables?" Aunt Gin asked, sounding horrified.

"Afraid so," Wax said, pulling the door closed.

The carriage lurched into motion, and Steris leaned out the window, waving farewell to the poor innkeeper.

"Framed for murder!" Steris called to her. "It's on page seventeen of the list I gave you! Try not to let them harass our servants too much when they arrive!"

A few hours later, Wax stepped up to a cliff in the darkness and let the mists enfold him.

He missed darkness. It was never dark in the city, not as it had been in the Roughs. Electric lights were only exacerbating the issue. Everything glowing, casting away the darkness—and with it, stillness. Silence. Solitude.

A man found himself when he was alone. You only had one person to chat with, one person to blame. He fished in his mistcoat pocket and was surprised to find a cigar. He thought he was out of these, good stout Tingmars brought down from Weathering.

He cut this one with his belt knife, then lit it with a match. He savored it, drawing in the smoke, holding it, then puffing it out to churn in the mists. A little bit of him to mix with Harmony. May He choke on it.

At his side, he turned a little metal spike over in his fingers. The earring VenDell had sent.

It was nearly identical to the one he'd used to kill Lessie.

Eventually, footsteps on pine needles signaled someone approaching. He pulled on his cigar, giving a warm glow to the mists and revealing MeLaan's face. Her feminine one. She'd finished changing, and was doing up the buttons on her shirt as she joined him.

"You going to get some sleep?" she asked softly.

"Maybe."

"Last I checked," she said, "humans still need it. Once in a while."

Wax pulled on his cigar, then blew out into the mists again.

"Suit wants you to go back to Elendel, I figure," MeLaan said. "He's trying to set it up so that you'll have no choice, so far as you see it."

"We're in a bad spot, MeLaan," Wax said. "The emissary that Aradel sends to a political rally ends up murdering the host? If the outer cities weren't tense before, they will be now. At the very best, it will be a huge political embarrassment. At the worst, I've started a war."

Wind blew, rustling pine branches he couldn't see. He couldn't even see MeLaan; clouds must have rolled in, blocking the starlight. Sweet, enveloping darkness.

"If there is war," she said, "Suit will have started it. Not you."

"I might be able to prevent it," Wax said. "Governor Aradel needs to know, MeLaan. If the outer cities are going to claim assassination—use it as the brand to start a bonfire—I can't just vanish. I *have* to get to Elendel. That way, I can claim I knew the New Seran justice system was corrupt, and so I fled to safety. I can make my case in the broadsheets before news spreads; I can convince Aradel I didn't kill the woman. If I do anything else, it will look like I'm hiding."

"Like I said," MeLaan said. "He's set it up so that you have no choice—so far as you see it."

"You see it differently?"

"I've been a lot of people, Ladrian. Seen through a lot of eyes. There's always another perspective, if you look hard enough."

He pulled on his cigar and held the smoke a long moment before letting it out in a slow dribble. MeLaan crept away. Did her kind need sleep? She'd implied they didn't, but he couldn't say for certain.

Alone with his cigar, he tried to sort through what he wanted to do. Go back to Elendel, as forced upon him by Suit's minions, or chase after the mystery—as forced upon him by Harmony's minions. He rolled the earring in his fingers, and confronted the hatred simmering inside of him.

He'd never hated God before. After Lessie's supposed death the first time, he hadn't blamed Harmony. Rusts, even after Bleeder had raised the question of why Harmony hadn't helped, Wax hadn't responded with hatred.

But now . . . yes, that hatred was there. You could take knocks, out in the Roughs. You lost friends. You sometimes had to kill a man you didn't want to kill. But one thing you never did: You never betrayed a companion. Friends were too rare a privilege out in those wilds, where everything seemed to want you dead.

By hiding the truth from him, Harmony had stabbed him square in the back. Wax could forgive a lot of things. He wasn't sure this was one of them.

His cigar eventually ran out. His questions lingered. By the time he hiked back toward their campsite, the mist was retreating for the night. He fed the horses—six of them, purchased at the New Seran bottom terrace shipping yards, along with a full-sized stagecoach used to do runs to the Southern Roughs.

They'd narrowly escaped New Seran. Galloping their carriage, they'd managed to descend the ramps before the police, but only after Wax had been forced to bring down a gondola line.

The police hadn't given chase after that, as if realizing they didn't have the resources to hunt someone like Waxillium Dawnshot, at least not without a lot of backup. Wax still wanted to be moving. Though he was tired to the bones, he couldn't let himself—or anyone else—rest long. Just in case.

As the others groggily piled into the vehicle, MeLaan took the reins from him and climbed up to the driver's seat. Wayne hopped into the spotter's seat beside her, and she gave him a grin.

"Where to, boss?" she asked, turning to Wax. "Back home?"

"No," Wax said. "We ride to Dulsing, the place Wayne and Marasi located." The direction of the building project.

"You found another perspective, I see," MeLaan said.

"Not yet," Wax said softly, climbing into the stagecoach. "But let's see if Harmony dares try to give me one."

PART THREE

17

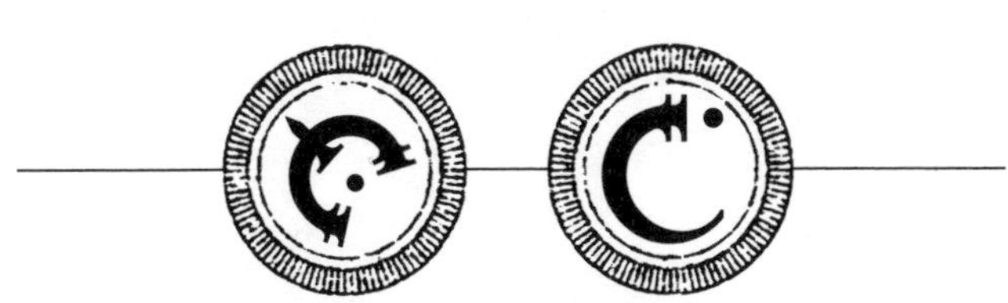

Marasi had read a lot about life in the Roughs in her youth, and knew what to expect of a stagecoach trip: boredom, dust, and discomfort.

It was wonderful.

She had to forcibly keep herself from hanging out the window as Wayne occasionally did, watching the scenery pass. They weren't in the Roughs, but this was close enough. The smell of the horses, the bumps in the road, the rickety creak of the wood and the springs . . . She had seen and done some remarkable things during her time with Waxillium, but *this* really felt as if she were living in an adventure.

Waxillium reclined across from her, feet up on the seat next to her, a wide-brimmed hat over his eyes, face bristly from a day without shaving. He'd removed his boots, which sat on the floor beside his shotgun.

It seemed surreal to remember she'd even considered a relationship with him, now that so long had passed with them working together. No, she was not interested, no longer. But she *did* admire the perfect image of him there—the gun, the boots, and the hat.

Of course, that image was distorted by the sight of Steris curled up on the seat beside him, snoring softly with her head on his shoulder.

In what kind of bizarre world did Marasi's punctilious half sister end up on the adventure? Steris belonged in a sitting room with a cup of tea and a dry book about horticulture, not riding cross-country in a stagecoach toward a potential army of Allomancers. Yet here she was, snuggled up against Dawnshot himself.

Marasi shook her head. She wasn't envious of Steris, which was—frankly—remarkable, considering their upbringings. It was very hard to hate Steris. You could be bored by her, confused by her, or frustrated with her—but hate her? Impossible.

Marasi got out her notebook to continue her report to VenDell and Constable-General Reddi, which she hoped to be able to send before reaching Dulsing.

Waxillium shifted, then tipped his hat back, eyeing her. "You should get some sleep."

"I'll rest when we stop."

"Stop?"

Marasi hesitated. They'd been going for half a day already, avoiding the main roads to evade potential pursuers from New Seran. They'd crossed several fields, and spent a full hour rattling along a stone ridge to bypass some farms below in a way that left little sign of their passage.

Their path lay almost directly northeast of New Seran, skirting the mountains to their right, staying to the foothills—which meant some ups and downs, but this was still good farmland. All of the Basin was, even here at the edges, where things were dryer than in the center.

"I thought that after stopping last night—" Marasi said. "Dear. You mean to go straight there?"

"'Straight' is an odd term," Waxillium said, "considering how much MeLaan has us weaving to avoid getting caught. But yes. Shouldn't be more than another four hours or so."

A train could have had them there in a fraction of that time, delivered in comfort. Maybe the outer cities did have reason to gripe about the way things were set up.

"Waxillium?" Marasi said as he shifted again.

"Mmm?"

"Do you think they're real? The Bands of Mourning?"

He tipped back his hat all the way. "Did I ever tell you why I went to the Roughs?"

"As a youth?" Marasi said. "It was because you hated the politics, the expectations. Polite society that was anything but polite."

"That's why I left Elendel," Waxillium said. "But why the Roughs? I could have gone to one of the outer cities, could have found a plantation somewhere to read books and live a quiet life."

"Well . . ." Marasi frowned. "I guess I thought you always wanted to be a lawman."

Waxillium smiled. "I wish I'd spotted it that easily. Should have. I spent my childhood tattling on other children for every little thing they did."

"Then what?"

He settled back, closing his eyes. "I was chasing a legend, Marasi. Tales of the Survivor's gold, riches to be had, stories to be made."

"You?" Marasi started. "You were a *gentleman adventurer*?"

Waxillium winced visibly at the term. "You make me sound like that fool in the broadsheets. I tell you, Marasi, those first months were hard. Every other town was full of the unemployed from the mines shutting down, and I couldn't enter a saloon without finding some fool baby-face like myself, up from the Basin with a head full of glory and treasure."

"So you started hunting bounties," she said. "You told me this part. Something about boots."

"Eventually, yes," Waxillium said, smiling. "Struggled for a long time up there before turning to bounties. At first, though, I had my eyes full of riches and gold. Took time to shake that out of me, but even then, becoming a lawman was about the cash. Started hunting men for money. And, well, there'd always been this streak in me that didn't like seeing people get pushed around. Ended up in Weathering. Just another forgotten, dried-out city in the Roughs with nobody to care about it. It was six years before someone gave me credentials and made it official."

The stagecoach cabin swayed on its straps. Up above, Marasi could hear Wayne and MeLaan chatting. So long as they weren't making out again while trying to drive.

"When VenDell told us about this, I didn't want the Bands to be real," Waxillium said, looking out the window. "I hated the thought of some foolish dream pulling me away again, after I'd finally found stability in Elendel. I didn't want that lure of excitement, the reminder of a world I'd come to love out there in the dust."

"So you think they *are* real."

"Here's the thing," he said, leaning forward, causing Steris to shift in her sleep. "My uncle hasn't had time to breed his Allomancers, as I suspect he's been doing. The plans he and the Set have concocted, they're long-term investments. But he promised *something* to Kelesina, and he really sounded like he thinks he can deliver. You have the device?"

Marasi pulled the small metal cube from her purse. Waxillium fished in his pocket and brought out his coin, the one some beggar had apparently given him. He held up the two next to each other, sunlight through the window gleaming off the cube and highlighting the otherworldly symbols on its sides.

"Something strange *is* going on, Marasi," Waxillium said. "Something important enough to draw my uncle's attention. I don't have the answers. I need to find them."

She found herself smiling at the intensity in his eyes. "It's not the treasure hunter that made you decide to go to Dulsing. It's the detective."

He smiled. "You were listening to what MeLaan said to me last night?"

Marasi nodded.

"You were supposed to be asleep," Waxillium said. He flipped the coin, caught it, then tossed the cube back to her. "Going to Aradel would have been the mature, prudent move, but I have to find the answers. And who knows? Maybe the Bands are real. If so, then getting them away from Suit is *at least* as important as informing the governor of what happened in New Seran."

"You think your uncle is trying to make Allomancers with technology, rather than by birth."

"A frightening power in the hands of a man like my uncle," Waxillium said, leaning back into his seat. "Get some sleep. We're probably going to infiltrate this building project in Dulsing during the night."

He settled with his hat over his eyes again. Marasi felt she should do as he said, and so tried to doze off. Unfortunately, there were too many thoughts in her head for sleep.

After some time, she gave up and returned to her letter. In it, she explained what they'd done and discovered. She needed to send this soon. Perhaps she could find a telegraph station when they changed horses, and send the letter in time for it to make a difference.

Once done with the letter, she moved to her notes about the missing kandra spike. Kelesina, acting on behalf of the Set, had tried to kill ReLuur, and had assumed success. When Suit had demanded proof, she'd ordered the spike dug up and sent to him in Dulsing. But where would it be kept there? Someplace secure, presumably. How in the world was she going to find it?

She held up the little cube. Suit had asked after this. Could she use that somehow?

Marasi frowned, turning the cube. The sides had little grooves between them. She looked closer, and in the sunlight spotted something she hadn't seen before. A tiny little knob hidden in one groove. It looked like . . . well, a switch. Nestled in, where it couldn't be flipped accidentally.

She used a hairpin to reach in and flip the switch. It moved just as she'd expect it to.

A switch. It seemed so . . . mundane. This was either a mystical relic or some kind of secret technology. You didn't use a switch on things like that; you held them up to starlight, or spoke the special command phrases, or did a dance on the last day of the month while eating a kumquat.

The switch didn't seem to have done anything. So, Marasi swallowed and burned a pinch of cadmium.

The cube began to vibrate in her fingers.

Then the entire coach lurched, rocking as if it had been struck by something very hard. Marasi hit her head on the roof, then was slammed back down onto her seat.

The horses screamed, but MeLaan somehow kept them under control. Within moments, the coach had pulled to a stop.

"What the hell was that?" Waxillium said, hauling himself up off the floor, where he had ended up in a jumble with Steris.

Marasi groaned, sitting up and holding her head. "I did something stupid."

"How stupid?" Waxillium asked.

"I was testing the device," Marasi said, "and used Allomancy."

Wayne's head appeared at the door a moment later, hanging down from above. "Was that a speed bubble?"

"Yes," Marasi said.

"That jolt damn near killed the horses," Wayne said.

"I'm sorry, I'm sorry."

Waxillium helped Steris sit up. "What . . . what went wrong?" she asked, befuddled.

"Marasi used a speed bubble while we were moving," Waxillium said. "We hit the threshold and towed her out of it, popping the thing and lurching us from one time frame to the next."

"But, she used it on the train," Steris said.

"Speed bubbles move with you if you're on something massive enough," Waxillium said. "Otherwise, the spinning of the planet would pop you out of every one you made. The train was heavy and fast. The stagecoach is small and just slow enough. So—"

"So I should have known better," Marasi said, blushing. "I haven't done that since I was a kid. But Waxillium, it *buzzed*."

"What?"

"The cube, it—" Marasi started, realizing she'd dropped the cube in the confusion. She searched around frantically before finally locating it near his foot. She held it up triumphantly. "It had a switch."

"A switch?"

She turned it to the side, showing them the little switch. "You have to slip something small in to move it," she said. "But it works now."

He looked at it, baffled, then showed it to Steris, who squinted. "What kind of eldritch device," Steris said, "has an *on switch*?"

"Makes sense, I guess," Waxillium said. "You don't want your eldritch devices turning on accidentally."

"Might end up almost killing your stagecoach drivers," Wayne grumbled.

"It didn't stop your Allomancy?" Waxillium asked Marasi, rubbing his chin.

She shook her head. She could still sense her metal reserves. "It didn't seem to do anything."

"Huh." Waxillium held it up. "Could be dangerous."

"So we're testing it, then?" Wayne asked, hanging into the window.

"Of course we are," Waxillium said. "But *away* from the coach."

Wax held the vibrating cube in his hand. It did respond to his metal burning, but didn't seem to do anything else.

They'd stopped near a stand of towering walnut trees, and Wayne was filling his pockets while Marasi watched Wax experiment from a safe distance. MeLaan watered the horses at a stream down the way. Nearby, a field of carrots grew with green sprouts, completely uncultivated. The air smelled fresh, of life untouched.

He held up the buzzing cube and let his metals die off. The cube stopped vibrating. He burned them again, and it responded—starting slowly, but picking up after about a second or two. But what did it *do*? Why didn't it blank his Allomancy as it had on the train?

Maybe it doesn't work on the person activating it, he thought. That would make some kind of sense, though he couldn't fathom how it could tell. "Hey, Wayne," he said.

"Yeah, mate?"

"Catch."

Wax tossed the cube to him. Wayne caught it, then jumped as

his belt—which held his metal vials and any coins on his person—ripped free from its breakaway straps and sprang away from him. He turned, watching it flop to the ground a good twenty feet down the hill, and when he approached it, it scooted away.

Wax ran toward him, and as he did, the shotgun in his leg holster pressed backward, as if being Pushed. The effect wore off a few seconds later, and by the time he reached Wayne, the cube had stopped buzzing.

Wayne held it up. "What was *that*?"

Wax plucked the device from his fingers as Marasi rushed over to join them. "It doesn't steal Allomancy, Wayne. It never did."

"But—"

"It takes the metal one is burning," Wax said, "and somehow . . . extends it. You saw. It Pushed your metal away, as if a Coinshot were there near you. The cube used Allomancy."

The three of them stood stunned, looking at the little device.

"We need to try it again," Wax said. "Wayne, hold this and burn your bendalloy. Marasi, go stand over there. Wayne, once you're ready, throw the cube to her."

They did as directed. Wax stood back. When Wayne ignited his metals, he suddenly became a blur inside his speed bubble. The cube zipped out an eyeblink later and soared through the air toward Marasi, deflected somewhat but still moving in the right direction.

It engaged just before reaching her, and she became a blur, zipping over to pick up the cube, then zipping back. It took a count of ten before the cube stopped working, dropping her into ordinary time.

"Did you see that?" Marasi said, awed, holding the cube. "It created a speed bubble for me. It *fed* off Wayne's Allomancy, and replicated it!"

"It's what we've been lookin' for, then?" Wayne asked, joining them, having dropped his own bubble.

"Not quite," Wax replied, taking the cube and holding it up. "But it's certainly encouraging. It looks like you have to be an Allomancer to use this—it doesn't grant new powers, but it does extend the ones you have. It's like . . . like an Allomantic grenade."

Marasi nodded eagerly. "Which means that the man on the train, the one who used this on us, is a Leecher. He can remove Allomancy in others, and he gave that power to the cube, which he threw at you."

"It engages a second or so after you throw it," Wax said with a nod. "Useful."

"And it's proof that Suit has technology he's been hiding," Marasi said.

"We knew that from the communication device," Wax said, "but yes, this is even more curious. I'm half tempted to think all this talk of the Bands of Mourning came from rumors about this technology the Set has been developing."

"And the symbols?"

"No idea," Wax said. "Some kind of cipher they developed?" He tapped the cube, then handed the thing to Marasi.

"Why me?" she asked.

"It's yours. You found it; you figured out how to turn it on. Besides, I have a feeling it's going to be the most effective in your hands."

She held it a moment, then her eyes widened. Being a Pulser wasn't very useful when you were catching yourself in a bubble where you moved slowly compared to everyone else. However, if you could trap someone *else* in that bubble . . .

Wayne whistled softly.

"I'll try not to lose it," Marasi said, tucking the device away. "We'll need to study it later, find out how it works."

I wonder . . . Wax thought, remembering something else. He played his hunch, reaching into his pocket and fishing out the golden bracelet that Kelesina had been wearing.

He tossed it to Wayne.

"What's this?" Wayne asked, holding it up toward the sky. "Pretty hoop o' gold, that is. Who'd you trade this off of? I could use this, mate. It would make a nice metalmind."

"I think it's already one," Wax said, deflating. It had been a silly idea in the first place.

Wayne gasped.

"What?" Marasi said.

"It's a metalmind," Wayne said. "Damn me, but it is. And I can *sense* it. Wax, you got your knife?"

Wax nodded, yanking his knife from his gunbelt, and when Wayne proffered his hand, he sliced a small cut along the back. It resealed immediately.

"Maaaate," Wayne whispered. "It's someone else's metalmind, but I can *use* it."

"Like VenDell said," Wax said, taking the bracelet from Wayne's fingers. "A metalmind with no Identity. Rusts. I have to flare my metal to even get the *faintest* line pointing to it. This thing must be stuffed full of power."

More than any metalmind he'd ever sensed, in fact. He could usually push on those without too much trouble. He'd barely be able to shift this one.

"Why didn't I notice what it was immediately?" Wayne said. "I had to be told. And, oh, rusts! This is proof of the Bands of Mourning, ain't it?"

"No," Wax said. "*I* can't sense a reserve in the bracelet—I can't use this, as I'm not a Bloodmaker. It's not a metalmind anybody can use, just one that anyone with the right powers already can use."

"That's still remarkable," Marasi said.

"And disturbing," Wax said, staring at that innocent-looking loop. The only way to have created this would involve using a Feruchemist with two powers. So either the Set had access to full-blooded Feruchemists, or his fears were coming true. They'd figured out how to use Hemalurgy.

Or it's a relic, he thought. *There's that possibility.* Perhaps this and the box were artifacts of another time.

He tossed the bracelet back to Wayne. "How much is in it?"

"A heap," Wayne said. "But it's not endless. The reservoir got smaller when I healed that cut."

"Hang on to it, then," Wax said, turning as he heard his name. MeLaan was at the edge of the glade, waving. Wax left Wayne and Marasi, striding over to the tall, slender kandra woman, still worried about what these discoveries meant. What did the bracelet indicate? Was there more to be discovered? Metalminds that granted anyone who touched them incredible powers? For the first time, he really started to wonder. What if the Bands *were* real? What would happen to society if Metalborn powers were simply something you could purchase?

He trudged up to MeLaan. "I think you'll want to see this," she said, waving for him to follow her up the side of a steep hill covered in foliage. At the top, they had a view of the land to the northeast. Some was cultivated in rows and rings, but much was like what they'd just left—wilderness blooming with random patches of fruits or vegetables. A cool breeze blew across him, barely enough to temper the heat of the sunlight above.

Seeing it all, feeling that perfect breeze, made Wax realize what annoyed him so much about the problems between Elendel and the outer cities. Did these people comprehend what life was like out in the Roughs, where planting was fraught with uncertainty, and the danger of starvation was real?

They think people are foolish for living in the Roughs, Wax thought, taking the old-fashioned spyglass that MeLaan handed him. *They don't understand what it's like to get trapped out there for generations, too poor—or too stubborn—to return to the Basin.*

Freedom in the Roughs came at a cost. Either way, the Basin was—literally—paradise, crafted for men by a God who wanted to compensate the world for a millennium of ashes and ruin. It seemed that even in paradise, men would find reasons to squabble and fight.

Wax raised the spyglass. "What am I looking for?"

"Check the road about a mile up," MeLaan said. "By that creek with the bridge over it."

He spotted a couple of men lounging in a field with axes. From the looks of it, they'd been cutting at the trunk of a dead tree. Another fallen tree crossed the roadway.

"What do you see?" MeLaan asked.

"A roadblock that doesn't want to look like one," Wax said. "That tree across the road is arranged to seem as if it just fell there, but the furrows on the ground indicate it was dragged there intentionally, and has been moved a time or two since being placed."

"Good eye," MeLaan said.

"You can't have it," he said, turning the spyglass and looking toward the farmsteads in the area. "Soldiers stationed in that farmhouse over there, I'd guess. And none of the other homes have smoke rising from them. Probably abandoned. You're unlikely to find a farmstead this time of day without dinner in the oven."

"They're waiting for us?"

"No, this is too extensive for that," Wax said. "This is a perimeter. They're trying not to have it look like one, to prevent word from spreading, but they've cordoned off this entire area. What the hell is happening in there?"

MeLaan shook her head, looking baffled.

"Well, we can't take the coach any farther," Wax said, handing back the spyglass. "How are you at bareback?"

"Well, I haven't thrown any riders off recently, but I don't get occasion to be a horse very often, so I can't say how I'll feel today."

Wax blinked.

"Oh, you meant *riding*," MeLaan said. "Yeah, I'm fine. I doubt I'm the one you'll have to worry about." She nodded back toward Steris walking into the grove, trailed by Wayne, who had filled his hat with walnuts.

"Right," Wax said.

Hopefully some of their horses would prove docile.

Twilight settled upon the land fitfully, like a tired eye struggling to stay open. It was the variety of the land down here in the south, Wax figured. One moment you could be riding through a wooded hollow, all in shadow, and the next you'd crest a hill into an open field and find that the sun hadn't quite dropped below the horizon yet.

Still, darkness did eventually arrive, but with it came no mists. Wax realized he'd been longing to feel them envelop him again.

MeLaan led the sortie, keeping to forested areas when possible. She or Wayne would scout ahead, listening for patrols, but the Set was attempting to hold such a large area that they obviously couldn't watch the whole wilderness. Marasi, of course, was an accomplished rider—and seemed pleased to have a reason to change into her new constable's trousers and jacket.

Steris surprised him. She did just fine, even riding in a skirt. She'd packed one full enough that she could tuck it beneath her and ride bareback without exposing too much. She took to it without complaint, as she'd done with practically everything else on this trip.

The few farmsteads or hunter's camps they passed on their ride were empty. Wax felt a mounting disquiet. Yes, this was a small, largely unpopulated region in the Basin's backwaters—but it was still profoundly disturbing that the Set could dominate it so fully.

Once they reached the final patch of trees near the village, MeLaan scouted ahead, then came back and waved for him to follow. He crawled up with her to peer at the village from the tree line.

Bright electric floodlights lit the perimeter around an enormous structure in what obviously had once been the center of the village of Dulsing. Wooden, windowless, huge, it was still under construction, judging by the scaffolding at the sides and the unfinished roof at the top. The town's buildings had mostly been torn down, leaving only a few at the perimeter untouched.

The roofless top of the building glowed with a warm light. Where were they getting so much electricity? MeLaan handed him the spyglass and he raised it, inspecting the perimeter. Those were definitely soldiers, wearing red uniforms with some mark on the breast that wasn't distinguishable at this distance. They carried rifles at their shoulders, and the floodlights created a bright ring around the place. Focused outward, not toward the building, which left plenty of shadowed areas inside that ring. So they'd have cover once they got past the perimeter.

"What do you think?" he asked. "Is that some kind of bunker?"

“Doesn’t look like any fort *I’ve* seen,” MeLaan whispered. “With those flimsy walls? Looks more like a big warehouse.”

A warehouse as large as a small town. Wax shook his head in bafflement, then spotted something near the far side of the village. A waterfall? It was outside the lights, but he thought he could see mist rising from where it plunged down, and a small stream did run through the village.

“High ground that direction,” he said.

“Yeah,” she said. “The maps mention the waterfall over there. Small but pretty, supposedly.”

“Must have hooked a turbine up to it,” he said. “That’s where the power is coming from. Let’s get back to the others.”

They crawled through the underbrush again to where Wayne, Marasi, and Steris waited in the dim woods. “They’re here all right,” Wax whispered. “We have to find a way to get in. Tons of soldiers. Well-guarded perimeter.”

“Fly in,” Steris suggested.

“Not gonna work,” Wayne said. “They had a Seeker back at the party; you think they won’t have one here? The moment one of us burns a metal, we’ll draw a hundred of Suit’s goons to welcome us with a handshake and a friendly bit of murderin’.”

“What then?” Marasi asked.

“I need to see,” Wayne said.

“There’s a better vantage on the other side, we think,” Wax said. He pointed, and MeLaan led the way in the darkness, walking her horse between the towering hardwoods. Wax fell in with Steris at the tail of the group, and lagged a little to be able to speak with her privately.

“Steris,” he whispered, “I’ve been considering how to proceed once we decide how to infiltrate. I’ve thought about bringing you in with us, and I just don’t see that it’s feasible. I think it would be best if you stayed and watched the horses.”

“Very well.”

“No, really. Those are *armed soldiers*. I can’t even fathom how I’d feel if I brought you in there and something happened. You need to stay out here."

"Very well."

"It isn't subject to—" Wax hesitated. "Wait. You're all right with this?"

"Why wouldn't I be?" she asked. "I barely have any sense of where to point a gun, and have hardly any capacity for sneaking—that's really quite a scandalous talent if you think about it, Lord Waxillium. While I *do* believe that people tend to be safest when near you, riding into an enemy compound is stretching the issue. I'll stay here."

Wax grinned in the darkness. "Steris, you're a gem."

"What? Because I have a moderately healthy sense of self-preservation?"

"Let's just say that out in the Roughs, I was accustomed to people always wanting to try things beyond their capacity. And they always seemed determined to do it right when it was the most dangerous."

"Well, I shall endeavor to stay out of sight," Steris said, "and not get captured."

"I doubt you need to worry about that all the way out here."

"Oh, I agree," she said. "But that *is* the sort of statistical anomaly that plagues my life, so I'll plan for it nonetheless."

With some difficulty, they navigated to the eastern edge of the town, where they left Steris and the horses. Wax dug some supplies off the pack animal. Metal vials, extra bullets, plenty of guns—including the aluminum one he'd stolen back at Kelesina's place. And the last of Ranette's ball-and-string devices, which he tucked into the pouch on his gunbelt.

After climbing up some switchbacks, they were able to settle onto a darkened ridge above the falls—which were nowhere near as impressive as he'd imagined—and study the town. Well, the remnants of it.

"I wish we could see into that building," Marasi said, handing back the spyglass.

Wax grunted in agreement. They were *almost* high enough to see what was going on inside. Certainly, those flickering lights bespoke considerable activity: people moving down below, passing before the lights in the large chamber. But what were they doing, and why were they still at it well into the night?

"Gonna be hard to sneak in there," Wayne said.

"You could kill one of the guards for me," MeLaan said, settling onto a rock. "I'd eat him, take his shape, and slip us in that way."

Wax blinked, then glanced at Marasi, who seemed sick.

"Really," MeLaan said, "you all need to stop staring at me like that when I offer pragmatic suggestions."

"It's not pragmatic," Marasi said. "It's cannibalism."

"Technically it's not, as we're different species. Honestly, if you look at our physiology, I share less in common with humans than you do with a cow—and nobody gasps when you eat one of *those*. You didn't have trouble with it back in the mansion with Innate's bodyguard."

"She was already dead," Wax said. "Thank you for the suggestion, MeLaan, but getting you a guard's body is out of the question."

"We don't like killin' folks," Wayne said. "At least, unless they start shootin' at us. They're just chaps what are doing their job." He looked to Marasi, as if for support.

"Don't look at me," Marasi said. "I'm reeling from watching *you* trying to take the moral high ground."

"Focus, Wayne," Wax said. "How are we going to get in? Shall we try a Fat Belt?"

"Nah," Wayne said, "too loud. I think we should do Spoiled Tomato."

"Dangerous," Wax said, shaking his head. "I'd have to do the placement just right, between the lit perimeter and the shadowed part near the walls."

"You can do it. You make shots like that all the time. Plus, we got this shiny new metalmind, full o' health waitin' to be slurped up."

"A mistake could ruin the whole infiltration, healing power or no," Wax said. "I think we should do Duck Under Clouds instead."

"You kiddin'?" Wayne said. "Didn't you get *shot* last time we tried that?"

"Kinda," Wax admitted.

MeLaan stared at them, baffled. "Duck under Clouds?"

"They get like this," Marasi said, patting her on the shoulder. "Best not to listen too closely."

"Tube Run," Wayne said.

"No glue."

"Banefielder?"

"Too dark."

"Blackwatch Doublestomp."

Wax hesitated. ". . . The hell is that?"

"Just made it up," Wayne said, grinning. "It's a nifty code name though, eh?"

"Not bad," Wax admitted. "And what type of plan is it?"

"Same as Spoiled Tomato," Wayne said.

"I said that was too dangerous."

"Nothin' else will work," Wayne said, standing. "Look, are we going to sit here arguing, or are we going to do this?"

Wax debated for a moment, eyeing the grounds, thinking. Could he get the placement right?

But then, did he have a better plan? That perimeter was very well guarded, but it was a dark night. If his life in the Roughs had taught him one thing, it was to trust his instincts. Unfortunately, at that moment they agreed with Wayne.

So, before he could talk himself out of it, he pulled his shotgun from its holster and tossed it to Wayne. The shorter man caught it with distaste—guns and Wayne didn't agree. His arms immediately started shaking.

"Try to hold on tight," Wax said. "Make an opening on the north side, if you can."

He increased his weight, flared his metal, and Pushed on the gun, using it as an anchor to hurl Wayne out off the rocky outcropping and over the camp. The man soared from the Push before dropping through the darkness, some fifty feet toward the ground below.

Marasi gasped. "Spoiled Tomato?" she asked.

"Yeah," Wax said. "Apparently it makes a mess sometimes when he lands."

To rust with that Wax, Wayne thought as he plummeted toward the ground, his hat blowing off. *Tossin' a gun to a fellow without even warnin' him. Why, that's just—*

He hit.

Now, there was a trick to falling to your death. Bodies hitting the ground were *loud*. Louder than anyone ever expected.

He mitigated this by hitting feet-first—his legs both snapped immediately—then twisted onto his side, breaking his shoulder, but dampening some of the sound by rolling with the impact. He tapped his fancy new metalmind right before his head smacked the ground, dazing him.

He ended up in a crumpled, broken heap beside a pile of rocks. *Of course* Wax would have sent him into a pile of rocks. As his vision cleared, he tried to glance at his legs, but he couldn't move. Couldn't feel anything, actually, which was quite pleasant. It was always nice when you snapped the spine—helped with the pain.

Not that the pain went *completely* away, mind you. But he and pain were old friends what shared a handshake and a beer now and then. Didn't much like one another, but they had a working relationship. Sensation—and agony—flooded back into him as his metalmind healed his spine, focusing on the worst wounds first. He drew in a deep breath. A snapped spine could suffocate a man. People didn't know that. Or, well, the ones who *did* know had suffocated already.

As soon as he could move—even while his legs were healing—he twisted and used his good arm to position one of the large rocks in the pile. Looked like these stones were here intended for shoring up the sides of the stream, perhaps to make a pathway across. Wayne put them to good use, reaching up with his other hand as his shoulder healed. Wax had placed him well, right in the dark area between the perimeter watchposts and the building. But that didn't mean he was safe.

Wayne stumbled to his feet, dragging Wax's gun, his leg twisting about and bones reknitting. Damn fine metalmind, that gold bracelet was. An extensive healing like this would have cost him months of saving up, but this metalmind was still mostly full.

He stumbled away as quietly as he could, leaving a large rock balanced on the others as he sought a place deeper in the shadows, then hid the gun near the building so his damn hand would stop shaking.

He got away none too soon. A pair of soldiers were approaching from the perimeter.

"It was over here," one said to the other. As they drew closer, one of the spotlights turned around and shone on the area, giving them light and quite nearly exposing Wayne. He froze in the shadows near a pile of work equipment, sweating as his toes popped softly, the bones grinding against one another as they knit back into their proper places.

The guards didn't hear. They stepped up to where he'd fallen—no tomato splat of blood this time, fortunately—and looked around. One nudged the stone accidentally, and it fell off the peak where Wayne had placed it, rolling down the side of the small pile and clattering against the other rocks. The men looked at it, then nodded, doing a quick sweep but heading back to their post and returning the light to its scan of the nearby area. The noise they'd heard had merely been some rocks shifting. Nothing significant.

Wayne stood up straight in the darkness and stopped tapping the bracelet metalmind. He felt good. Renewed, like he always did after a big healing. Felt like he could do something impossible, run up a mountain, or eat the entire boar and chips plate at Findley's all on his own.

He crept off through the shadows, about important business. Fortunately, he found his hat almost immediately, near another rock pile. That done, he moved on to less important matters, like making an opportunity to help the others sneak in.

Wax had said north side. *Let's see. . . .* He kept close to the building, and even resisted the urge to go sneaking in on his own to find out what in Ruin's name was in there.

Time to think like a guard. It was hard, as he didn't have a guard's hat. He settled into the shadows and listened as a pair of them passed on patrol, digesting their accents like a nice snack of pretzel sticks with mustard.

After about fifteen minutes of watching, he picked out a likely candidate and kept pace as the man did his rounds, though Wayne stayed in the shadow. The lanky fellow had a face like a rabbit, but was tall enough he could probably have picked all the walnuts he wanted without needing a stepladder.

Here I am, Wayne thought, *in the middle of nowhere! Guarding a big old barn. This isn't what I signed up for. I haven't seen my daughter in eight months. Eight months! She's probably talking by now. Rusts. This life.*

The man turned to go back the other way on his rounds, and someone barked out at him from one of the stations with the floodlights, saying something Wayne couldn't hear. The tone was unmistakable.

And my superiors, Wayne thought, turning and slinking along in the shadows, still keeping pace with the man. *Oh, how they lean on me! Every little thing gets me a talking-to. Shouting. That's all this life is. Being yelled at day in and day out.*

Wayne smiled, then scuttled ahead of the man, looking for something he'd stepped over earlier. A set of black cords, each as thick as his finger, plugged into a big box near the building. As the guard came strolling past, not paying much attention, Wayne carefully lifted the cords.

The guard's foot caught on them. In that moment, Wayne yanked them from the hub.

The floodlights nearest to him went out.

Men immediately started shouting. The guard panicked in the darkness. "I'm sorry!" he shouted. "I didn't mean to. I wasn't watching my feet!"

Wayne slipped away and found a nice quiet nook between two

stacks of sandbags as the guards shouted and argued, and the poor man was chewed out. Some people came in to fix the cords, though Wayne had tossed them to the side, so it took some time searching in the dark to find the ends and get them connected.

The lights came back on. Wayne was taking a long swig from his leather canteen as Wax, Marasi, and MeLaan joined him in the shadows. "Nice," Wax whispered.

"It wasn't, actually," Wayne whispered. "It was pretty mean. That poor guard ain't done nothin' wrong, and everybody keeps yellin' at him."

Wax took the lead at that point, prowling along the side of the big barnlike building. The roof wasn't the only thing still unfinished—the entrances were open, not fitted with proper doors. They stopped beside one and Wayne pointed, whispering to Wax where his shotgun was.

Wax fetched it, then snuck through the doorway. They followed, Wayne last of all. The cavernous interior was lit by a few electric lanterns here and there, and they passed a long light lattice that was obviously going to be installed in the ceiling, once the roof was done. It was brighter than outside in here, but not by much, and there were stacks of boxes and supplies arranged in rows, which let them sneak through and stay hidden. Once they got to the front of the rows of boxes, Wax hesitated, and the two women peered around him. Nobody gave Wayne a good view, which was how it always went. First he got yelled at on the job, then this.

He wiggled between them, getting a good elbow into Marasi's midriff—which earned him a glare, as if she didn't know that proper crowd-wiggling protocol involved getting friendly with one another's extremities. He managed to peek between Wax and MeLaan, finally getting a glimpse at what had stopped them.

It was a boat.

Of course, the common word "boat" didn't do the thing justice. Wayne stared at the massive construction, searching for a better description. One that would capture the majesty, the incredible scale, of the thing he was seeing.

"That's a *damn big boat,*" he finally whispered.

Much better.

Why would they be building a ship here, miles and miles from the ocean? The thing couldn't be easy to move. It filled almost the entire building, with a curved bottom and a prow—unfinished on one side—that was easily three stories high. The thing had two long, armlike extensions at the sides. Pontoons? They were big, and one wasn't finished yet, ending in a jagged line of construction.

Jagged? Wayne frowned. That didn't look like the way you built something. In fact, now that he studied it, that prow looked more *crumpled* than *unfinished*.

"Someone broke it," Wayne said, pointing. "They were trying to move it, and cracked off one pontoon."

"It has to be a warship," Marasi said. "They *are* preparing for a war."

"I think Wayne is right," Wax said. "Look at the gouges in the dirt, the damage to the hull. They were transporting this thing through here, and it rolled free and cracked. So the Set constructed this building to cut it off from the view of anyone outside while they repair it."

"Engineers," Wayne said, pointing at some people who were *obviously* smart types, walking along the outside of the ship and pointing, carrying clipboards and wearing dark brown suits and skirts. The type teachers at schools would wear, thinking they were the height of fashion.

"It's not like any ship I've seen," Marasi said, shouldering her purse and clutching her rifle.

"You brought your purse," Wayne said, "on a darin' infiltration?"

"Why not?" she said. "Purses are handy. Anyway, if the Set has technology like that speaking telegraph, what will they put on a ship like this? And why did they build it away from the sea in the first place?"

"Suit will have answers," Wax said, eyes narrowing. "Marasi, I assume you're still after the spike?"

"Yes," she said, determined.

"I'm going to find my uncle. Who do you want? Wayne or MeLaan?"

"MeLaan this time," Marasi said.

Wax nodded. "Stay hidden, but if Wayne and I get spotted, try to help. We'll do the same for you. If you find that spike, return to this point and lie low. If all goes well, we'll slip back out together."

"And if all doesn't go well?"

"Which it won't," Wayne added.

"Meet back where we left Steris and the horses," Wax said, sliding a gun from the holster at his side. MeLaan did the same, only her holster was her *leg*. Like, the skin split and she reached in through a slit in her trousers and slipped the gun out—a sleek, long-barreled thing.

Wayne whistled softly. She grinned, then gave him a kiss. "Try not to get shot too many times."

"You neither," he said.

They split up.

18

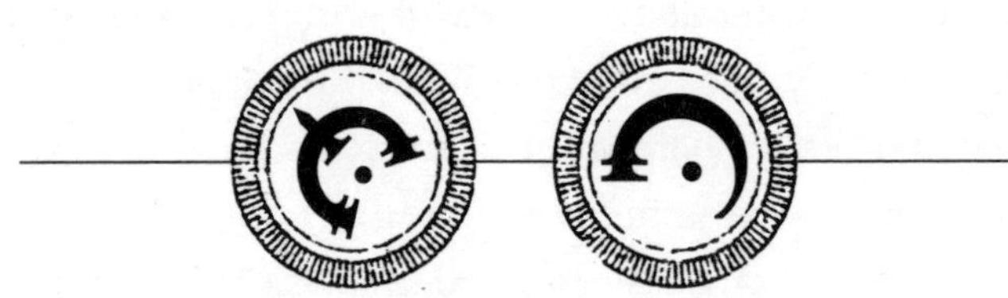

Marasi snuck through the warehouse, her rifle's strap an uncomfortable weight on her shoulder. She was glad for the trousers—they were quieter than rustling skirts—but she kept worrying that the scientists and workers in the room would notice the sound of her boots on the packed earth.

Probably not. The warehouse was hardly silent. Though it was night, and activity was muted, some people were still working. Along one side of the room, a few carpenters sawed lengths of wood, each stroke echoing back from the walls. The group of engineers made exclamations as they discussed aspects of the large vessel.

They seem surprised by it, Marasi thought. *As if they're not the ones who built it in the first place.* Were they new to the project, then?

Guards dotted the warehouse, but there weren't nearly as many as outside. She and MeLaan kept to the shadowed edge of the chamber, near the piles of boxes and supplies, but still had to pass uncomfortably close to a group of soldiers sitting at a small table playing cards.

The soldiers didn't notice them. Eventually, MeLaan and Marasi managed to reach the south wall, which was one of the long sides of the rectangular building. Here, rooms had been built into the structure, and they were more finished than the rest, complete with doors and the occasional window.

"Living quarters?" Marasi whispered, pointing.

"Maybe," MeLaan replied, crouching beside her. "So how are we going to find the spike?"

"I'd assume it's inside a safe of some sort."

"Maybe," MeLaan said. "Or it could be in a desk drawer in one of those rooms, or packed away in a box . . . or hell, they may have just thrown it away. Suit only seemed to want it because he required proof that poor ReLuur had been dealt with."

Marasi took a deep breath. "If that's the case, we'll have to interrogate Suit once Waxillium finds him. But I don't think they threw it away. We know the Set is researching ways to make Allomancers, and we know they're interested in Hemalurgy. They'd study the spike instead of tossing it."

MeLaan nodded thoughtfully. "But it could still be practically anywhere."

Not far away, the scientists—led by a man with a limp—walked up a plank ramp, peering into the open side of the boat. *It's him,* Marasi thought. The same one from the train robbery. He was showing the newcomers around the project.

They stepped inside.

"I've got an idea," Marasi said.

"How crazy is it?"

"Less crazy than tossing Wayne off a cliff."

"Not a high bar, but all right. How do we start?"

Marasi pointed at the hole in the hull that the scientists had entered through. "We get in there."

Wax moved along behind the supply pallets in the direction opposite Marasi's, feeling as if he were stepping through the shadow of progress. He'd pondered the transformations that Elendel had undergone during his absence: motorcars and electric lights, skyscrapers and concrete roads. It was like he'd left one world and come back to another.

That seemed only the beginning. Enormous warships. Technology that enhanced Allomancy. Bracers that one Feruchemist could fill, and another could use. He couldn't help but feel intimidated, as if this behemoth ship were a soldier from another time, come to stamp out all the dusty old relics like Wax.

He pulled up beside the last stack of planks in the line, Wayne joining him. The man yanked out his canteen, which was of sturdy, stiff leather, worked to the shape of a small bottle. He took a swig and offered it to Wax, who accepted it and downed a drink.

He coughed softly. "Apple juice?"

"Good for the body," Wayne said, tucking the canteen away.

"I was not expecting that."

"Gotta keep the stomach guessin', mate," Wayne said. "Or it'll grow complacent and all. How're we gonna find your uncle?"

"Perspective?" Wax asked, nodding toward the middle reaches of the warehouse, where a complex network of temporary construction catwalks ringed the inside of the building. They were unpopulated in the night. "We'd have a view of the entire area, but wouldn't be too noticeable from below."

"Sounds good," Wayne said. "You up for it, though? You're gonna have to climb up like a regular person. No Steelpushes."

He didn't have any metal inside of him—too easy to use reflexively. His vials sat unused on his belt.

"I'll be fine," Wax said dryly. He waited until nearby guards and workers had passed, then led the way in a low run along the shadows of the building. The lights were aimed on the ship, away from the walls. He had to hope that the few workers walking about weren't focused on the dark reaches of the large chamber.

Two full-sized catwalks ran the length of the wall up high, and leading toward them were a series of ladders and shorter catwalks as landings, to hold supplies. He grabbed the bottom ladder and climbed up one level, then another. By the third one, his arms were aching. He made himself lighter, which helped, but he still had to stop and catch his breath on the fifth tier. Just as making his body heavier granted him the strength to move his oversized muscles, getting lighter always seemed to cost him some of his strength.

"Gettin' old," Wayne said with a grin, passing him and starting up the next ladder.

"Don't be dense," Wax said, grabbing the ladder below him and climbing. "I'm trying to pace myself. What if we reach the top and have to fight?"

"You can throw your wooden teeth at 'em," Wayne said from above. "Do some cane waggin' as well. I'm sure you're cross about stayin' up so late."

Wax growled softly and climbed up onto the next tier, but in fact he was winded to the point that arguing was taxing. The younger man seemed to realize it, and had a wide grin on his face as they climbed up the final two tiers to the bottom catwalk.

"I should deck you right in your grin," he grumbled as he joined the still-smiling Wayne on the catwalk. "But you'd just heal."

"Nah," Wayne said. "I'd fall over and groan. Considerin' your age, it's more important to make you feel you've accomplished somethin' in a day."

Wax shook his head, turning and stepping to the side along the catwalk. The board under his foot immediately cracked. His leg slipped through, and though he caught himself and yanked the foot out, for the first time in ages he felt a little of what others must feel at being up so high. That ground was far, far below, and he didn't have any metals in him at the moment.

He growled and stepped around the hole. "That was *not* my fault. The board was weak."

"Sure, sure," Wayne said. "It's okay, mate. Most folks put on a little weight as they hit their twilight years. 'S natural and all."

"If I shot you," Wax said, "nobody would blame me. They'd probably just say, 'Wow. You lasted that long? I'd have shot him years ago.' Then they'd buy me a pint."

"Now, that hurts, it does," Wayne said. "I—"

"Who are *you*?"

Wax froze, then both he and Wayne looked upward toward the person leaning out over the railing of the upper catwalk, staring down at them. An engineer, by the looks of it, in a white coat over vest and cravat. He frowned at them, then seemed to recognize Wax, his eyes widening.

"Rust," Wax swore, raising his hands as Wayne moved immediately, jumping up. Wax gave him a boost, and he kicked off and grabbed the railing of the upper catwalk. The engineer started to cry out, but Wayne snatched the man's ankle, toppling him with a thump.

Wayne swung up in a heartbeat, and another thump sounded. Wax waited, nervous. Moments passed.

"Wayne?" he hissed. "Are you up there?"

A moment later, the engineer's unconscious face appeared over the side of the catwalk, eyes closed.

"Of course he's up here," Wayne said from up above, imitating the voice of the unfortunate engineer and wiggling the head like a puppet's. "You just tossed that bloke up here, mate! You've forgotten already? Memory loss. You must be gettin' *real* old."

Technically, every person in the world was dying—they were merely doing it very slowly. Irich's curse was not that he was dying. It was that he could *feel* it happening.

As he shuffled down the hallways of the enormous wooden ship, he had to keep close watch on the floor, because the slightest dip or cleft could cause him to trip. When he gestured toward the wall where they'd found the burned maps—explaining to the other scientists—his arm felt as if it were strapped with a ten-pound weight.

His left hand barely worked anymore; he could grip his cane, but he couldn't stop his hand from trembling as he did so—and he practically had to drag his left leg with each step. The shortness of breath had begun. His physician said that one day, he simply wouldn't have the strength to breathe.

On that day, Irich would suffocate alone, unable to move. And he could feel it coming. Step by excruciating step.

"And what is this, Professor Irich?" Stanoux asked, gesturing toward the ceiling. "Such a fascinating pattern!"

"We aren't certain," Irich said, leaning on his cane and looking upward—a task that was surprisingly difficult. Rusts. He hadn't had trouble tipping his head back before, had he?

Step by step.

"It looks like a ship," Stansi said, cocking her head.

Indeed, the golden pattern on the corridor ceiling *did* look something like a small ship. Why paint it here? He suspected it would take years to sort out this vessel's many secrets. Once, Irich would have been content to spend his entire life picking through these oddities, writing about each and every one.

Today however, his "entire life" seemed far too short a period to be spent on such endeavors. Suit and Sequence wanted their weapons, and they could have them, for Irich desired only one thing.

A miracle.

"Please, continue with me," Irich said, walking down the corridor with his latest gait. He had to develop a new one every few months, as more of his muscles grew too weak or refused to function. Step, cane, shuffle, breathe. Step, cane, shuffle, breathe.

"What marvelous woodwork!" Stanoux said, adjusting his spectacles. "Aunt, do you recognize what kind of wood this is?"

Stansi stepped up beside him, waving over the guard with the lantern so she could admire the strange hardwood. Irich had shown similar interest in the ship's details at first, but each day his patience grew more strained.

"Please," Irich said. "You shall have all the time you wish to study, prod, and theorize. But only *after* we have solved the primary problem."

"Which is?" Stansi asked.

Irich gestured toward an arched doorway ahead, guarded by a soldier with another lantern. She saluted as Irich passed. Technically, he was an Array—a rank of some influence within the Set. Suit and his people had a high regard for scientific thought. The power and prestige, however, were meaningless to him. Neither could grant him additional breaths of life.

Past the doorway, he waved for his group of five scientists to gaze upon the grand machinery that filled the hold of the strange vessel. It was like nothing he had ever seen, without gears or wires. It looked more like a *hearth,* only constructed of a lightweight metal with lines of other metals running away from it along the walls. Like a spiderweb.

"This ship," Irich said, "is filled with enigmas. You have noticed the odd patterns on the ceilings, but questions like those are barely the *beginning.* What is the purpose of the room hung with dozens of black hoods, like those worn by an executioner? We have found what appear to be musical instruments, but they seem incapable of making any sounds. The ship has an ingenious system of plumbing, and we have identified facilities for both men and women—but there is a *third* set of rooms with an indecipherable marking on the doors. For whom were these built? People of the lower class? Families? A *third* gender? So many questions.

"One question tops them all, and we feel that answering it will provide the very linchpin. It is why I have called for you, the most brilliant minds of the outer cities. If you can answer this, we will gain the technological might to secure our freedom from Elendel oppression once and for all."

"And what question might that be?" Professor Javie asked.

Irich turned back to them. "Why, how this thing *moves* of course."

"You don't know?"

Irich shook his head. "It defies all scientific knowledge available to us. Some mechanisms were undoubtedly damaged in the crash, but as you can see, the vehicle is mostly intact. We *should* have been able to ascertain its method of propulsion, but so far it eludes us."

"What of the navigators?" Stanoux asked. "The crew? Did none survive?"

"They have been uncooperative," Irich said. *And somewhat fragile.* "Beyond that, the language barrier has so far proven insurmountable. That is why I invited you, Lord Stanoux, as one of the world's foremost experts on ancient, anteverdant languages. Perhaps you can decipher the books found on this ship. Lady Stansi, you and Professor Javie will lead our engineers. Imagine the power we would have with a fleet of such ships. We would dominate the Basin!"

The scientists shared looks. "I don't know that I want *any* group having access to such power, Professor," Lady Stansi said.

Ah, right. These were not politicians. He should not employ the same rhetoric he had used when Suit sent him to gather funds from the wealthy. "Yes," he admitted, "it will be a terrible burden. But surely you can see that this knowledge is better off in our hands, rather than in the hands of those at Elendel? And think of what we will *learn,* what we could *know.*"

They took that better, nodding in turn. He would have to speak with Suit—these people must not see themselves as serving a totalitarian army, but a benign freedom movement seeking knowledge and peace. That would be difficult, with all these rusted soldiers marching about and saluting everyone.

He prepared for an explanation of what they knew, intending to divert the scientists with promises of knowledge, when he heard a voice echo down the hallway. "Professor Irich?"

He sighed. What now? "Excuse me," he said. "Lady Stansi, perhaps you will wish to inspect this fixture, which appears to provide some kind of power to the ship. It does not have electricity, so far as we can discern. I would value your unbiased opinions before I tell you what we have concluded. I must go deal with something."

They seemed amenable to this—enthusiastic even. He left them and limped down the hallway. *Too slow, too slow,* he thought, both of his walk and the possibility of progress from the scientists. He couldn't wait upon research, experimentation. He needed answers *now.* He had thought that on the train, they might find . . .

But no, of course not. An idle hope. He should never have left this project. Back in the hallway, he found no sign of the person who had called to him. Frustrated, he made it all the way back to the doorway before turning and searching down one of the side hallways.

They should know better than to call for him! Could they not see the difficulty he had in traversing even a short distance?

He started back up the hallway, but hesitated as he noticed a small storage compartment that had popped open on the wall. There were hundreds of these scattered throughout the ship, containing ropes or weapons or other items. But this one had dropped something to the floor. A small, silvery cube.

His heart leaped in excitement. Another of the devices? Such luck! He had thought all these compartments searched by now. He struggled to pick it up, going down on his good knee and fishing for it, then lurched back to his feet.

A plan was already forming. He would tell Suit that it had been recovered by one of his spies in New Seran. His punishments would be lifted, and perhaps he would be allowed to move to the second site, perhaps join the expedition.

Excited, he sent a soldier to watch the scientists, then hobbled out of the ship, glad that something was finally going *right* for him.

Marasi cracked a closet door within the strange ship, then looked after the man called Irich, who limped through the gaping hole in the wall. MeLaan slipped out of a closet across the hallway from her and held up a warding hand to Marasi, then snuck to the opening to watch where Irich went.

Marasi waited, anxious. Though her duties as a constable usually related more to analysis and investigation, she'd gone on her share of raids in Elendel. She'd thought herself hardened, but *Harmony,* this mission was starting to rub her nerves raw. Too little sleep, and so much sneaking about, hiding, knowing that at any moment someone could turn a corner and find you there, looking guilty as sin.

MeLaan finally waved her forward, and she scrambled out of the closet and knelt beside the kandra at the entrance.

"He went into that room," MeLaan said, pointing at a door along the wall. "Now what?"

"We wait just a bit longer," Marasi said. "And see if he comes back out."

Wax prowled along the wooden planks of the interior scaffolding. MeLaan's spyglass let him get a good look at the ground floor, though he'd have much preferred binoculars. He scanned the whole area, noticing with interest as Marasi and MeLaan entered the ship.

That ship . . . something about it bothered him. He hadn't been on many boats, but the decks atop the enormous thing seemed off to him. Where were the masts? He'd assumed them torn down, but from above, he could see no broken stumps. So, was this ship propelled through the water by a steam engine, perhaps? Gasoline?

After rounding the entire building on the catwalk, he saw no sign of his uncle.

"Still nothing?" Wayne asked as he lowered the spyglass a last time.

Wax shook his head. "There are some rooms built into the north side of the structure. He could be in there. He might also be inside the ship."

"So what do we try next?"

Wax tapped the end of the spyglass against his palm. He'd been struggling with the same question. How did he find his prey without alerting the guards camped outside?

Wayne nudged him. Down below, the limping man came back out of the boat. Wax focused the spyglass on him, watching as he crossed to one of the nearby rooms.

"Did he look anxious about somethin' to you?" Wayne asked.

"Yeah," Wax said, lowering the spyglass. "What did those two women *do* in there?"

"Maybe they—"

"I don't want to hear your guess," Wax said. "Really."

"Fair enough."

"Come on," Wax said, leading the way back around the shadowed catwalks toward the ladders.

"You have an idea?" Wayne asked.

"More of an impression," Wax said. "Suit doesn't like talking to minions. Everyone we've interviewed indicates the same thing—he chooses underlings with some power and repute and lets them handle things. Miles, the Marksman. My uncle loathes being bothered."

"So . . ."

"That man with the limp," Wax said, "probably has a similar role here. He's an Allomancer, and I heard him referenced in Lady Kelesina's mansion; he's an important underling, though perhaps not in favor right now. Either way, he likely reports directly to my uncle."

"So follow him long enough . . ." Wayne said.

". . . and we should find Suit."

"Sounds good," Wayne said. "Unless he reports every afternoon at tea, which would have us waitin' a *long* time."

Wax paused by the ladder, noticing with surprise that the man with the limp had already left the rooms. Wax's view was partially obscured by the massive ship, but he did catch sight of the man hobbling around the front of the vessel, again walking with a determined air.

Wax held up a hand to Wayne, then crouched down with the spyglass. The limping man crossed the warehouse to a solitary room, much like a guard chamber, built into the southwest corner. A soldier here stepped aside, letting the limping man enter. As the door swung open, Wax got a good glimpse of the room beyond.

His sister was inside.

He almost dropped the spyglass. The door swung shut, so he couldn't get a second glimpse, but he *had* seen her. Sitting at a small table, loomed over by the large Coinshot brute Wax had fought on the train.

"Wax?" Wayne asked.

"It's Telsin," Wax whispered. "She's being held inside that room." He found himself rising and reaching for one of his metal vials.

"Whoa, *whoa,* mate," Wayne said, grabbing his arm. "I'm all for charging in recklessly and whatnot, but don't you think it would be best to talk this through? You know, before we get all 'Let's shoot this place up.'"

"She's *here*, Wayne," he said. "This is why I came." He felt cold. "She'll know things about our uncle. She's the key. I'm going in after her."

"All right, all right," Wayne said. "But Wax, doesn't it strike you as worryish that *I'm* havin' to be the voice of reason here?"

Wax looked down at his friend. "It probably should."

"Yeah, I'll say. Look, I've got an idea."

"How bad an idea is it?"

"Compared to burnin' Allomancy, going in shooting, and inevitably drawing the attention of all those guards, not to mention the Set's kill squads? I'd say compared to that, it's a pretty *damn* good idea."

"Tell me."

"Well, see," Wayne said, sticking his gum to one of the catwalk's support beams, "we've got this *very* nice engineer's outfit over there on the unconscious fellow, and ever since that party half a year back, I been workin' on my smart-person talk. . . ."

19

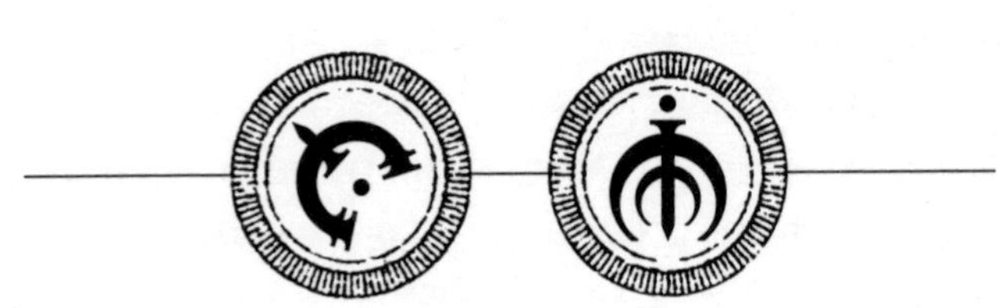

Marasi waited inside the ship, forcing herself—with effort—to remain calm. How did Waxillium do it? He and Wayne could be so relaxed, it seemed like they could take a nap in the middle of a firefight.

Well, she stood her ground—or rather, knelt it—and was rewarded. Through the hole in the ship's hull, she watched the wall of the warehouse where the rooms were. Irich soon hobbled out of one, then shuffled off and called toward some guards.

"What was that he said?" Marasi asked.

"He told them to 'Send to Mister Suit,'" MeLaan said. "You think he really stashed that device in the same place as they're keeping the spike?"

"That's the hope," Marasi said.

"Shall we?"

Marasi nodded, then prepared herself for another nerve-racking experience. MeLaan led, strolling down the planks and out into the open. Marasi followed, keeping her head high as MeLaan had told her. *Look like you belong,* the kandra had said. *The first rule of impersonation is to* belong.

She felt completely exposed, as if she were dancing naked in the middle of Elendel's Hub. They reached the bottom of the gangway, walking with excruciating slowness, and crossed the floor of the warehouse to the door. Was Marasi walking too stiffly? She couldn't check over her shoulder—MeLaan had warned her about that. But surely a quick glance wouldn't hurt anything. . . .

Stay firm. MeLaan tried the door, and blessedly it opened. The two of them stepped through into an empty hallway, and Marasi shut the door. No shouts of alarm followed. She was positive one of the carpenters had glanced at them, but nobody had said a word.

"Nice work," MeLaan said.

"I feel like I'm going to puke."

"Must run in the family," MeLaan said, leading her along the hallway. It had bare wooden walls and smelled of sawdust, and a solitary electric light hung from the ceiling. Melaan stopped at the simple door at the end, listened carefully, then tried the knob. This one was locked.

"You can open it?" Marasi said. "Like you did before?"

"Sure," MeLaan said, kneeling by the doorknob. "No problem. I'll try something more mundane first." She cocked her hand, and a set of picks *sprouted* from the skin of her forearm. She plucked them free and started working on the door.

"Handy," Marasi said.

"Pun intended?"

"That depends," she said, checking over her shoulder. The hallway was still empty. *Fool girl.* "How many times have you heard that joke?"

MeLaan smiled, focused on her lockpicking. "I've been alive pushing seven hundred years now, kid. You'll have trouble finding jokes I *haven't* heard."

"You know, I should really interview you sometime."

MeLaan cocked an eyebrow in her direction.

"You kandra have a unique perspective on society," Marasi explained softly. "You've seen trends, movements across large scales."

"I suppose," MeLaan said, twisting her lockpick. "What good does it do?"

"Statistics show that if we make subtle changes to our environment—the way we approach our legal system, or employment rates, maybe even our city layout—we can positively influence the people living in that environment. Your head may hold the key to what those changes should be! You've seen society evolve, move; you've watched the shifting of peoples like the tides on a beach."

"My thigh," MeLaan said, twisting the doorknob with a click, then pushing the door open a crack. She nodded, standing up straight.

"Your . . . what?" Marasi asked.

"You said my head might hold the key," MeLaan said, striding into the chamber beyond—a small, surprisingly well-furnished room. "It's actually my thigh, right now. A kandra stores its cognitive system through its entire body, but my memories right now are in a solid metal compartment in my thigh. Safer that way. People aim for the head."

"So what's in your head?"

"Eyes, sensory apparatus," MeLaan said. "And an emergency canteen."

"You're kidding."

"Nope," MeLaan said, hands on hips, scanning the room. Another door on the left led farther into the system of rooms built along the side of the warehouse, but there were no windows out to the main chamber, which was good.

Though the room smelled of new sawdust, like the rest of the building, here that was mixed with a scent of wood polish and a faint odor of cigar smoke. Light from a small electric desk lamp revealed a tidy study, with rows of books in a bookcase, two plush chairs with a maroon and yellow pattern in front of the desk, and several decorative plants that probably had to be rotated outside each day to keep from wilting.

Marasi trailed through the room, noting its oddities. Every room had them—marks of individuality, clues to the life of the occupant. The desk drawers had wide, exaggerated handles on them. The stand lamp in the corner had been bolted to the wooden floor, as had the chairs, likely to keep them in place should Irich stumble into them. Marasi was not familiar with the man's disease, but it appeared he liked his chambers to accommodate a little fumbling.

MeLaan went straight for the bookcase, then began pulling books off, toppling them to the ground. "It's always behind the books," she said. "People don't like to read, they like to be seen as someone who reads. I—"

"MeLaan?" Marasi said, then pointed to the large safe in the corner.

"Ah," MeLaan said, mid-ransack. She knocked the last few books off the shelf, perhaps for completeness's sake, then strode to the safe. "Hmm . . . This is going to be a little tougher. Can't crack something like this with a set of picks."

"Can you manage it?" Marasi asked.

"Patience," MeLaan said. "Bring over that lamp."

Marasi took it from the desk, stretching out the cord to its fullest and directing its light for MeLaan.

"Hmmm . . ." MeLaan said, then pressed her hand against the safe, ignoring the dial. Her fingers and palm went translucent, and then her flesh began to *wiggle,* squeezing into the joints, leaving behind crystalline bones held together with the barest of sinew.

Marasi swallowed, mouth suddenly tasting bitter. She'd known MeLaan could do this, but watching it was something else. She busied herself propping the lamp on the arm of the desk chair to give MeLaan light, though the kandra now knelt with eyes closed, so who knew if she needed it any longer? Marasi then started rummaging through the desk drawers to see if she could find anything important.

Harmony send that Irich goes back to the scientists after this, Marasi thought, *instead of returning here to catch up on paperwork.*

"The world back then," MeLaan said suddenly, "wasn't all that different from the one now."

Marasi hesitated. MeLaan still knelt with her eyes closed, her strange bones exposed. The flesh had gone translucent all the way up to her elbow.

"What do you mean?" Marasi asked.

"People talk about that time," MeLaan said. "The time of the Lord Mistborn, right after the Catacendre. They speak of it in hushed tones as if it were some time of legends."

"It was," Marasi said. "The Counselor of Gods, Hammond, Allrianne Ladrian. They forged a new world."

"Yeah, sure," MeLaan said. "But they also squabbled like children, and each one had their own vision of what this 'new world' should be. Half the reason you're having troubles now was because they didn't care about settlements outside of Elendel. The Originators were big-city people, through and through. You want trends? Want to know what I've seen? People are people. Hell, even *kandra* act the same, in our own way. Life then was like life now, only you have better street food."

Marasi pondered this, then turned back to the desk. She'd still want to interview some kandra—but perhaps ones who were a little more . . . reflective than MeLaan.

In the desk, she found a notebook with some of Irich's observations and sketches about the ship, written in a shaky scrawl, along with a map of the area. The more she discovered, the more certain she was that the Set *hadn't* built this vessel. They were studying it as much as repairing it.

Marasi tucked the book into her purse. *See, handy,* she thought. After that, she rose to check the other door out of the room. She wouldn't want to have some random carpenter wander in. She cracked it open and peeked into a completely dark room, and was immediately hit with a pungent odor like that of the slums. Unwashed bodies, dirt and grime. Frowning, she opened the door wider.

The shaded illumination of the lamp—which faced the wrong way to give direct light—crept hesitantly into the room. Shadows stretched long from a few bare tables and a stack of boxes. And beyond them . . . were those *cages*? Yes. Perhaps four feet tall, with thick bars, the cages looked like the type you might use to contain a large animal.

They were empty. "MeLaan?" Marasi asked, glancing at the

kandra—who did not respond. She looked utterly absorbed by her task.

Marasi inched into the room, wishing for another light. What did they keep in here? Guard dogs? She hadn't seen any of those at the perimeter. She stopped near one of the three large cages, bending over to see if she could determine what kind of animal had been kept in it.

Something rustled in the next cage over. Marasi's breath caught. What she'd mistaken for a lump of blankets or pillows was *moving.* She glanced toward the desk in the other room, where she'd set her rifle.

The thing lurched and slammed against the bars.

Marasi gasped, jumping away, her back crashing against the stack of nearby boxes. Inside the cage, dim light reflected from a too-flat face of red and black. Dark pits of eyes.

The pictures. Marasi had forgotten the pictures that ReLuur had left. Horrible faces of red and black, with those deep, dark eyes. Images as if from a nightmare, drawn in frantic, scribbled strokes.

The monsters were real. And there was one in the cage here, swathed in thick fur, face of polished red. It regarded her, silent, then reached out between the bars with a shockingly human hand and whispered a single word through lips that somehow didn't move.

"Please."

Wayne turned down his saunter and added a fair measure of scramble to his step instead. This engineer, he didn't like being here, among all these soldiers. He'd spent his life building houses and working on skyscrapers, and now here he was, basically in the middle of a bivouac!

That ship *was* marvelous, but he had a distinct worry. It was secret. And secret projects were the kind where little men like himself disappeared when everything was finished.

No, something's wrong, Wayne thought, halfway across the floor of the warehouse. He didn't stop walking, but he turned his steps in a little circle, like he was pacing. Something was wrong, but what *was* it?

"Wayne?" Wax hissed from the shadows nearby, crouched beside a barrel of pitch.

Wayne ignored him, continuing his loop. He . . . he was a scientist. No, no, an engineer. He was a working man. Learned enough, but not some fancy professor who was paid to stand all day and talk. He built things, and he hated being in this place, with all its guns. He encouraged life, and the soldiers were the opposite of that. They, they . . .

No, he thought again, raising hands to the sides of his head. Wrong, wrong, wrong!

Shape up, Wayne. This was your *plan. You've gotta make it work.*

What was wrong? He . . . He was a . . .

He stopped. Then reached into the pocket of his vest and took out a charcoal pencil. He held it up, inspecting it, before slipping it behind his ear. He let out a long sigh.

He was an engineer. A no-nonsense man who saw that things got done. He liked it here, as they had a military way about them—they said what they wanted, and were straight with him. Men were rewarded for hard work.

He didn't like all those guns. And he certainly didn't like the men in charge of this place. There was something *off* about them. But he held his tongue.

Relaxing, Wayne crossed the rest of the way to the door guard. False nose, mustache, a little extra air in the cheeks to fatten his face, and a perpetual squint in the right eye. Came from looking at plans all the time, he figured. But he didn't need a monocle. Those things looked downright stupid.

He stepped up to the guard. "The lattice supports of the apricity are completely liminal!"

The man blinked at him.

"Don't just stand there!" Wayne said, waving toward the walls of the warehouse. "Can't you see that the forebode malefactors are starting to bow? We could have a full-blown bannock on our hands at any minute!"

"What . . ." the guard said. "What am *I* supposed to—"

"Please," Wayne said, pushing him aside—the man let him—and pulling open the door.

The scene beyond was as Wax had described it. That was Telsin, all right. Dark hair, rugged body. Almost like a Roughs woman. He'd seen her evanotypes all over the mansion. Looked older now. Being a prisoner could do that to somebody.

Tweaked-leg and thick-neck stood beside her table, and both turned with annoyance toward him.

Now, Wayne thought, focusing on tweaked-leg, *the real test.*

"We've got a serious problem," Wayne said. "I've been checking the integrity of the structure, and the caronals are completely nepheligenous out there! We are about to have a full-blown case of ximelolagnia if somebody doesn't do something."

The bespectacled man looked at Wayne, blinked once, then said, "Well, of course we will, you idiot. But what do we *do* about it?"

Wayne held back a smile, tucking it into his pocket for later use. It seemed to him that the smarter a man was, the more likely he was to pretend he knew more than he did. Like the way the drunkest fellow at the pub was always the one who was most sure he could handle another pint. Tweaked-leg would sooner sell his own grandmother as a footstool than admit he didn't know what Wayne was talking about.

"Quickly," Wayne said, gesturing. "We've got to hold it up while I ratchet the saprostomous underlays! You'll need to supervise while I work!"

Tweaked-leg sighed, but walked out. Thankfully, his thick-necked companion followed. Within moments, Wayne had this guy pushing against the supports of the ship's pontoon while tweaked-leg observed, a few guards joining in to help.

A soft thump from behind indicated that Wax had dealt with the guard at the door. Normally Wayne would feel left out, since he didn't get to do any hitting. This time though, Wayne got to make a bunch of idiots stand with their hands pressed against some wood, thinking they were keeping the ship from tipping over.

So it evened out.

"Please."

The creature spoke with a strange accent, but the voice was unmistakably human. Marasi breathed in and out in sharp breaths, regarding that hand reaching for her. A human hand.

Lips that didn't move . . . polished skin . . . That wasn't a face, but a *mask*. This wasn't some horrible creature, but a person in a wooden mask, the eyeholes caught by the shadows. What Marasi had mistaken for fur was thick blankets clutched around the person's shoulders.

"Marasi?" MeLaan asked. The kandra appeared in the doorway. "I got it open. What are you doing— What the hell is *that*?"

"It's a person," Marasi said. The masked one turned toward MeLaan, and the new angle lit the holes in its mask, illuminating human eyes with brown irises.

Marasi stepped forward. "Who are you?"

The person turned back to her and said something completely unintelligible. Then it paused, and said, "Please?" That was a man's voice.

"We've got to go," MeLaan said. "Safe is open."

"Is the spike inside?" Marasi asked.

"See for yourself."

Marasi hesitated, then hustled into the other room, passing MeLaan.

"Please!" the man cried, huddled against the bars, reaching out.

The safe gaped open in the corner of the room. The top shelf was cluttered with objects, including the little Allomantic grenade. Prominent among them was also a length of silvery metal. Kandra spikes, as proven in the Bleeder case, were smaller than Marasi might have once imagined—less than three inches long, and slender, not at all like the spikes in Death's eyes.

She knelt beside the safe, taking it out.

"We have it," Marasi said, turning toward MeLaan. "Do you want to carry it?"

MeLaan shook her head. "We don't touch one another's spikes."

Marasi frowned, remembering the stories. "Didn't the Guardian—"

"Yes."

MeLaan's face remained impassive, but her tone was stern. Marasi shrugged, tucking the spike into her purse, then searched in the safe. She left the banknotes—stupid, she knew, but it felt more like really robbing to take those—and took back the little cube that stored Allomantic charges.

Beside it were several other small relics—each was coinlike, with cloth bands attached to the sides. They too bore the strange inscriptions in an unknown language. Marasi picked one up, then looked over MeLaan's shoulder into the other room, where the man in the mask slumped against his bars.

Marasi tucked the disc in her purse, then reached farther into the safe, taking out something she'd noticed earlier. A small set of keys. She stood up and strode through the room.

"Marasi?" MeLaan asked, sounding skeptical. "It might have some kind of disease."

"He's not an *it*," Marasi said, stepping up to the cage.

The figure twisted to regard her.

Hand quivering only a little, she unlocked the cage, getting the right key on the second try. As soon as the lock clicked, the figure lunged for the cage door, throwing it open. Outside, he stumbled—he obviously hadn't been allowed to stand up straight for some time.

Marasi backed away until she was beside MeLaan. The tall kandra woman watched with a skeptical expression, arms folded, as the masked figure staggered up against the boxes, holding to them. He panted, then lurched away from the boxes toward the back of the room. There was a door there that Marasi hadn't noticed in the gloom, and the man frantically shoved it open, stepping into the next room. Lights flicked on as the man found a switch within.

"If he alerts the guards, I'm blaming you," MeLaan said, joining Marasi as they walked after the man. "I would hate to have to tell Wax that . . ." MeLaan trailed off as they reached the next room over.

"By the Father and the First Contract," MeLaan whispered.

The floor was stained red. Operating tables of sleek metal crowded one wall, gleaming garishly compared to the macabre floor. On the wall hung a dozen wooden masks like the one the man wore.

He had fallen to his knees before them, looking up. Dried blood stained the wall where it had dripped from a few of the masks.

Marasi raised her hand to her mouth, taking in the gruesome scene. There were no bodies, but the blood bespoke a massacre. The man she'd rescued lifted his mask with a trembling hand, tipping it back so it rested on the top of his head, exposing his face. A young face, much younger than she'd imagined. A youth not yet twenty, she guessed, with a short, wispy beard and mustache. He stared up at those masks, unblinking, hands spread to the sides in disbelief.

Marasi stepped forward, moving to lift the hem of her skirt so as not to brush that bloody ground—before remembering she had on trousers.

As she reached the youth, he turned to her.

"Please," he whispered, tears in his eyes.

Wax stepped into the room.

Telsin sat twirling a pencil in her hand. There was a speaking box before her on the table, but making no sound. She turned lazily to see who had entered, then froze in place, gaping.

He closed the door quietly, aluminum gun in his other hand. He started to speak, but Telsin leaped from her chair and threw herself into his arms. Head against his chest, she started weeping softly.

"Rusts," he said, holding her, feeling awkward. "What did they do to you, Telsin?" He wasn't certain what he'd expected from their reunion, but this hadn't been it. He didn't think he'd ever seen her cry. He certainly couldn't remember it.

She shook her head, pulling back, sniffling and setting her jaw.

She looked . . . old. Not that she was ancient, but he remembered her as a youth, not a middle-aged woman.

Stupid though it sounded, he hadn't expected age to come for Telsin. She had always seemed invincible.

"No other ways out of this room?" Wax asked, glancing about.

"No," she said. "Do you have another weapon?"

He pulled out one of his Sterrions and handed it to her. "Do you know how to use it?"

"I'm a fast learner," she said, looking far more comfortable now that she had a gun in hand.

"Telsin," Wax said. "Is he here? Our uncle?"

"No. I was just speaking with him through that device. He likes . . . he likes to check in on me. I have to tell him how wonderful I think my accommodations are. He pretends I'm his guest, even still."

"Well, you're not. Not anymore. Let's go." Hopefully Wayne's distraction was still working.

Telsin, however, sat down in her chair again. She gripped that gun in both hands, held before her, but she stared unseeingly. "There's so much to ask. Why did you come back? Rusts . . . why did you *leave*, Waxillium? You didn't come when I sent to you, when I was engaged to Maurin, when our parents died—"

"There isn't time," Wax said, seizing her by the shoulder.

She looked up at him, dazed. "You were always the quiet one. The thoughtful one. How did you get here? I . . . Your face, Waxillium. You're old."

The door suddenly slammed open. The tall, thick-armed man that Wax had fought on the train stood there, looking stunned. He turned from Wax to Telsin, and opened his mouth.

Telsin shot him.

"We need to go," MeLaan said.

"We're bringing him," Marasi said, pointing to the man.

"Why?"

"Haven't you figured it out, MeLaan?" Marasi asked. "That ship out there *wasn't* built by the Set. It's from somewhere else, someplace distant and alien. It probably wrecked near our coast, and the Set brought it here to be studied."

MeLaan cocked her head. "Harmony does say odd things sometimes, about other peoples, not from the Basin—" She blinked, focusing on the man kneeling on the bloody floor. "Wow. *Wow.*"

Marasi nodded. Proof that there was life past the Roughs, and the deserts beyond. She couldn't let him stay here, particularly not with the Set.

"Bring him then," MeLaan said, moving out of the room. "And let's get back to the meeting point."

Marasi gestured toward the way out, trying to usher the masked man along. He just knelt there on the bloody floor, looking up at those hollow masks on the wall.

Then, with a trembling finger, he reached up and slid his mask back down over his face. He stood and pulled his blankets tight, shambling after Marasi as she crossed the room with the cages and entered the study.

MeLaan was already out in the hallway beyond. Marasi fetched her rifle and moved to join the kandra. Rusts, what was Waxillium going to say when he found out she'd picked up a stray? She could almost hear his voice. *You freed him, Marasi, but for all he knows you're a member of the same group who apparently killed his friends. Be careful.*

She stopped at the door and looked back, gripping her rifle more tightly. Waxillium could be a curmudgeon, but he was right more often than not. The masked man might be dangerous.

He had stopped inside the room with the safe, looking about, seeming dazed. How long had he been in that little cage, trapped in the darkness? Listening as his friends were taken, tortured, and killed.

Rust and Ruin . . .

His eyes found the safe, fixating upon it, and then he crossed the room in a shuffle. He reached inside, and for a moment she assumed he was going for the banknotes. But of course not—he pulled out one of the little discs with the straps.

He held it up, seeming awed, then shucked off the blankets he'd been wearing like a cloak. She'd expected him to be wearing a loincloth or something savage underneath, but instead he was dressed in trousers that went down to just below his knees, under which he wore tight white socks. His shirt was loose and white, and over it he wore a snug red vest—matching his mask in coloring—with a double row of buttons up the front.

She'd never seen clothing like it before, but it was hardly *savage*. The man yanked up one sleeve, exposing his arm, and strapped on the disc by its cloth ties. He let out a relieved sigh.

Looking toward her again, he seemed more confident now. He was a short man, even a few inches shorter than Wayne, but seemed to have grown a foot by standing up straight and discarding those thick blankets. But rusts, how were they going to sneak him out? He was hardly inconspicuous with that mask. Perhaps Marasi and MeLaan could openly move short distances in here without drawing attention, but this man certainly couldn't.

A series of gunshots rang out in the warehouse.

Perhaps sneaking wouldn't be an issue.

20

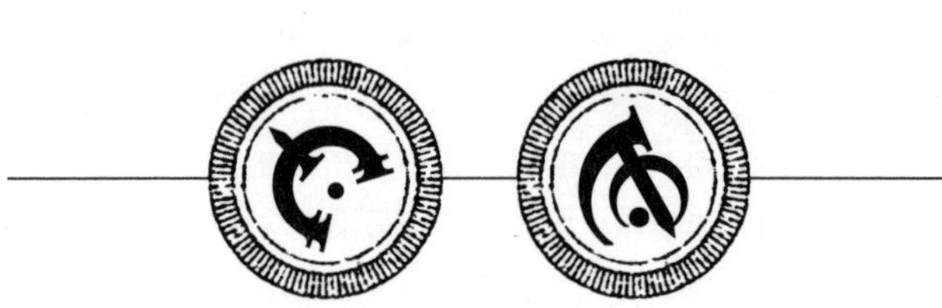

The corpse slumped into the room, one hand still on the doorknob, face frozen in an expression of shock. Telsin had fired four times and had only hit twice, but that was enough.

Wax cursed, grabbing his sister by the arm and towing her across the room. With his other hand, he found a vial of metal flakes on his belt.

"I'll kill them all, Waxillium," she whispered. "Each and every one of them. They held me. . . ."

Great. On one hand, he couldn't blame her. On the other hand, this was going to be rusting inconvenient. He downed the metal vial, then peeked out of the doorway to see the engineers and carpenters scattering for cover as guards came running toward Wax's position. A few were very near, the ones Wayne had led away, and one pointed at him and shouted.

The room's flimsy walls seemed like they'd be about as effective against bullets as stern words were against the town drunk. As the first soldier took a shot at him—Wax shoved back with a Steelpush—he made a decision.

"Hang on to me," he said, pulling Telsin to his side. He took one step out of the room, fired into the ground, and sent them on a Push up into the air. Soldiers pointed, leveling guns, but in a moment he was on the top of the large ship. As he'd seen earlier, it was wide and flat up here, though the planks were smoother than the deck of any ship he'd seen, and the gunwales were like the crenellated tops of a fort or old tower.

He dropped Telsin. "I'll be back soon," he promised, leaping over the side of the ship. The man who had shot at him earlier wasn't giving up, and fired more rounds. Splinters popped off the sides of the ship as Wax fired Vindication and dropped the man. Wax landed, bounced off a stray nail, then skidded to a stop beside a stack of boxes where Wayne was hiding.

"What?" Wayne asked. "Get impatient?"

"My sister shot one of them."

"Nice."

Wax shook his head. Soldiers had started to pour into both ends of the large structure. "Not nice. There will be kill squads mixed among those soldiers, Wayne. Aluminum bullets. We need to get Marasi and MeLaan and go. Fast."

Wayne nodded. Wax took another draught of steel flakes, in case he lost his gunbelt, then nodded. "Speed us to the other side."

Wayne ran out, and Wax followed. Gunfire sounded, but Wayne popped up a speed bubble. It only covered about ten feet, but that was plenty to throw off aim. Wayne let Wax pass him, then they charged through the edge, side by side. The bubble collapsed, and bullets zipped through the air back where they'd been.

They ran on, but about the time the soldiers got another bead on them, Wayne created another bubble. This lurched them forward again, and shortly they were able to dive behind the broken section of the ship's pontoon and take cover. Soldiers cried out, confused by the Allomancy—but if there were kill squads among them, trained hazekiller hit men, they wouldn't be so easily fooled.

Wax led the way, darting along the front of the ship, in its shadow. As soon as someone started firing, Wayne tossed up another bubble, and the two of them repositioned. Wayne made to run out, but Wax stopped him, arm on shoulder.

"Wait."

Safely inside this speed bubble, Wax looked back across the cavernous hall. They were close to the eastern side, and soldiers in slow motion set up a perimeter, clogging the doorway and kneeling in ranks. Captains at the rear yelled, pointing, and bullets flew toward the last spot where Wayne and Wax had been seen.

Uncomfortably, more shots streaked through the air where—if they'd been following their previous pattern—they would have exited the speed bubble.

"Damn," Wayne said, eyeing the bullets. He tossed over his canteen. Wax took a drink, judging distances and feeling the surreal sensation of standing calmly in a maelstrom of gunfire, sipping apple juice.

"They're goin' all-out," Wayne said.

"Our reputation precedes us. How much time have you got left?"

"Two minutes, maybe. I've got more bendalloy on the horse, in case. The kandra stocked me up before we left."

Wax grunted. Two minutes could go very quickly. He pointed at the large hole in the ship's side, where a plank ramp led to the thing's insides. "I saw the ladies go in there."

"Funny," Wayne said, "'Cuz *I* see them peekin' out over there."

Wax followed his gesture, and indeed saw MeLaan's face behind a barely opened door out of one of the rooms at the side of the warehouse. Wax took a deep breath. "All right. Those armies will cut us apart, Allomancy or no, if we don't hide quickly. Those rooms will do. We can move through them toward the outer wall of the building, I can break through it, and we flee into the night that direction."

"Right," Wayne said. "And your sister?"

"She should be safe for the moment," Wax said. "Once we break out, I'll launch myself to the roof, then come back down through the open part and grab her."

"Sounds good," Wayne said, "'cept for one thing."

Wax handed back the canteen. "Here."

"Ha!" Wayne said, taking it. "But I was talkin' about *that*." He pointed toward the ship. A figure was climbing down one of the rope ladders that hung over the side of the ship. Telsin had *not* stayed put.

"Rust and *Ruin*," Wax snapped.

"Under a minute left, mate."

"Get her inside a bubble!" Wax shouted, gesturing. "I'll join the other two. Go!"

They split, the speed bubble falling. A sudden storm of gunfire assaulted Wax's ears as he dropped to the ground, feet forward, and Pushed against the metal supports in the ship behind him. He skidded across the packed dirt of the floor, bullets flying overhead, and reached the door that MeLaan flung open for him. His heels hit the threshold—the corridor had a wooden floor—and he popped up onto his feet, landing inside with a dusty thump.

"I'll have you know," Marasi said, "that *we* managed to do our job without alerting anyone."

"I'll send you a plaque," Wax said, pointing toward a strange, short man standing behind her. "What the hell is that?"

The man pointed back.

"His people must have built the ship," Marasi said. "They had him caged in there, Waxillium."

"Damn," MeLaan said from the doorway. "That army isn't playing games." It was hard to hear her over the gunfire.

"I found my sister," Wax said. "Suit's people must know how angry that will make him. We need to—"

"Wax!" MeLaan said, pointing.

He squeezed back up beside her. Wayne had almost reached his sister, who pressed herself against the ship's side, eyes frantic. But Wayne had been hit. He lurched in place, holding his shoulder, as another bullet hit him right in the neck. He fell in a spray of blood.

Wayne could heal from that, with his new, strange metalmind. Unfortunately, the soldiers didn't stop firing. Another bullet hit Wayne's side as he dropped and played dead, then another. In an eyeblink he was healed and up, but then another round dropped him.

They were prepared. They knew. You want to kill a Bloodmaker? Knock him down and keep shooting.

Seeing his friend bleeding, facing some fifty men on his own, awakened something primal in Wax. He didn't think; he didn't shout orders. He tore from the hallway in a furious Push on the nails in the walls, soaring out into the warehouse proper a foot or so above the ground, pulling up dust in his wake.

The soldiers had been waiting for this. They had formed up on both sides of the warehouse, using boxes as cover, and they sent out twin waves of bullets—completely uncaring that they risked catching one another in the crossfire. Killing an Allomancer was worth the danger.

They could only wish to be so lucky.

To Wax's eyes, the room became a frantic network of blue lines, a loom full of a mad weaver's threads. He shouted, Pushing to both sides, shoving sprays of bullets in either direction and creating a ballooning hub of open space.

Several bullets continued to fly, though he noticed them only because one clipped him on the shoulder. Wax spun and yanked Vindication from her holster. A second volley came, and—his mind instantly matching blue lines with bullets fired—he shot once, dropping one of the men among the ranks who had fired an aluminum bullet.

More bullets came in a storm, but Wax swept them aside like dishes off a table. He was at the mercy of anyone firing aluminum, so he kept moving, dashing across the floor and leaping, Pushing behind himself and severely reducing his weight once he'd finished Pushing. The result was immediate; he sped up like an arrow, flying through the air with a roar of wind in his ears.

He landed before Wayne in a skid and Pushed bullets away from the healing man with a roar, then increased his weight and *Pushed* on the hull of the ship nearby. The wood crumpled, nails popping free of joints and planks tearing away before his fury, creating a second hole.

"Inside!" he shouted at his sister, prone on the ground nearby.

She nodded, scurrying in, and Wayne—still bleeding from a dozen different places—joined her in a crawl, throwing himself in through the opening.

Can't let them stay there, Wax thought, Pushing himself away as another round of bullets pelted the area. One didn't deflect when he Pushed it, but he couldn't pick out the owner from among the dozens of firing men. Damn.

The ship was a death trap. Yes, it would provide cover, but if they took refuge there the troops would surround them. But Wayne needed a moment to heal. That meant keeping the soldiers—

Three men in jet-black suits launched in succession over the hunkered-down soldiers. The guns they bore had no Allomantic metal trails. Wax cursed, dropping Vindication and ripping the shotgun from its holster on his leg.

The first of the Allomancers to land Pushed on Wax. He felt it as a jolt on the shotgun as he leveled the thing—increasing his weight and setting it against his shoulder—to fire.

The Allomancer smiled, Pushing on the slug as it left the barrel. But the huge powder load of the gun—designed to bring down Thugs—sent the man sprawling backward from his own Push. Dazed, he was just able to glance up as the next slug hit him in the face.

Thanks, Ranette.

The other two Allomancers ducked down as they landed, expecting more fire, but the powerful shotgun held only two rounds. Wax dropped it into its holster as he knelt, grabbing Vindication.

Behind! If there was a kill squad from one direction, they'd likely send another for him the other way too. The regular soldiers were mostly a distraction.

He twisted, Pushing around himself and leveling Vindication to surprise a man and woman in suits sneaking up on him. He dropped the woman.

The male Allomancer opened fire. Too many shots. No metal lines. Wax—

The bullets froze in the air.

Wax blinked, and then noticed something that had fallen to the ground near the enemy Allomancer: a small metal cube. Marasi crouched inside the doorway where she'd been hiding, MeLaan standing over her and drawing fire—absorbing bullets with her flesh like it was no big deal.

Wax grinned, then stepped aside. The Allomantic grenade ran out a second later, and the man who had been trapped inside the bubble fired again, trying to kill a Wax who was no longer there.

Wax leveled his own gun and killed the fellow.

Marasi wished she knew where her earplugs had gotten to. Honestly, how did Waxillium survive without them? The man had to be half deaf by now.

A bullet popped up dust on the ground near her. MeLaan knelt beside Marasi, giving her cover from one direction and taking another series of hits. She grunted. "This doesn't hurt," she said. "But it's not particularly *pleasant* either."

Ahead, Waxillium dodged shots from two more members of the kill squad and scooped up the device. Marasi leveled her rifle, trying to concentrate. Everyone was moving so quickly, and the *bullets*. They zipped in the air all around her. She brought down several soldiers, trying to focus on the ones that were firing in her direction. Many had taken shelter behind boxes on either side, so they weren't firing in coordinated volleys anymore. They seemed to know that their job was to make a lot of noise and try to distract Wax while others, better equipped and better trained, actually tried to take him down.

Still, it was remarkable he didn't get hit. Waxillium dashed past, mistcoat tassels flying, and swept bullets from the air. Then he launched himself toward the catwalks above.

Two men in suits followed. Allomancers. Marasi took aim at one and fired, but her shot was deflected.

Speaking of which . . . Though gunfire still popped in the huge room, no bullets hit the ground near Marasi, and none seemed to be striking MeLaan.

But why? Then Marasi spotted the little cube nearby. Waxillium had charged and then dropped it in front of them as he ran by. Marasi grinned, fishing an aluminum round from her purse. She could feel the device Pushing on her gun, but it was far enough away that it didn't matter.

A hand fell on her shoulder. She jumped, then found the small masked man behind her. Rusts! She'd almost forgotten about him. His other hand was frozen halfway toward his mask, and behind it his eyes were wide.

She followed his gaze, which was focused on Waxillium, who landed beyond them. He must have increased his weight manyfold, for he was able to Push a group of boxes by their nails and send them flying backward, along with many soldiers.

"Fotenstall," he whispered in awe.

"Allomancer," Marasi said with a nod.

"Hanner konge?"

"I have no idea what that means," Marasi said. "But that cube thing will soon stop buzzing, so we need to move. MeLaan? Do we retreat back?"

"Please," the masked man said, gesturing toward the ship. He pointed frantically. "Please!"

Marasi ignored him, scrambling across the ground—entering the warehouse proper—and grabbing the device. It had indeed stopped buzzing.

Waxillium landed nearby, sweeping a round of shots away from her, and Marasi charged the thing in her hand. It seemed like last time . . . yes, by burning just a tad of her cadmium she was able to get it buzzing, yet not slow herself down too much. She somehow poured the power into the device and tossed it at the people who landed nearby, chasing Waxillium.

It froze them in place.

"Nice work so far," Waxillium said. "But we're going to have to split up. Get back into those hallways. I'll follow soon. You're too exposed out here!"

The men lurched out of her speed bubble. Waxillium started firing at them, but they ducked, and one grabbed the little cube.

Marasi brought him down with the aluminum bullet she'd chambered.

Waxillium grinned. "Go!" he said, charging the other man, who yelped and leaped into the air, Pushing himself away. Waxillium scooped up the little cube as he passed, then he too launched into the air.

"Come on," MeLaan said, grabbing Marasi by the shoulder. A bullet took the kandra in the face, ripping off a chunk of her cheek and exposing green crystalline bone underneath.

The masked man cried out in fear, pointing and mumbling in his language.

"You should see me in the mornings," MeLaan said. She gestured back toward the hallways. Marasi moved to follow.

The masked man pulled on her arm, pointing more frantically at the ship. "Please, please, *please*."

Marasi hesitated. A bad idea in the middle of a firefight. Fortunately, most everyone seemed to be concentrating on Waxillium.

Something bit her in the left side. She looked down to see what it was, and was surprised to see red blooming on her coat around a hole.

A bullet hole.

"I've been shot!" she said, more surprised than pained. Shouldn't that hurt? She'd been *shot*!

She stared at the blood, *her blood,* until the masked man grabbed her by the shoulders and started towing her toward the ship. MeLaan cursed and helped him. Marasi realized she'd dropped her gun, and struggled against them, trying to reach for it, suddenly frantic that she *not* leave it behind.

That made almost no sense, and part of her acknowledged it, but rusts—

Shock, she thought. *I'm going into shock.*

Oh, hell.

Wax soared high above the floor of the warehouse, zipping past the catwalks, where several gunmen with rifles had set up. He flipped

Ranette's ball device outward—catching it around the railing of the catwalk—and hung on tight, pivoting sharply in the air. The gunmen started, trying to draw a bead on him as he landed behind them.

He stepped back and Pushed one gunman out at just the right moment, shoving him into the air as the last of the kill-squad Allomancers shot up past the catwalks, bearing a stunned expression at Wax's sudden change of direction. He collided with the rifleman in midair, and Wax turned, Pushing the other rifleman away. The poor man screamed as he fell.

Farther down the catwalk, two more men had set up with crossbows and wooden shields. Lovely.

Wax increased his weight. The entire catwalk shattered as he crashed downward through the wood, destroying the supports. He Pushed himself off a falling bar, shooting back out into the air, spinning Ranette's ball device on its cord. Above him, the suited man shook off the frantic gunman, dropping him and Pushing off to send himself into the air.

Wax flipped Ranette's ball upward and let go of the cord, still falling backward. The confused Allomancer caught the device by the cord as it passed.

Wax shot him in the chest.

Shouldn't drop your Allomantic shield, Wax thought, twisting in the air as he fell. *Even to catch a neat toy.*

As he approached the ground, Wax slowed himself on a spent bullet, then landed with a flare of mistcoat tassels. The dead Allomancer thumped to the ground beside him.

The ball dropped from his fingers and rolled toward Wax. "Thanks," Wax said, scooping it up. Where was—

Marasi. Down and bleeding, being dragged into the ship. *Damn!* Wax growled, launching himself into the air again as more soldiers fired. This place was a mess. Too many soldiers, many of whom were advancing on the ship, hiding a group of men with modern crossbows behind them. As one got close to the ship, Wayne peeked out.

"Wayne!" Wax shouted, passing overhead. He pocketed Ranette's ball and pulled out the Allomantic grenade—which was buzzing furiously—and dropped it.

Wayne looked up just in time to snatch the thing from the air, then looked down at it with surprise. When the first bullet curved away from him, Wayne grinned instead, then let out a whoop and flung it at the men in front of him. The thing rolled among them, tossing weapons aside with its power.

Wax sighed, landing on the top of the ship. Of *course* he'd throw it.

Wayne followed by jumping among the approaching soldiers, energetically laying about with his dueling canes. A bullet came startlingly close to Wax. More aluminum? As Wayne enthusiastically busted heads, Wax launched off the ship and landed among the advancing soldiers, increased his weight, and Pushed outward with a flare of strength. That tossed people away from him in a blast.

When the bodies fell, three men stood, stupefied, holding guns Wax couldn't sense.

He brought them down with a Sterrion—his other guns were out of bullets—then turned as he heard something distant. Horns blaring, a command. He leaped to the side, enough men dead or dropped that he could get a clear view out one of the doors into the night.

Men were streaming out of the buildings in the village. Dozens. He had a sinking feeling of dread. How long until his metals gave out? How many could he fight until someone with a crossbow or an aluminum bullet got lucky and hit him? He roared, launching himself upward in a leap over the fallen men he'd Pushed. Many were climbing to their feet. He was one man, not an army. He needed to run.

"Back!" he shouted at Wayne, who already had a crossbow bolt sticking from his thigh. The shorter man joined him, running toward cover inside the wrecked ship.

Marasi squeezed her eyes shut against the pain. It had finally come, arriving with a vengeance. MeLaan had given her a painkiller to chew, but it hadn't done anything yet.

"Dieten," the masked man said, putting her hand on her wound, which he'd bound with a strip of cloth from his shirt. She cracked an eye and saw him nod encouragingly, though with the mask down over his face she could see only his eyes.

Well, she wasn't dead. Even if *rusts* it hurt. And she thought she remembered reading somewhere that getting shot in the stomach—even on the side—wasn't good.

Don't think about that. What was going on? She gritted her teeth, shoved down her panic at being wounded, and tried to assess their situation. MeLaan watched the battlefield from beside the hole in the ship. Waxillium's sister stood nearby, cradling a handgun, eyes intense. Outside, gunfire, grunts, and screams accompanied Waxillium and Wayne doing what they did best: creating havoc.

Apparently the havoc quota had been filled, for a few moments later Waxillium swooped in through the hole. He nodded to MeLaan, his face shining with sweat, breathing heavily. Wayne scrambled in a moment later. He had a *crossbow bolt* sticking from his leg.

"Well, that was fun," Wayne said, plopping down and taking a deep breath. "Ain't been whooped so bad since the last time I played cards with Ranette."

"Marasi," Waxillium said, walking over to her. He pushed the masked man aside. "Thank Harmony you're alive. How bad is it?"

"I . . . don't really have much to compare it to," she said through clenched teeth.

Waxillium knelt beside her, lifting the bandage and grunting. "You'll live, unless that nicked the intestines. That could be bad."

"What kind of bad?"

"Painful bad."

"I might be able to do something," MeLaan said. "I'll check it out once we're safe. Speaking of which, how exactly *are* we going to get away?"

Waxillium didn't respond immediately. He looked exhausted. He glanced up at his sister, who was still muttering and holding her pistol. Outside the ship, it had gone unnervingly quiet.

"Our best bet is still going out through one of the warehouse's

walls," Waxillium said. "We're going to have to push toward those rooms Marasi and MeLaan were in."

"That's gonna be dangerous, Wax," Wayne said, stumbling to his feet, *still* ignoring the bolt in his thigh. "They'll have formed up, knowing we're going to try to make a break for it."

"We can manage," Waxillium said. "With me Pushing, we get to those rooms, find an outer wall, then break through."

"And if they're waiting on the other side?" MeLaan asked.

"Hopefully they won't be. It—"

"Guys," Wayne said. "I don't think we have time to plan!"

Gunfire sounded outside again, and bullets started snapping against the hull. Wayne scrambled away from the opening. Marasi thought she could hear Irich out there, shouting for the soldiers not to damage the ship, but the firing continued. It seemed someone had overruled him.

"Please," the masked man said, taking Marasi by the arm and pointing.

Marasi managed to get to her feet, though the pain made her eyes water. The masked man gestured, holding her by the arm.

She followed. Easier than trying to complain.

"We're going to have to push through it," Waxillium said from behind.

"I want to *kill* them," Waxillium's sister said. "I need more bullets."

"Yeah, let's have you focus on running, Telsin. Everyone get ready on my mark. Wayne, did you happen to grab that grenade?"

"Yup."

"We'll use it to make a speed bubble at the halfway point," Waxillium said.

"No luck there," Wayne said. "Completely outta bendalloy."

"Damn," Waxillium said. "Then we . . ." He trailed off. "Marasi? Where are you going?"

She continued limping along with the masked man. "He wants to show us something," Marasi said.

"They're coming!" Wayne shouted, peeking around the corner. "Fast!"

Marasi focused on moving down the corridor, one hand holding to her wound. She heard Waxillium curse, then gunfire sounded in the hallway. Waxillium was firing on men trying to pile in through the hole after them. *Trapped in here,* Marasi thought.

The masked man let go of her suddenly, then scrambled up the hallway ahead. "Don't—" Marasi said, but he stopped, threw open a panel in the wall, then reached in and pulled something.

A section of the ceiling, painted with one of the strange golden patterns, fell open. A rope ladder dropped down, hanging only halfway to the floor. The masked man jumped up and grabbed it.

"There's a hidden room here!" Marasi called.

"Better than nothing," Waxillium called back. "Everyone up!"

Wayne went next, jumping up and catching the ladder and climbing it with a lithe step. MeLaan could touch it without needing to jump, and she hoisted herself next. Waxillium's sister barely managed to grab the thing, but she climbed up with a hand from MeLaan.

Marasi stood looking with despair at the ladder, trying to imagine climbing it with her pain, until Waxillium seized her around the waist and Pushed them both up in a spinning leap. They landed inside the trapdoor, finding themselves in a narrow, low-ceilinged room fitted with a few chairs that were bolted to the floor. A single small window to the left looked out of the hull, letting in a sliver of light. The place looked like a railway compartment.

"Great," Wayne said. "At least now we can die in relaxed positions."

The masked man was fiddling with something near the wall. Some kind of trunk? He got it open and pulled out another one of those small, coinlike medallions with the straps on the sides. He pulled off the one he was wearing, and immediately gave a visible shiver, then slapped this one on instead.

"How's that?" he asked, looking back at them.

Marasi blinked in shock. He'd said it in her language—strangely accented, true, but intelligible.

"No?" the man asked. "You're looking at me confused, still. These things never work right. She swore that—"

"No, it works!" Marasi said. "At least, *I* can understand you." She looked to the others, who nodded.

"Aha!" the man said. "Great, great. Put these on." He tossed a medallion at each of them. "Touching the skin, please, maskless barbarians. Except you, Metallic One. You will not need one, yah?"

Marasi took hers and settled down on one of the seats, feeling dizzy. The painkiller seemed to finally be doing something, but she was still exhausted.

Below, shouts sounded in the hallway.

"Somebody better shut that door," the masked man said, crawling down on the floor and fiddling with something underneath a counter.

Wayne obliged, pulling up the ladder, which was tied to the trapdoor. It clicked closed, leaving them in even greater gloom. A gunshot sounded below, then another. Marasi jumped as the bullets *hammered* against the floor of the room.

"Does this place have any other exits?" Waxillium asked.

The masked man yanked on something, and the room shook with a jolt. "Nope," he said.

"Then why did you lead us here?" Waxillium demanded, grabbing him by the arm.

The masked man looked back at him. "Medallions on, yah?"

More bullets pelted the floor, but didn't penetrate into the room, fortunately.

"What do they do?" MeLaan asked.

"Make you lighter," the masked man said.

As soon as he said it—as soon as she knew what it did—something inside of Marasi understood. She was holding metal that, somehow, she could *feel*. It wanted something from her, and she poured it in, filling the metal . . . the *metalmind*.

She grew lighter, rising on her seat, the force of her body pushing less on her backside. Telsin gasped, obviously experiencing a similar sensation.

"Now that," Wayne said, "that's *right* strange."

"Great Metallic One," the masked man said, glancing at Waxil-

lium, "I, of course, wouldn't *dare* give orders to one of your stature, even if you wear your bare face out at all times. Who am I to judge? Even if you look equally crass as these others—even the cute one—I'm sure you're not. But, if I may be so bold as to suggest—"

"What?" Waxillium asked.

"A little Push," the masked man said, pointing downward. "On my mark."

"If I Push downward," Waxillium said, "I'll just fly up and hit the ceiling." He hesitated as the masked man pointed to a pair of straps connected to the floor, with wooden handholds at the ends. Waxillium looked at them, then looked at the masked man, who nodded eagerly.

Even in the darkness, Marasi could see the curiosity on Waxillium's face. Despite the men shouting below, the muffled sound of gunshots, he was still the lawman—the detective. Questions teased him. He stepped over to the straps, picked them up, and held them firmly, bracing himself with his feet on the floor.

"Ready," he said.

"A moment," the masked man said, reaching for a lever. He yanked it hard, and the entire room shook, then *slid* sideways. Out of the hull, like a drawer in a dresser being opened. Marasi could see out of the front end now, which proved to have a large glass window that had been blocked by wood earlier.

"Go!" the man said.

Waxillium must have Pushed, for the room shook, then rose into the air. They weren't in a room at all, but in a small boat that could detach from the main vessel.

n answer.
(Continued on back.)

m stood the haunted man. nen last we'd met, he'd rn a mistcloak, the hood which had obscured his e, but now I could see him arly.

Lightning flashed in his ld eyes and wind disarnged his sand-colored ir. In one hand, he held the lled tapestry like a baton. ith the other, he pointed alien-looking pistol at me. o doubt the origin of the ost he'd launched earlier.

The runes on the pistol's le flared emerald. I burnt romium and lunged forard into a Baz-Kor move eant to stop Coinshots efore they fill you full of les. Just as the green runes rned red, my hand touched e metal of the device.

When I drain a Misting of etal reserves, I feel someing I can only describe as ulling power from the metal nd returning this power to me external source. The etal remains, but the power gone.

I imagined that same innt as I touched the pistol. I ulled power from the device nd returned it . . . elsewhere.

The red glowing runes ent out like candles in wind.

It worked! The haunted deice was certainly something f another world—neither eruchemical nor Allomanic—yet my chromium touch ad affected it.

The haunted man glanced at the pistol and gritted his teeth. "What in helmore did you do?"

He touched a few of the runes on the side of his pistol-like device, and the symbols began to glow again. He pointed the gun at me, this time mere inches from my face. My chromium trick had not broken the pistol as I'd hoped. If I couldn't permanently leech its power, I'd have to relieve the haunted man of it altogether.

My Baz-Kor training took over, and I executed a movement meant to knock a gun from an aggressor's hands. One smooth maneuver took me behind my opponent and out of range of the pistol. Now the haunted man stood between me and the gondola's rusted opening. My next move sent the alien pistol flying from the man's grip and out into open air.

The haunted man spun to meet me, surprise registering in his eyes. I took the instant to seize the map.

Unfortunately, I was only able to grab one end, and it unrolled between me and the haunted man. Each of us held tight to the long ends of the map. I only needed to find the pouch on it with my father's instructions sewn inside. After that, it did not matter to me whether this thief took the rest of the tapestry or not.

"Shadows, woman!" said the man. "Leave me alone!" He clutched his end of the map and jumped from the hole in the side of the car.

The sudden jolt on the tapestry pulled me to the ground and dragged me across the floor till my head and arms dangled out over the void, though I still managed to hang on with both hands to my edge of the map, the only thing keeping the haunted man from falling to his doom.

"Bloody helmore!" he yelled. "Would you just let go!"

"I will *not*!" I gripped the fabric tighter.

"It's just a stupid map." He studied the tapestry. Adjusting his grip a few inches to the side, he crumpled the linen between his fingers and began to climb.

"It's my inheritance!" I yelled back.

"I don't care if it's the Survivor's bathrobe. *Just give it to me!*"

"You are entirely disagreeable!" I said.

"Then you're starting to figure me out."

I trust you will not judge me too harshly if the pleasant timbre of the comic stranger's voice had me completely enchanted. His hair like gold, his eyes like blue ice. If you ever meet me in person, I will gladly give a more detailed description.

"Truthfully," I said, "a little politeness on your part could have avoided this whole debacle, and you wouldn't be hanging fifty feet above death from the threads of a poorly rendered map. Climb in. Let's come to an agreement."

He reached up as if to take my offer, but something in his hand flashed in the light of the stars. Instinctively, I burnt metal, releasing one hand to touch the device.

It was an everyday hunting knife.

"Politeness," he said with a grumble. "That's not how I work."

He clutched his side of the tapestry and cut through the top of it with his knife. Between us, a V shape formed just before the map ripped completely in half.

I gasped as he fell backward into the mist, clutching his piece of the tapestry.

I pulled away from the edge, frantically searched my half of the map for the hidden pocket, and found it almost immediately. The lack of a knife, however, meant I would have to wait to open it until I returned to the mansion. Still, I was relieved that although the haunted man was gone and my father's map ruined, I had the information I needed to continue my quest. I do admit, though, that if the haunted man still lives, he wound up with the better half of the map.

After disembarking the lift, I walked to the location where my foe would have hit the ground. I found no trace of him, and though no one witnessed his fall, a young white-haired man was there and offered to tell me a story. I declined.

It was not until I had returned home that I lit up the electric lamp and found Pinecone Allomouser the Third asleep with her kittens on my bed. Careful not to disturb them, I used a sewing knife to make quick work of the tapestry's hidden pocket. Inside was a folded piece of vellum written on in my father's flowing penmanship.

My dearest Nicelle,

In this letter I am at long last able to disclose to you the secrets of the Unknown Constructs of Antiquity. . . .

—Continued next week!!—

21

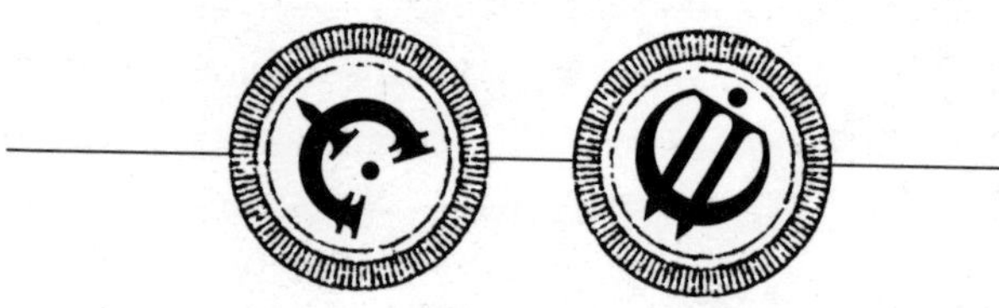

Wax stood in the center of the small vessel, Pushing against some kind of plate down below, designed—obviously—for this very purpose. It would be attached to the shelf the vessel had been on—not something that rose with it, but some kind of launchpad for an Allomancer to use as an anchor.

This vessel, though tiny, should still have been too heavy to lift. He should have broken those straps he held to, or been crushed by the force of his own Push. Yet he managed it. He held to those straps—essentially hitching himself to the ship—and lifted it, with all the people inside, off a ledge that had extended from the mother vessel.

It's those medallions, he realized. *They allow everyone to do as I do—to make themselves light, nearly as light as air.* That meant he was really only lifting the ship itself, along with their equipment.

The vehicle was small—barely six feet wide, though it was maybe twice as long—and had wide openings like doorways on either side. Those had faced walls inside the pocketlike shelf they'd popped out of, but now they exposed the air.

All in all, the thing felt like the cab of a motorcar with the doors ripped off. As the craft rose, small pontoons on extended arms folded

down and clicked into place. Wax had a brief view of surprised soldiers on the portion of the catwalk he hadn't broken, and then they were out, rising through the opening in the warehouse roof.

The strange man in the red mask scrambled through the vehicle and leaned out one of the holes in the walls to look downward. He looked solemn as he saluted the ship below, then bowed his head, whispering something.

Finally, he turned to Wax. "You are doing great, O Divine One!"

"I'm not going to be able to Push it much higher," Wax said with a grunt. "The anchor is too far away."

"You shouldn't need to," the man said, scrambling past Marasi—he patted her on the shoulder—then fiddling with some controls at the front of the machine. "I'll need the primer cube, please," he said, holding out a hand to Wayne.

"Huh?" Wayne said, looking away from where he'd been hanging out the other door to look down. A few distant gunshots sounded as soldiers took potshots at the hovering vehicle. "Oh, this?" Wayne took out the Allomantic grenade.

"Yah," the man said, snatching it. "Thanks!" He spun and pressed it against Wax's arm until—as he was still burning steel to keep them afloat—it started buzzing.

The little man turned and snapped the cube into place under the shelf at the front of the ship. The machine shook, and then something started thumping underneath them. A fan? Yes, a very large one, blowing downward, powered by an unseen motor.

"You can let go, Great Being of Metals," the man said, looking back at Wax. "If it suits your divine desires."

Wax eased off on his Push. They immediately started to sink.

"Reduce your weight!" the man cried. "I mean, if it is aligned with your magnificent will, O Metabolic One."

"Metabolic?" Wax asked, filling his metalmind and decreasing his weight. The ship stabilized in the air.

"Uh," the masked man said, seating himself at the front, "well, we're supposed to use a different title each time, yah? I've never been very good at this, Your Magnificence. Please don't launch a coin di-

rectly into my skull. I'm not insolent, just stupid." He pushed a lever forward, and smaller fans began whirring at the ends of the pontoons.

"They're not boats," MeLaan whispered. "Not this one, not the big one below. They're flying ships."

"Harmony's Bands," Marasi said. She was very pale, holding to her wounded stomach.

Flying ships that ran on some kind of Allomancy. Rust and Ruin. Wax felt the world seem to lurch around him. If electricity had changed life so dramatically, what would *this* do? Wax forced himself to shake out of his stupor and looked to the short masked man. "What's your name?" Wax said.

"Allik Neverfar, Tall One," the man said.

"Wait here a moment then, Allik."

"Whatever you desire, O—"

Wax jumped out of the vehicle before he could be praised—or insulted, he couldn't tell which these were—again. He got a better look at the small airship as he left. Yes, it looked more like a long motorcar cab than it did a boat, with that flat bottom. The large fan was separated from the ship by a short space, allowing air intake above. The doorways on the walls didn't seem to close; it was fortunate the seats had straps.

Wax dropped through the sky, afraid to Push off the small airship, but was able to use anchors down below to slow and direct himself toward the forests north of the camp.

He wanted to be quick. That ship wasn't up so high that it would be safe if they had access to cannons. He dropped into the forest and surprised Steris, who sat on her horse with the others in a line, all packed and ready to go.

"Lord Waxillium!" she cried. "I assumed you'd be coming, and prepared—"

"Great," Wax said, walking to his horse. "Get down, and grab your pack and Marasi's."

She did so without objection or question, pulling off her small pack of essentials, then fetched that of Marasi. Wax did the same for MeLaan and Wayne.

"We're leaving the horses?" Steris asked.

He released the horses, then grabbed Steris around the waist. "Turns out we've found something better." He pulled out one of his older guns, then dropped it—he'd need a large chunk of metal to get them high enough—and Pushed, launching them from the forest and into the sky.

He'd worried about maneuvering—doing so up high wasn't easy without skyscrapers to Push against. However, Allik steered the ship toward him, allowing him to get Steris one of the armbands, then set her into the vessel before climbing in himself. It managed to accept the new weight of the supplies, though Allik had to pull a lever to keep them from sinking.

"Seven people," the masked man said. "And supplies. Above the weight *Wilg* is supposed to carry, but she should manage. Until our metal runs out. The question is, where do you want her to take us?"

"Elendel," Wax said, walking toward the front of the little ship.

"Great," Allik said. "And . . . where is that?"

"North," Wax said, pointing. The little shelf at the front of the vehicle—like the dash of a motorcar—had a compass set into it. "If you head west first though, and find the river, we can—"

"No." Telsin seized Wax by the arm. "We need to talk."

Gunfire sounded below, followed by an echoing boom. Great. They *did* have a cannon.

"Just get us away from here," Wax said to Allik as he let Telsin tow him toward the back of the small ship. He passed Wayne, still hanging halfway out of one of the two open doorways and gawking. Marasi was on the floor, with MeLaan checking her wound, while Steris had already started packing their bags into an efficient pile between two of the seats.

The fans whirred and the ship began to move—not quickly, but steadily—away from the enemy camp. Wax settled onto a bench at the back of the ship with his sister. Rusts . . . Telsin. Finally. It had been a year and a half since he'd promised to stop his uncle and free her. Now here she was, sitting beside him.

She looked like a modern woman, with her hair in curls, wearing

a stylish dress of contemporary fashion—thin material, hem up right below the knees, a neckline to emphasize a long neck and delicate drooping chains. If you didn't look at her eyes, you could have assumed she was a fine lady on her way to a ball.

If you did look into her eyes, all you found was coldness.

"Waxillium," she said softly, "there's a weapon of some sort to the south, hidden among the mountains separating the Basin from the Roughs. Uncle Edwarn has found it. He's on his way there."

"How much do you know?" Wax asked, taking her hand. "Telsin, do you know what he's planning? Is it a revolution?"

"He doesn't tell me much," she said. Her voice was so calm, so cold, compared to how it had been before. Always full of passion, ever nudging him to do things he should not. It seemed like they'd leeched the life out of her, during her months of captivity. "We have dinner together most nights when he is here, but he grows angry if I ask about his work. He wanted me for one of his . . . his projects, originally, but my age makes that impossible. Now I am just a pawn. To use against you, I believe."

"No longer," Wax said, squeezing her hand. "No more, Telsin."

"And if he finds this weapon?" she asked. "He seems *convinced* it is there, and that it will give his group the power to dominate the Basin. Waxillium, we *can't* let him have it." Some passion returned to her eyes, some of the Telsin he remembered. "If he seizes the Basin, then he will take me again. He will kill you, and he *will take me*."

"We'll get to Elendel, inform the governor, and then send an expedition."

"And if that takes too long?" Telsin said. "Do you know what the weapon is? The thing he is searching for?"

Wax looked down at the medallion strapped to her arm. "Feruchemy and Allomancy anyone can use."

"The Lord Ruler's own power, Waxillium," Telsin said, passionate. "The Bands of Mourning. We could find them, use them before he does. He has to travel by foot on a treacherous mountain trail. I heard them preparing for it. We, however . . ." She looked out the

doorway, toward the passing landcape. This was a view few ever saw. A view once reserved only for Coinshots.

"Let me check on Marasi," Wax said. "Then we'll decide."

Marasi soared above the world, looking at a land bathed in starlight. Trees like shrubs. Rivers like streams. Hills like little lumps. The land was Harmony's garden. Was this how He saw it, with God's perspective?

The Path taught he was all around, that his body was the mists—that he saw all and *was* all. The mists were pervasive, but visible only when he wanted them to be. She'd always liked this teaching, as it made her feel His nearness. Yet other aspects of the Path bothered her. There was no structure to it, and because of that everyone seemed to have their own idea of how it should be followed.

Survivorists, like Marasi herself, regarded Harmony differently. Yes, he was God, but to them he was more a *force* than a benevolent deity. He was there, but he was as likely to help a beetle as he was to help a man, for all were the same to him. If you *really* wanted to get something done, you prayed to the Survivor, who had—somehow—survived even death.

Marasi winced as MeLaan continued to work. "Hmm, yes," MeLaan said. "Very interesting."

Marasi lay on the floor of the vehicle, near the doorway, head on a pillow made from a wadded-up jacket. The wind wasn't too bad, contrary to what Marasi would have expected, as they weren't moving terribly fast—though the fans did make a fair amount of noise.

MeLaan had spread Marasi's uniform aside in a very improper way, barely keeping the most important bits covered. Nobody seemed to care though, so Marasi didn't make a fuss. Besides, that was far less disconcerting than what MeLaan was doing to her. The kandra woman knelt over Marasi, hand on her side, the flesh having liquefied and run down *into* the wound.

It was discomfortingly like what had happened when she'd picked the lock, as if Marasi were just another puzzle to be manipulated.

Rusts, she could *feel* MeLaan poking around in there with bits of flesh that had become tentacles.

"I'm going to die, aren't I?" Marasi asked softly.

"Yes," MeLaan said. Light from a small lantern from their packs illuminated her face. "Nothing I can do about that."

Marasi squeezed her eyes shut. It served her right, running about like some lawman from the Roughs, scrambling through firefights and assuming she was invincible.

"How is it?" Waxillium's voice asked. Marasi opened her eyes to see him leaning over, and she found herself blushing at her state of near-nudity. Of course. Her final emotion would be embarrassment because of damned *Waxillium Ladrian*.

"Hmm?" MeLaan asked, pulling her arm out, the flesh forming back over her crystalline bones. "Oh. I caught a hole in the intestines, as you'd guessed. Sewed that up tight, using some catgut I made from some spare intestines I had brewing. I patched it with some of my flesh, grafted on."

"She'll reject the flesh."

"Nah. I took a bite and replicated her skin. Her body will think it's hers."

"You *ate* part of me?" Marasi said.

"Wow," Waxillium said. "That's . . . wow."

"Yeah, well, I'm incredible," MeLaan said. "Excuse me." She reached her hand out the open side of the flying vehicle, then dropped a stream of something vile. "Had to slurp up things inside there to clean everything out. The safest way." She eyed Marasi. "You *owe* me."

"Is that the part of me you . . . um . . . ate?" Marasi asked.

"No, just what was leaking," MeLaan said. "That grafted patch over the wound should hold until you heal on your own—I melded it to your veins and capillaries. It's going to get itchy, but don't scratch it, and let me know if it starts to go necrotic."

Marasi hesitated, then prodded at her wound with exploratory fingers. She found only tight flesh, like that from a scar, patching the hole. It barely hurt, more a dull pain like a bruise. She sat up, amazed. "You said I was going to die!"

"Of course you're going to die," MeLaan said, cocking her head. "You're mortal. Can't turn you into a kandra by just— Oh, you thought *today*. Hell, girl. That shot barely clipped you."

"You're an awful person," Marasi said. "You realize this."

MeLaan grinned, nodding to Waxillium, who offered a hand to help Marasi up. She quickly straightened her uniform, though MeLaan had cut it in ways that made modesty difficult. She'd have to dig into her pack for something new, but how would she ever change in the vehicle's crowded confines?

She sighed, taking Waxillium's hand and letting him pull her to her feet. For now she kept one hand at her waist, preventing her trousers from falling off. He offered her his mistcoat and, after a moment's hesitation, she put it on.

"Thanks," she said, noting that underneath the coat he had been wearing a bandage of his own, upper left arm, right below the shoulder. Had he also been shot during the fighting? He hadn't said anything, which made her feel even more foolish.

Waxillium nodded his head toward the front of the vehicle, where Allik sat with his feet up on the dash, leaning back. Due to the mask, it was impossible to read his expression, but she felt his posture was reflective.

"You feel up to talking with him?" Waxillium asked.

"I suppose," Marasi said. "I'm a little light-headed and a lot humiliated. But other than that, I'm fine."

Waxillium smiled, then took her arm. "You got ReLuur's spike?"

"Yes," Marasi said, though she fished in her purse to make sure, to have her fingers on it, just in case. She held it up.

"These degrade if they're out of a body, don't they?" Waxillium said, glancing at MeLaan, who had settled in a doorway with her legs dangling out, completely ignoring the perfectly good seats.

"How do you know about that?" she asked.

"The book Ironeyes gave me."

"Oh, right," MeLaan said, her expression darkening. "That. You know, the Lord Mistborn was wrong to create it."

"I've read it, regardless."

MeLaan sighed, looking out. "The longer it's away from ReLuur, the more its Blessing will weaken. But they are powerful, and can last some time—besides, even if the Blessing degrades, the spike will still restore his mind anyway. With some . . . loss of memory." Her voice caught on that last part, and she turned away.

"Well, we have it thanks to you," Waxillium said, looking at Marasi. "And I have my sister. So we should turn back to Elendel and find out what Allik knows."

"We should," Marasi agreed. "But your uncle—"

"You heard my conversation with Telsin?"

"Enough of it." When she hadn't been distracted by the fear that she was dying. *Stupid kandra.*

"And what do you think?" Waxillium asked.

"I don't know, Waxillium," Marasi said. "Did we really come here for the spike, or even your sister?"

"No," he said softly. "We came to stop Suit."

Marasi nodded, then dug a little more in her purse, bringing out the notebook she'd stolen from Irich's study. She flipped to the page with the map and held it so both she and Waxillium could see it.

It had a spot clearly labeled *Second Site,* some kind of base camp in the mountains. And beyond that, something high up among some other peaks, indicated as dangerously high. Notes from Irich said, *Temple reported to be here.*

"The weapon," Waxillium said, brushing the map with his fingers. "The Bands of Mourning."

"It's real."

"My uncle thinks it is." Waxillium hesitated. "And I do too."

"Can you imagine him as a Mistborn," Marasi said, "and a Full Feruchemist? Immortal—like Miles, only far worse. Possessing the strength of all metals. Like the Lord Ruler come again."

"My uncle said he was going to the second site," Waxillium said, studying the map. "It's possible that his expedition hasn't gotten to the temple yet, though. They know where it is, from their interrogations, but they were still planning their expedition. With this machine, we could beat him there."

Waxillium drew in a deep breath, then nodded toward Allik up in his seat. "Will you talk to him? Find out what he knows."

"The man's been through a *lot*, Waxillium," Marasi said softly. "I think they must have tortured and murdered his friends. He doesn't deserve an interrogation right now."

"We don't deserve a lot of things that happen to us, Marasi. Talk to him, please. I'd do it, but the way he treats me . . . well, I think you'll get better answers."

She sighed, but nodded and climbed past Wayne, who was—unsurprisingly—slumped in a seat and snoring away. Steris sat with hands in her lap, content, as if riding in a flying machine were an everyday occurrence. Telsin sat in the very back.

Marasi wobbled. Rusts, she *was* light-headed. Fortunately, the front of the vehicle had two seats, the one Allik used and a smaller stool next to him. Allik glanced at her, and she realized she'd been wrong about his posture. He wasn't pensive, he was *cold*. He sat there with arms wrapped around himself, and even shivered a little.

She was surprised. It was colder up here than down below, true, but she wasn't particularly cold herself. Then again, she was wearing Waxillium's coat now.

Allik turned back toward the windshield as she settled down on the stool. "I had assumed," he said, "that everyone up here in the land of the Sovereign was a barbarian. Nobody wears masks, and what your people did to my crewmates . . ."

He shivered again. This didn't seem to be the cold.

"But then you let me out," he continued. "And you had one of *them* with you, a grand Metalborn of the precious arts. So I'm left confused."

"I don't feel like a barbarian," Marasi said. "But I doubt all but the most barbarous of people *feel* like one. I'm sorry about what happened to your friends. They had the misfortune of running across a group of very evil people."

"There were fifteen masks on the wall," Allik said. "But *Brunstell*'s crew was nearly a hundred, yah? I know that some died in the crash,

but the rest . . . do you know where they might be?" He looked to her, and she could see pain in his eyes behind the mask.

"Maybe," Marasi said, surprised to realize she might. She turned the notebook around, showing the map. "Do you know anything about this?"

Allik stared at it. "How did you get that?"

"I found it in the desk of one of your captors."

"They couldn't communicate with us," Allik said, taking the notebook. "How did they get this from us?"

Marasi grimaced. While torture was a terribly ineffective method of interrogation, at least as far as legal cases were concerned, she suspected it *was* a powerful motivator for overcoming barriers.

"You think they're here," Allik said, pointing at the map. "You think the men who captured them, the evil men, brought my crewmates to find the Sovereign's temple."

"It sounds like something Suit would do," Marasi said, glancing back at Waxillium, who had settled into a seat behind her and leaned forward to listen. "Bring guides, or experts, just in case. He's on his way here, the leader of those who killed your friends."

"Then that is where I must go," Allik said, sitting up and changing the direction of the ship. "*Wilg* and I will drop you somewhere, if you demand it, for I'm not *about* to make that one angry." He thumbed over his shoulder at Waxillium. "But I've got to find my crewmates."

"Who is the Sovereign?" Waxillium asked from behind.

Allik winced. "Surely he was not as great as you, Remarkable One."

Waxillium said nothing.

"He's staring at me, isn't he?" Allik asked softly of Marasi.

She nodded.

"Eyes like icicles," Allik said, "drilling into me from behind." He spoke more loudly. "The Sovereign was our king from three centuries ago. He told us he was your king first. And your god."

"The Lord Ruler?" Waxillium said. "He died."

"Yes," Allik said. "He told us that too."

"Three hundred years ago," Waxillium said. "Exactly?"

"Three hundred and thirty, Persistent One."

Waxillium shook his head. "That's after Harmony Ascended. Are you *sure* about those dates?"

"Of course I'm sure," Allik said. "But if you wish me to revise my beliefs in order to—"

"No," Waxillium said. "Just speak the truth."

Allik sighed, rolling his eyes, an odd expression to see from one in a mask. "Gods," he whispered to her. "Very temperamental. Anyway, the Sovereign came about ten years after the Ice Death happened, yah? Silly name, but you've got to call it something. The land was beautiful and warm, and then it froze."

Marasi glanced toward Waxillium, frowning. He shrugged. "Froze?" she said. "I don't recall hearing of freezing."

"It's frozen right now!" Allik said, shivering. "You had it here too, you must have. Over three centuries ago, the Ice Death came."

"The Catacendre?" Waxillium said. "Harmony remade the world. Saved it."

"*Froze* it," Allik said, shaking his head. "The land was soft and warm, and now it is harsh and broken and frozen."

"Harmony . . ." Marasi whispered. "Allik's from the South, Waxillium. Haven't you read the old books? The people from the Final Empire never went in that direction. The oceans boiled, supposedly, if you got too close to the equator."

"The people who lived down south adapted," Waxillium said softly. "No Ashmounts to fill the sky with ash, to cool it . . ."

"So, the world nearly ended," Allik continued. "And the Sovereign, he came and he saved us. Taught us this." He gestured toward the armband he wore, with the medallion, then paused. "Well, not *this* one in particular. This one." He reached into his desk and took out the other medallion he'd worn, the one he'd taken out of the safe back in the warehouse. He put it on, swapping it for the language one, and sighed in contentment.

Marasi watched him, then raised her hand as if to touch his, and he nodded, allowing it. His skin grew warmer even as she sat there.

"Heat," she said, glancing toward Waxillium. "This medallion stores heat. That's a property of Feruchemy, right?"

Waxillium nodded. "The most archetypal. In the ancient days, my Terris ancestors dwelled in the highlands, often traveling through snow-filled mountain passes. The ability to store their heat, then draw upon it, allowed them to survive where nobody else could."

Allik sat, basking in his warmth for a time, before—with obvious reluctance—pulling off his medallion and swapping it quickly for the one that somehow allowed him to speak to them.

"Without these," he said, holding up the first medallion, "we'd be dead. Gone. All five peoples extinct, yah?"

Marasi nodded. "And he taught you this? The Sovereign?"

"Sure did. Saved us, bless him. Taught us that the Metalborn were pieces of God, each one of them, though we didn't have any of those at first. He gave us devices, and started the Firemothers and Firefathers, who live to fill these medallions so the rest of us may leave our homes and survive in this too-cold world. After he left, we used his gifts to figure out the rest, like these that make us fly."

"The Lord Ruler," Marasi said, "seeking redemption for what he did up here by saving the people down there."

"He was *dead*," Waxillium said. "The records—"

"Have been wrong before," Marasi said. "It had to be him, Waxillium. And that means the Bands . . ."

Waxillium moved up beside Allik, on the other side. The masked man eyed him, as if made very uncomfortable by his presence.

"These," Waxillium said, plucking the heat-giving medallion off the dash. "You can create these, as you wish?"

"If we have the Metalborn to do so, and the Excisors, yes. The Excisors are the gifts the Sovereign made for us."

"So with one of those devices, a Metalborn can create a medallion like this—one for *any* Allomantic or Feruchemical ability?"

"Holy words," Allik said. "But if anyone can say them, it is you, O Blasphemous One. Yes. Any."

"And did one of you create a medallion that grants *all* of the powers?" Waxillium asked.

Allik laughed.

Marasi frowned. "Why laugh?"

"You think us gods?" Allik said, shaking his head. "You see that? The one you hold? It is very complicated. It is stored with the ability to give yourself a sliver of holiness."

"Investiture," Waxillium said. "This inner ring is nicrosil. You tap it, and it grants you Investiture—turning you into a temporary Feruchemist who has the ability to fill a metalmind with weight." He held up the medallion. "The iron on this is for convenience, right? You can fill it, but so long as you're tapping the Investiture, you could touch any source of iron and turn it into a metalmind."

"You know much about this, Mysterious One," Allik said. "You are wise and—"

"I learn quickly," Waxillium said, glancing at Marasi. She nodded for him to continue. This was fascinating . . . but the Metallic Arts was not one of her areas of expertise. Waxillium had a passion for it though. "What's this other ring built into the medallion?"

"That grants the warmth," Allik said. "It is a grand combination—*two* attributes, from separate rings. Took us long to make these work, yah? The one I wear now, also grants two. Weight and Connection. I've *seen* medallions with three. Twice in my life only. Every attempt at four has failed."

"So wear multiple medallions," Waxillium said. "Strap thirty-two to your body, and have all the abilities."

"I'm sorry, great Wise One," Allik said. "You are obviously very knowledgeable about this, and know things that none of us would *ever* think to try. How could we be so foolish as to not realize that we could simply—"

"Shut it," Waxillium growled.

Allik flinched.

"Doesn't work?" Waxillium asked.

Allik shook his head. "They interfere with each other."

"So to create one with multiple powers . . ."

"You must be very skilled," Allik said. "More skilled than any who has lived among us. Or . . ." He chuckled. "Or you'd have to have all

the powers, rather than adding yours to the medallion, then passing it to another to have it added to! If that were the case, you'd be a great god indeed. As powerful as the Sovereign."

"He *did* create one of these," Waxillium said, rubbing the medallion with his thumb. "One with all of the abilities. A bracer, or a set of them, that granted all sixteen Allomantic abilities and all sixteen Feruchemical abilities."

Allik wilted.

"That's why you're here, isn't it, Allik?" Waxillium asked, looking into the man's eyes.

Marasi leaned forward. Waxillium said he wasn't good at reading people, but he was wrong. He was great at it—so long as reading them involved bullying them.

"Yes," Allik whispered.

"You traveled from your lands to find the Bands of Mourning," Waxillium said. "Why are they up here?"

"Hidden away," Allik said. "When the Sovereign left us, he took them with him, along with his priests, his closest servants. Well, some of them eventually returned, yah? With stories to tell. He'd taken them on a great journey, and had them build a temple for him in a hidden range of mountains. He'd left the priests there, with the Bands, and told them to protect them until he returned for them. And, that was dumb, yah? Because we could *really* use those to fight the Deniers of Masks."

"Deniers of masks? Like us?"

"No, no," Allik said, laughing. "You're just barbarians. The Deniers are *really* dangerous."

"Hey," Wayne called from behind them, hair whipping in the wind, hat held in his hands. When had he woken up? "We knocked your big ship outta the sky, didn't we?"

"You?" Allik said, laughing. "No, no. You could not have so harmed *Brunstell.* He fell to a great storm. It is a danger of our ships—so light, so easily troubled by storms. We would have landed *Brunstell,* but we were in the mountains, searching. We were so close to the temple, but then . . . yah. Blown out of the mountains over your

lands. Smashed into that poor village. The barbarians there were nice at first. Then the others came."

He shrank down in his chair.

Waxillium patted him on the shoulder.

"Thank you, Wonderful One," Allik said. He heaved a sigh. "Well, ever since the Sovereign's elite told us the stories, we've tried to find the bracers."

"Find them?" Waxillium said. "You told us he'd left the Bands there for himself."

"Well, yah, but everyone interprets it as a challenge. A test sent by the Sovereign? He was fond of those. Why would he let priests tell us about them, if he didn't want us to come claim them?

"Only, after years of searching, everyone started thinking the temple was some fancy legend, lost in time. Everyone's uncle had a map, yah? The type worth less than the paper it's written on? But then, recently, some interesting stories started circulating. Talk of lands up here, and of mountains nobody had explored. We sent several scout vessels, and they returned with stories of your people, in this land.

"Well, five or six years back, the Hunters sent a big ship up with a quest to finally find the temple. And they succeeded, we think. One skimmer came back with a map of where they'd been. The rest froze to death; a blizzard in the mountains overwhelmed their medallions."

Wind rocked the small ship as Allik fell silent.

"We're going after that temple, right?" Marasi asked, looking at Waxillium.

"Damn right we are."

22

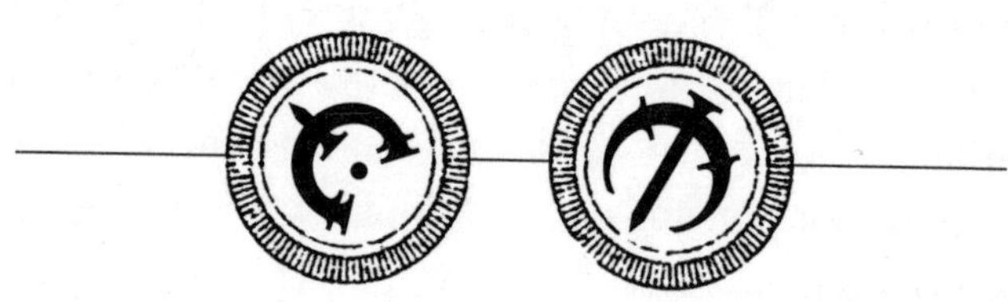

Marasi had plenty of time to think as they traveled southward toward the mountains. Allik guessed the trip would take about two hours, which surprised her. She'd imagined an airship to be a fast-moving vehicle, but this was likely slower than a train. Still, being able to proceed there in a straight line instead of having to follow the landscape was a distinct advantage.

Even with the fans whirring in their casings, the airship seemed to spend much of its time gliding. Allik would increase their height or lower it, trying to find favorable winds—and he complained that he didn't know the airstreams of this area. He did his navigation using devices she didn't recognize along with some startlingly accurate maps of the lower Basin. How often had these people prowled through the skies up here, hidden in the darkness, observing and making their maps?

Most of the others slept, comfortably tapping warmth as Allik had taught them. When Marasi considered sleeping herself, she could not banish the image of falling from one of those doorways and awakening just as she hit the ground—even with the waist belts tying them all in.

Wayne gave her something else to help with the pain, though he

wouldn't say what it was. It felt good though, and she could mostly ignore her aching side. She settled into the seat beside Allik and chatted with him. She felt guilty, as that required him to wear the medallion that let him translate, but he seemed as eager to talk as she was. She could not say whether that was because he was starved for interaction following his incarceration, or if he wanted to be distracted from thinking about the friends he'd lost during his journey.

Over the next two hours, he told her more about the medallions they wore, and the legends of the Bands of Mourning. In Allik's lore, the Lord Ruler had filled them with a great deal of every attribute—but had also crafted them to grant any person who used them the ability to draw those forth. A kind of challenge to mankind to find them, along with a warning not to. Allik didn't seem to consider this a contradiction at all.

He also spent more time telling her about life where he was from—a place over the mountains, across the entire Southern Roughs and the wastelands beyond. A distant, wonderful place where everyone wore masks, though not everyone wore them in the same way.

Allik's own people preferred to change masks according to their professions or moods. Not each day, certainly, but it wasn't uncommon for them to change their mask as often as a lady in Elendel might change her hairstyle. There were other groups though. One gave a mask to each child, and those only changed once, when they reached adulthood. Allik claimed that these people—called Hunters—even grew *into* their masks somehow, though Marasi found that difficult to believe. Still other people, to whom he referred derisively, wore only plain, unpainted masks until they did something to earn a more ornate one.

"They are the Fallen," he explained to her, wagging one hand before himself in a gesture she didn't understand. "They were our kings, yah? Before the world froze. They offended the Jaggenmire, which is why everything went wrong, and—"

"Wait," Marasi said, speaking softly so the others could sleep, "the . . . yayg—"

"Jaggenmire?" he asked. "It didn't translate? You don't have a word for it in your language, then. It's like a god, only not."

"Very descriptive."

Surprisingly he lifted his mask, something she'd only seen him do that once, when he'd knelt before the masks of his friends. He didn't seem to consider it an infraction of any sort, and kept talking. She liked being able to see his face, even if his wispy beard and mustache looked a little ridiculous—it made him look younger than he really was, unless he was lying about being twenty-two.

"It's like . . ." he said, grimacing, "like a thing that runs the world, yah? When something grows, or dies, the Jaggenmire make that happen. There is Herr, and his sister Frue, who is also his wife. And she makes things stop, and he makes things go, but neither can—"

"—make life on their own," Marasi said.

"Yah!" he said.

"Ruin and Preservation," she said. "The old Terris gods. They're one now. Harmony."

"No, they were *always* one," Allik said. "And always apart. Very odd, very complex. But anyway, we were talking about the Fallen, yah? They work doing anything they can to relieve their burden of failure. A compliment means a lot to them, but you have to be careful, because if you tell them they did well, they might take your compliment to heart and travel back to their people to tell everyone. Then *you* might be called in to testify about how good a job they did, so they can change their mask. And their language, that's a *real* pain. I speak a smattering of it—always useful, so you don't have to wear the medallion—and it makes my head spin as if I'd been flying too high for way too long."

She smiled, listening to him go on, gesturing wildly as he spoke—which she figured was only natural, if everyone's faces were covered all the time.

"Do you speak many languages?" she asked, as he took a breath, finally pausing his narrative.

"I don't even speak my own that well," he said with a grin. "But I'm trying. Seems like a good skill for a skimmer pilot to have, since

it's often my job to pilot *Wilg* and take people between ships or towers. And if I'm going to sit half the day in a class, I figure it should be something useful. Though mathematics has—"

"Class?" Marasi asked, frowning.

"Sure. What do you think we do all day on the ship?"

"I don't know," Marasi said. "Swab decks? Tie ropes. Um . . . trim . . . stuff. Deckhand types of things."

He looked at her, eyes bulging, then slapped his mask down. "I'm going to pretend that you did *not* just compare me to a common *lowship*man, Miss Marasi."

"Ummm . . ."

"You have to be something more special than that, if you want to fly. We're expected to be gentlemen and ladies. We've thrown people *overboard* for not knowing the proper dance moves."

"What, really?"

"Yah, really." He hesitated. "All right, so we tied a rope to his foot first." He made a gesture she had started to realize was something like a smile or a laugh. "He dangled there below *Brunstell* for a good five minutes, cursing up a storm. He never got the cistern three-step wrong again, though! And Svel always said to him . . ."

Allik trailed off, growing silent.

"And?" Marasi prodded.

"Sorry. His mask . . . Svel, I mean. On the wall . . ."

Oh. The conversation died, Allik staring out the front of the ship, then making a few adjustments to their heading. Outside, the landscape was dark save for a few pinpricks of towns, now far to their left. Though they'd initially skirted the Seran Range, Allik had moved the skimmer into the mountains about a half hour back. Now they flew over the tops of the peaks, having ascended higher than they'd been when flying over the Basin.

"Allik," Marasi said, resting her hand on his arm. "I'm sorry."

He didn't respond. And so, hesitantly—fully aware that she was probably doing something taboo—she reached out and lifted his mask. He didn't stop her, and the motion revealed eyes staring sightlessly, a tear trickling down each cheek.

"I'm never going to see them again," he said softly. "*Brunstell* is crashed; I'll never serve on him again. Hell, I'm never going to see *home* again, am I?"

"Of course you will," Marasi said. "You can fly there."

"*Wilg* won't last on the stone I've got," he said, wiping the tears from first one cheek, then the other.

"The stone?"

"Fuel," Allik said, glancing at her. "What, you think *Wilg* flies on clouds and dreams?"

"I thought it flew on Allomancy."

"Allomancy Pushes the impellers," Allik said. "But ettmetal is what supports it."

"I don't think that one translated either," Marasi said, frowning.

"Here, see," Allik said, kneeling down and opening the compartment where he'd put the little cube that Waxillium called an Allomantic grenade. It was attached to a metal shell, which glowed softly at the center. Allik pointed, and to the side she could see a greater light blazing with a pure whiteness. A stone, burning like a limelight.

Or like Allomancy itself, Marasi realized. "What kind of metal *is* it, though?"

"Ettmetal," Allik said, shrugging. "There's a little bit in the primer cube too, to make it work. A lot more to make a ship like *Wilg* go, and a lot, *lot* more to get *Brunstell* into the air. You don't have this metal?"

"I don't think so," Marasi said.

"Well, what we have in *Wilg,* it'll be enough to fly us a day or two. After that, we'd need an Allomancer Pushing full-time. So unless His Greatness the Drowsy One back there wants to fly with me all the way back, I'm stuck, yah?"

"You said there was more on *Brunstell.*"

"Yah, but *they* have it." He grinned. "At first, the evil ones didn't know how to care for it. Got some wet. *That* was a good day."

"Wet?"

"Ettmetal explodes if it gets wet."

"What kind of metal *explodes* if you put it in water?"

"This kind," he said. "Anyway, your evil men, they got most of ours."

"And we're going to stop them," Marasi said firmly. "We'll get your crewmates back, stick you on your ship—or some of these skimmers, if the big one won't fly anymore—and send you home."

He settled back in his seat, closing the panel under the dash. "That's what we're going to do," he agreed, nodding. Then he eyed her, his mask still up. "Of course, your people don't have what we do. No airships at all. So they'll simply let me and mine soar away, no information demanded, with this technology?"

Rusts. He was clever. "Maybe we can give the governor some technology," she said, "like a few medallions. Then promise him trade between our two peoples, fueled by the goodwill of having helped you and yours get home. That will erase some of the shame of what Suit did."

"There are those from my lands who might find your Basin up here . . . tempting, with no defenses against attack from above."

"All the more important to have allies among your people."

"Maybe," he said, pulling his mask back down. "I appreciate your genuine nature. You have no mask to hide your emotions. So odd, but welcome in this case. Still, I have to wonder if this will be more complicated than you say. If we do find the relics, what you call the Bands of Mourning, who keeps those? They are ours, yet I cannot see your Metalborn lord letting them slip away from him."

Another difficult question. "I . . . I honestly don't know," Marasi said. "But you could say we have as much a claim to them as you, since it was *our* ruler who created them."

"A ruler you killed," he pointed out. "But let us not argue about it, yah? We will find what we find, and then determine what to do." He hesitated. "I must tell you something, Miss Marasi. It is possible we will find nothing at the temple but destruction."

She frowned, settling on her seat, wishing he still had the mask up so she could read his face. "What do you mean?"

"I told you of the ones who came seeking the temple," Allik said.

"The Hunters," Marasi said.

He nodded. "They were warriors, in the time before the freezing. Now they hunt answers to what happened to us, and secrets to making it never happen again. Miss Marasi, I have known many, and they can be a good people—but very, very stern. They believe that the Bands of Mourning were left with us as a test—but opposite the one we all assume. They think the Sovereign intended to see if we would take the power when we should not. And so . . ."

"What?" Marasi asked.

"Their ship," he said, looking toward her, "that came up here first. It carried bombs, great ones, made from the ettmetal. Intended to *destroy* the Bands. They did not succeed, it is said. But anything could have happened. The place of the temple is said to be frozen beyond anything else in this world. A dangerous place for my kind." He shivered visibly, then looked longingly at the medallion set on the desk before him.

"Go ahead," Marasi said, "put it on."

He nodded. They'd had to do this several times during the flight so far, letting Allik warm himself with the Feruchemical device. Marasi wore one herself, comfortably warm—though up this high, the air was probably freezing.

Allik settled back, and Marasi—curious—picked up the Connection medallion that he had set down. She turned it over in her fingers, noting the sinuous lines down the center, dividing it into separate metals. Iron for weight, duralumin for Connection, and most importantly nicrosil, to give her the ability to tap metals in the first place.

She knew enough Metallic theory to identify the metals, but Connection . . . what did it actually do? And how did that make him speak a *language* of all things?

Suddenly feeling foolish, she smiled and took off her medallion. The ship immediately dipped due to her restored weight. She let out a squeal of alarm and immediately donned the weight/Connection one instead, then blushed—making herself light again—as Waxillium whipped his gun out and leaped to his feet. So he hadn't been

sleeping, but eavesdropping. He looked around to see what had caused the lurch.

None of the others stirred. Wayne kept snoring.

Marasi held up the disc to Allik, then tapped Connection. She waited for some reaction inside of her, but it didn't seem to do anything.

"We've been foolish," she said. "I could have been wearing this all along, and speaking *your* language. Then you could have been warm the entire time."

Allik grinned at her, then said something completely unintelligible.

"What's going on?" Waxillium said from behind her.

"Nothing," Marasi said, blushing again. It wasn't working. Why wasn't it working?

Allik gestured to her, and she switched back to her previous medallion—working very carefully this time to avoid causing a jolt, but mostly failing. How did he transition between them so smoothly?

He made a gesture, like a hand drawn across his face, that she thought indicated a smile. "Clever, but it won't work on you."

"Why?"

"Because we're in your lands," he said. "The visitor always has to wear the medallion. It's filled with Connection, yah? Blank Connection, to no place. But Connection can't just be connected to *nothing*, so when you tap it, it reaches out and connects you to the place where you are. Makes your soul think you were raised in this place instead, so your language changes."

Marasi frowned, though Waxillium perked up, pulling up between their two seats. "Curious," he said. "Very curious."

"It is the way of the world," Allik said with a shrug.

"Then why do you have an accent still?" Marasi asked. "If your brain thinks it was raised here?"

"Ah," Allik said, raising his finger. "My soul thinks I was raised here, in your lands, but it knows that I am Malwish by descent, and that parents are from Wiestlow, so I cannot help but have an accent, yah? I got it from them. It is how the medallions always work."

"Strange," Marasi repeated.

"Yah," Allik agreed. But Waxillium was nodding, as if it made perfect sense to him.

"Those mountains to the right," Waxillium said, pointing. "Those are some taller peaks than the ones we've been passing."

"Yah!" Allik said. "Good eye, O Observan—"

"Stop with the titles."

"Yes, um, O Confusing . . . er . . ." Allik took a deep breath. "Those are the peaks we're seeking. Getting close. We'll have to climb *Wilg* up even higher. Cold temperatures, dangerous altitudes."

He hesitated as Waxillium pointed at something ahead. Difficult to see, but distinct once Marasi noticed it. Light, hovering in the darkness—only a glimmer, but stark against the blackness.

"The Seran Range is uninhabited," Waxillium said, "except in a few of the valleys. Too cold, too many storms."

"So if there's a light . . ." Marasi said.

"Suit has left on his expedition," Waxillium said, standing up straight. "Time to wake the others."

23

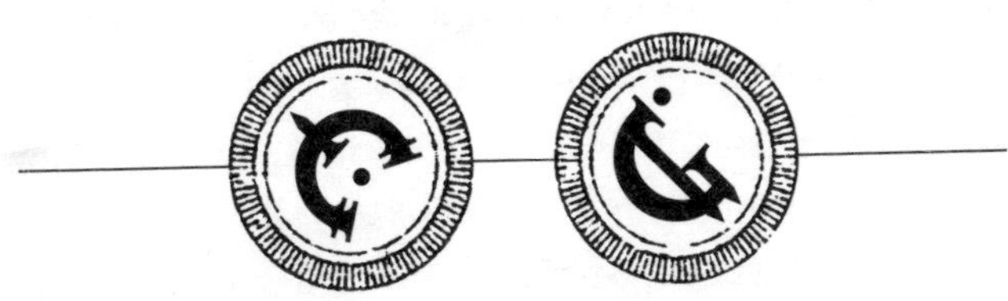

Wayne was awakened quite rough-like, in a manner unbefitting his grand dreams, in which he was king of the dogs. Had a crown shaped like a bowl and everything. He blinked his eyes, feeling nice and warm, and got hit with a blast of air. Drowsy, he remembered he was flying in some kind of rusting *airship* with a fellow what had no face. And that was almost as good as that dog thing.

"Can you bring us down closer?" Telsin asked.

"If I do," the masked guy said, "they'll hear us, even with *Wilg*'s fans on low speed. We need to pass over those people below, but I will keep us very high."

Rusts! Wax's sister hung half out of the machine's open side, looking down, though Wayne could barely make her out with the light so low. He hadn't figured that Telsin would be the adventurous type, what with Wax being all calm and careful most of the time. Yet there she was, doing her best imitation of a pub sign flapping in the wind. He nodded in appreciation, then untied his little belt thing, and got up to look at what she was seeing.

He stepped over their packs, which had toppled from the neat stack Steris had made, then leaned out next to Telsin. That let him

look down at a long line of people—lit by lanterns—trudging through what appeared to be waist-high snow. Poor sods.

Wax stepped up to the other opening, looking down with his spyglass. Wayne couldn't see much, himself. He held on with one hand and took out his box of gum, shaking it. Only one ball left. Damn. Well, at least it had plenty of powder on it. That would help perk him up, it would.

"Do you see him?" Telsin asked.

"I think so," Wax said. "Wait. Yes, that's him. I'll bet they left on their expedition the moment they got word of what happened with us at the warehouse." He reached into his holster and took out one of his guns. He gave the rusting things names, but Wayne could never keep them straight. It was one of the ones with the long tubey thing on the front what spat bits of metal at the bad guys.

"Let me do it," Telsin said, voice passionate.

Wayne hesitated, ball of gum halfway to his mouth. That was quite the bloodthirst this woman had.

"You can't make a shot like this," Wax said. "Not sure if I can either."

"Let me try," Telsin begged. "I don't care what it takes. I want him dead. Another will take his place, but I *want him dead*."

Wax sighted for a long moment, and everyone in the ship seemed to hold their breath. Finally, Wax lowered his gun. "No," he said. "Your testimony in court will do more against the Set than killing a man for no reason other than vengeance. And I'd rather have him to interrogate anyway." He holstered the gun.

Wayne nodded. Reliable chap, that Wax. Steady. The same on a good day and a bad. Wayne moved to retreat into the ship's interior, but as he scrambled over the seats, he somehow got tangled a little with Telsin and, in the process, kicked one of the packs out the opening.

Wayne stared down, aghast, as it fell and actually *hit* one of the men on the head.

"What did you do?" Telsin demanded.

Wayne winced.

"What did Wayne do now?" Marasi asked, a sense of resignation in her voice.

"He kicked that pack out right on top of them," Telsin said.

"'S not my fault," he said. "Wax woke me up too soon. Put me off balance." He looked back at the ship's other occupants. Wax sighed, moving up beside the pilot. Steris and MeLaan sat on the back bench, out of the way—MeLaan lounging in a rather attractive way, Steris bent over a large notebook. Taking notes? What was *wrong* with that woman?

Down below, the men in the snow held their lanterns high and scanned the sky, seeming confused.

"Move us away," Wax said to the masked pilot, pointing. "Go the direction they're hiking."

"Yes, Decisive One," the pilot fellow said, and the fans at the sides of the thing grew louder. "Hold on, everyone."

The ship shifted. Not quickly, but it did start moving again. Neat trick that had been, staying in place while flying. Birds couldn't do that, just Coinshots. Wayne moved forward, sidling past Marasi to get a good look out the front of the ship.

"Wind is picking up," the pilot mentioned. "Might be a storm, as if things weren't cold enough already."

"There," Wax said, pointing. "What was that?"

"I'll bring us around," the pilot fellow said, swinging the ship, which rocked precariously. Another gust of wind brought flakes of snow in through the openings in the ship's walls.

"That's it," Wax said, peering through the curtain of snow. "Harmony's Rings . . . it's really here."

"I don't see anything," Wayne said, squinting.

"Hold on to something," the pilot fellow said. "Or make sure you're strapped in. I'm going to land."

So Wayne grabbed the man's arm.

"Something *else*."

Wayne grabbed the chair's back, and good thing he did, since the ship pitched to the side as it came down. The landing wasn't too bad, assuming you liked getting shaken about and then having your face smacked into the wall.

Wayne blinked, finding himself in blackness. A moment later MeLaan managed to relight her lantern and hold it up, showing that the ship had settled halfway on its side, one of the fan wings—which could fold up so the thing could fit in the larger ship—having bent up on its hinges, with a big heap of snow pushed in through the hole in the ship's side.

"Is that how it usually goes?" Wax asked, standing up shakily on the sloping floor.

"Landing is difficult," the pilot fellow admitted.

"Technically," Marasi said from the back, "it's not. It's probably the easiest thing to do with a flying ship, assuming you're not picky."

Wayne snorted, climbing across the ship to the side that was pointed upward, and hopped out. The snow crunched when he dropped into it. He hadn't expected that—the only snow he'd seen had been the occasional flurry up in the Roughs, and it never got anywhere *near* this deep. Why would it crunch? The stuff was made of water, not cereal flakes.

He stumbled out of the high pile of snow onto a windswept rocky portion of ground. Snow pelted him like grains of sand, but it didn't seem to be coming from the sky, just getting blown in from the side. He shivered and tapped more warmth. The clouds happened to roll out of the way, releasing starlight like a bouncer stepping back and letting folks into the night's most exclusive club.

That light cascaded down, white and calm, upon a rusting *castle* in the middle of the mountains. A bleak stone fortress, cut of the same stone as the field. It looked to be only one story, hunkered down against the wind, but it glowed in the starlight like the spirit of some ancient building from anteverdant days.

Wayne breathed out slowly, his breath making white mist before him. "Nice," he said, nodding. "Nice." The folks that built this, they had *style*.

Marasi clambered out of the ship, wearing Wax's mistcoat for some reason, and almost fell face-first in the snow. She stood on top of the white fluff, a gust of wind almost knocking her over again, until suddenly she sank down into it farther with a crunch. She'd finally remembered to stop filling her weight metalmind. Easy mistake to make, if you weren't accustomed to being a Feruchemist.

She pushed through the snow and joined Wayne, wiping melted snow from her brow. She looked to be doing well, considering that she'd been shot.

"Suit and his people aren't far off," she said. "And they know we're here, now."

"Then we find the Bands first," Wax said from behind them. It was seriously unfair how he glided up out of the machine, then soared on a quick jump to land next to them, no stumbling in that snow. Seriously. Why had Harmony made the stuff? Didn't seem to serve much of a purpose. "Everyone grab your things. Allik, remove the grenade from the ship, just in case."

They all hurried to obey, Marasi climbing back in the machine, then joining Steris in handing the packs out. Allik emerged, wearing that mask of his still, and stood on the side of his ship, staring at the fortress and shaking his head. He then turned and patted his ship, like it was some kind of puppy, until Steris appeared and chased him away for some reason. A few moments later Marasi climbed out, wearing a dress instead of her uniform, but with trousers on underneath. She tossed Wax his mistcoat.

Figures. A woman *would* have to change outfits for this. Can't infiltrate a remote, ancient temple without properly accessorizing. Wayne ran his hand through his hair, then had a moment of panic. His *hat*! He scrambled back toward the ship, looking around frantically, but then spotted it peeking from a snowdrift nearby, having fallen free as they landed. He picked it up with a sigh of relief.

"Everyone back," Wax said, steadying himself with a stable footing, the wind blowing his mistcoat tassels back and whipping them about. The others moved away from the ship, and Wax grunted, Pushing. The ship skidded back softly into the snow, piling it up in a wave. Wax Pushed until the thing was completely buried.

"Nice," Wayne said.

"Let's hope one of their Coinshots or a Lurcher doesn't spot it beneath the snow," Wax said, turning toward the temple and shouldering his shotgun. "Come on, let's get out of this wind."

They picked up the packs and started across the stone field toward the fortress. Steris had found another lantern somewhere, and lit it. Wayne hurried his step and fell in beside that pilot fellow with the mask.

"You know," Wayne said, "I'm an Allomancer too."

The man said nothing.

"I figured you'd want to know," Wayne said, "since it seems like this is your religion and all. In case you wanted someone else to worship."

Again no reply.

"I'm a Slider," Wayne said. "Speed bubbles, you know? Those fancy titles would work for me just fine, I think. Handsome One. Smart One. Um . . . Guy wif the Great Hat."

The only sound was that of their footfalls and the gusting wind.

"Now, see," Wayne said, "this is unfair. Wax doesn't want you to worship him, right? But you *gotta* have someone to worship. It's human nature. It's ingratiated in us. So, I'm willin' to be accommodatin' and let you—"

"He can't understand you, Wayne," Marasi said, marching past. "He's swapped metalminds to keep himself warm."

Wayne stopped in place as they all hiked onward. "Well, when he gets his brain back, someone tell him I'm a god, all right?"

"Will do," Wax called from up ahead.

Wayne sighed, moving to catch up, but then stopped. What was that off to the side? He shouldered his pack and hiked over, ignoring Marasi's call that he turn back. There *was* something there, near the cliffs. A hulking shape bigger than a house, the exposed bits covered in frost.

Wax strode over, squinting against the wind, and grunted. "Another ship," he said. "The one that the Hunters sent."

"The who?"

"Group of people from Allik's region," Wax said. "They came here to destroy the place. Fortunately, it seems they didn't succeed." He turned to go, but Wayne nudged him, nodding toward a hand sticking from one of the snowbanks. Looking more closely, he was able to pick out a dozen corpses, perhaps more, lying there in this icy place, frozen for all time.

Wax nodded, then they hiked back toward the others. Marasi and Steris had waited, along with the masked man—who had crossed half the distance to the new ship, then stopped, staring at it. Telsin had strode on ahead, MeLaan tailing her. He quickly joined the rest of them as they followed after Telsin and MeLaan.

"Your sister," Wayne said to Wax, "is kinda . . ."

"Severe?" Marasi said.

"I was gonna say bonkers," Wayne admitted. "Though I'm not sure if it's the good kinda bonkers or the bad kind, as of yet, as I haven't had time to give it the proper evaluatin'."

"She's been through a lot," Wax said, eyes ahead. "We'll get her home and give her some physicians to talk to. She'll mend."

Wayne nodded. "Course, she won't fit in wif us anymore if she does."

They continued, and that fortress, *rusts* it was impressive. Made of broad stone blocks, the type that some poor fellow probably broke his back lugging about, it had steps out front leading up to an enormous statue. At first he was surprised, as all the way out here seemed an odd place for a sculpture—but then, the ones back in Elendel had been shat on by about a million birds, so perhaps this was the *best* place to keep your statue.

The group of them made their way up the steps, fighting the wind. The medallion meant the wind wasn't cold enough to chill his nethers, but it was still annoying. At the top of the steps they had to walk around that statue, which was in the shape of a fellow in a long coat holding a spear to his side, its tip resting on the stones. Wayne scratched his face, stepping back and craning his neck.

"What's wrong with his eye?" Wayne asked, pointing.

Marasi stepped up beside him, squinting in the darkness. "A spike," she said softly. "Like on that coin of Waxillium's."

Yup, that was it. One spike, jutting through his right eye. Wayne rounded the statue, which had snow piled about its base.

"One spiked eye," Wax said, thoughtful. "This place was built by the Lord Ruler. Why would he have them make a statue of him with one eye spiked through?"

"He carries a spear," Marasi said. "For the one that he used to kill the Survivor?"

"A metal spear," Wax noted. "But no lines. Aluminum. Looks like some on his belt too. Expensive."

Marasi nodded. "The Lord Ruler was run through with three spears, by the Lord Mistborn's testimony. 'Once stabbed by a beggar, for the poverty he brought. Once stabbed by a worker, for the slavery he enforced. Last stabbed by a prince, for the lords he corrupted.' The spears didn't hurt him."

"Come on," Telsin called from inside the building, where she'd been joined by Steris.

Wax and the masked fellow moved off, but Wayne kept looking up at the statue.

"So I've been thinkin'," Wayne said as MeLaan passed him.

"Yeah?" she asked, glancing at him.

Rusts. Wax might think it weird, considering she was like a billion years old or something, but it seemed like even *longer* since a woman had looked at him like that. It wasn't a lusty look or anything like that, it was . . . what was the word . . .

Fond.

Yup, that would do.

"Wayne?" she asked.

"Oh, right. Um, well, this place is abandoned, right? So none of the stuff in it belongs to anyone."

"Well, I'm sure a lot of people would *claim* it," MeLaan said. "But ownership would be tough to prove."

"So . . ."

"So I'd say don't touch anything anyway," MeLaan said.

"Oh. Right."

She smiled at him, then continued on in through the open doorway behind the statue. It was big, gaping, like a fellow's mouth after you kick 'im right in the canteen.

He looked back at the statue, then poked at the spearhead with his toe. Then he hit it with his heel. Then he hit with a rock. Finally, he twisted it a few times.

It fell right off, clanging to the stone beneath. It had been practically *hanging* free. And Wax was wrong, only the head was of metal—the oversized spear was wood. *Aluminum, you say?* Wayne thought with a smile.

Now, he didn't care much for what rich folks said was worth money. Unless it was, by itself, worth more than a house. Little Sophi Tarcsel, the inventor, did need more funds.

He wrapped the big spearhead, which was as large as his palm, with a handkerchief to keep it from freezing his fingers off, and started whistling as he jogged after the others. As he passed, he noticed that there once *had* been gates on this doorway, big ones, but they lay in frozen splinters.

The others had gathered inside, where the temple had some kind of entryway. It had murals on either side, just like the ones that the strange kandra chap had shown back in Wax's mansion. Wayne stepped up to one, beside Wax, who was inspecting it.

Yup. Same mural. One depicting a pair of bracers on a pedestal, the other—across the way—depicting the Lord Ruler wearing them.

"We've found the place for certain, then," Wax said. "The statue was enough evidence, but this seals it. ReLuur was here."

Together they left the entryway, stepping through its only door into a long, dark hallway. What were those lumps ahead? MeLaan and Steris held their lanterns higher, though nobody seemed to have any inclination to be the first one to proceed.

The masked fellow, though, he was muttering something in funnytalk. He seemed to be following something with his eyes. A metal pattern on the wall? He stepped to the side, and dug the little grenade from his pocket. He did something, opening its side, then used tweezers to extract what looked like a small nugget of metal. He shoved it into a cavity in the wall, then pulled down a lever.

Wayne heard what he thought was distant humming, then a series of small blue lights started glowing on the walls. As was appropriate to match the atmosphere of this rusting place, they were creepier than Steris in the morning. There were no bulbs or anything rational like that, just sections of the walls that seemed to be made of translucent glass that glowed in a downright gloomy way.

It *was* enough to light up the lumps on the floor. Bodies. A right disturbing number of them, lying in awkward positions. And those pools around them . . . frozen blood.

Wayne whistled softly. "They *really* went far to give this place a creepy look."

"Those bodies weren't here originally," Wax said dryly. "I think they must be— Wayne, what the hell is that?"

"It fell right off," Wayne said, clutching the spearhead, which was cold to the touch, even through the handkerchief. The tip was peeking out on one side. "I didn't even look at it, Wax. Musta been loosened by the wind. See, it has a hole on the bottom for screwing off and—"

"Don't touch anything," Wax said, pointing at him. "Else."

MeLaan gave him a look.

"You shut up," Wayne said to her.

"Didn't say a word, Wayne."

"You *implied* one. That's worse."

Wax sighed, looking at the pilot fellow, who was inspecting some carvings on the wall. "Allik?" Wax said, then tapped the medallion he'd tied to his wrist.

The masked man sighed, but swapped out one of his medallions for the other. He immediately shivered. "I have now been to hell," he said. "These mountains will rise all the way there for certain."

"You think hell is in the *sky*?" Steris asked, standing close to Wax, practically clinging to him.

"Of course it is," Allik said. "Dig down deep enough in the ground, and things get warm. Hell must be the other way. What did you want of me, Great Metallic Destroyer?"

Wax sighed. "Bodies," he said, nodding down the hallway. "Traps?"

"Yes," Allik said. "The ones who built this place were charged with protecting the Sovereign's weapon. They knew others would eventually follow, and so the builders were bound to make it difficult, knowing that they could not remain to guard in person. Not in this place of ice and death. But . . ."

"What?" Wax said.

"Those masks," Allik said.

"The masks of Hunters?" Wax asked.

Allik looked at him, shocked. "How did you recognize them?"

"I didn't," Wax said, walking forward carefully. Wayne joined him, as did MeLaan. Wax waved for Marasi, Steris, and Telsin to remain back, though he gestured for Allik to join them.

Together, the four of them walked to the first set of corpses. Wax knelt down beside the pool of frozen blood. The closest fellow had died miserably, with a spike through his chest. Wayne could see the trap now, the tip of it still jutting from the wall. The poor fellow's mates must have tried to pull him free of the spike, but then had gotten caught in traps themselves.

The masks were different from Allik's, that was for sure. Made of wood with bits of glass stuck to them, each in a different, odd pattern. And these ones showed the mouth, covering the top half the face, then running down the sides. The skin there, at the sides of the mask, seemed to have *melded* with the wood—though that might be because everything in here was as cold as a spinster's bedroom.

Wax nudged the mask. "You said the Hunters came to destroy this place."

"Yes," Allik said.

"Well, I think they either lied to you, or changed their minds." Wax nodded toward the busted doors, then down the hallway, littered with bodies. "The lure of the Bands was too powerful for these fellows. I'd guess the dead ones we found near the ship were the ones determined to go through with blowing up the whole place. Got betrayed, but then these betrayers in turn fell to the traps. The ones who returned home; what happened to them? Vanished?"

"Yes," Allik said, cocking his head. He raised his mask, revealing a wonderfully silly mustache and beard, then regarded Wax with awed eyes. "They went back to the Hunters. Then . . . gone. Returned to their families, it was said."

"Executed," Wax said, rising. "It was discovered they helped murder the rest of their crew, then tried to steal the Bands. They turned back because of the traps killing too many of their fellows, took a skimmer because it was all they could man, and returned with a made-up story of a blizzard. They were going to gather another crew and try again. Their superiors caught them first."

Allik seemed befuddled. "How . . . how did you figure that—"

"He does this all the time," Wayne said. "Best not to encourage him."

"Just a theory," Wax said. "One supported by the evidence though. Steris, Telsin. I want you to stay behind while—"

"I'm going with you," Telsin snapped. She walked forward, cold as the dead blokes on the floor. "I won't be shoved aside, Waxillium. I won't be left for our uncle to catch up to us and take me again."

Wax sighed, looking toward Steris and Marasi.

"I'll stay," Steris said. "Someone needs to watch the entrance for Suit and his people."

Wax nodded, glancing at Wayne. "You keep an eye on her." Then he looked to Marasi. "You keep an eye on *him*. We'll come get you if we find anything."

Marasi nodded. Wayne sighed.

"You intend to go forward?" Allik said, standing up, eyes bulging. "O Great Impetuous One, far be it from me—a lowly pilot—to question your ridiculous intentions, but . . . seriously? Didn't you see the *corpses*?"

"I saw them," Wax said. "MeLaan?"

"On it," she said, striding forward.

"Great One," Allik said, "I cannot but think they have traps designed to kill your kind. If they thought of all this, they will have prepared for one such as you."

"Yes," Wax said. "That spike was all wood."

Allik grew more frantic. "Then why would you—"

MeLaan stepped on a pressure plate, causing a spear to launch out of one of the many small holes in the wall. It moved jarringly fast, piercing right through MeLaan's torso, coming out the other side.

She sighed, looking down. "This is going to absolutely ruin my wardrobe."

Allik gawked, then lifted his hand as if to raise his mask, only it was already up. He fumbled, unable to take his eyes off MeLaan, who yanked the spear out with a casual gesture.

"Traps," Wax said, "are somewhat less threatening when you have an immortal along."

"Unless they have explosives," MeLaan said. "If I lose a spike, you'd better be ready to stick it right back in. And I was serious—this is going to be *awful* for my clothing."

"You could do it without," Wayne said hopefully.

She thought for a moment, then shrugged, reaching to grab her top.

"I'll buy you new clothing, MeLaan," Wax said, interrupting her. "We don't want to make poor Allik fall over dead."

"Actually," Allik said, "I don't think I'd mind."

"Good man," Wayne said. "Knew I liked you."

"Ignore them," Wax said. "Wayne, help guard the door. Allik, I need you with me, in case something is written in your language."

The man nodded, then put back down his mask. Made sense why he wore one now. Wayne couldn't grow a proper beard either, but at least he had the sense to shave.

MeLaan strolled down the hallway. "Telsin, stay behind me," Wax said, "and step exactly where I step. Same for you, Allik."

They left Wayne and the two ladies behind. Ahead, a large spiked log swung out of a hidden compartment and *crushed* MeLaan against the wall. She shook it off like a champ, stumbling on down the hallway while her leg re-formed.

"You know," Wayne said, looking toward Steris and Marasi, "she might be even better at the Blackwatch Doublestomp than I am."

24

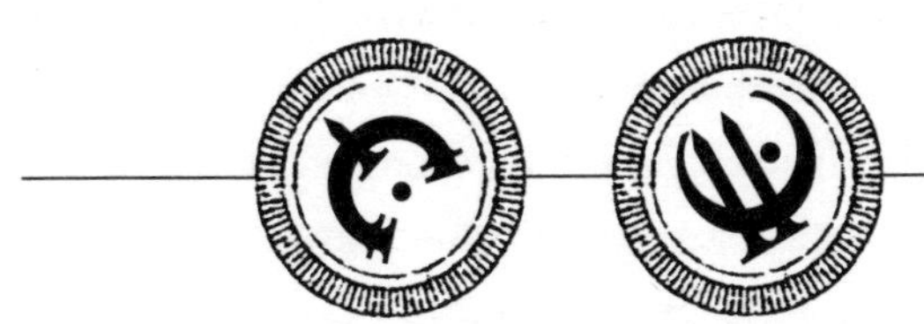

Marasi settled in beside Wayne and Steris, watching the approach to the temple. Distant lanternlight showed Suit's group. But they were getting closer.

What would they do if the man got here? Fight? For how long? Eventually their medallions would run out of heat, and they had almost nothing in the way of supplies.

They'd simply have to count on Waxillium finding the Bands quickly; then they could escape on the skimmer and be away before Suit could do anything. The idea of that infuriating man stuck up here in the snows—having slogged miles and miles to find an empty temple—appealed to her.

At the very least, imagining his reaction distracted her from her own annoyance.

Sit here, Marasi. Stay out of trouble. Babysit Wayne. She knew that wasn't what he meant, but it was still galling.

Rather than sit and simmer in her own petulance, Marasi dug in her purse, pulling out the little spike that belonged to ReLuur. Such a small thing, and so clean—a shining sliver of . . . pewter, was it? Staring at it in the light of Steris's lantern, she wished she didn't know its history. A person had been killed to make this, their soul ripped apart so a piece could be used to make a kandra.

Even though it had been done long ago, to someone who would have been centuries dead by now anyway, she felt as if there should be blood beneath her fingers, making the spike slippery. It should not be so clean.

Yet, she thought, *where would mankind be without the kandra, acting as Harmony's hands—guiding and protecting us? Such good to come of something so awful.* Indeed, according to the Historica, without the work the kandra had done through the ages collecting atium, mankind would likely have been destroyed.

The Lord Ruler is the same, Marasi thought. *He was a monster. He created this spike by killing someone. And yet he somehow managed to get to Allik's people and save their entire civilization.*

Waxillium sought justice. He had an open heart—he'd spared Wayne's life all those years ago, after all—but in the end, he sought to uphold the law. That was shortsighted. Marasi wanted to create a world where law enforcement wouldn't be *needed*. Was that why she was so annoyed with him lately?

"You bein' careful with that?" Wayne asked, nodding toward the spike. "You don't want to prick yourself and turn into a kandra."

"I'm pretty sure that's not how it works," Marasi said, tucking it back into her purse.

"Never can tell," Wayne said. "I think I should carry it. Just in case."

"You'd swap it for the first trinket we passed, Wayne."

"No I wouldn't." He paused. "Why? You see somethin' good back there?"

Marasi rose and walked to Steris, who had settled primly on a stone shelf along the wall of the temple's vestibule. She sat in a ladylike posture, knees forward, back straight, writing carefully on a notebook by lanternlight.

"Steris?" Marasi asked.

The woman looked up and blinked. "Ah. Marasi. Perhaps you can help me with a topic. How useless am I?"

"Excuse me?"

"Useless," Steris said, holding her notebook. Not her little pocket one; her larger one, full-sized, which she'd brought in her pack. She used it for brainstorming lists.

Today, she'd been writing on the back of it. "I've been trying to quantify it, for reference purposes," Steris said. "I am under no illusions as to my position in this group. I am the baggage, the accident. The person who needs to be left with the horses, or sent to stay away from traps. If Lord Waxillium could have sequestered me somewhere safe along the way and left me, he certainly would have."

Marasi sighed, slumping down on the shelf beside her sister. Was this actually something the two of them could *relate* on? "I know how you feel," she said. "I spent the first year around him feeling unwelcome, as if Waxillium considered me some little puppy nipping at his heels. And now, when he finally does seem to have accepted me, he treats me as merely a tool to be used or put back on the shelf as required."

Steris cocked her head at Marasi. "I think you mistake me."

Of course I do, Marasi thought with resignation. "How?"

"I did not mean to say I *minded* being treated this way," Steris said. "I was merely stating facts. I am quite useless on this expedition, and I think that is only fair, considering my personal life experience. However, if I wish to improve, I need to know how far I have to go. Here."

She turned her notebook to show Marasi the back, where she'd been writing. Why use the back? Either way, she'd drawn a small graph with points plotted on it. Usefulness was listed on one axis, and it had names up the other. Rusts—she'd assigned a *number* to everyone's level of worth on the mission. Waxillium was a hundred, as was MeLaan. Wayne was a seventy-five.

Marasi was an eighty-three. She hadn't expected that.

"I would say that ten is the threshold below which one's uselessness outweighs the little one does add to the project. I'm thinking I might be a seven, as there are instances where it is better to have me along, though they are few. What do you think?"

"Steris," Marasi said, pushing the notebook aside. "Why do you care about being useful here in the first place?"

"Well, why do you?"

"Because this is who I am," Marasi said. "Who I want to be. But not you—you're perfectly happy sitting in a parlor digging through ledgers. Yet here you are, on the top of a mountain in a blizzard, waiting for a gunfight."

Steris pursed her lips. "I assumed," she eventually said, "that I would be of help to Lord Waxillium at the party, and I was. It was my original understanding that this would be primarily a political enterprise."

Of course. So analytical in everything. Marasi settled back, glancing out the doorway at those approaching lights. Wayne, fortunately, was watching carefully. He acted the fool sometimes, but he took his duties seriously.

"And then," Steris said softly, "perhaps I came along because of the way it feels. . . ."

Marasi looked sharply back at her sister.

"Like the whole world has been upended," Steris said, looking toward the ceiling. "Like the laws of nature and man no longer hold sway. They're suddenly flexible, like a string given slack. We're the spheres. . . . I love the idea that I can break out of it all—the expectations, the way I'm regarded, the way I regard myself—and *soar.*

"I saw it in his eyes, first. That hunger, that fire. And then I found it in myself. He's a flame, Waxillium is, and fire can be shared. When I'm out here, when I'm with him, I *burn,* Marasi. It's wonderful."

Marasi's jaw dropped, and she gawked at her sister. Had those words left *Steris's* mouth? Careful, monotonous, *boring* Steris? She glanced toward Marasi and blushed.

"You actually love him, don't you?" Marasi asked.

"Well, love is a *strong* emotion, one that requires careful deliberation to—"

"Steris."

"Yes." She looked down at her notebook. "It's foolish, isn't it?"

"Of course it is," Marasi said. "Love is always a foolish emotion. That's what makes it work." She found herself reaching over and pulling Steris into a hug with one arm. "I'm happy for you, Steris."

"And you?" Steris asked. "When will you find someone to make you happy?"

"It's not about finding someone, Steris. Not for me."

But what was it about? She gave Steris another hug and, distracted by her own jumble of thoughts, went to check on Wayne.

"What'cha thinkin' about?" Wayne asked as she joined him beside the outer doorway.

"I just had my long-held assumptions about someone shattered in a brief moment. I'm wondering if every person I pass has similar depths, and if there's any way to avoid the mistake of judging them so shallowly that I'm rocked when they show their true complexity. You?"

"I was lookin' at you two," Wayne said, contemplative as he regarded the snowy landscape outside rather than her, "and wondering. Do sisters ever *really* get sexy with one another for a fellow to watch, or does that only happen in pub songs?"

Marasi let out a long breath. "Thank you for restoring my ability to trust my judgment, Wayne."

"Anytime."

"Those lights are still distant," Marasi said. "You think they got trapped in the snows?"

Wayne shook his head.

Marasi frowned, noting his posture—seeming relaxed, but he'd gotten out one of his dueling canes and rested it across his knees.

"What?" she asked.

"I figure," Wayne said, "that if *I* knew I'd been spotted, the best way to sneak up would be to leave my lights behind and make it *seem* like I'm goin' slowly."

Marasi looked again. She ignored the lights this time, scanning a nearer darkness full of shifting snow. And there, almost to the windswept patch of rock before the temple, she caught movement. Shadows in the shadows.

"Time to call for Waxillium?" Marasi asked.

"I think . . ." He trailed off, and Marasi pulled her rifle up, nervous.

"What?" she asked.

Wayne pointed to an approaching shadow. It bore a little flag, crossed with an X. The symbol for parley.

Wax pulled on the rope, helping MeLaan climb from the pit. She crawled over the edge, then flopped down. She'd been right about her clothing—it was ragged, pierced in several dozen places, her left trouser leg ripped completely at the thigh.

She'd compacted her body, somehow. Most of her fatty curves had become taut muscles instead, and she'd taken *off* her hair, storing it in the pack Allik carried, leaving her bald.

Wax knelt beside her, glancing down the hallway with its spikes, pits, poison darts, and other strange mechanisms. The entire temple seemed to be one long passage, intended to be as hard to move through as possible.

Something about this is wrong, Wax thought. But what?

MeLaan stirred on the ground.

"Rest a moment," Wax said, hand on her shoulder.

"I don't know if we *have* a moment, Ladrian," she said, sitting up and accepting a canteen of water from the nervous Allik. Telsin stood nearby with arms folded, obviously annoyed at how long this was taking. She kept glancing over her shoulder, as if at any moment she expected to find Suit there to take her again.

"How are your bones?" Wax asked MeLaan.

She held up her left arm—or tried to. It had snapped at the middle of the humerus, and the rest of her arm dangled.

Wax breathed out. "You're sure that doesn't hurt?"

"Turned off the nerves that cause pain," she said. "A trick we've learned over the last centuries. And since my bones are crystal, they can't feel." She grimaced as the arm straightened, the break seeming to heal. But it hadn't, Wax knew—she couldn't make bone, or heal it. "Another patch?"

She nodded. She had stretched ligament along the sides of the break to hold it tight. She'd done that with many of her bones already.

MeLaan moved to rise.

"We can find another way," Wax said, standing. "Break in through one of the walls up ahead, or the roof maybe."

"And how long will that take?"

"Depends on how much we care about what's inside."

"And wouldn't it be silly to come all this way, then *ruin* the Bands of Mourning because of our impatience?"

Wax looked down the hallway. They were most of the way through it, so he put off pushing her further. He could see a door ahead.

"You might not have to do much more anyway," Wax said. "I think I have the pattern figured out."

"What pattern?" MeLaan asked.

"Pressure plate under the second stone to your right," Wax said. "Shoots darts."

She glanced at him, then stepped forward and tapped it with her toe. Darts spat from the wall, passed before her, and bounced against the opposite wall.

"Next one is two stones ahead," Wax said. "There's a hint of a metal line leading underneath it. So far, those have been wall traps."

Another toe press. A portion of the wall opened, dropping a very large spiked log.

"Nice," MeLaan said.

"Last one should be a pit trap," Wax said, joining her in walking around the fallen log. "Check your rope. The stones those are under are raised slightly."

She tugged on it, using her right hand because the fingers of her left had been crushed. The crystal had broken beyond repair, and she now walked with the hand permanently shut, splinters of bones fused together by tendons.

"I hate the pit ones," she said. "They just keep going down. Makes me afraid of what might be at the bottom."

She stepped on the section of floor he indicated, and Wax held tightly to his side of the rope, which was tied about his waist. But instead of a pit trap, the ceiling opened, dropping a block of something. MeLaan jumped back, and the block of strangely colored ice banged to the stones beneath. It was wet, its surface oddly oily-looking.

"What in Harmony's Rings—" MeLaan said, squatting to inspect the ice.

"Acid, maybe?" Wax said. "It looks like whatever they stored up there was a liquid, but it separated over time, and half froze."

MeLaan stared at it a long time.

"What?" Wax asked.

"Nothing," she said, shaking her head. "So that's it?"

"Best as I can tell." Together, they stepped up before the end of the hallway, at a door made of stone. But there was no handle. The rest of the wall was thick stone as well.

There were some markings carved into the door, if indeed that was what it was. Circles, with symbols in them, inlaid in silver. Wax looked to Allik.

"I don't recognize any of those," the pilot said after swapping his metalminds. "If they're writing, it's not a language I understand."

"What do you want to do?" MeLaan asked.

"Let's get the others," Wax said, thoughtful. "More brains to solve this will be helpful, and Marasi might recognize those from ReLuur's notes."

They started back, letting MeLaan go first again—though Wax kept his eyes open for any indicators of traps. It was still slow going, as she wanted to be careful they'd caught everything.

Telsin fell in beside Wax, glancing once over her shoulder at the door, arms wrapped around herself, though with the medallion she couldn't be cold. Allik trailed behind them, wearing his warming medallion.

"Do you ever wonder, Waxillium," Telsin said softly, "how you got where you are?"

"Sometimes, I suppose," he said. "Though I figure I can trace it. I don't always like it, but it makes sense, if I stop and think it through."

"I can't do the same," she said. "I remember being a child, and assuming the world belonged to me. That I'd be able to seize it when I grew older, accomplish my dreams, become something great. Yet as I've aged, I feel like less and less is under my control. I can't help thinking it shouldn't be that way. How could I have been so in control as a youth, yet often feel so helpless as an adult?"

"That's our uncle's fault," Wax said. "For keeping you captive."

"Yes, and no. Wax, I'm an adult—with greying hair and over half my life behind me. Shouldn't I have a clue as to what this is all about?" She shook her head. "That's not Edwarn's fault. What have we done, Waxillium? We're alone. Our parents are dead. *We're* the adults now, yet where are our children? What's our legacy? What have we accomplished? Don't you ever feel like you never actually grew up? That everyone else did, but you're secretly faking?"

No, he didn't feel that way. But he grunted in agreement anyway—it was good to hear her show a side of herself other than feverish hatred of Suit and his people.

"Is that why you're so keen to come here?" Wax asked. "You think that what we find in there will accomplish something?"

"At least it will help society," Telsin said.

"Unless it destroys society."

"Pushing society forward is no destruction. Even if, in doing so, it leaves us behind."

She withdrew into herself again. He couldn't blame her, after her ordeal. He wished there had been time to go back to Elendel, see her situated in someplace warm and safe, before flying back here.

They retraced their steps, passing the traps they'd already set off. Fallen blocks of stone from the ceiling, darts and spears from the walls, even a stone wall that had dropped to block them, though

MeLaan had kept it from falling all the way by slamming a large rock underneath. Wax had been able to wiggle into the space and Push a few coins upward to lift it farther, then they propped it up with rocks in the tracks at the sides. They still had to stoop to go underneath.

They did find two more traps, which they set off as well. Wax found himself increasingly dissatisfied. *So much work,* he thought, noting again the wall section that had fallen in to release scythes that cut the air. That trap had gotten entangled on itself, and so hadn't endangered them at all—but the ingenuity required to put it together was marvelous.

"Allik," he said, prompting the short man to swap back to his Connection medallion. "Why would your people build such an obvious resting place for the Bands? Why make this temple, which proclaims that something precious is inside, then go to the effort of making all these traps? Why not just hide the Bands someplace unassuming, like a cave?"

"They are a challenge, like I said, Thoughtful One," Allik said. "And it was not *my* people who did this, not specifically. The original priests who crafted this place were of no people currently living among us."

"Yes," Wax said, "and you told me the Sovereign left his weapon here with orders to protect it because he was going to return for it. Right?"

"That is the legend."

"These traps don't make sense, then," Wax said, waving back down the hallway. "Wouldn't they have been worried for your king's safety?"

"Simple traps could not affect him, Unobservant Master," Allik said with a laugh. A nervous laugh. He'd glanced at MeLaan again. "The traps are a declaration, and a challenge."

They walked on, but still Wax felt unsatisfied. Allik's explanations made a sort of sense—as much sense as building the temple up in the mountains. It was everything Wax would have expected from such a place, down to the smallest details.

Perhaps that was the problem.

"Wax!" Wayne's head poked into the corridor before them. They were almost back to the front entryway. "Wax, there you are. Your uncle, mate. He's here."

"How close?" Wax asked, speeding up.

"Close, close," Wayne said. "Like, on our doorstep and demandin' rent money close."

He'd hoped to have the Bands before that happened. "We'll need to try to collapse the entryway," Wax said as he reached Wayne. "Or maybe this hallway. Seal them out while we finish in here."

"We could do that," Wayne said. "Or . . ."

"Or what?" Wax asked, stopping in place.

"We've got him captured," Wayne said, thumbing over his shoulder. "Marasi has a gun to his rusting head."

Captured? "Impossible."

"Yeah," Wayne said, sounding troubled. "He walked right up to us, carrying a flag. Says he wants to talk. To you."

25

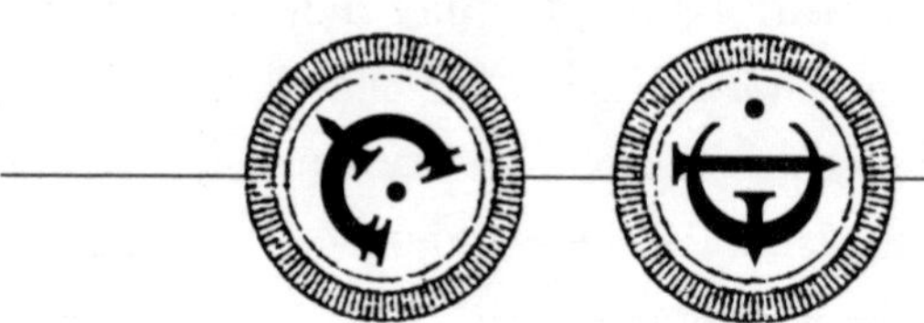

Wax passed from the temple's vestibule onto the landing outside. Edwarn Ladrian, his uncle, stood at the top of the steps, just beneath the statue of the Lord Ruler. Wax was accustomed to seeing this man in a sensible suit, surrounded by luxury—so it was somehow both strange and satisfying at the same time to find Edwarn in a thick coat, hood up, fur brushing cheeks red with the cold. His beard was stuck with snow, and he smiled at Wax, gloved hands resting atop an ivory walking stick.

Marasi knelt in the doorway, her rifle trained directly on him. Edwarn stood alone, though his people—at least a hundred, perhaps more—were setting up tents and dumping supplies in piles on the stone approach.

"Waxillium!" Edwarn said. "Speaking out here in the cold would prove unpleasant. Might I join you and yours inside?"

Wax studied the man. What trick was he planning? Edwarn would never place himself solely in Wax's power, would he?

"You can put the gun down," Wax said to Marasi. "Thank you."

She rose, hesitant. Wax nodded to Edwarn, who cheerily walked through the doorway. Edwarn was a stout man, plump and round-faced. As Wax stepped into the doorway after him, Edwarn pulled off his gloves and put down his hood, revealing a head of hair that was more silver than black. He removed his parka; beneath it he wore stout trousers, suspenders, and a thick white shirt. However, as he folded the parka over his arm, his cheeks returned to a normal color and he stopped shivering.

"You *do* know what the medallions do," Wax said.

"Certainly," Edwarn said. "But their reserves of heat are not eternal, and we don't know how to refill them. We had to reserve their use for those who were suffering greatly from the cold during our trip." He glanced toward Allik, who had moved up beside Marasi, taking her arm in one hand and staring death at Edwarn.

Telsin, Wax thought, seeking the woman out. If she shot their uncle as she had that man in the warehouse . . .

She stood all the way across the vestibule, just outside of it, in the hallway with the traps. Wayne had wisely sauntered over and stood nearby, back to the doorway. He nodded lazily to Wax. He was watching her.

"I see you stole one of my savages," Edwarn said, gesturing at Allik. "He taught you to use the medallions? Both heat and weightlessness?"

Wax pursed his lips and didn't reply.

"No need to act stupid, Nephew," Edwarn said. "We could judge their nature from the type of metals involved, of course. It is a pity we didn't discover the smaller flying machines hidden in the large one. That would have made my trip so much easier."

"Why did you come here, Uncle?" Wax demanded, stepping out of the doorway and casually putting his back to the wall, in case there was a sharpshooter outside. He noticed, impressed, that Marasi had done the same.

"Why did I come? For the same reason as you, Nephew. To find a weapon."

"I meant," Wax said, "why did you come in here, to be taken by me. You're giving yourself up?"

"Giving myself— Nephew, I came to *negotiate*."

"I have no need to negotiate," Wax said. "I have you now. You're under arrest for treason, murder, and kidnapping. Allik will stand witness against you."

"The savage?" Edwarn said, amused.

"I also have—"

Edwarn rapped his cane on the stones. It was banded in metal. Foolish; Wax could use that against him.

"No need, no need," Edwarn said. "I am *not* in your custody, Nephew. Stop entertaining this fantastical delusion that you can achieve anything by harassing me. Even if you *were* to somehow drag me back to Elendel and throw me in a cage, I'd be released in days."

"We'll see," Wax said. He raised Vindication, pointing it right at Edwarn's head. "Run. Give me an excuse, Uncle. I dare you."

"So dramatic," Edwarn said. "Did they teach you that in the Roughs, then?" He shook his head. "Have you looked outside? I have *twenty* Allomancers and Feruchemists here, son. All well trained, and all ready to kill. You're in *my* custody, if anything."

Wax cocked Vindication. "Lucky that I've got you, then."

"I am not so important to the Set as all that," Edwarn said with a smile. "Don't think they wouldn't shoot through me to get to you. But it won't come to that. You won't use me as a hostage. What would there be for you to gain? We've already dug out your little flying ship. You aren't getting out of here alive. Not unless I order it."

Wax clenched his jaw as Edwarn walked to the side of the entryway and settled down on a stone shelf there. He fished in his pocket and brought out a pipe, then nodded in greeting toward Steris, who had been seated on the shelf but immediately moved away.

"Could I borrow that lantern?" Edwarn asked.

Steris held out the lantern. He stuck a lighting stick into it, then used that in turn to light his pipe. He puffed at it a few times, then leaned back, smiling pleasantly. "So?"

"What do you want from me?" Wax said.

"To accompany you," Edwarn said. He nodded toward the hallway beyond. "Our interrogation of the savages—now that we've been able to force them to speak properly—indicates that there is a hallway full of traps beyond here. And . . ." Edwarn hesitated. "Ahh, so you've been *through* the traps, have you? Then you know about the door?"

"How do *you* know this?" Allik said, stepping forward, fists clenched. Marasi put a warning hand on his shoulder, holding him back. "What have you done to my crewmates?"

"You've made yours talk too, I see," Edwarn said. "A pity the Lord Ruler gave his fantastic knowledge to them, don't you think? Barely men. They must hide their—"

"How do you know?" Allik continued, speaking more loudly. "About the hallway? About the door?"

"Your captain knew many things you did not, I believe," Suit said. "Did she tell you about the group of Hunters she carried as subcaptain in her youth? How she got them drinking, and listened to their secrets? They were planning to return here, she said, for the prize."

"My captain," Allik said, voice strained. "She lives?"

Suit smiled, puffing on his pipe, then turned to Wax. "I can get you through the door. I have the key, passed from the lips of a dying priest, to a doomed Hunter, to an airship captain, and now at last to me." He spread his hands, smoking pipe in one.

"You're trying to trick me," Wax said, narrowing his eyes.

"Of course I am," Suit said. "The question is, can you best me? Without an accommodation, we are at an impasse. My men outside can't get in here. It's too fortified a position, and we can't risk explosives lest we damage the prize. You, however, can't get *out*. You can't get the Bands without my help, but you can't pass my army of Allomancers either. You'll starve in here."

Wax ground his teeth. Rusts, he hated this man. Edwarn . . . Suit . . . he was the infection that ate at the wounds of noble society. Spreading his disease. Bringing fever. He was the very definition of the games Wax hated.

"Waxillium," Telsin said from the doorway. "Don't trust him. He'll trick you. He'll win. He always wins."

"We'll try it your way, Uncle," Wax said reluctantly. "I'll let you open the door, but then you must return here."

Edwarn sniffed. "I get to go inside, past the door, and see what is there. Otherwise, you will get no help from me."

"You'll be under guard. I'll have a gun to your head."

"I have no objection to this." He puffed on his pipe, held the smoke in his mouth, then let it out between the teeth of his smile.

Wax gave his uncle a thorough frisk. He had no Allomantically reactive metal on his body save for that on his cane, but he didn't have any aluminum either. At least not in a large enough concentration to be dangerous.

"You first," Wax said, waving his gun toward the doorway. He ignored Telsin's glare. Wayne stood up and held her to the side as Edwarn sauntered through, trailing pipe smoke. Marasi fell in beside Wax as he followed, gripping her rifle with white knuckles. Allik, Steris, and MeLaan came next. Wayne and Telsin took the rear, keeping Wax's sister as far from Uncle Edwarn as possible.

"You sure about this?" Marasi asked as they passed rubble, strewn spears, and darts.

Wax didn't answer. He thought furiously about what his uncle could be planning. What had Wax missed? He had several theories by the time they reached the door.

Edwarn stood before it, looking the symbols up and down. "Push on that one," he said, pointing toward one of the engraved circles. "With Allomancy."

Wax cleared everyone back save Wayne. The shorter man nodded, wearing the bracelet that would let him heal great amounts, speed bubble at the ready in case somehow Edwarn planned the activation of the door to be a trap.

Wax Pushed. Something clicked.

"Now there," Edwarn said, pointing. "The one with the triangular shape."

Click.

"Finally this one," Edwarn said, tapping one with the back of his hand.

"That's it?" Wax said.

"Get them wrong and the thing freezes shut, I'm told," Edwarn said idly. "It has a clockwork timer. Won't be ready again for ten years. You could spend a lifetime guessing, and still have only a small chance of opening it." He looked at Wax and smiled. "Apparently these symbols spell out something the Lord Ruler would have understood."

Wax glanced back at Allik, who shook his head, baffled. "They really make no sense to me."

Wax turned around, held his breath, and Pushed on the final symbol. It clicked. Then, with a deep scrape of stone on metal, the entire thing *slid* to the side, opening a path. Edwarn stepped toward it, but Wax leveled his gun, causing the man to hesitate.

"I'll have you know," Edwarn said, "that I worked a very long time to find what was in this place. It seems unfitting that another should pass that door before me."

"Tough," Wax said, grabbing Telsin's shoulder as she tried to slip by him and enter. "MeLaan?"

"Right," the kandra said. Rusts, she limped as she passed through the door. One of her legs was longer than the other, because of the breaks. She said she didn't feel pain, but if she chose to lie to him, he'd never know.

She stepped into the other room, which had a soft blue glow coming from it. More of those glass lights in the walls.

"Nothing hit me on the way in," she said from within. "Want me to walk around a bit?"

"Just around the doorway area," Wax called to her, gun still held on Edwarn. "Make sure it's safe for us."

They waited a tense few moments. No traps activated in the other room that he could hear.

"How can you wait?" Telsin asked. "Knowing what could be back there? A wonder beyond understanding."

"It isn't going anywhere."

"You never want to know what's beyond the door," Telsin whispered. "You never did chase the horizon. Where is your curiosity?"

"It's alive and well. The things I'm curious about are simply different from the ones you find exciting."

"All clear," MeLaan said from the other room.

Wax nodded for the others to go first, everyone but him and Edwarn. "Stay near the door," he told them.

Once they were inside, he stepped closer to his uncle.

"Threatening," Edwarn said, looking him up and down. "You separated us from the others, Waxillium. Planning a little intimidation?"

"I care for the people in that room," Wax said softly. "I suspect more than a monster like you can ever know."

"You think me emotionless?" Edwarn said, his voice stern. "I tried to spare *your* life, Waxillium. I argued before the Set on your behalf. There was a time when I loved you like a son."

Wax raised Vindication again.

"When we're done with this," Wax said, "you're going to give me names. The others in the Set. I'm going to drag you back to Elendel, and there you'll talk."

"And you'd brutalize me to get those names, no doubt," Edwarn said.

"I follow the law."

"Which can be changed—or bent—to suit your needs. You call me a monster; you hate me because I seek rule. And yet you serve those who do the very same things as I. Your senate? It strangles the life from children with its economic policies." Edwarn stepped forward, a motion which put the barrel of Wax's gun right at his temple. "The longer you live, Waxillium, the more you'll know I am right. The difference between *good* and *evil* men is not found in the acts they are willing to commit—but merely in what *name* they are willing to commit them in."

"Waxillium?" Marasi appeared at the stone doorway. "You'll want to see this."

Wax ground his teeth together and felt his eye twitching. He pulled the gun away from his uncle's head and waved it toward the door.

Edwarn sauntered in, pipe trailing smoke. Wax followed, and entered the solitary room at the center of the fortresslike temple. The dais here was the one depicted in the mural at the temple's entrance.

It rose from the center of the room, gilded and slender, with steps leading up to it. On it was a small square pedestal topped with red velvet and a golden rack suitable for the display of a precious relic. A soft white light, not blue like those at the sides of the room, shone from above the dais and illuminated the whole thing.

The whole empty thing.

Shattered glass lay on the floor of the dais. Wax could pick out corners; it was the remains of a glass box that had once topped the pedestal, enshrouding what had lain there.

The room was quiet and still, frost on the floor in places, dust disturbed by the opening of the stone door floating in the air. There were no other doors or openings in the walls.

"Gone," Wax whispered. "Someone beat us here."

26

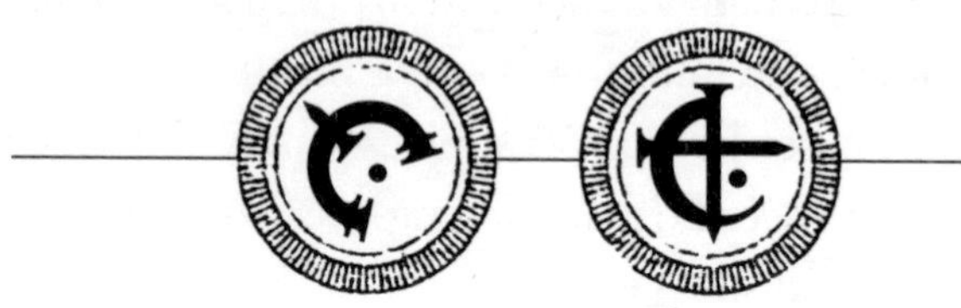

"Why's everyone looking at me?" Wayne said.

"Natural reaction," Marasi said. She held a gun on Edwarn, as did MeLaan.

Wax carefully picked his way across the floor. *Looks like a throne room,* he thought absently. The others started to follow, and he held them back with an upraised hand.

"Stay in this center row walking toward the dais," he ordered them, not looking. "There's a pit trap on either side, and that slightly depressed square over there? It'll drop a sharpened blade from the ceiling."

"How does he know that?" Steris asked. She clutched her notebook, within which she made lists.

"Wax has a natural affinity for things what kill people," Wayne said. "You're all still lookin' at me. Rusts, you think I somehow got in here and lifted the rusting thing?"

"No," Marasi admitted. "But someone did. ReLuur the kandra?"

"No," Wax said, crouching and picking among the pieces of glass on the steps leading up to the pedestal. "These have been here a long time, judging by the dust."

There was no way the kandra had gone down that corridor outside. Too many traps were left, and all the ones that had been sprung had bodies near them.

It was likely that the kandra had snapped his pictures and wisely returned home to gather more of his kind and mount a proper expedition. Kandra were immortal; he wouldn't be hasty in trying to get in here. He'd have planned to take years studying the temple and extracting its secrets.

Who, then?

Telsin passed him, stepping to the dais. Glass crunched under her feet, and Wax glanced up to see her staring at the empty pedestal, aghast. "How?" she murmured.

MeLaan shook her head. "What would *you* do, if you'd secretly stolen the thing? Leave the place gaping open to let everyone know, or reset the traps and sneak away?"

No, Wax thought. Reset the traps? Unlikely. He glanced at his uncle, who stood with pipe in hand, staring at the dais with bristling anger. He was surprised by this.

Or was that an act? Was this all a setup, after taking the Bands, to throw Wax off? Wax brushed the dust from a piece of glass, then dropped it and selected a larger chunk, one of the corner pieces. Wax eyed it critically, then took another piece and set it alongside.

"This *is* a disappointment," Edwarn said. He seemed genuinely troubled.

This wasn't him, Wax thought, stretching out one of his mistcoat tassels and using it judge the length of the shard of glass. *No, this goes back way further than that. . . .*

He stood up, the arguments of the others becoming a distant buzz to him as he regarded the supposed resting place of the Bands of Mourning. A small velvet-topped pedestal, frozen in time.

"I guess that is that," Edwarn said. "Time for this to end, then."

Wax spun, whipping out his gun. He pointed it not at Edwarn, but at his sister.

She stared him down, hand at her pocket. Then she slowly removed a gun. Where had she gotten that? He couldn't sense it. Aluminum.

"Telsin," Wax said, voice hoarse.

Edwarn wouldn't have come in here without a mole. She made the most sense. But *rusts.*

"I'm sorry, Waxillium," she said.

"Don't do this." He hesitated. Too long. She raised the gun.

He fired. She did the same. His shot swerved away from her, Pushed by Allomancy. But her shot—aluminum—took him just below the neck.

Marasi moved before she had time to think. Her rifle already in position, she shot at Suit. Whatever was happening, having him dead couldn't hurt.

Unfortunately, her bullet veered as well, missing Edwarn. Then her weapon flew backward from her hands. Suit smiled at her with infuriating unconcern.

At the pedestal, Waxillium stumbled back. He'd been hit right where the collarbone met his neck. He tried to remain on his feet, but Telsin shot him a *second* time, in the abdomen. Waxillium collapsed, rolled down the steps to the base of the dais, and groaned.

Edwarn was an Allomancer.

Telsin was in the Set.

Again, Marasi reacted before she knew what she was doing. Wayne leaped for Suit, but Suit took a hit from the dueling canes without flinching, then used his own cane—which was banded in metal—and Pushed it against Wayne.

Wayne was flung toward Marasi, canes clattering to the floor. He grunted, hitting the ground as Marasi tried to leap for Suit. Perhaps if she caught just him in a bubble with her, Wayne could—

Her metal reserves were gone. Wayne stumbled up behind her, looking similarly confused. Telsin had tossed something between the two of them.

A small metal cube. Another Allomantic grenade. She was an Allomancer too. She tossed a bag of something to Suit. Coins.

Wayne recovered from his surprise, leaping toward Edwarn again.

But the man Pushed a handful of coins. Wayne cursed, flinching in midair as the coins ripped through his body. Marasi watched in horror, and nearby someone screamed.

Shock. No. She wouldn't let herself be stunned. She hurled herself at Suit, though he casually shoved her aside. She briefly caught hold of his shirt as she fell, but then her fingers slipped. Her head knocked against the stones as she hit.

Dazed, she was able to see Waxillium stumble to his feet. He lurched, bleeding, as Telsin fired again. Then he charged: but not for the doorway, or for Suit. He scrambled toward the side of the room, away from everything. The only thing in that direction was a corner, surely trapping him—

The floor dropped, plunging Waxillium into the pit.

Nearby, Wayne climbed to his feet.

"Keep him down!" Suit shouted, launching coins at Wayne.

Telsin, atop the dais, fired on Wayne. She wasn't a terribly good shot, but between her and Edwarn, they managed to hit several times.

That didn't drop him, not with the gold metalmind. He made a rude gesture and ran out the door, healing from the wounds almost as soon as he was hit.

Suit growled as Telsin's weapon clicked, out of bullets. Marasi tried to grab Suit by the legs and maybe trip him, but he kicked her in the chest. She grunted, breath knocked out of her, and Suit put his foot against her throat.

"Wayne!" Suit yelled. "Come back or I'll kill the others!"

No reply. Wayne, it seemed, had taken the chance to escape down the hallway outside. Good. He wasn't abandoning them; he had correctly realized that their chances were best if he escaped.

"I'll do it!" Suit yelled. "I'll kill her!"

"You think he cares about that?" Telsin asked.

"Honestly, I can't tell with that one," Suit said. He waited a moment to see if Wayne replied, then sighed, taking his foot off Marasi's neck.

Dazed, still having trouble breathing, she took stock of the situation. MeLaan was writhing on the floor. When had that happened? Allik and Steris stood frozen with wide eyes. This had all taken place in a flash. A few years back, Marasi would have been like those two, stunned and confused. She was impressed, on one level, that she'd been able to react as quickly as she had.

Her growth hadn't been enough. Edwarn picked up her rifle, sighting it on her. "Over you go," he said, gesturing with the gun for Marasi to crawl to Steris and Allik so he could cover them all at once. She considered trying something, but what? Her metal reserves were gone, and the import of what had just transpired was settling upon her.

Waxillium was maybe bleeding to death at the bottom of that pit. Wayne had escaped, but had no bendalloy. MeLaan was down.

She might have to do something about this herself.

"Please," Allik said, frantically grabbing Marasi by the arm as she joined the other two. "Please."

He was panicked, but she couldn't blame him. He'd seen Waxillium—the man he worshipped—fall, and was once again in Suit's hands. Steris narrowed her eyes at Telsin.

Waxillium had seen the truth, but too slowly. He hadn't searched her, and he'd hesitated instead of firing. For all his cleverness, Waxillium had a hole in his judgment regarding Suit and Telsin. He always had.

Not that you did any better, Marasi thought.

Telsin walked calmly down the steps, holding her handgun before herself. "That was bungled."

"Bungled?" Edwarn said. "I thought it went well."

"I let Waxillium escape."

"You shot him thrice," Edwarn said. "He's as good as dead."

"And you're going to trust that?" Telsin asked.

Edwarn sighed. "No."

Telsin nodded, her expression calm as she slid a knife from her pocket, then knelt and plunged it into MeLaan. Steris cried out, stepping toward them.

"What did you do to her?" Marasi asked.

They didn't answer, but Marasi suspected the truth. There were liquids that, when injected into kandra, immobilized them and made them start to lose their shapes. It was temporary, but Marasi could only guess that while she had been focused on Suit, Telsin had somehow used one of those on MeLaan. With her arms twisted, her legs broken, the kandra's skeleton hadn't been in any shape for her to fight.

Telsin worked for a gruesome moment and came out with a spike. She tucked it into her pocket, then kept working. Suit walked over to Marasi, and through his ripped shirt Marasi caught a glint of metal peeking between two of his ribs. Not a large spike like the one Ironeyes had. Something more subtle.

They hadn't just been experimenting with Hemalurgy—they'd used spikes to grant themselves powers.

Telsin finally got the second spike out of poor MeLaan and pocketed it. The kandra melted, a mess of greenish-brown flesh and muscles without anything to cling to—oozing out of her clothing, leaving her bones and her skull of green crystal to gaze vacantly at the ceiling.

Telsin pointed toward the pit Waxillium had fallen into. "Chase him down."

"Me?" Suit said. "Surely we can wait for—"

"No waiting," Telsin said. "You know him best. You hunt him down. He is still alive. I've met rocks less durable than my brother."

Suit sighed again, but nodded this time, swapping guns with Telsin so he'd have the aluminum pistol, then reloading it. He walked toward the pit. Marasi glanced at Telsin, who watched MeLaan's remains but held the rifle at the ready.

Should Marasi charge her? Suit obeyed *her.* She wasn't simply a member of the Set; she outranked Waxillium's uncle. And she was obviously an Allomancer; the way she'd used the Allomantic grenade proved that.

Suit climbed down, using a rope. Shortly after that, Marasi heard footsteps outside, and soon an array of soldiers in uniforms like those from the warehouse piled in.

"The short one," Telsin said, urgent. "Wayne. Did you pass him?"

"Sir?" one of the soldiers asked. "No, we haven't seen him."

"Damn," Telsin said. "Where did that rat get to? I need as many men as we can get scouring that hallway and the plain outside. He's *extremely* dangerous, particularly if he has another vial of bendalloy."

Marasi turned to Steris, who was still dazed, eyes wide, still looking at the hole where Waxillium had fallen. Allik held Marasi's arm, his eyes visible behind his mask.

"I'll get us out of this," she whispered to them.

Somehow.

27

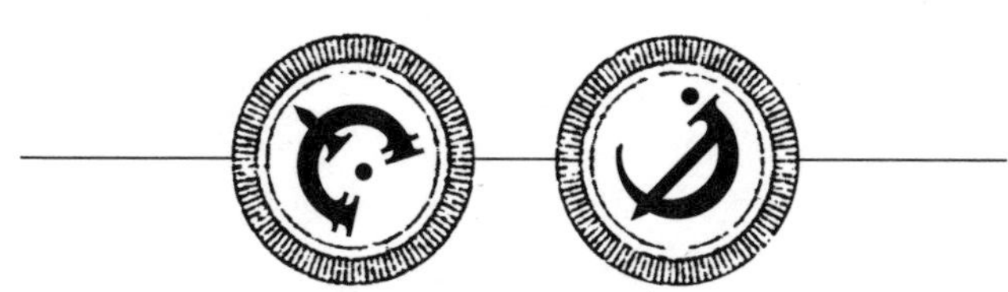

H*e'll tell on us. . . . You know he will.*

Wax rolled onto his back, staring upward. Darkness. The pit had twisted during the fall—he remembered ramming into one of its curves—and deposited him here.

Rusts . . . how could his vision swim when he couldn't *see* anything? He fumbled at his gunbelt and came up with a vial, which he managed to down, replenishing his metal reserves.

You coming? Of course you're not. You never want to risk trouble.

No. He *could* see something. A lone candle in a black room. He blinked his eyes, but it was gone. A vision of the past. A memory . . .

Light in a dark room. Set there to distract . . .

That was what the dais up above had been. The Bands had *never* been there. The people who had built the place left the broken glass, the empty rack, the dais and the pedestal—all as a ruse. But they'd made a mistake.

The glass box they'd broken had been too large to fit on the pedestal.

Candle in a dark room . . . Wax thought. That meant the Bands were somewhere else. He blinked, and thought—as his eyes adjusted—he actually could pick out light.

He wasn't in a narrow pit. That hole had dumped him out somewhere. He heaved himself over in a twist, coming to his knees, and felt at his gut. Blood there. A bad hit, all the way through, judging by the wetness he felt trickling down the back of his thigh. He'd taken a shot to the leg too, but that didn't matter. He'd broken that leg in his fall anyway.

The shot near his neck was the worst. He knew this without even touching it, knew it by the way his body worked—by the way pieces of him were growing numb, the way certain muscles didn't respond right.

That light. A soft blue. Not a candle, but one of the built-in lights of the building. He crawled toward the light, dragging his broken leg, scraping on stone, sweat streaming down the sides of his face and mixing with the blood he spilled to the ground.

"Harmony," he whispered. "Harmony."

No reply. Now he prayed? What of his hatred?

For a time, that light was everything to him. An hour could have passed as he crawled, or perhaps it had been only a minute. As he neared, he saw sentries in the darkness. People sitting arrayed before the light, casting long shadows into the depths of the room. The ceiling was low, barely taller than a man could stand. That was why . . . why the people had to sit. . . .

Focus! he thought at himself, flaring his metal. The sentries had metal on them. And . . . yes, one other faint line, pointing toward a spot on the floor up ahead. Another trap.

The flared metal seemed to bring him clarity, helping him push back the muddled sensation. Blood loss. He was fading quickly. Still, a shade more alert, he saw those sentries for what they were. Corpses. Seated, somehow, draped in warm clothing. He passed the first row of them and looked in on frozen faces, shriveled with the passing of time but remarkably well preserved. Each held a mask in its lap. They sat in four concentric rings, looking at the light up ahead.

Here, the ones who had built this place had died. Then how . . . how had word of the key to the door been passed on. . . .

Wax crawled among the huddled dead, frozen despite their warm clothing. He could imagine them seated here, waiting for the end, as the heat in their metalminds dwindled. The cold, creeping in as night does after sunset, a final, consuming darkness.

And ahead, another pedestal. Smaller, carved of white rock. A simple light glowing on its top revealed a set of metal bracers. No fancy trimmings here, just the silent reverence of the dead.

Something sounded behind him, a scrape of boots on stone; then a light flooded the room from there.

"Waxillium?" Edwarn's voice called.

Wax huddled down.

"I know you're here, son," Edwarn said. "That's quite the trail of blood you're leaving. This is over, as you must realize."

He's an Allomancer now, Wax thought, remembering what Edwarn had done to Marasi's gun. The man carried a pistol, the aluminum one that Telsin had used.

Telsin . . . How long had she been working with them? He hated that he'd guessed, hated that his first instinct—even if he'd been right—had been to pull a gun on his only sibling. It just made too much sense. She'd caused Wayne to knock the backpack out the door. She'd killed the brute in the warehouse, when he'd been about to speak—potentially addressing her, outing her as a member of the Set.

Suit wouldn't . . . wouldn't have come into the temple with them unless he had the upper hand. . . .

He needed to stay focused. Edwarn was approaching. Wax was tempted to Push a bullet toward the man, but held himself back. Edwarn raised the light, illuminating the vast emptiness and looking slowly around himself. He didn't seem to have spotted Wax, and the bodies all had some metal on them, so Edwarn's steelsight wouldn't reveal Wax. But the blood trail would soon betray him.

Still, Wax waited. He bowed himself, huddling down in the line of figures, imitating their stooped postures.

Have to get those bracers . . .

He'd get shot before he could reach them. If he could even make it that distance without passing out.

"I *did* try to protect you," Suit said.

"What did you do to my sister?" Wax demanded, his voice echoing in the darkness.

Suit smiled, walking forward, scanning the bodies. If he could draw the man closer . . .

"I didn't do anything to her," Suit said. "Son, *she* recruited *me*."

"Lies," Wax hissed.

"The old world is dying, Waxillium!" Edwarn said. "I told you that a new one will soon be born, a world where men like you don't belong."

"I can find my place in a world of airships."

"That's not what I'm talking about," Suit said. "I'm talking about the secrets, Waxillium. The world where constables exist only to make people feel secure. It will be a world of shadows, of hidden government. The shift is already happening. Those who rule these days are not the men who smile at crowds and make speeches."

Edwarn moved around a corpse, then followed Wax's blood trail with his eyes. Only a few more steps.

"The day of kings has passed," Edwarn said. "The day of mighty men to be worshiped has gone, and with its passing goes the right of Allomancers to power. No more will their gifts hinge on the whims of fate. Instead, the powers will come to those who deserve them. Who can *use* them."

He raised his foot to step, then hesitated, looking down. He grinned, moving his foot backward and making Wax's heart fall. "Trying to goad me into stepping onto the trap? Such a brash plan, Waxillium." He glanced upward. "Looks like it's rigged to drop this entire section of ceiling. You'd be caught in it too."

Edwarn turned and looked right at where Wax was sitting, trying to hide among the corpses.

Wax raised his head. "It would have been worth the cost." He still had his shotgun, but doubted he had the strength to use it. Instead, kneeling, he held out a single bloodied hand, clutching a bullet in it. "Shall we see how good you are, Uncle?"

A duel. Perhaps he could win a duel.

Edwarn regarded him, then shook his head. "I think not."

He stepped on the pressure plate, triggering the trap.

Telsin marched Marasi and the others out of the temple. And, once they were outside, Telsin reached to Marasi's arm and ripped free the medallion there.

Marasi gasped, clutching her purse as the cold descended upon her like a swarm of insects, nipping at every bit of exposed skin. Her dress suddenly seemed flimsy, useless. She might as well have been naked. Telsin repeated the process for Steris, then reached for Allik's arm.

"Please," Marasi said. "He—"

Telsin grabbed the medallion. Allik tried to pull away, but one of the guards cuffed him across the face, cracking his mask and sending him to the snowy ground. The guard reached down, ripping off the medallion.

Allik gasped loudly, huddling on the cold stone. Beyond them, the field was a flurry of activity. Tents flapped in the wind, and men scurried around the fallen Hunter airship. A group of people in masks were being marched across the field to a particularly large tent—so, Allik's crewmates were still alive.

One man with a red uniform beneath his thick coat hiked up the steps. "Lady Sequence," he said to Telsin as he reached the top. "We've located what we think must be the weapon."

"The Bands?" Marasi asked.

Telsin looked at her drolly. "The Bands were a possibility. An engaging one, yes, and I will not deny my disappointment. Irich will be particularly displeased. But we didn't come here for them."

The airship, Marasi realized, looking toward it. *Bearing a bomb intended to destroy the temple.*

A bomb that had never been used. Men moved about the large airship, investigating it. *This* was what Suit and the others had come for.

Marasi stepped forward, but one of the guards grabbed her while another dug in her purse to check for anything dangerous. Another batted Steris's notebook from her fingers, then began to frisk Steris none too gently.

"The ship is in good repair despite the elements, Sequence," the soldier told Telsin as Marasi watched helplessly. "It didn't crash as the other one did."

"Excellent," Telsin said. "Let's see if that thing has any of the powering metal left in it." She started down the steps, her warming medallion letting her ignore the freezing cold. She seemed like a spirit in her sleek, airy gown beside men in full winter gear. She hesitated, looking back at Marasi and the others.

"Search them thoroughly," she informed the men. "I sensed faint metal from the older woman, but it's gone now. Her notebook must have metal bindings. I don't believe that they have any aluminum guns—besides the one that Waxillium had. Either way, keep watch on them. They're insurance against the short one, who is still out here somewhere."

The roof fell in on them.

Wax shouted, diving toward the pedestal and the two simple bracers. Suit took a different tack; he Pushed himself back away from the bracers, out of the path of the stones.

Rock hit Wax like a fist slamming him to the ground. Bones crunched inside of him. He gasped, but got a mouthful of dust.

He knew how bad it was when the pain faded. As the dust settled, he found he couldn't move any part of his body. A weight rested on his back, pinning him with his head to the side. One of his hands hung within his view, the fingers mangled. He couldn't feel them. Nothing. Just his face. Enough to feel the tears of pain and failure on his cheeks.

Steel. He tried burning it.

He felt a few wisps of it inside of him, a warmth that became the only thing he could sense.

Rubble shifted nearby, and rocks clattered. A second later Suit appeared, a cut in his arm resealing. He dusted himself off and glanced at Wax.

"The trouble with Hemalurgy is in its limitations," he said. "If you kill a man and steal his Metallic abilities, the resulting gift to you is weakened. Did you know that? What's more, if you spike yourself too much, you become subject to Harmony's . . . interference. Indeed, by the stories, you might open yourself to the interference of any idiot Soother or Rioter with enough talent." He shook his head. "I am limited to three boons, even if we have discovered how to make someone else be weak, while we gain the benefit."

He glanced toward the bracers. "But if there is a way to gain more powers, and not be subject to Harmony . . . now that would be something. I see why Telsin was so eager."

He left Wax, passing the frozen corpses of the dead masked ones, bits of them sticking from beneath fallen rocks. Crushed. Some even looked to have shattered.

Suit stepped up to the pedestal. "Behold me, Waxillium. Today, I become a god."

Wax tried to cry out, but his lungs wouldn't hold enough air. He tried to heave himself free, but his body no longer worked. He was dying. Though steel burned fitfully inside of him, he was dying.

No. He was already dead. His body just hadn't quite realized it yet.

Suit held the Bands. Wax twisted his head as best he could, pinned as he was, to see it. The bearded man smiled broadly, waiting.

Nothing happened.

Suit strained, his face darkening. Then he turned the bracers around, looking them over. He put them on.

Still, nothing happened.

"Drained," he said with disgust. "After all this, we find them *empty* of attributes. What a waste." He sighed, then walked over to Wax, sliding the aluminum gun from his pocket. "I have no doubt that Irich's scientists will be able to puzzle out how the Bands were made. Take that thought with you into the eternities, Waxillium. Be sure to shake Ironeyes's hand for me. I intend to never meet him."

He pressed the gun against Wax's head.

And then something slammed into Suit. The man cried out, and a scuffle followed, along with the gun discharging. Suit cursing. Feet on stone.

A second later, Wayne scrambled into view. He knelt beside Wax and looked him over, seeming horrified.

"Wayne," Wax croaked. "How . . . ?"

"Ah, 's nothing," his partner said. "Slipped out and fell down another of those holes. That one ended in spikes, I'm afraid. But I was able to heal up and climb out, once the soldiers had passed, then slip into this pit. You picked a better hole to fall in than I did, for sure."

"Suit . . ."

"He ran," Wayne said. "Didn't want to face me himself, not with me healing. Right cowardly, that one. . . ." He trailed off, looking down at Wax's body, pinned by the rock. "I—"

"Find Steris and Marasi," Wax croaked. "Help them escape."

"Wax," he said, shaking his head. "No. *No.* I can't do this without you."

"Yes you can. Fight."

"Not that part," Wayne said. "The rest of it. Livin'. We . . . we'll get you out of this." He rubbed his eyes with the heels of his palms, then looked at the stone on top of Wax, then down at the blood pooling beneath.

Then he sat back, running his hands through his hair, eyes wide, as if in shock. Wax tried to urge him on, but his lips wouldn't move.

Not enough strength.

Marasi huddled on the cold ground with Steris and Allik, surrounded by armed men who searched their possessions. It was still night out here, but sunrise had to be close.

Waxillium would have found a way out of this.

Stop comparing yourself to him, she thought. *Is it any wonder you stand in his shadow, when that's all you can see yourself doing?*

She needed to solve this. A dozen plans ran through her head, all stupid. The guard nearby still had her purse.

ReLuur's spike, it might be in there. Since it was Hemalurgically Invested, it might not have registered to the eyes of an Allomancer looking for metals on her. The guard dumped the purse out, spilling the contents onto the cold stone.

No spike. Instead, among her notebooks and handkerchiefs tumbled a palm-sized wedge of metal. The aluminum spearhead from the statue?

Wayne, I'm going to . . . She gritted her teeth. When had he swapped her for the spike? That man!

"I searched that purse already," another guard noted. "No weapons."

"Well then, what's this?" the first guard said, picking up the wedge-shaped piece of aluminum.

The second guard snorted. "You're welcome to try to kill someone with that if you want. It's dull."

Marasi wilted, feeling stupid. Even if she had the spike, what would she do? She couldn't overpower armed guards.

Then what *could* she do?

Someone fell through the sky and thumped to the ground nearby. She perked up, thinking it must be Waxillium. Instead it was Suit, clothing ripped and dusty, carrying a gun. The guards saluted, the one with her purse dropping it and the metal wedge. One of her glass makeup jars rolled away.

Poor Allik huddled beside Steris. He'd stopped shivering, and his skin was turning blue. Steris met her eyes, and looked resigned.

Suit strode past. He looked far more intimidating dropping through the air using Allomantic abilities than he had bundled up for the weather and standing on the steps of the temple.

"Is my brother dead?" Telsin demanded, turning from her group of engineers nearby.

"Yes," Suit said. "Though I encountered the short one."

"You killed him?"

"Left him distracted," Suit said. "I thought you'd want to see what I found." He held up something that gleamed in the powerful lights the crew had set up. Two silvery bracers, each as long as a forearm. "There was a hidden chamber down there, Sequence. And my, what a secret it contained."

Telsin shoved between her scientists and scrambled up to Suit. She took the bracers, awed.

"They don't work," Suit noted.

"What do you mean?"

"They're out of attributes, I think. Their reserves gone."

"But they grant Allomancy too," Telsin said, putting them on and waving toward one of the guards, who tossed her a vial of metals. She downed it, eager.

"Well?" Suit asked.

"Nothing."

A decoy, Marasi thought. Like the glass case and the empty pedestal . . . yes, that had been one too. She could see now why Waxillium had been doing his measuring.

Waxillium. He couldn't really be . . .

No. What could she do? Not fight. But think. These Bands were a decoy. A second layer of falsehood to confuse intruders.

So where were the real ones?

Candles in a dark room.

They're another decoy, Wax thought, mind muddled. *Those bracers were too perfect, just like the stories. They were left to fool us.*

Like the symbols of Wax's old adversary, painted on the door of a mansion. Meant to distract. Delay.

This place was made for the Lord Ruler, Wax thought. *Those traps . . . those traps are stupid. What if one* did *catch him? The whole thing has to be a decoy.*

So what? There was another temple out there? Maybe they *had* hidden it in a cave?

He could barely see anymore. Wayne held his hand, tears streaming down his face. Everything was fading. The cold . . . coming . . . like darkness . . .

No, Wax thought, *it wouldn't be somewhere else. He'd need to be able to find it. He'd recognize it. . . .*

It was.

It was here!

Wax gasped, and tried to form the words, eyes wide. Wayne gripped his hand, knuckles white.

He couldn't feel it.

The darkness arrived, and Wax died.

28

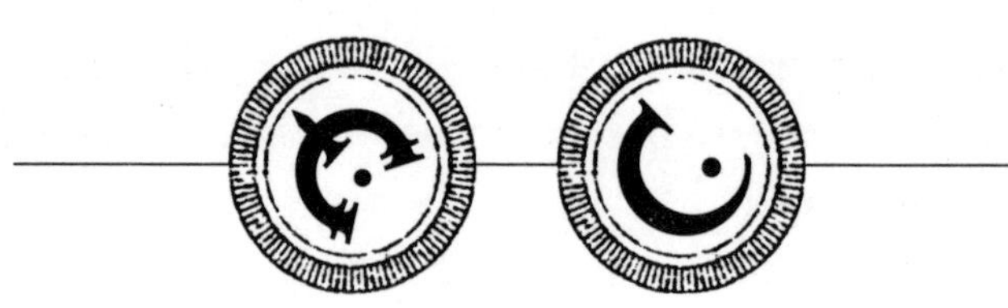

Wax stilled.

Wayne let the hand fall limp. He wanted to just sit here. Stare at nothing like those fellows in rows nearby, the ones that weren't crushed. Sit and become nothing.

All his life, only one man had believed in him. Only one man had forgiven him, had encouraged him. The rest of this damned race could burn away and become ash, for all Wayne cared. He hated them all.

But . . . what would Wax say?

He left me, the bastard, Wayne thought, wiping his eyes. In that moment, he hated Wax too. But then, Wayne loved him more than the hatred. He growled, and stumbled to his feet. He had no weapons; he'd dropped his dueling canes above.

He stared at Wax's body, then knelt and felt along the man's leg. He got ahold of something and yanked it free. The shotgun.

Wayne's hands immediately started shaking.

"You stop that," he hissed at them. "We're done with that."

He cocked the shotgun, then went looking for a way out of this tomb.

The whole temple is a decoy, Marasi thought, trembling in the cold. *So where are the actual Bands?*

The place was built for the Lord Ruler, who would supposedly return to claim his weapon. Where would you put that weapon?

He'd know what it looked like, Marasi thought. *He built it. We think it was in the shape of bracers, but it didn't have to be. Could be anything.*

That would be smart, if you were making a weapon. These metalminds, you had to know what they did before they worked. You could protect yourself, so only someone who knew what to look for could use your weapon.

And in that case, the people who built the temple could have left the weapon where the returning Lord Ruler would see it, but everyone else would pass right by, digging farther into the temple to encounter traps, pits, and decoys—all designed to either kill them or convince them that they'd successfully robbed the place.

Where did you put the weapon? On the doorstep, under the sign of the Sovereign himself, in his very own hand. Marasi turned, frantic, searching out the oversized spearhead.

It lay right beside her, where the guard had dropped it. Waxillium had called it aluminum because he couldn't sense it, but he hadn't looked closely enough.

If he had, he'd have seen it was made of different interwoven metals, wavy, like the folds forged into the blade of a sword. He couldn't Push on it, not because it was aluminum.

But because it was a metalmind, stored with more power than any they'd ever seen.

Around Wax, everything became misty and indistinct. The cavern, the rocks, the ground itself—all just mist. He could stand on it somehow.

Harmony stepped up beside Wax in the misty darkness. They fell in beside one another, walking as was natural for men to do. God looked much as Wax had always imagined Him. Tall, peaceful, hands laced before Himself. Face like a long oval, serene and human, though He towed behind Him a cloak of timelessness. Wax could *see* it, trailing after. Storms and winds, clouds and rain, deserts and forests, all reflected somehow in this creature's wake. His robe was the Terris V pattern, where each V was not a color, but an age. A *strata* of time, like those of a deep rock uncovered.

"They say," Wax said softly, "that You come to all people when they die."

"It is a duty I consider to be among my most sacred," Harmony said. "Even with other pressing matters, I find time to take this walk." He had a quiet voice, familiar to Wax. Like that of a forgotten friend.

"I'm dead then."

"Yes," Harmony said. "Your body, mind, and soul have separated. Soon one will return to the earth, another to the cosmere, and the third . . . Even I do not know."

Wax continued walking. The shadowy cavern vanished, and Wax had a feeling of *blurring*. Mists became darkness, and all he could see was a distant light, like the sun below the horizon.

"If You can take time to walk with us," Wax said, bitter, "why not come a little earlier? Why not *stop* the walk before it must begin?"

"Should I prevent all hardship, Waxillium?"

"I know where this is going," Wax said. "I know what You're going to say. You value choice. Everyone theorizes about it. But You *can* help. You've done it before, in placing me where I needed to go. You intervene. So why not intervene more? Prevent children from being killed. Make certain that constables arrive in time to stop deaths. You don't have to take away choice, but You *could* do more. I know You could."

He left the last part unsaid.

You could have saved her. Or at least told me what I was doing.

Harmony nodded. It felt bizarre to be demanding things, but rusts . . . if this was the end, Wax wanted a few answers.

"What is it to be God, Waxillium?" Harmony asked.

"I don't think that's a question I can answer."

"It is not one I ever thought I'd have to answer either," Harmony said. "But obviously, it has been forced upon me. You would have me intervene and stop the murders of innocents. I could do this. I have considered it. If I were to stop every one, what then? Do I stop maimings as well?"

"Of course," Wax said.

"And where do I hold back, Waxillium? Do I prevent all wounds, or do I prevent only those caused by evil people? Do I stop a man from falling asleep so that he will not tip a candle and burn down his house? Do I stop all harm that could ever befall a person?"

"Maybe."

"And once nobody is ever hurt," Harmony said, "will people be satisfied? Will they not pray to me and ask for more? Will some people still curse and spit at the sound of my name because they are poor, while another is rich? Should I mitigate this, make everyone the same, Waxillium?"

"I won't be caught in this trap," Wax said. "You're the God, not me. You can find a line where You prevent the worst. *You* can find a line where You're stopping the worst that is reasonable, while still letting us live our lives."

The light ahead suddenly rolled outward, and Wax found that they'd been rounding a *planet*. They stood high above it, and had stepped from darkness into sunlight, which let Wax see the world below, bathed in a calm, cool light.

Beyond that hung a haze of red. All around, pressing in upon the world. He could feel it choking him, a miasma of dread and destruction.

"Perhaps," Harmony said softly, "I have already done just as you suggest. You do not see it, because the worst never reaches you."

"What is it?" Wax asked, trying to take in that vast redness. It beat inward, but he could see something, a thin strip of light—like a bubble around the world—stopping it.

"A representation," Harmony said. "A crude one, perhaps." He looked to Wax and smiled, like a father at a wide-eyed child.

"We're not done with our conversation," Wax said. "You let her die. *You let me kill her.*"

"And how long," Harmony asked softly, "must you hate yourself for that?"

Wax clenched his jaw, but couldn't force down the trembling that took him. He lived it again, holding her as she died. Knowing he'd killed her.

That hatred *seethed* inside of him. Hatred for Harmony. Hatred for the world.

And yes. Hatred for himself.

"Why?" Wax asked.

"Because you demanded it of me."

"No I didn't!"

"Yes. A part of you did. An eventuality I can see, one of many possible Waxilliums, all you—yet not set. Know yourself, Waxillium. Would you have had another kill her? Someone she didn't know?"

"No," he whispered.

"Would you have had her live on, a slave in her mind? Corrupted by that *cursed* spike that would forever leave her scarred, even if replaced?"

"No." He was crying.

"And if you had known," Harmony said, holding his eyes, "that you'd never have been able to pull that trigger unless your eyes were veiled? If you'd realized what knowledge of the truth would do to you—stilling your hand and trapping her in an endless prison of madness—what would you have asked of me?"

"Don't tell me," Wax whispered, squeezing his eyes shut.

The silence seemed to stretch until eternity.

"I am sorry," Harmony said with a gentle voice, "for your pain. I am sorry for what you did, what we had to do. But I am not sorry for making you do what had to be done."

Wax opened his eyes.

"And when I hold back, staying my hand from protecting those below," Harmony said, "I must do it out of trust in what people can do on their own." He glanced toward the red haze. "And because I have other problems to occupy me."

"You didn't tell me what it was," Wax said.

"That is because I do not know."

"That . . . frightens me."

Harmony looked to him. "It should."

Down below, a tiny spark flickered on one of the landmasses. Wax blinked. He'd seen it, despite the incredible distance.

"What was that?" he asked.

Harmony smiled. "Trust."

Marasi clutched the spearhead in two hands.

And tapped *everything*.

Power flooded into her, lighting her up like an inferno. Snow hung motionless in the air. She stood up and reached to the belt of one of her captors, removing one of his vials of metal. She took them all, several from each guard, and drank them. She was tapping a metalmind, letting her move at a speed so fast that when she lifted her hand, she could briefly see the pocket of vacuum left behind. She smiled.

Then she burned her metals. All of them.

In that one transcendent moment, she felt herself change, expand. She felt the Lord Ruler's own power, stored in the Bands of Mourning—the spearhead clutched in her fingers—surge through her, and she felt she would burst. It was as if an ocean of light had suddenly been pumped into her arteries and veins.

Blue lines exploded from her, first pointing at metals, then multiplying, changing, *transforming*. She saw through it all, everything in blue. There were no people or objects, just energy coalesced. The metals shone brilliantly, as if they were holes into someplace different. Concentrated essence, providing a pathway to power.

She was using the reserves with startling quickness. She slowed her speed, and for some reason the people beside her jumped, holding their ears. She cocked her head, then *PUSHED*.

The Push flung the guards a good fifty feet. That left her facing Suit and Telsin, who regarded her with horrified expressions. They were glowing energy to her, but she recognized them. They had spikes inside of them.

Convenient. Those spikes resisted Pushes, but not enough to bother Marasi now. She lifted a hand and flung both of them away by the very metals they'd used to pierce themselves.

All around, guards grabbed guns and turned on her. She swept them backward, then lifted herself off the ground, Pushing on the trace minerals in the stone beneath her.

She hung there, and was surprised to see something spinning around her. Mist? Where was it coming from?

Me, she realized.

She hovered in the sky, flush with power. In that moment, she *was* the Ascendant Warrior. She held the fullness of what Waxillium had barely tasted his whole life. She could be him, eclipse him. She could bring justice to entire peoples. Holding it all within her, having it and measuring it, she finally admitted the truth to herself.

This isn't what I want.

She would not let her childhood dreams hold sway over her any longer. She smiled, then threw herself through the air in a Push toward the temple.

Steris watched her sister *fly away.*

"Unexpected," she said. And here she assumed she'd been prepared for anything. Marasi starting to glow, throwing people around with Allomancy as if they were dolls, then streaking away and leaving a trail of mist . . . well, that hadn't been on the list. It hadn't even made the *appendix.*

She looked down at poor Allik, so cold he'd stopped shivering. "I shall have to enlarge my projections of what is plausible during activities such as this, don't you think?"

He mumbled something in his language. "Foralate men!" He waved his hand in a gesture. "Forsalvin!"

"Telling me to flee without you?" Steris said, walking over and retrieving her notebook. "Yes, running while they are all confused would be wise, but I don't plan to leave yet." She opened the notebook, which she'd hollowed out with Wax's knife in the rear of the skimmer, while Marasi was talking with Allik up front and the others slept. "Did you know that when I evaluated everyone's usefulness on this expedition, I gave myself a seven out of a hundred? Not very high, yes, but I couldn't reasonably give myself the lowest mark possible. I do have my uses."

She turned the large notebook, showing an extra medallion from the skimmer's emergency store settled protectively into the gouged-out section she'd made.

She smiled at Allik, pulled it free, and pressed it into his hand. He let out a long, relieved sigh, and the blown snow that had stuck to his face melted away.

Nearby, soldiers were regaining their feet and shouting to one another.

"And now," Steris said, "I think your earlier suggestion has merit."

"Now what?" Wax asked Harmony. "I fade off into nothing?"

"I don't believe it's nothing," God said. "There is something beyond. Though perhaps my belief is merely my own desire wishing it to be so."

"You are not encouraging me. Aren't You omnipotent?"

"Hardly," Harmony said, smiling. "But I believe that parts of me *could* be."

"That doesn't make any sense."

"It won't until I make it do so," Harmony said, extending His hands to either side. "In answer to your question, however, you don't fade just yet. Though soon. Right now, you make a choice."

Wax looked from one of the deity's hands to the other. "Does everyone get this choice?"

"Their choices are different." He proffered His hands to Wax, as if offering them for him to take.

"I don't see the choice."

"My right hand," Harmony said, "is freedom. You can feel it, I think."

And he could. Soaring, released from all bonds, riding upon lines of blue light. Adventure into the unknown, seeking only the fulfillment of his own curiosity. It was glorious. It was what he'd always wanted, and its lure thrummed through him.

Freedom.

Wax gasped. "What . . . what is the other one?"

Harmony held up His left hand, and Wax heard something. A voice?

"Wax?" it said.

Yes, a frantic voice. Feminine.

"Wax, you have to know what it does. It will heal you, Wax. Waxillium! Please . . ."

"That hand," Wax said, looking at it. "That hand is duty, isn't it?"

"No, Waxillium," Harmony said gently. "Although that is how you've seen it. Duty or freedom. Burden or adventure. You were always the one who made the *right* choice, when others played. And so you resent it."

"No I don't," Wax said.

Harmony smiled. The understanding in His face was infuriating.

"This hand," Harmony said, "is not duty. It is but a different adventure."

"Wax . . ." the voice said from below, choked with emotion. It belonged to Marasi. "You *have* to tap the metalmind."

Wax reached toward the left hand, and Harmony—shockingly—pulled it away. "Are you certain?"

"I have to."

"Do you?"

"I *have* to. It's who I am."

"Then perhaps," Harmony said, "you should stop hating that, my son." He extended the hand.

Wax hesitated. "Tell me one thing first."

"If it is within my means."

"Did she come here? When she passed?"

Harmony smiled. "She asked me to look after you."

Wax seized the left hand with his own. He was immediately pulled toward something, like air being sucked through a hole. Warmth bathed him; then it became a *fire.* Pulling breath into his lungs, he screamed, heaving, throwing the boulder off. It clattered to the side, and he found himself in the low-roofed chamber beneath the temple.

Such strength! He hadn't thrown that rock with muscles, but with *steel.* His body reknit even as he launched himself to his feet by Pushing on tiny traces of metal in the ground beneath him. He landed and looked down at his left hand. The one that had been dangling, broken, before his face as he died.

Clutched in it was an oversized spearhead crafted from sixteen different metals melded together. He looked up from it and toward Marasi, who regarded him with tearstained eyes, but a broad smile.

"You found it," Wax said.

She nodded eagerly. "Just took a little old-fashioned detective work."

"You saved me," Wax said.

Rust and Ruin . . . such *power.* He felt as if he could level cities or build them up anew.

"Suit and your sister are outside," Marasi said. "I left the others there. I don't— Well, I wasn't thinking straight. Or maybe I was thinking too much. Here." She handed him a vial of metals.

Wax took it, then held up the Bands. "You could have done this yourself."

"No," Marasi said. "I couldn't have."

"But—"

"I couldn't have," Marasi said. "It just . . . isn't me." She shrugged. "Does that make sense?"

"Surprisingly, yes." He flexed his hand around the Bands.

"Go," Marasi said. "Do what you do best, Waxillium Ladrian."

"Which is what? Break things?"

"Break things," Marasi said, "*with style.*"

He grinned, then downed the vial of metals.

29

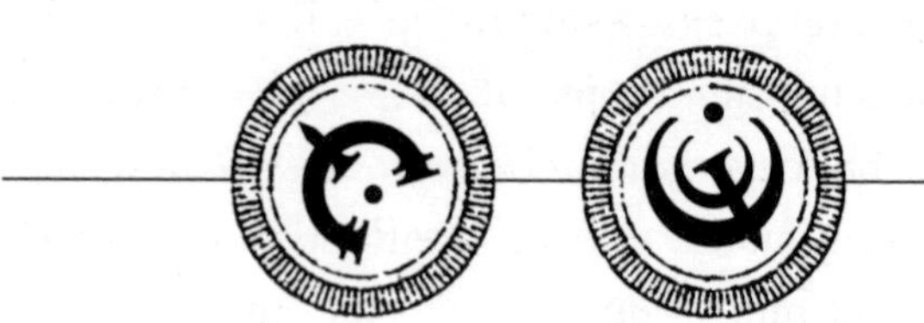

"Waxillium's followers have the Bands!" Suit whispered to himself as he crossed the dark, stony field. Snow had begun falling—a bitter, icy snow, nothing like the soft flakes he'd occasionally seen in the eastern Basin. "It is a crisis. They will be coming for us. We must move up our timetables!"

He chewed on the words, mulling them over as he pulled his coat tight. Warming device notwithstanding, that wind was *annoying*.

Would they buy his argument? No, not dire enough.

"Waxillium and his people have the Bands!" he whispered to himself. "This will undoubtedly let the kandra devise the means of creating metalminds anyone can use. We must move up our timetables and seize Elendel now, or we will find ourselves technologically outmatched!"

Yes. Yes, that was the idea. Even the most careful of the Series would be distressed by the prospect of being technologically outmaneuvered. This would convince them to give him the leeway he desired.

Anything could be an advantage. He'd wanted the Bands for himself, but in lieu of that, he'd find something else.

Suit *always* found the advantage.

He passed soldiers scurrying about and unloading weapons on the frozen plain of rock. They'd planned for a potential fight here, as he'd worried he might encounter more of the masked savages.

"Sir!" one of the men called. "Orders?"

He gestured toward the sky. "If anyone other than the Sequence drops from the air or approaches your position, *shoot* them. Then keep shooting, even after they are down."

"Yes, sir!" the soldier said, waving to a group of his men. He turned toward an empty rack, then paused. "My rifle? Who took my rifle!"

Suit continued on past, tossing the fake Bands of Mourning into the snow and leaving the troops to—hopefully—slow down Waxillium's minions. He eagerly marched aboard the new airship. Now this device, *this* was an advantage. The Bands could serve one man, make a deity out of him. A fleet of ships like this could deify an entire army.

The wooden hallway inside had gaslights set into lamps with austere metal housings. It was all distinctly plainer than the ship that had crashed in Dulsing—the wood here was unornamented, unpolished. The other ship had felt decorated like a den. This one, a warehouse.

Probably cheaper to build this way, he thought, nodding his head in approval.

Footsteps clattered above as men charged through one of the corridors on another deck, and Suit brushed the snow from his arms as a technician ran up to him, bearing the red uniform of the Set's Hidden Guard.

"My lord," the man said, proffering one of the medallions. "You'll need this."

Suit took it and rolled up his sleeve to strap it to his upper arm. "Is this ship operational?"

The man's eyes lit up. "Yes, sir! The machinery is operational, sheltered as it was from the weather. Sir . . . it's *amazing*. You can *feel* the energy pulsing off that metal. We did have to send men out to unclog the fans—a few of the Coinshots helped—and we have them moving now. Fed is down below, priming the weight-changing machinery with her Feruchemy, to lighten the ship. That should be the last step!"

"Then lift us off," Suit said, walking toward where he assumed the bridge would be found.

"My lord Suit?" the man called after him. "Aren't we waiting for the Sequence?"

He hesitated only briefly. Where had she gotten to?

Another advantage? he thought. He could stand being Sequence.

"She will join us aloft if she can," he said. "Our priority is to get this ship, and its secrets, to a secure location."

As the technician saluted and ran to obey, Suit filled his medallion, becoming lighter. So much easier than getting his spikes had been. It was hard not to feel that their experiments in Hemalurgy had been a waste, a dead end.

The ship quivered, and the fans started up with a much louder sound than he had expected. Before he reached the bridge, the thing rocked, and he heard ice cracking above the sound of the fans. He leaned over to a porthole, looking out as the ground retreated.

It *worked*. Immediately, implications flooded his mind. Travel. Shipping. Warfare. New regions could be settled. New types of buildings and docks would be needed.

It would all flow through him.

He suppressed a smile—best to celebrate *after* he was safely away—but he could not stop the heady sensation. The Set had been planning for events a century or more away, putting careful plots into motion at his suggestion. He was proud of those, but truth be told, he'd rather they rule in *his* lifetime.

And with this, he could do so.

Jordis huddled in the tent, watching her crew die.

It had been long coming, this death. The last ember of the fire, refusing to give up its spark. During the terrible march through the dead rain, her people had been given tiny sips of warmth from a metalmind. Enough to barely keep them alive, like plants locked in a dark shed for most of the day.

But now, in this place, the cold was too pervasive—and the hardships of the march too devastating. She crawled among her crew and whispered encouragement, though she could no longer feel her fingers or toes. Most of the men and women of the ship couldn't even nod. A few had started removing their clothing, complaining of heat. Chillfever had struck them.

Not long now. The maskless devils seemed to know this; they'd posted only a single guard at the tent. Her people could have snuck away out the back, perhaps. But what would they sneak toward? Death outside in the winds rather than death inside here?

How do the maskless survive it? she wondered. They must be devils indeed, born of the frost itself, to be so capable of withstanding the cold.

Jordis knelt beside Petrine, the enginemaster and eldest of her crew. How had the woman survived so long? She was by no means feeble, but she was past her sixth decade. Petrine lifted her hand and gripped Jordis's arm—though her wrinkled eyes were shadowed by the mask, Jordis needed no gesture or expression to know Petrine's emotions.

"Do we attack?" Petrine asked.

"For what purpose?"

"We could die by their weapons instead of the cold."

Wise, those words. Perhaps they could—

A loud thump came from outside the tent. Jordis found her feet, surprisingly, though most of the others remained huddling where they lay. The front of the tent burst open and a man with a familiar—but broken—mask appeared there.

Impossible. Was the chillfever striking her too?

The man raised his mask and displayed a bearded, youthful face. "I am sorry to have come in unannounced," Allik said. "But I bear gifts, as is traditional for visiting someone's house unannounced, yes?"

He held up a gloved fist, which clutched a bundle of medallions by their cords.

Jordis looked from the medallions to young Allik, then back. For once she didn't even care about how free he was with raising his mask. She stumbled to him, seizing one of them, unable to believe.

The wonderful warmth ran through her, like a sunrise within. She sighed in relief, her mind clearing. It *was* him. "How?" she whispered.

"I," Allik proclaimed, "have made friends with some of the devils." He gestured to the side and a female maskless one almost toppled in, wearing one of the long dresses that were popular here, carrying an armful of rifles.

She said something in her language, dropping the guns to the floor of the tent and dusting off her hands.

"I think she wants us to start shooting the other ones," Allik said as Jordis quickly grabbed the other medallions and began distributing them to the most severely afflicted of her people. "I, for one, am *more* than happy to oblige."

Petrine continued the distribution as Jordis armed herself with one of the guns. Though the warmth was wonderful, she still felt weak, and she didn't want to look in her boots to see if her toes had frostbite. "I don't know that we will put up much of a fight."

"Better than no fight at all, yes, Captain?" Allik asked.

"This is true," Jordis admitted, and made a sign of respect, touching her right shoulder with her left hand, then lowering her hand to touch her wrist. "You did well. Almost I forgive you for your terrible dancing." She turned to Petrine. "Arm the men and women with these weapons. Let's kill as many of the devils as we can."

Wax ripped from the temple in a burst of might and Allomancy. He spun above the building, rocks flung by his explosive exit tumbling in the air around him, trailing mist. Below, a storm of gunfire broke out on the previously quiet mountainside, though they weren't firing at him.

Above it, an airship lumbered through the sky, fans whirring powerfully on its two pontoons. It was awesome to behold, but the ship was obviously not spry. It moved with the ponderous motions of something very large, and very heavy—even with the weight reduction granted by the medallions.

Wax was tempted to crush the ship. Push the nails from their mountings, rip the thing apart in a storm of destruction, dumping Suit and his traitorous sister to the frozen ground below. He almost did it. But . . . rusts. He wasn't an executioner. He was a lawman. He'd rather die than betray that.

Well, die *again*.

He dropped, then used the trace metals in the stonework of the temple as an anchor to send himself soaring across the ground in a swoop. A few of the soldiers below took halfhearted shots at him, but most seemed engrossed in a gunfight with a group of people in masks who had taken up a position behind a rocky shelf.

Steris, Allik, Wax thought, identifying them. *Good.*

He landed among the soldiers and flung them aside. He grabbed an aluminum pistol from one of their racks, loaded it, then waved to the masked people before hurling himself into the sky after the airship.

He was strong. Incredibly strong. The Bands, still clutched in his left hand, somehow gave him not just Allomancy, but *ancient* Allomancy. The potency of those who had lived long ago, during the time of the Lord Ruler. Perhaps even more. Was that possible?

What did you create? he wondered. *And how long will it last?*

His resources were diminishing. Not merely the metals inside of him, but the reserves stored inside the Bands. Stores that changed his level of Investiture.

He should have held back, he knew—reserved it for study, or for use in a future emergency—but *rusts* it was intoxicating. He reached the airship easily, despite only having a few shell casings to Push upon below. He soared up and landed on the ship's nose, then smashed his hand through one of the windows to the bridge, any cuts healing immediately.

Inside, Suit sat alone. There was no sign of pilots, technicians, or servants. Just a wide, half-oval deck, not even carpeted, and Suit in a chair.

Wax climbed in and raised the aluminum pistol. His boots thumped on the wood. He did a quick scan. *People in the hallway outside,* he thought. *And a bit of metal in Suit's mouth.* The old coin-in-the-mouth trick, a way to hide metal from an Allomancer. Anything inside the body was very hard to sense.

Unless you were bearing the very powers of creation, that is.

"And so," Suit said, lighting his pipe, "our confrontation comes at long last."

"Not much of a confrontation," Wax said, still alight with power. "I could destroy you a hundred different ways right now, Uncle."

"I don't doubt that you could," Suit said, shaking out his match, then puffing on the pipe. Trying to hide the coin. Talking around a pipe let him have a reason to sound odd. "And here I can only destroy you *one* way."

Wax leveled his pistol.

Suit looked right at it and smiled. "Do you know why I've always beaten you, Nephew?"

"You haven't beaten me," Wax said. "You've refused to fight. That is an entirely different thing."

"But sometimes the only way to win *is* to refuse to fight."

Wax strode forward, wary of traps. He thought faster, moved faster than normal. The blue lines spread from him as a brilliant web, seeking sources of metal smaller—and farther away—than he could normally sense. At times this seemed to flicker, and for a moment he saw the *radiance* inside of each person and thing. It felt as if he might be able to move those too.

An awed voice in the back of his mind whispered, *They're all the same. Metal, minds, men, all the same substance. . . .*

"What have you done, Uncle?" Wax asked softly.

"And here I must answer my own question," Edwarn said, shaking his head and standing. "I beat you, Waxillium, *not* because of preparation—though it is extensive. I beat you not because of wit or strength of arm, but because of a unique ability of mine. Creativity."

"You're going to bludgeon me with paintings?"

"Always quick with a wry comment!" Suit said. "Bravo."

"What have you done?"

"I armed the bomb," Suit said. "It is set to explode in mere moments. Unless I stop it."

"Let it explode," Wax said, holding up the Bands—metallic strata weaving across the triangular chunk of metal. "I'm pretty sure I'll survive it."

"And those below?" Suit asked. "Your friends? My captives? From the sounds of it, they're fighting quite vigorously for their freedom. How sad it will be to see them vaporized by an explosion I've been told should be enough to destroy a large city all on its—"

Wax increased the speed of his thoughts, tapping zinc. He sorted through a dozen scenarios. Find the explosives and Push them away? How far could he get them? Would Suit detonate the bomb before he could arrive?

His speed of body was nearly tapped out—Marasi must have used that in getting to him—so yes, Suit would have time, though would he actually *do* it? Would he blow himself up, along with this ship, to defeat Wax?

If this were an ordinary criminal, Wax would have bet strongly against it. Unfortunately, Suit and the Set in general had demonstrated a level of fanaticism he had not expected. Like the way Miles had acted as he was executed. These people were not just thugs and thieves; they were political reformers, slaves to an ideal.

What else? What else could Wax do? He discarded scenario after scenario. Get Marasi and the others to safety: too slow. Shoot Suit now: the man could heal himself, and Wax might not have time to get to the bomb and remove it before the blast happened anyway. Push the ship upward? He wouldn't be able to do that fast enough; unless he Pushed slowly, he'd rip the vessel apart.

"—own," Suit said.

"What do you want?" Wax demanded. "I'm not going to let you go."

"You don't need to," Suit said. "I have little doubt that you'd chase me across the world, Waxillium. I might be creative, but you . . . you are *tenacious*."

"What, then?"

"You drop the Bands out the window," Suit said. "I order the bomb disarmed. Then we face one another as men, without unnatural advantages."

"You think I'd trust you?"

"You don't need to," Suit said. "Just give me your word you'll do it."

"Done," Wax said.

"Disarm the device!" Suit shouted toward the door. He strolled to the front of the ship and spoke into a tube there. "Disarm it and stand down."

Feet thumped away from the door. Wax could actually watch them go—not by their metals, but by the signature their souls made. In moments, he could see nobody there, or hiding anywhere around the bridge.

A voice soon echoed up through the tube. The tin Wax burned let him hear. "Done, my lord." A pause. "Thank Trell for that." The voice sounded relieved.

Suit turned to Wax. "There is a tradition in the Roughs, is there not? Two men, a dusty road, guns on their hips. Man against man. One lives. The other dies. A dispute settled." He patted the sidearm at his hip. "I can't give you a dusty road, but perhaps we can squint and pretend that the frost is playing that role."

Wax drew his lips to a line. Edwarn looked entirely sincere. "Don't make me do this, Uncle."

"Why?" Suit said. "I know you've been *itching* for this exact opportunity! You have an aluminum gun, I see. The same as mine. No Steelpushing to interfere. Just two men and their sidearms."

"Uncle . . ."

"You've dreamed of it, son. The chance to shoot me, no questions asked, and not be running afoul of the law. Besides, to the law I'm already dead! Your conscience can rest. I won't give in, and I'm armed. The only way to stop me is to shoot me. Let's do it."

Wax fingered the Bands of Mourning, and felt himself smiling. "You don't understand at all, do you?"

"Oh, I do. I've seen it in you! The hidden hunger of the lawman, wishing to be cut free so he can kill. It's what defines you and your type."

"No," Wax said. He unhooked the holster from his leg, the one that had held his shotgun, and slipped the Bands into its leather pouch. His remaining bullets and metal vials followed, leaving him with no metals, save the aluminum gun.

"Perhaps I have felt hidden hunger," Wax said. "But it isn't what defines me."

"Oh, and what does?"

Wax tossed the leather holding the Bands out the broken window, then slipped his gun into his side holster. "I'll show you."

Telsin scrambled in the snow, climbing through it, frantic.

Suit was an idiot. She'd always known this, but today made it manifest. Flying away in the ship? That was the *first* place they'd go to chase him. He was as good as dead.

Today was a disaster. An unparalleled disaster. Waxillium knew of her subterfuge. The Set was exposed. Their plans were crumbling.

Something had to be salvageable. She stumbled to a small clearing in the snow, near the temple entrance, where her people had deposited the skimmer that she and Waxillium had ridden in on. Still functional, hopefully. She knew how it worked—she'd watched carefully during their trip. All she needed to do was—

Something *banged* behind her.

She blinked at the sudden spray of redness on the snow all around her. Flakes of it.

Her blood.

"You killed one of my friends today," a ragged voice said from behind. "I'm not going to let you take a second."

She fell to her knees before the craft, then turned her head.

Wayne stood behind her in the snow, his face haggard, holding a shotgun.

"You . . ." Telsin whispered. "You can't . . . guns . . ."

"Yeah," Wayne said, cocking the shotgun. "About that."

He lowered the barrel to her face and fired.

Marasi climbed the previously hidden steps back into the room with the broken glass and the ornate pedestal. She didn't know what had opened this hidden path, but she was glad for it. Ever blunt, Waxillium had simply ripped himself a hole out of the catacombs, going straight up through the stone—half this chamber had collapsed as a result—but following his route would have been an arduous climb.

The power was gone. She'd handed it over to Waxillium, but instead of feeling deflated, she felt . . . peaceful. Hers was the serenity of a woman who'd lain stretched out on a perfect summer day, feeling the sun as it slowly sank. Yes, the light was gone now, but *oh* what a joy it had been.

Poor MeLaan was still here, and her form had started to incorporate the bones, slowly assembling them in a strange configuration. With no spikes, she'd become a mistwraith. Marasi knelt beside her, but wasn't certain what comfort she could offer. At the very least, MeLaan seemed to still be alive.

Marasi rose, then hurried down the hallway with the traps, reaching the entryway with the murals. Outside, a war was going on, hundreds of gunshots echoing in the cold, snow-filled night. She was surprised to see that the people in masks seemed to be winning. The soldiers had been pushed back to the edge of the stone field, their backs to a series of gulfs and cliffs. They had nowhere to retreat, and many of their number lay dead or wounded.

She thought she saw Waxillium's influence in the way some of those bodies lay, as if tossed through the air to land crumpled. Marasi nodded in satisfaction. Let him do the job he came to do.

She still had one of her own to finish. She strode out of the temple, down the steps past the statue of the Lord Ruler holding what now, with the spearhead removed, appeared to be only a staff.

Now where would she find—

A loud gunshot from quite nearby. She swiveled her head, searching for the source. A second one sounded.

A moment later, Wayne emerged through the snowstorm, head down, expression shadowed. He carried a shotgun on his shoulder, and clutched not one, but *three* small metal spikes in his other hand.

Wax stood quietly on the bridge of the ship, waiting for his uncle to move.

This didn't work the way it did in the stories. You didn't outdraw a man; couldn't happen, not without Feruchemical speed. If you waited for him to start moving, you would be too slow. He'd tried it with blanks on the fastest men he knew.

The man who drew first got the first shot. That was that.

Suit drew.

Wax Pushed on the metal window frame behind him. He crossed the distance between them in a blur, even as Suit fired. The bullet hit Wax in the shoulder, but Wax collided with the surprised Suit, knocking them both to the floor of the bridge.

Suit grabbed his arm. Wax's metal reserves vanished.

"Aha!" Suit said. "I made myself a Leecher! I can drain the metals from anyone who touches me, Waxillium. You're dead. No Bands. No Allomancy. I win."

Wax grunted, clinging tight to Suit as they rolled. "You forget," he said. "I'm not surprised. You've always hated it. I'm a *Terrisman,* Uncle."

He increased his weight manyfold.

He tapped everything he had in his arm bracer, hundreds of hours spent being lighter than he should have been. He brought it all out in one moment of desperation.

The airship lurched. And then the floor shattered.

Wax clung to Suit as they fell, holding him tight, though one hand was weakening from the gunshot. They crashed through two levels of the ship—Suit's body, which tapped healing, bearing the brunt of the damage—before smashing out the bottom, battered, bleeding, and thrashed by splintered wood.

Suit looked horrified. "You fool! You—"

Wax spun them in the air, pointing Suit downward as they plummeted. Snow-filled air was a roaring wind around them, flakes streaking past.

Suit screamed.

And then he Pushed.

Suit dropped the coin from his mouth and used his Allomancy to Push it downward in a straight shot. It hit the approaching ground and slowed the two of them with a lurch.

Wax decreased his weight just enough that Suit's Push was sufficient to keep them alive. They crashed into the snow, some distance from the plateau with the temple.

Wax recovered first. He lurched to his feet and pulled Suit up by one hand, the two of them standing alone in a field of white. Suit looked up at him, dazed by the fall and the impact.

"The definition of a lawman, *Uncle,* is easy," Wax said, feeling blood from a dozen cuts trickle down his face. He lifted Suit by the front of his clothing, bringing him close. "He's the man who takes the bullet so nobody else has to."

With that, Wax decked him across the face and dropped him to the snow, unconscious.

MeLaan swam in a sea of terror. Terror within her own mind; a piece of her knowing this was not right. This being ruled by instinct, this craven set of impulses.

But this was what she did. Food. She needed food.

No. First a place to hide. From the trembling sounds. Hide away, find a crack. She continued building a body that would let her walk. Flee.

So cold. She didn't understand coldness. It wasn't a thing that should be. And she couldn't taste dirt, just stone. Stone everywhere.

Frozen stone.

She felt like screaming. Something was missing. Not food. Not a place to hide, but . . . something. Something was horribly, horribly, horribly wrong.

An object dropped on her. It was cold, but not stone. This wasn't food. She enfolded it and intended to spit it away, but then something happened.

Something wonderful. She gobbled up the second one as it was dropped, and began to undulate, frantic. It came *back*. Memory. Knowledge. Rationality.

Self.

She exulted in it, ignoring the little holes that were now poked in her memory. She remembered most of the trip here, but something had happened in the room with the Bands. . . . No, the Bands hadn't been there, and . . .

She formed eyes first, and she knew what she would see when she opened them. She'd already tasted him on the air, and knew his flavor.

"Welcome back," Wayne said, grinning. "I think we won."

30

Marasi accepted the canteen from Allik. It steamed from the top although it was only lukewarm to the touch. She sat on the steps up to the temple, swathed in about forty blankets. She'd surrendered her medallion to one of the Malwish people until more could be secured from the airship.

And its recovery was an interesting sight to say the least. Waxillium stood on the rocky section before the plateau, heaving with two hands and Pulling on nothing visible. Up ahead, the rogue airship slowly sank through the snow-filled sky, drawn toward Waxillium on an invisible tether.

"Will it break apart?" Allik asked.

She looked at him with surprise, then down at his language medallion.

"Warm choc and a blanket will do me for a minute," he said, settling down and pulling his blanket around him. "Others are in greater need, yah? The ship. Will it break?"

Marasi looked up toward it. She could imagine Suit's people aboard, trying desperately to make the engines work harder, the fans blow more powerfully. It sank anyway. Waxillium Ladrian—bearing the Bands of Mourning and supremely annoyed—was like a force of nature.

She smiled and sipped her drink.

"Rusts!" she said, looking at it. "What is this?" It was sweet, thick, warm, chocolaty, and *wonderful*.

"Choc," he said. "Sometimes it is a man's only succor in this frozen, lonely world, yah?"

"You *drink chocolate*?"

"Sure. Don't you?"

She never had. Plus, this was far sweeter than the chocolate she was used to. Not bitter at all. She took a long, soothing draught. "Allik, this is the most wonderful thing I've ever experienced. And I just held the powers of creation themselves."

He smiled.

"I don't think your ship is in danger," Marasi said. "He's Pulling on it evenly, and slowly. He's a careful man, Waxillium is."

"Careful? It seems to me he is very proficient at breaking things. That doesn't sound particularly careful, yah?"

"Well," Marasi said, sipping her drink, "he does it with amazing precision."

Indeed, it wasn't long before the airship settled down onto the rocks, still in one piece. Waxillium held it in place, then raised the Bands of Mourning in one hand, winds, snows, and even traces of mist swirling around him.

The fans slowly powered down. A short time later, soldiers exited with hands up. Wayne and MeLaan scurried up to them, gathering weapons while Allik's people boarded the ship to secure it and search for anyone lurking inside.

Marasi waited through it all, sipping her melted chocolate and thinking. ReLuur's spike lay safely wrapped in a handkerchief, tucked into her pocket. In her mind's eye, she saw Wayne again as he had been, trudging through the snow, gun to his shoulder, a pattern of frozen blood flaking his skin. Alongside this image was the glee with which Waxillium had launched into the sky to chase down his uncle.

There was a darkness to these men that the stories hadn't conveyed. Marasi was glad for it, but she had stepped to that ledge, then turned back. Proud though she was of having fulfilled her mission for the kandra, she had decided that things would be different for her in the future. She was all right with that.

It was what she had chosen.

"Frosts," Allik said after some time. "We'd better go do something, yah?"

She looked up from her now-empty canteen of chocolate to follow Allik's gesture. The Malwish airship crew had returned from their inspection, and the enemy soldiers had been led away—to be safely locked in the ship's brig, Marasi believed.

Suit was still where Waxillium had put him: tied to the top of the Lord Ruler's spear, feet dangling. He'd been gagged, he'd had his metalminds removed, and Waxillium had used Allomancy to leech away his metals. And this *still* seemed like it might not be cautious enough. He still had his spikes, as they weren't sure how to remove them without killing him. He shouldn't be able to do anything without metals, but she couldn't help being worried.

Steris had joined Waxillium on the field, and he'd put his arm around her shoulders. Marasi smiled. Now *that* was an image she'd never thought she'd find comforting. But they would do well together.

Unfortunately, trouble approached Waxillium and Steris in the form of Allik's captain and some of her airmen. The two groups faced one another, MeLaan and Wayne falling in beside Waxillium—Wayne casually carrying that shotgun, MeLaan standing a good two inches taller than anyone else, arms folded, her posture unyielding.

Right. "Let's go," Marasi said to Allik.

Allik's captain, Jordis, wore one of the translation medallions—and she didn't flinch before the gust of wind that accompanied Marasi as she arrived.

"We thank you for your help," Jordis was saying, her voice touched by the same accent Allik had. "But our appreciation does not allow us to ignore thievery. We expect that our property will be returned."

"I don't see any of your property here," Waxillium replied coldly. "I see only an artifact *we* recovered. Well, that and my airship."

"Your—" Jordis sputtered. She stepped forward. "Since crashing in your lands, my crew has been incarcerated, tortured, and *murdered*. You seem to be itching for a war, Allomancer."

Drat. Marasi had been hoping she'd share Allik's reverence for Waxillium. Indeed, much of the crew seemed nervous about him, but the captain obviously didn't mean to back down.

"If there is to be war," Waxillium said, "giving you a powerful weapon does not seem the method to save my people. I cannot help what Suit and his people did to you—they are outlaws, and what they did was deplorable. I will see them brought to justice."

"And yet you steal from us."

"Do you deny," Waxillium asked, "that this temple was *empty* upon my arrival? Do you deny that this airship was from nation other than your own? I cannot steal what was not owned, Captain. By right of salvage, I claim this relic and that ship. You may—"

Marasi was about to step between them when, curiously, Steris spoke up, interrupting Wax.

"Lord Waxillium," she said. "I think it prudent to let them take the ship."

"What? Like hell I'm going to—"

"Waxillium," Steris said softly. "They're tired, miserable, and a long way from home. How do you suggest, otherwise, that they are to return to those they love? Is that justice?"

His lips tightened. "The Set has one of these ships to study, Steris."

"Then," Steris said, looking to Jordis, "we will beg—in return for the generosity of this gift—that the Malwish people open trade with us. I suspect we can purchase ships from them more quickly than the Set can build their own."

Marasi nodded. *Not bad, Steris.*

"If they'll sell," Waxillium said.

"I think that they will," Steris said, looking to Jordis. "Because the good captain will persuade them that access to our Allomancers is worth relinquishing a technological monopoly."

"That's true," Marasi said, stepping up to the rest, Allik with her. "We're rare among you, aren't we?"

"We?" Allik asked as the captain looked to her.

"I'm an Allomancer too," she said, amused. "You didn't see me charging the cube device back in the warehouse?"

"I was . . . a little distracted. . . ." he said, sounding woozy. "Oh dear. Um. Great One."

Marasi sighed, looking to Jordis.

"I can promise you nothing," the captain said to Steris, sounding reluctant. "The Malwish are but one of many. Another nation among us may see you up here as weak and decide to strike."

"Then," Steris said, "you *might* want to inform them that the Bands of Mourning are here, ready to punish those who attack."

Jordis hissed. Marasi couldn't see her features behind the mask, but the hand swipe she made did not look pleased. "Impossible. You give me the lesser prize to distract me from the greater, yah? We will not give you the Sovereign's weapon."

"You're not giving it to *us*," Steris said. She looked to MeLaan, who watched with crossed arms. "Allik. Your people have stories of creatures like her, do you not?"

"Tell the others," Marasi said to Allik. "Please."

He removed his medallion and launched into a furious explanation in his language, waving his hands, then gesturing at MeLaan. She cocked an eyebrow, then made her skin translucent—displaying a skeleton that was so cracked and mangled, Marasi was left momentarily stunned. How was MeLaan still standing?

The captain took this in.

"We," Steris said, "will give the Bands to the immortal kandra. They are wise and impartial, tasked with serving all people. They will promise not to let us use the Bands unless we are attacked by your kind."

There was no way to tell what Captain Jordis thought, her expression hidden behind that mask. When she did speak, she made a few curt gestures—but those could be faked far more easily than facial expressions, Marasi figured. What did one make of a society where everyone hid their true feelings behind a mask, only letting out calculated reactions?

"This is an unpleasant accommodation," Jordis said. "It means I will limp back to my people, half my crew dead and my ship exchanged for one decades out of date."

"True," Steris continued at Waxillium's side—he merely stood there with arms folded, *looming,* as he was so good at doing. "But Captain, you will return with something more valuable than an old relic or even your fallen ship. You'll have new trading partners in a land brimming with Metalborn. Has it been mentioned that my lord Waxillium holds an important seat in our government? That he has a dramatic influence over trade, tariffs, and taxation? Those among your people who secure favorable treaties with us could become very rich indeed."

Jordis regarded them, then folded her arms, facing Waxillium directly. "It is still unpleasant." Jordis was much shorter, but she managed to loom pretty well herself. In fact, Marasi got the distinct impression that the woman wanted to shout at them, attack in a rage, seek retribution for what had been done to her and hers. Anything but just simply trade.

Perhaps some emotions were too strong to be hidden even by a mask.

Jordis finally nodded. "Very well. Let it be done. But I will not leave without a draft agreement—a promise of intentions, if nothing else."

Marasi breathed a sigh of relief, shooting Steris a nod of appreciation. Still, she did not miss the stiffness in Jordis's posture as she and Waxillium shook hands. The Basin had not made a friend this day. Hopefully some last-minute scrambling had prevented them from making an enemy.

"I have one further request," Waxillium said to her.

"What?" Jordis asked, suspicious.

"Nothing terrible or costly," Waxillium said. "Honestly, I'd just like a ride."

The Southerners agreed, fortunately. They didn't particularly want to carry a brigful of enemy soldiers all the way south. Wax had to make it very clear they couldn't keep Suit himself, and the captain relented with minimal argument. She seemed to realize that her best chance of seeing justice done to all of those who had brutalized her crew lay in letting Wax do some thorough interrogations.

He kept his relationship to the man quiet.

As the Malwish crew prepared the ship for travel, Wax stood before the statue of the Lord Ruler, with that single spike in his eye. He'd checked the belt, which was aluminum. No kind of charge. If there had ever been two bracers, he had to assume they'd been made into this one spearhead.

Marasi passed behind him. "I'm going to go check our skimmer for supplies we might have left behind."

Wax nodded. *I held your power,* he thought toward the statue, *if only a tiny bit of it. Rusts . . . I think I understand.*

He'd given the Bands to MeLaan, and she had made them vanish into her flesh. He was *glad* to know that they were effectively out of his reach. Too much power.

He raised his finger in farewell to the Lord Ruler, then jogged off after Marasi.

"Aradel and the Senate won't like this deal," Wax noted as he reached her. "Particularly the part about us giving away the Bands."

"I know," Marasi said.

"As long as I can tell him it wasn't my idea."

She glanced at him. "You don't seem too broken up about losing the Bands."

"I'm not," he admitted. "I was worried, honestly. The Bands are drained, mostly, but we could probably recharge them by compounding. The power they offer is something . . ."

". . . Sublime and devastating at once?" Marasi asked. "Dangerous because of what it could do in the wrong hands, yet somehow *more* dangerous in your own?"

"Yes."

They shared something in that moment, swept by winds. Something they'd touched, something—hopefully—only they would know.

They turned together without a word, seeking the skimmer. Jordis would want to load it on the ship, but first there was a corpse Wax needed to see. He didn't blame Wayne for what he'd done to Telsin. Yes, taking her to Elendel for justice—and interrogation—would have been better. And yes, he found that he'd rather have pulled the trigger himself. Harmony was right about that.

But either way, Telsin was dealt with. That meant—

Blood on the snow.

No skimmer.

More importantly, no body.

Marasi froze in place as they drew near, but Wax approached the empty patch of ground. She had slipped away, again. He found he was not surprised, though he was impressed. She'd gotten the skimmer aloft and away during the fighting, escaping during the chaos.

Wayne should have known she might be able to heal herself, Wax thought, going down on one knee beside the eerie pattern of blood drops that seemed to outline a body.

"It's not done, then," Marasi said.

Wax brushed the drops of blood, frozen to the ground. He'd spent the last eighteen months trying to save this woman. And when he finally had, she'd killed him.

"It's not done," he said. "But in some ways, that's better."

"Because your sister isn't dead?"

He turned toward Marasi. It seemed that despite hours in this frozen place, the cold had only just reached inside of him.

"No," he said. "Because now I have someone to hunt."

31

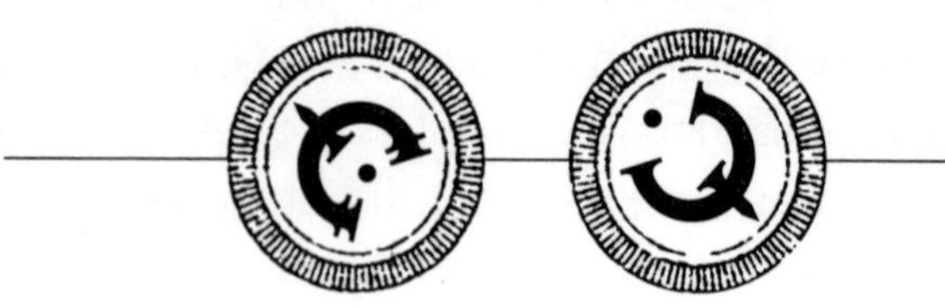

"Wax, you *gotta* see this!"

Wax tipped his head back, bleary-eyed. These bunks were not particularly pleasant, but at least the airship flew in a calm, smooth manner. That was nice, as the skimmer had always felt as if it were one gust of wind away from plowing nose-first into a hillside.

Wayne hung halfway out of the room's large window.

"That window opens?" Wax asked, surprised.

"Any window opens," Wayne said, "if you push hard enough. Look, you've *gotta* see this."

Wax sighed, climbing up and leaning out of the window beside Wayne. Beneath them, Elendel spread out as a vast sea of lights.

"Like rivers of fire," Wayne mumbled. "Look how it follows patterns. Rich areas more lit, roads all in lines. Beautiful."

Wax grunted.

"That's all you can say, mate?"

"Wayne, I see this basically every night."

"Now, that there, that ain't fair. You should feel guilty."

"For being a Coinshot?"

"For cheatin' at life, Wax."

"How about I feel appreciative instead?"

"Suppose that'll do."

Wax settled down on his bunk, then pulled on his boots, doing the laces. He ached like a man beaten senseless. He wished he could blame the strain of the last few days, but he'd held the Bands of Mourning and had been healed completely.

That meant these aches came merely from sleeping a few hours on this bunk. Rusts. He *was* getting old. Upon considering that, however, he found that mortality didn't frighten him as it once had.

"We should get up to the bridge," he suggested, standing. It had been a full day since they'd left the mountains. They'd stopped at a town to telegraph ahead at Wax's insistence, then waited until the next night to fly the rest of the way. He had had no intention of bringing a massive flying warship anywhere near the city without at least giving warning first.

Jordis had been amenable, once he'd promised her supplies for their trip home in repayment. Marasi worried about the captain, he knew, but he had looked into the woman's eyes behind the mask. She was a soldier, a killer, despite her claims of hers being a simple trading vessel.

She knew. Wax had held the Bands. He could have swept the Malwish away and stolen their ship without a second thought. Instead, he'd given in to Steris's compromise. Strong words notwithstanding, Jordis realized she'd gotten more out of this deal than she had any reason to expect.

Wayne joined him outside their room, and they stepped aside as a few wearied airmen passed. He couldn't see their faces, but could read a world of emotions from their hunched backs and subdued speech.

"They've been broken," Wayne whispered, looking over his shoulder as the airmen continued on. "Ain't fair what happened to these folks, Wax."

"Is life ever fair?"

"It has been to me," Wayne said. "More than fair, I reckon. Considering what I deserve."

"Do you want to talk about it?" Wax asked.

"What?"

"You used a gun, Wayne."

"Bah, that was a shotgun. Barely counts."

Wax rested a hand on his friend's shoulder.

Wayne shrugged. "Guess my body figured, 'What the hell?'"

"I thought it meant you'd forgiven yourself."

"Nah," Wayne said. "I was just real mad at your sister."

"You knew, didn't you?" Wax asked, frowning. "That she'd heal?"

"Well, I didn't wanna kill someone in cold blood—"

"That's good, I suppose."

"—but there weren't no fire around to light her with first."

"Wayne . . ."

The shorter man sighed. "I saw the metalminds peekin' outta her sleeves. Figured, if you're gonna give yourself one power from a Feruchemist, you'd wanna be able to heal. I ain't gonna kill your sister, mate. But I didn't mind makin' her jump a bit, and I needed MeLaan's spikes."

Wayne's gaze grew distant. "Shoulda stayed there, I suppose. To stop her from runnin', you know? But I wasn't of sound mind, so to speak. I thought you were *dead,* mate. Really thought it. And I kept thinkin' to myself, 'Would Wax kill her for real? Or would he give her another chance, like he gave me?' So I let her be. I stayed my hand, 'cuz it was the last thing I could do for you. Does that make sense?"

Wax squeezed Wayne's shoulder. "Thank you. I'm glad you're learning."

It felt disingenuous to say that when inside, in truth, he wished Wayne had stripped off her metalminds and left her a frozen corpse.

Wayne grinned. Wax nodded in the direction the airmen had gone. "I'll meet you up there."

"Going to go fetch your woman?" Wayne said. "She's gonna have a hard time adjustin' to life back here, away from her native habitat of the frozen, icy, desolate wastes up—"

"Wayne," Wax interrupted, soft but firm.

"Hum?"

"Enough."

"I was just—"

"Enough."

Wayne stopped with his mouth open, then licked his lips and nodded. "Right, then. See you up above in a few, mate?"

"We'll be right along."

Wayne scampered off toward the bridge. Wax trailed through the hallway, heading down several doors to the room Steris and Marasi had been sharing. He raised his hand to knock, but it was cracked, so he peeked in. Steris lay on a bunk, wrapped in a blanket, sleeping softly. There was no sign of Marasi; she'd mentioned wanting to watch the approach to the city from the bridge.

He hesitated at the door, watching her sleep. He almost left; she'd been through so much these last few days. She had to be exhausted. Once they reached Elendel, they'd still have to unload the prisoners and bring the supplies on board—it could be hours before the ship had to leave. She could sleep a little longer, couldn't she?

The door creaked as he leaned against it, and Steris started awake. Her eyes found him immediately. Then she smiled, relaxing, and huddled up against her pillow. She was wearing a travel dress under the blanket.

Wax stepped into the room and took a seat on the bunk across from Steris; there was so little space in this room that his knees touched her bunk after he sat. And these were the rooms the airmen considered large. He leaned forward, taking Steris's hand in his.

She squeezed it, eyes closed once more, and they sat there. Still. Everyone else could wait a few minutes.

"Thank you," Wax said softly.

"For what?" she said.

"Coming with me."

"I didn't do much."

"You were extremely helpful at the party," Wax said. "And your negotiations with the Malwish . . . Steris, that was incredible."

"Perhaps," she said. "But I still feel that I was basically luggage for most of the trip."

He shrugged. "Steris, I think we're all like that. Shuffled from place to place by duty, or society, or God Himself. It seems like we're just along for the ride, even in our own lives. But once in a while, we *do* face a choice. A real one. We may not be able to choose what happens to us, or where we'll stop, but we point ourselves in a direction." He squeezed her hand. "You pointed yourself toward me."

"Well," she said, smiling, "being near you *is* generally the safest place. . . ."

He cupped her face with his hand, all callused and rough. *Another adventure.*

Eventually, an airman came looking for them, and Wax reluctantly stood, helping Steris up. Then they walked—arm in arm—through the hallways of the ship and up to the bridge, where the others waited.

Here, Wax was able to appreciate what Wayne had seen. With the panoramic view from the bridge, the city really was gorgeous at night. *Is this a sight that will become commonplace?* Wax thought as Steris squeezed his arm, grinning at the sight. This airship technology was new, but not many years had passed since he'd seen his first motorcar on the road.

Marasi had been directing Captain Jordis through the city. Wax couldn't read anything in the captain's posture, or those of her crew. Were they impressed by the size of the city and the height of the skyscrapers? Or were these things commonplace in the South?

They approached Ahlstrom Tower, and Wax could only imagine the stories this would prompt in the broadsheets the next morning. Good. He hated subterfuge; let the people of Elendel know, to a man, that the world had just become a much larger place.

Ahlstrom Tower, in which Wax had an ownership interest, had a flat top. The captain had assured him that she could land her ship "on a nail, so long as the head is smooth enough." True to her word, they set it down.

"You're certain you don't want to stay?" Marasi asked Jordis. "Visit our city, find out what we're *actually* like?"

"No. Thank you." The words sounded forced, to Wax. But who was to say, with the accent muddying things? "We will take your offer of supplies and be away tonight."

Time to debark. Together—the others filing after—Wax and Steris made their way through the halls again.

"It almost feels," Steris said softly, "like this entire experience was a dream. I need to write it all down quickly, lest it fade."

Wax found himself nodding as he thought of his meeting with Harmony.

The hallway led to a junction where the wall had opened and a long docking bridge had been settled in place, leading down to the rooftop. Below, Wax picked out several figures craning their necks to look at the ship. Governor Aradel had come in person.

Allik stood at the door, and he lifted his mask as Wax approached. No bow or nod, just the mask lift. Among this people, perhaps that was the same thing—as behind him, the other airmen did the same.

"Mighty One," Allik said to Wax. "May your next fire be known to you."

"And you, Allik."

"Oh, it is," he said with a grin. "For *my* next fire is home, yah?" He looked to Marasi, and then reached up and removed his mask—the broken one, which he had glued. He held it out with two hands, which caused a few gasps behind him.

"*Please,*" Allik said. The word had more accent to it than the way he'd been speaking before.

The captain, who had not lifted her mask to Wax, grew stiff at the gesture. Marasi hesitated, then accepted the mask. "Thank you."

"Thank you, Miss Marasi," Allik said. "For life." He took a flat, unornamented mask from his waist and pulled it on by the leather strap. It was really nothing more than a curved piece of wood with holes for the eyes. "I look forward to my homecoming, but my next fire after that may be here again. I plan to take you up on your offer to visit this city."

"So long as you bring some more choc," Marasi said, "you can visit any time you like."

Wax smiled, and then the five of them relinquished their weight medallion metalminds to the captain, a formality they'd been instructed was customary. Jordis had already presented Wax with one of each, translation and heat-storing, as a gift for him to keep. Wayne had likely stolen another set, though Wax intended to wait until they were off the ship to ask.

Wax led them down the gangway, Steris on his arm.

"Seriously, Waxillium," Marasi said, walking up beside them. "You need to import that chocolate of theirs. I don't know what they put in it, but it's amazing. You think the airships are going to be big? Wait until you *taste* this stuff."

"Hey," Wayne said, pulling up on his other side, but then twisting his neck to look at the people in the ship behind them. "Marasi, I think that pilot fellow *fancies* you."

"Thank you," Marasi said, "for lending us your brilliant powers of observation, Wayne."

"That could be useful politically," Steris noted.

"Please," Marasi said. "He's practically a *child* compared to me. And don't you snicker."

"I wouldn't dare," Wax said, eyes ahead. He didn't miss how reverently Marasi carried the mask, however.

Ahead, a group of the governor's aides and guards clustered together in a protective bubble, as if they could stave off the weirdness before them—and what it represented—through collective body heat. Aradel himself stood apart, as if he'd pushed out of the group.

Wax strolled up to him, Steris on his arm, and waited.

"Damn," Aradel finally said.

"I *did* warn you," Wax replied.

Aradel shook his head in awe, eyes wide. "Well, maybe this will distract everyone from the disaster you all started in New Seran."

"Bad?" Steris asked.

Aradel grunted. "Senate's had my balls over the fire for two days straight, screaming about war and irresponsible leadership. As if I *ever* had any influence over you people." He started, finally ripping his gaze from the airship, and coughed—as if realizing what he'd just said, and whom he'd said it to.

Wax smiled. Aradel was blunt, but usually displayed more tact than this. You couldn't go far as a constable without *some* understanding of how to deal with people's egos.

"Apologies, Lady Harms," he said. "Ladrian, I need to hear what happened in New Seran. The honest truth of it, from your own mouth."

"You'll have it," Wax promised. "Tomorrow."

"But—"

"Governor," Wax said. "I appreciate your position, but you have *no idea* what we've been through these last few days. My people need rest. Tomorrow. Please."

Aradel grunted. "Fine."

"Did you prepare the thing I requested?" Wax asked.

"It's below," Aradel said, turning back toward the airship. "In the penthouse." The governor took a deep breath, looking at that enormous airship again. Constable-General Reddi had led a group of constables up to accept the transfer of prisoners.

Wax could now see that the ship had landed only *half* on the building. One fan spun lazily, keeping the ship in place. *Likely done that way on purpose,* he thought of the landing, *as a message. The crew wants to remind us that while we might get this technology soon, we'll still be many years behind them in its use.*

"I think we'll be fine," Wax said to Aradel. "If the outer cities had thoughts about attacking us, I suspect this might stall them. Spread the knowledge that an *airship* flew through central Elendel and let me off—then left peaceably."

"We have initial treaties in place, Your Honor," Steris added. "Favorable to us for trade. That should give the hawks pause, and could buy us time to smooth things over."

"Yes, perhaps," Aradel said. "It's going to be a tough metal for the Senate to swallow though, Ladrian. Not the airship itself, but the fact that I'm—apparently—just going to let it fly off." He hesitated. "I haven't told them what you said about the other item."

"Bands of Mourning?" Wax said.

Aradel nodded, too politic to say what Wax was certain he was thinking. *What have you gone and done to me this time, Ladrian?*

"MeLaan?" Wax asked. "Would you mind taking over here?"

"Sure," she said, striding toward them. She wore an outfit borrowed from the Southlanders, a man's breeches and boots that went up to midcalf. She rested an arm on the governor's shoulder.

"Holy One," Aradel said, his voice strained but reverent. He eyed Wax. "You realize precisely how unfair it is to deal with you, when you can fall back on heavenly messengers to talk you out of trouble?"

"That's nothing," Wax said, guiding Steris toward the steps down. "Ask me sometime about the conversation I had with God the last time I died."

"That was vicious," Steris said as they reached the steps.

"Nonsense," Wax said. "He's a politician now. He needs practice being thrown off balance in conversations. Helps him prepare for debates and such."

She eyed him.

"I'll be better," he promised, holding the door open for her. Marasi moved to join them, but Wayne caught her by the arm and shook his head.

"Better?" Steris asked from the stairwell. "So this means no more complaining about parties."

"Of course I'll gripe," Wax said, following her into the stairwell, leaving the others behind. "It's a defining character feature. But I'll try and confine the worst of it to you and Wayne."

"And I," Steris said, "shall promise to be properly amazed by your exploits saving everyone from everything." She smiled at him. "And to always carry a few vials of metal with me, just in case. By the way, where are we going?"

He grinned, guiding her down to the top floor of the skyscraper, a regal penthouse that—currently—was unoccupied, the tenants having moved to Elmsdel for an extended holiday. Seated in a chair in the hall outside the apartment proper was a tired-looking man in the garb of a Survivorist priest, his formal mistcloak—really more of a shawl—worn over robes adorned with stitching up the sleeves representing scars.

Steris looked to Wax, curious.

"I was wondering, Steris," Wax said, "if you'd be willing to be my bride."

"I've already agreed—"

"Yes, but last time I asked with an expectation of a contract," Wax said. "It was the lord of a house asking a woman of means for a union. Well, that request stands, and thank you. But I'm asking again. It's important to me.

"Will you be my bride? I want to be married to you. Right now, before the Survivor and that priest. Not because words on a paper say we have to, but because we want to." He took her by the hand, and spoke more softly. "I'm painfully tired of being alone, Steris. It's time I admitted that. And you . . . well, you're incredible. You truly are."

Steris started sniffling. She pulled her hand free of his and wiped her eyes.

"Is that . . . good crying or bad?" Wax asked. All these years dealing with women, and he still couldn't tell the difference sometimes.

"Well, this wasn't on any of my lists, you see."

"Ah." He felt his heart lurch.

"And," she continued, "I can't remember a time when I missed something for one of my lists, only to have it be so wonderful." She nodded, red-nosed and sniffly. "And it is. Thank you, Lord Waxillium." She paused. "But tonight! So soon? Don't the others deserve to attend a wedding?"

"They *did* attend one," Wax said. "It's not our fault there wasn't a marriage at the end. So . . . what do you think? I mean, if you're tired from the trip, don't let me pressure you. I just thought—"

In response, she kissed him.

EPILOGUE

Marasi found it invigorating to work by candlelight. Perhaps it was the primordial danger of it. Electric lights felt safe, contained, harnessed—but an open flame, well, that was something raw. Alive. A little spark of fury which, if released, could destroy her and everything she worked on.

She worked with a lot of such sparks these days.

Spread on her desk in the octant constabulary headquarters were notes, files, interviews. She'd been present for most of them over the last two weeks, advising Constable-General Reddi. The two of them worked so closely these days, it was sometimes hard to remember how difficult he'd been to her during her early days in the constabulary.

Though Suit himself hadn't broken, many of his men had talked. They knew just enough to be infuriating. They'd been recruited from among the dissident young men of the outer cities—their ears stuffed with stories of the Survivor and his fight against imperial rule. They'd been trained in cities like Rashekin and Bilming, far from central rule. In closed compounds that were much more extensive than anyone had known.

Aradel and the others had focused on these details. Troops, timetables, technology—like the long-distance speaking device Waxillium had stolen from Lady Kelesina's mansion. They geared up for war, all the while talking peace.

They were scared, and legitimately so. Decades of not-so-benign neglect had created this snarl. Hopefully it could still be peacefully untangled. Marasi left that to politicians. She cut through the jingoism, the rhetoric, and turned her attention to something else. Stories among the men of something unusual, beyond the rumors of airships and new Allomantic metals.

She held up one sheet covered in notes. Half mentions, admissions made with sideways glances, always spoken of in whispers. Tales of men with red eyes who visited in the night. She added the stories to her files of research about Trell, the ancient god that people were somehow worshipping again. A god that had crafted spikes to corrupt the kandra Paalm, and whose name was on the lips of many of the prisoners.

She'd spent months researching, and so far felt like she knew nothing. But she *would* find answers, one way or another.

Suit's captors thought to shock him with the austerity of his quarters. A common cell in the prison's nethers, with a bucket for facilities and one blanket on the bed. A tired, pointless tactic. As if he'd known only rose petals and feather beds in his life; as if he'd never slept on a stone slab.

Well, they would see. Anything could be an advantage. In this case, it was a chance to prove himself. He would not break, and they would see.

So it was that he wasn't at all surprised when, after two weeks of captivity, the door to the corridor outside his cell clicked open one night and a stranger stalked in. Male this time, with a ragged beard and wild hair. A beggar stolen off the street, Suit guessed.

You could tell them by the way they walked. Never a stroll, never leisurely. Always fast, determined. Purposeful.

Of course, the softly glowing red eyes were another sign. So far as Suit had been able to determine, Waxillium and his fools had no knowledge of these creatures. They didn't understand, couldn't understand.

The Set had Faceless Immortals of its own.

Suit stood, pulling down the sleeves of his prisoner's jumpsuit and swiping the wrinkles from his shoulders. "Two weeks is longer than I expected."

"Our timeline is not yours."

"I was not complaining," Suit said. "Merely observing. I am perfectly willing to wait upon Trell's pleasure."

"Are you?" the Immortal asked. "It is our understanding that you push for an acceleration."

"I was merely stating my perspective," Suit said. "So that a proper discourse can be engaged."

The creature studied him through the bars. "You didn't break or spill secrets."

"I did not."

"We are impressed."

"Thank you."

Advantage. Even two weeks in prison can be used to prove a point.

"The timeline will be accelerated, as you have requested," the Immortal said.

"Excellent!"

The creature reached into its pocket and removed a device like a small package wrapped in wires. One of Irich's early attempts at creating an explosive device from the metal that powered the airships. It had proven ineffective, barely more explosive than dynamite, when they needed something that could end cities.

"What is that?" Suit asked, growing nervous.

"Our accelerated pace will no longer require the Set to have its full hierarchy."

"But you need us!" Suit said. "To rule, to manage civilization on—"

"No longer. Recent advances have made civilization here too dangerous. Allowing it to continue risks further advances we cannot control, and so we have decided to remove life on this sphere instead.

Thank you for your service; it has been accepted. You will be allowed to serve in another Realm."

"But—"

The creature engaged the explosive device, blowing itself—and Suit—to oblivion.

Wax started awake. Had that been an explosion?

He looked around the quiet bedroom suite of the tower penthouse. Steris curled up on the bed next to him, perfectly still in her sleep, though she held lightly to his arm. She often did that, as if afraid to let go and risk all this ending.

Looking at her there in the starlight, he was shocked by the deep affection he felt for her. His surprise didn't concern him. He could remember many a morning waking next to Lessie, feeling that same surprise. Amazement at his good fortune, astonishment at the depth of his own emotion.

He gently lifted her hand away, then pulled the sheet up around her before slipping from the bed and strolling bare-chested across the room toward the balcony.

They'd stayed here in the penthouse through the honeymoon, rather than returning to the mansion. It felt like a good way to have a new beginning, and Wax was starting to think he might like to relocate here more permanently. He was a new person for what seemed like the hundredth time in his life, and this was a new age. This was no longer an era of quiet mansions and smoking-room conversations; it was an era of bold skyscrapers and vibrant downtown politics.

The mists were out, curling around outside, though the skyscraper was tall enough he thought he could see stars and the Red Rip through that mist. He moved to push open the doors and step out onto the balcony, but paused, noticing his dressing table, upon which Drewton had set out a row of objects. The valet had gone through Wax's things, from his pockets and from his possessions recovered from the hotel in New Seran. Drewton probably wanted to know which should be kept, and which disposed of.

Wax smiled, brushing his fingers over the wrinkled cravat he'd worn to the party with Steris. He remembered tossing it to the ground as he changed to trousers and mistcoat in his room, prior to their quick escape from the city. Drewton had laid it out, along with a napkin from the party, monogrammed, and even a bottle cap he'd swiped in case he needed something to Push on. But Drewton had set it out on its own little cloth as if it might be the most important thing in the world.

Wax shook his head, resting a hand on the door out to the balcony. Then he froze and looked back at the table.

It was right there. The coin he'd been given by the beggar, shining in the faint starlight. Drewton must have found it in his pocket. Wax reached out, hesitated a moment, and then slipped it from the table before stepping out into the mist.

Could it be? he wondered, holding up the coin. Two different metals. One was silvery. Could that be nicrosil? The other was copper. A Feruchemical metal. Though the pattern printed on the face wasn't the same, and the coin itself was smaller, this didn't look all that different from one of the Southerner medallions.

As soon as he thought of it—as soon as he knew what it might do—the metalmind started working, and he found a store within him, a reserve he could tap. Wax gasped.

They called them copperminds. A very special kind of Feruchemical storage. One that stored memories.

He tapped it.

Immediately, Wax was in a different place. A barren land, with no one in sight and only dust blowing around him. It was a difficult perspective to experience, for only half of the viewer's eyesight was normal.

The other was all in blue, lines everywhere. The vision of a man spiked through the eye.

The figure crossed those desolate reaches, passing half-tended crops left to die and rattle in the wind. Ahead lay a town—or the remnants of one.

He heard his own boots on the dirty rock, the wind blowing, and felt cold. He continued on into the town, passing foundations marked by old, burned-out fires. Somehow, he knew that the inhabitants here—as in other villages and towns he'd passed—had torn down their own walls for firewood, in desperation to survive.

Bodies lay in the street, stripped. Their clothing had been taken for burning after they'd frozen in what most men would consider only mildly cold weather.

Ahead stood a bunkerlike stone dwelling. Long and narrow, it reminded him of something—not something Wax knew, but a memory in the mind of the man storing this experience. A memory of something long ago that flickered in his consciousness, then was lost in a moment.

The traveler continued, stepping up to the doorway, which was open. They'd burned the door.

Inside, a mass of people huddled together for warmth, wrapped uselessly in blankets. No fires left.

They'd burned even their masks.

The traveler moved among them, drawing some concern, though most people stared with dull eyes. Awaiting death. He found the leaders near the center, the elders, aged and wearing cloth masks on their faces—the only things they had left. One ancient woman looked up at him and lifted her mask.

He saw her normally in one world, and outlined in blue in another. The traveler reached out and took the woman by the shoulder, kneeled down, and whispered a single word.

Wax came out of that memory with a shock, dropping the coin, startled and stepping back.

The coin plinged against the balcony and settled to a stop near his feet.

That arm . . . That *arm*. Lined with a network of scars layered atop one another, as if made by scraping the skin time and time again. The haunting word he'd spoken echoed in Wax's mind.

"Survive."

POSTSCRIPT

Marasi, Wax, and Wayne will return in *The Lost Metal*, the epic finale of Mistborn: Era Two. I plan to release this after *Oathbringer*, the third volume of the Stormlight Archive, which I'm hard at work writing at this moment.

To tide you over until *Oathbringer*, I have just released a special digital-only novella that is intended to be read after *The Bands of Mourning*, though it takes place during the events of the original Mistborn Trilogy. Ten years in the making, *Mistborn: Secret History* might answer a few of your questions.

There's always another secret.

Brandon Sanderson
January 2016

ARS ARCANUM

METALS QUICK REFERENCE CHART

METAL	ALLOMANTIC POWER	FERUCHEMICAL POWER
Iron	Pulls on Nearby Sources of Metal	Stores Physical Weight
Steel	Pushes on Nearby Sources of Metal	Stores Physical Speed
Tin	Increases Senses	Stores Senses
Pewter	Increases Physical Abilities	Stores Physical Strength
Zinc	Riots (Enflames) Emotions	Stores Mental Speed
Brass	Soothes (Dampens) Emotions	Stores Warmth
Copper	Hides Allomantic Pulses	Stores Memories
Bronze	Allows One to Hear Allomantic Pulses	Stores Wakefulness
Cadmium	Slows Down Time	Stores Breath
Bendalloy	Speeds Up Time	Stores Energy
Gold	Reveals Your Past Self	Stores Health
Electrum	Reveals Your Own Future	Stores Determination
Chromium	Wipes Allomantic Reserves of Target	Stores Fortune
Nicrosil	Enhances Allomantic Burn of Target	Stores Investiture
Aluminum	Wipes Internal Allomantic Reserves	Stores Identity
Duralumin	Enhances the Next Metal Burned	Stores Connection

ALUMINUM: A Mistborn who burns aluminum instantly metabolizes all of his or her metals without giving any other effect, wiping all Allomantic reserves. Mistings who can burn aluminum are called Aluminum Gnats due to the ineffectiveness of this ability by itself. Trueself Ferrings can store their spiritual sense of identity in an aluminum metalmind. This is an art rarely spoken of outside of Terris communities, and even among them it is not yet well understood. Aluminum itself and a few of its alloys are Allomantically inert; they cannot be Pushed or Pulled and can be used to shield an individual from emotional Allomancy.

BENDALLOY: Slider Mistings burn bendalloy to compress time in a bubble around themselves, making it pass more quickly within the bubble. This causes events outside the bubble to move at a glacial pace from the point of view of the Slider. Subsumer Ferrings can store nutrition and calories in a bendalloy metalmind; they can eat large amounts of food during active storage without feeling full or gaining weight, and then can go without the need to eat while tapping the metalmind. A separate bendalloy metalmind can be used to similarly regulate fluids intake.

BRASS: Soother Mistings burn brass to Soothe (dampen) the emotions of nearby individuals. This can be directed at a single individual or directed across a general area, and the Soother can focus on specific emotions. Firesoul Ferrings can store warmth in a brass metalmind, cooling themselves off while actively storing. They can tap the metalmind at a later time to warm themselves.

BRONZE: Seeker Mistings burn bronze to "hear" pulses given off by other Allomancers who are burning metals. Different metals produce different pulses. Sentry Ferrings can store wakefulness in a bronze metalmind, making themselves drowsy while actively storing. They can tap the metalmind at a later time to reduce drowsiness or to heighten their awareness.

CADMIUM: Pulser Mistings burn cadmium to stretch time in a bubble around themselves, making it pass more slowly inside the bubble. This causes events outside the bubble to move at blurring speed from the point of view of the Pulser. Gasper Ferrings can store breath inside a cadmium metalmind; during active storage they must hyperventilate in order for their bodies to get enough air. The breath can be retrieved at a later time, eliminating or reducing the need to breathe using the lungs while tapping the metalmind. They can also highly oxygenate their blood.

CHROMIUM: Leecher Mistings who burn chromium while touching another Allomancer will wipe that Allomancer's metal reserves. Spinner Ferrings can store fortune in a chromium metalmind, making themselves unlucky during active storage, and can tap it at a later time to increase their luck.

COPPER: Coppercloud Mistings (a.k.a. Smokers) burn copper to create an invisible cloud around themselves, which hides nearby Allomancers from being detected by a Seeker and which shields the Smoker from the effects of emotional Allomancy. Archivist Ferrings can store memories in a copper metalmind (coppermind); the memory is gone from their head while in storage, and can be retrieved with perfect recall at a later time.

DURALUMIN: A Mistborn who burns duralumin instantly burns away any other metals being burned at the time, releasing an enormous burst of those metals' power. Mistings who can burn Duralumin are called Duralumin Gnats due to the ineffectiveness of this ability by itself. Connecter Ferrings can store spiritual connection in a duralumin metalmind, reducing other people's awareness and friendship with them during active storage, and can tap it at a later time in order to speedily form trust relationships with others.

ELECTRUM: Oracle Mistings burn electrum to see a vision of possible paths their future could take. This is usually limited to a few seconds. Pinnacle Ferrings can store determination in an electrum metalmind, entering a depressed state during active storage, and can tap it at a later time to enter a manic phase.

GOLD: Augur Mistings burn gold to see a vision of a past self or how they would have turned out having made different choices in the past. Bloodmaker Ferrings can store health in a gold metalmind, reducing their health while actively storing, and can tap it at a later time in order to heal quickly or to heal beyond the body's usual abilities.

IRON: Lurcher Mistings who burn iron can Pull on nearby sources of metal. Pulls must be directly toward the Lurcher's center of gravity. Skimmer Ferrings can store physical weight in an iron metalmind, reducing their effective weight while actively storing, and can tap it at a later time to increase their effective weight.

NICROSIL: Nicroburst Mistings who burn nicrosil while touching another Allomancer will instantly burn away any metals being burned by that Allomancer, releasing an enormous (and perhaps unexpected) burst of those metals' power within that Allomancer. Soulbearer Ferrings can store Investiture in a nicrosil metalmind. This is a power that very few know anything about; indeed, I'm certain the people of Terris don't truly know what they are doing when they use these powers.

PEWTER: Pewterarm Mistings (a.k.a. Thugs) burn pewter to increase their physical strength, speed, and durability, also enhancing their bodies' ability to heal. Brute Ferrings can store physical strength in a pewter metalmind, reducing their strength while actively storing, and can tap it at a later time to increase their strength.

STEEL: Coinshot Mistings who burn steel can Push on nearby sources of metal. Pushes must be directly away from the Coinshot's center of gravity. Steelrunner Ferrings can store physical speed in a steel metalmind, slowing them while actively storing, and can tap it at a later time to increase their speed.

TIN: Tineye Mistings who burn tin increase the sensitivity of their five senses. All are increased at the same time. Windwhisperer Ferrings can store the sensitivity of one of the five senses into a tin metalmind; a different tin metalmind must be used for each sense. While storing, their sensitivity in that sense is reduced, and when the metalmind is tapped that sense is enhanced.

ZINC: Rioter Mistings burn zinc to Riot (enflame) the emotions of nearby individuals. This can be directed at a single individual or directed across a general area, and the Rioter can focus on specific emotions. Sparker Ferrings can store mental speed in a zinc metalmind, dulling their ability to think and reason while actively storing, and can tap it at a later time to think and reason more quickly.

ON THE THREE METALLIC ARTS

On Scadrial, there are three prime manifestations of Investiture. Locally these are spoken of as the "Metallic Arts," though there are other names for them.

Allomancy is the most common of the three. It is end-positive, according to my terminology—meaning that the practitioner draws in power from an external source. The body then filters it into various forms. (The actual outlet of the power is not chosen by the practitioner, but instead is hardwritten into their Spiritweb.) The key to drawing this power comes in the form of various types of metals, with specific compositions being required. Though the metal is consumed in the process, the power itself doesn't actually come from the metal. The metal is a catalyst, you might say, that begins an Investiture and keeps it running.

In truth, this isn't much different from the form-based Investitures one finds on Sel, where specific shape is the key—here, however, the interactions are more limited. Still, one cannot deny the raw power of Allomancy. It is instinctive and intuitive for the practitioner, as opposed to requiring a great deal of study and exactness, as one finds in the form-based Investitures of Sel.

Allomancy is brutal, raw, and powerful. There are sixteen base metals that work, though two others—named the "God Metals" locally—can be used in alloy to craft an entirely different set of sixteen each. As these God Metals are no longer commonly available, however, the other metals are not in wide use.

Feruchemy is still widely known and used at this point on Scadrial. Indeed, you might say that it is more present today than it has been in many eras past, when it was confined to distant Terris or hidden from sight by the Keepers.

Feruchemy is an end-neutral art, meaning that power is neither gained nor lost. The art also requires metal as a focus, but instead of being consumed, the metal acts as a medium by which abilities within the practitioner are shuttled through time. Invest that metal on one day, withdraw the power on another day. It is a well-rounded art, with some feelers in the Physical, some in the Cognitive, and even some in the Spiritual. The last powers are under heavy experimentation by the Terris community, and aren't spoken of to outsiders.

It should be noted that the interbreeding of the Feruchemists with the general population has diluted the power in some ways. It is now common for people to be born with access to only one of the sixteen Feruchemical abilities. It is hypothesized that if one could make metalminds out of alloys with the God Metals, other abilities could be discovered.

Hemalurgy is widely unknown in the modern world of Scadrial. Its secrets were kept close by those who survived their world's rebirth, and the only known practitioners of it now are the kandra, who (for the most part) serve Harmony.

Hemalurgy is an end-negative art. Some power is lost in the practice of it. Though many throughout history have maligned it as an "evil" art, none of the Investitures are actually evil. At its core, Hemalurgy deals with removing abilities—or attributes—from one person and bestowing them on another. It is primarily concerned with things of the Spiritual Realm, and is of the greatest interest to me. If one of these three arts is of great import to the cosmere, it is this one. I think there are many possibilities for its use.

COMBINATIONS

It is possible on Scadrial to be born with ability to access both Allomancy and Feruchemy. This has been of specific interest to me lately, as the mixing of different types of Investiture has curious effects. One needs look only at what has happened on Roshar to find this manifested—two powers, combined, often have an almost chemical reaction. Instead of getting out exactly what you put in, you get something new.

On Scadrial, someone with one Allomantic power and one Feruchemical power is called "Twinborn." The effects here are more subtle than they are when mixing Surges on Roshar, but I am convinced that each unique combination also creates something distinctive. Not just two powers, you could say, but two powers . . . and an effect. This demands further study.